Nicole Laurent

Nicole Laurent

**Elizabeth Baroody
aka Christy Demaine**

Copyright © 2010 by Elizabeth Baroody aka Christy Demaine.

Library of Congress Control Number: 2009914305
ISBN: Hardcover   978-1-4500-2374-0
             Softcover   978-1-4500-2373-3
             Ebook   978-1-4500-2375-7

All rights reserved. No part of this book may be reproduced or transmitted in any form or by any means, electronic or mechanical, including photocopying, recording, or by any information storage and retrieval system, without permission in writing from the copyright owner.

This is a work of fiction. Names, characters, places and incidents either are the product of the author's imagination or are used fictitiously, and any resemblance to any actual persons, living or dead, events, or locales is entirely coincidental.

This book was printed in the United States of America.

To order additional copies of this book, contact:
Xlibris Corporation
1-888-795-4274
www.Xlibris.com
Orders@Xlibris.com
71065

This book is dedicated to Elizabeth Baroody. May she rest in peace.

Also by Elizabeth Baroody

Approximately 115 articles, short stories, and poems have been written and published since 1972. A book, written under the name of "Christy Demaine," entitled "A Matter of Revenge," was published in 1977 and is still available on the internet and used book stores.

Chapter One

The Recruit

The long, black Lincoln Town car idled along the spiked fence that surrounded the mansion and finally arrived at the rear entrance. It paused at the ornate iron gates, and the driver admired the lions' head that decorated the exact centers. The lions' mouths were open and inside each one, was the letter "G." The headlights of the Lincoln blinked twice. The gates swung inward, the car passed through and preceded to a remote ell of the massive Georgian brick house where a slight, dark figure of a man waited in the glow of light from an open door. He stepped forward, smiling.

"Come in quickly, Ed. These Washington summers can be hell even out here in the Maryland suburbs."

"Yes, I heard it got up to ninety-eight degrees."

The two men entered the house together and shut the simmering humidity outside. The room, a library, had a high ceiling, the walls were covered in a cranberry red damask to match the carpet, and the furniture was dark cherry. Little oriental rugs had been placed here and there. In the center of the back wall, there was a fireplace flanked by bookcases that reached to the ceiling and on the opposite wall was a large-screen television and DVD player, which were recessed behind open doors.

"So you think you have found us a live one?" asked the small, dark man. "We certainly need recruits. In our business, attrition is swifter than most. Let's see what you've got, Ed." G. Edmund Hammer paused and looked thoughtfully down at the videotapes he held in his hand and closed his briefcase.

"She's damned intriguing. I have followed her myself and had her followed for seven months in three different countries, and yet, I could never really touch on what makes her so exciting. She is totally unique, Gazar, totally unique."

"You sound like a man who is falling in love," Gazar chuckled. "Never get emotionally involved."

"I know the rules. She will probably never see me again after we have negotiated a contract," he promised. He slid the DVD into the player and glanced around for the remote. "But if things were different . . . do you want my notes now or after you have seen the film?"

"Can't you just give me a voice-over on the pertinent facts as we view the video? And run it at slow speed so I can ask questions as we move along."

Hammer punched in the Play button, and a scene of the Paris airport, Orly, came into view. A common sight, passengers converging on a plane, was also shown.

"Pay attention to the small blonde woman in the black linen Channel suit, with a briefcase and carry-on bag, black, leather shoulder bag. And note those legs: shapely but muscular. She is an athletic as you will see shortly."

Gazar sat forward sharply. "Hmmmmm."

The scene switched to the interior of the plane, and the subject removes her dark glasses and stashes her carry-on under the seat but continues to hold tightly to her briefcase. The camera comes in for a side view of her face, but the plane is taking off, and it is rough on the runway, the picture is indistinct and shaky.

"Damn! Is this the best you can do?" fumed Gazar, staring at the screen. "Well, at least you can tell me this creature's name. Where does she live?"

"Her name is Nicole Longet Laurent, and she is twenty-four years old. She will be twenty-five on the ninth of next month, August. Her mother is a seamstress for several designers. She does what they call detail work. The mother's name is Yvette Longet, never married, but has a longtime lover, Enrico Garibaldi."

"And I suppose this Nicole is the Italian's love child?" Gazar guessed.

"No, she isn't. According to the concierge at their apartment house, and they have lived there forever on the third floor, so he knows everything about them, this Garibaldi arrived on the scene about twelve, maybe fifteen years ago. He has a wife and children in Italy but seems devoted to the mother. We located Nicole's birth certificate, and it reads 'Father Unknown.' We tried to trace any possible boyfriends who were around about that time but came up empty. And there is a grandmother who lives with Yvette Longet. She also sews handwork, as they term it. Her name is Mimi."

The camera work was still unsteady, and Gazar was becoming frustrated as he peered at the flickering screen. He pounded the arm of his wingback desk chair.

"Sorry, lots of turbulence. The rest are better," apologized Hammer. "This one is just about over."

The scene went suddenly dark, came back showing the terminal in New York and the subject rapidly disappearing from view. Hammer hit Stop, then Eject, and pulled the first film from the machine as he continued to explain.

"You notice how she is holding the briefcase close to her side. It probably contains either gems or rare coins that she is delivering to a client somewhere in New York or closeby. She is the courier for her husband's business. He is Rene Laurent, fairly well known as a custom jewelry designer, as well as a shop owner in Paris."

"Husbands can be trouble," snorted Gazar. "Is he the jealous type?"

"She is straight as an arrow. Works in the shop, goes to church on Sunday with the mother and grandmother, seems to be in love with her husband, who is much older but a good-looking guy, very suave, cosmopolitan. He has a mistress however, a woman his age who lives on a farm outside the city."

"That is interesting," mused Gazar. "Usually the other way around. Roll the next tape, and it better be better than the last one."

Hammer pushed the second video into the machine, and it again showed an airport scene. This time the small blonde was in a navy and white Oscar de la Renta suit with a navy shoulder bag with the same briefcase and carry-on. She walked toward the camera up the steps of the plane, smiled briefly, and passed into the body of the plane.

"Something about her appearance doesn't quite fit. The brows are dark and straight, and the eyes, very dark. There is something almost Spanish or perhaps Greek in her features and yet, despite her light skin. What is wrong?" puzzled Gazar, staring.

"It is the hair. It fooled me too until I realized that she uses a number of wigs when she travels, and oddly enough, while she works in the shop."

Another, completely different scene rolled into view. It was obviously taken on a country road, trees all around, no houses, no person . . . and then a lone runner came down the road wearing a black, spandex running suit and a black knit watch cap pulled low. He ran at a fast pace along a stone fence. In the distance, one could see a fairly new farmhouse with several sheds around it. Closer to the stone fence were the crumbling walls of the original farmhouse, a crude sod house with roof long gone, and chimneys standing drunkenly at each end as if ready to fall. Nearby, a broken wooden pail and chain lay next to a gaping circle of rotted wood, covering an abandoned well. Two placid cows grazed by the fence, ignoring the runner as he flew past as if they were used to this happening. A common thing, nothing to note.

"Is this the country house where Rene Laurent's mistress lives?"

"No," said Hammer.

"Well, who is that kid?" demanded Gazar. "Look at that pace! He hasn't broken stride in a mile! He is the one you should be recruiting, Ed."

"Keep watching. Coming around the turn now. Our cameraman switches right here. He's beside the broken-down car with the hood up. Here it comes up, close and natural."

Close up. The face of the runner fills the screen. Hammer holds the action. Beneath the knit cap were the dark straight brows, the oval face, that perfect mouth.

"My god," gasped Gazar. He struggled to unwrap a cigar and put it between his lips. His hand felt around for the lighter on the desk, but he accidentally knocked it off onto the carpet. He took the cigar out of his mouth and simply held it. He stared as the runner took off her hat, wiped the sweat from her face, and ran on. The camera followed down the fence line until she disappeared from sight. Her natural hair appeared to be very dark, chopped off in damp spiky bangs in front, short to the ears in back, thick and tending to curl, unlike the several wigs she favored while traveling.

"A chameleon!" exclaimed Gazar as he felt around on the floor for the lighter. "I could have sworn it was a young boy. She runs like a deer. What else do you have on her as to her childhood? This father, or no father, thing is a bit unsettling and is she well enough educated for the work? She does speak English well, I presume?"

"A minor accent. She is also proficient in Spanish and Italian," said Hammer. "French, of course, and possibly others I'm not aware of, yet."

Gazar's cigar lay unlit between his fingers as he stared at the blank screen and as Hammer thrust the last tape into the machine, he held up his hand, indicating that the tape be put on hold for the moment.

"And what would motivate this little frog to jump into the game? You know, Ed, these are not ordinary types that we deal with, and you were considering putting her into the field, were you not?" pondered Gazar, finally managing to light his cigar. "You must have seen something. I define the necessary quality of the best agents as the psychotic edge, an almost total absence of fear, and an irrational compulsion that what they do is right, no matter what it entails to complete the mission."

G. Edmund Hammer seemed to think this philosophy over and apply it generally to Nicole Laurent, but no one could actually judge that psychotic edge until the agent was on the job and called upon to act on his own.

"Well, there is motivation and opportunity. She has a natural cover to travel, she is somewhat bored with her present existence . . . , and she needs money," Hammer finally said, "Laurent uses her. He dresses her up in designer clothes and plasters them with his best jewelry to attract customers. They go to art exhibits, charity affairs, and numerous fancy parties of the very rich."

"What do you mean, she needs money?"

"Laurent is extended. He buys gems on credit. He has his clothes made in England. The farm he shares with his mistress as well as the building he owns that contains his shop, and the living quarters over it are mortgaged. He makes it. He spends it. He gives Nicole no salary, just a small allowance, and she seems to work harder at the business than he does. One reason she's frustrated about finances is because she is desperate to move her mother and grandmother into a larger apartment in a very good neighborhood."

"How do you get this stuff?"

"I found out where the ladies lived and sent Richard Leach over to see them. He pretended to be selling life insurance, and he took them a really nice gift basket just to listen to his spiel. Of course, by the time he was ready to leave, he mentioned a sizable monthly payment, and they were horrified but not until he started them talking about Nicole and Rene and got all the information on the family we needed. They were thrilled with the basket."

"Good. Richard Leach heads that little Paris office. In fact, he is the Paris office with just that little money, man, and a clerk, who is a nonagent and thinks that they run a travel agency," said Gazar, with a laugh. "In fact, it is a working cover. They do sell tours if someone wanders in now and then."

"Shall I run this last tape?"

Gazar went to the bar, poured each of them a scotch and water, then settled back into his chair. "Let it run."

The scene was a gala in a country house. Nicole stood against a wall, dressed in something gold and long. Emeralds gleamed on her ears and a brooch that nestled in her cleavage shot green sparks in the lights of an overhead chandelier. More emeralds on her fingers. She held a drink in one hand but as the tape moved on, she never seemed to drink anything from the glass. Fade out. End of party. Over to a museum. Again, Nicole stood against a wall of paintings this time, dressed in something black and soft that moved when she moved. Diamonds dangled from her ears. A starburst of diamonds glittered on one shoulder, all very elite and understated. Drink in hand. The tape ran on and finally she moved to a tall fern and poured the drink into the marble base in which it rested.

"Wait—isn't that Prince Charles right there in that kilt thing?" asked Gazar, peering at the screen through thick glasses.

"And that is Camilla, a few steps behind," said Hammer, "right there. Here she comes."

"That woman has spent too much time around horses," commented Gazar.

The tape rolled on, keying in to two more social occasions where a stunning but obviously bored Nicole stood silently, noticing nothing, saying nothing.

"And just where is Monsieur Laurent at these affairs while his gorgeous wife is holding up the wall and tossing good booze in the floral arrangements?"

"Working the crowd. Mr. Personality. He gets invited everywhere. He is well read, interesting, funny, and good-looking, a true egocentric. Her mother related a story about a posh party they went to where Nicole borrowed a maid's uniform and actually served Rene three courses at dinner, and he never looked up, nor did his dinner companions, so involved with themselves that they didn't notice. Sad, isn't it?"

On the tape, Nicole glanced at her watch and yawned.

"Well, do you think she is agent material?" Hammer asked.

"How is her accent? We need someone in the eastern states division."

"Almost none. Four years as a foreign exchange student in the United States and then four years on scholarship at American University in DC."

The tape ran on. Nicole in the shop. Nicole renting a car at Dulles Airport. Lunch in a small Chinese restaurant. And back to the stone fence, where she was running, and running, running, through the countryside outside Paris.

"Before you contact this girl, this woman," said Gazar, thoughtfully, as he poured each of them a second scotch and water, "I feel she has to be tested under fire to see how she handles a tough situation. I want to set her up and see what flies. Is it her habit to go to that same Chinese restaurant when she has a delivery in Washington?"

"Well . . . come to think of it, she has gone there twice in four months," recalled Hammer. "Of course, we don't know when she's coming back to the Washington area."

"We would, if I bought something very nice from Rene Laurent," suggested Gazar, as his narrow, dark eyes crinkled in a half smile. He crushed his cigar almost viciously into a glass ashtray as he turned to Hammer. "Set it up!"

Hammer removed the last disc and put it in his briefcase.

"What did you have in mind?"

"Suppose we steal the jewels from her. How will she react? Will she call 911? Scream for help? Burst into tears?" Gazar rubbed his hands together in anticipation as if relishing the prospect of unexpected violence. He definitely enjoyed his role of control. He glanced up to see Hammer staring at him intensely.

"If you're worried about the snatch, we'll return the jewels, anonymously of course, to Rene Laurent, by mail to Paris. See? No harm done."

"Of course," echoed Hammer. "Tell me what you want me to do."

* * *

Nicole looked down at the street below and knew that it would be another hot day because although it was not yet ten o'clock, steam was already wafting up from water in the street where the flower vendor had sprayed his wares earlier this morning.

"Paris," hummed Nicole. "When it sizzles."

Even though she knew how hot it was outside of the air-conditioned apartment, she regretted missing her daily run around the old farm on the outskirts of the city. The run cleared her mind and invigorated her body for whatever the day would bring. Running gave her such a sense of freedom as the trees flew past, the dew of morning cleansed her face, and her muscles pumped, urging her to go faster and faster . . . but on this particular day, Rene had wakened very early. He was thrilled over a new, big order he had received from an unfamiliar person in the States, a client who had said he had admired a necklace that Rene designed several years ago for a friend, and he desired a similar one for his wife. He generally described what he wanted, and Rene recalled the one he was interested in, a quality piece and quite expensive.

"Do we have the right stones in the vault, or will I need to call Kenya or Brazil?" he asked Nicole, absentmindedly fondling her breasts, as they lay nude on the bed. Although he seemed higher on the idea of the new necklace than on making love, she responded by turning toward him and fitting her body closely into his.

"Oh, Rene, I'd have to see the original design," she murmured sleepily as she lifted her mouth for a kiss.

"So many small stones," he remembered, burying his face into her neck.

"Hmmmmm, a lovely piece," she breathed into his ear.

"And so are you," he answered, turning her over onto her back.

They moved together easily with the familiarity of two people who knew each other well, and afterward Nicole had fallen deeply asleep in that dreamlike aftermath when time ceased to matter, and the world outside held little or no importance.

When she woke and found Rene's side of the bed empty, she hurriedly jumped up and went into the shower. She dressed and found her keys on the dresser, then looked out of the window to see the steaming sidewalks that promised another hot day. She went down the stairs, locked the door behind her, and walked around the back parking lot to the sidewalk that ran along the side of the building. The windows on the street side had been bricked in years ago for additional security for the shop. Continuing on to the front of the building, she paused and admired the brass plaque, which read, *Rene Laurent, custom jewelry and rare coins*. The narrow, glass show windows had tiny white strips that triggered the alarms. She tapped on the door and a smiling Henri-Paul welcomed her inside.

"Monsieur Rene is already at the drawing board!" he announced. "And I must say he is in an excellent mood this morning!"

"The better for us all then, no," she agreed.

Nicole walked to the rear of the shop, lightly tapped on the workroom door, and went inside. Rene was seated at his design table, his back to her.

"Ah, my darling, it is still so beautiful, is it not!" he exclaimed.

"Yes, Rene, beautiful," she agreed, smiling. She came up behind him and kissed the top of his head, thinking about the intimate moments they had just shared in the early hours of dawn.

He swiveled his chair around, and she realized that he was holding in his hands the original drawings of the necklace he had been commissioned to duplicate. As he regarded his own handiwork, she understood that he had been commenting on the jewelry, and her smile abruptly faded.

"Very nice, Rene. When will it be ready to deliver?" she asked flatly.

"By Thursday. I'll book a flight for you for Friday morning, and of course, you must look nice for the delivery. When you get to Washington, wear that little red jacket with the brass buttons and the black skirt," he directed. He turned back to the drawing board. "Now, don't disturb me for the rest of the day. Oh, yes, and have Henri-Paul bring me a hot carafe of coffee, two warm croissants, and some marmalade."

She stared at the back of his head. "One plane ticket, red jacket, black skirt, coffee, croissants, marmalade," she repeated through clenched teeth. "What kind?"

"Orange or grapefruit and tell him to warm the jar."

Nicole turned and left the room. She walked to the front of the shop where Georges was in the process of removing the night covers from inside the showcases, and Henri-Paul was arranging the fresh flowers from the vendor across the street on the low tables beside the chairs where customers could rest and be shown their choices.

"I am going to the cafe on the corner for my breakfast," she informed them as she buzzed herself out of the door. "And Henri-Paul, if you find a spare moment, would you please bring Monsieur Rene a cup of coffee? No hurry."

* * *

By Friday, the heat of the last few days had broken and when Nicole reached Charles de Gaulle, a gentle rain was falling. The red jacket and black skirt were hung carefully in a suit bag, and she was wearing blue jeans and a white shirt covered by a huge, clear plastic raincoat with a hood. The large, black shoulder bag contained a zippered pocket that held the ornately wrapped necklace in the Laurent box.

In the airport waiting room, a sullen-faced Chinese woman in a nondescript green pantsuit took a seat several yards away from the row where Nicole was waiting for her flight to be called. The woman uneasily checked the time of departure, took a slip of paper from her purse, and moved swiftly to the bank of telephones.

At the sound of the man's voice on the other end, she said breathlessly, "Here Chung Pu in de Gaulle Airport. You say to me, get briefcase. She no got briefcase."

"Then it is on her somewhere. What's she got with her?"

"Big bag, see clothes in there. Big pocketbook on shoulder," she reported.

"No package?"

"No package."

"Then, when you land in the States, you must try to snatch the shoulder bag," ordered Gazar, "and get rough if you have to. Shut her up before she can summon help and bring the bag to the post office. Someone will be waiting by the boxes."

"He will have my money?" the woman demanded as she leaned forward to make sure Nicole had not gotten up and walked out of her sight.

"Give him the bag, and he gives you your money," Gazar answered gruffly.

"Okie Dokie," the woman agreed into the empty air of the long distance connection. Gazar had hung up.

The flight to Dulles was called over the loud speaker. The woman grabbed her cheap, green, plastic purse, and overnight bag, and keeping to the end of the line in the boarding crowd of passengers, followed the figure ahead of Nicole Laurent, the mark. She kept her head down and despite the cloudy day, put on dark glasses, a disguise she adapted from the movies. Her flat, cloth shoes were soggy from the water on the metal steps, and she had not thought to bring another pair. She had been given two sharp hatpins, which were imbedded in, and seemed to be part of the metallic handles of her purse. The tips were saturated with a heavy sedative provided by the eerie little man, Gazar. She only had to wait, find herself alone with the little Frenchwoman, and quick! It would be done like the ugly, American man wished it done and at last, she would have enough money to go back to Hong Kong.

Nicole folded her suit bag and placed it carefully under her seat. She reached into her shoulder bag, reassured herself that the necklace was secure, brought out a new roll of mints, unwrapped the package, and popped one into her mouth. A second mint leapt out of the roll and hurtled down the aisle. It landed at the feet of a Chinese woman in damp cloth shoes, who recoiled as if she had been shot. The woman averted her eyes and drew up her feet to one side.

"Pardon," said Nicole, laughing. "It wished to run away!" She retrieved the mint and wrapped it in a tissue.

The Chinese woman turned her head and made no reply but others nearby smiled at the little incident, then returned to their laptops and earphones as Nicole made her way back to her seat.

The flight was uneventful, and the movie, in English, was one she had seen, so time passed slowly even though her seat companion kept trying to begin a conversation. He had also seen the movie and was trying to explain his version of the plot until she finally put her fingers to her mouth to indicate that he shut his own. Then he began to apologize profusely while she attempted to take a short nap. Finally, they touched down at Dulles; the passengers got off the plane and wandered away to their various pursuits, fighting off jet lag. Nicole went off to rent a car.

The Chinese woman was picked up by a long, black, Lincoln Town car, and she climbed into the passenger seat. They waited near an exit for Nicole to appear in the rental car.

"You bring my money?" the woman asked hopefully.

G. Edmund Hammer looked at her. "You know I don't have your money. It was understood it would be at the post office when the job is done."

"How I can trust you?" whined the woman. "Give me half part now."

"Shut up! Here she comes in a blue Escort."

The little blue car zipped past, moving erratically. The driver was obviously inexperienced with this model and was driving much too fast. Even so, two other vehicles cut in between, and Hammer swore out loud, afraid he would lose her once she left the vast grounds of the airport and headed onto the highway.

"Go! Go!" shouted Chung Pu, clutching her lethal purse as he accelerated. "She getting away!"

The big, black car roared after the small, blue one, but when about two miles ahead, he rounded a curve in the road, the Escort had completely vanished from sight. He slowed and looked for a place to turn around as he remembered seeing a shopping center entrance about half a mile back. They drove back to the center, and there it was, the blue Escort in a corner of the parking lot, and closeby, between a dry cleaner and a gift shop was the Chinese restaurant. The windows were painted with red flowers and stone Foo dogs flanked the red door of the entrance.

"Go in," said Hammer. "Sit near the door. When she pays the cashier, follow her outside and grab that shoulder bag. I'll be here with the motor running." He seemed to consider a second plan. "Or make the snatch at the blue car when she is getting out the car keys and is momentarily distracted."

"What I do then?" Chung Pu began to look doubtful.

"Think of the money waiting for you at the post office."

"Okie Dokie," she said. "I stick her with needle and run very fast."

"What?" said Hammer startled. "What are you talking about?"

Chung Pu tried to laugh. It was obvious that Hammer had not been told about the two needles in the handles of her purse. "Oh, I just make joke."

She got out of the car quickly before he could ask her anything more. Perhaps Gazar wanted it to be a big secret between the two of them. As she scuttled across to the restaurant, she pulled one of the needles from the handle and hid it in her sleeve.

"Maybe I not run too fast so I fix that stupid French woman first one big time. Maybe she die. What I care? I be gone," panted Chung Pu as she huffed and puffed her way across the parking lot to the restaurant.

The place was not crowded, but the booths nearest the door were occupied, so she was forced to sit further back. She considered this a bad omen. Already that part of the plan had gone wrong. Chung Pu hesitated, thinking that perhaps she should go back outside and wait, but a small kimonoed girl approached with a menu in hand, so she took a seat at one of the tiny tables in the center of the room.

The French woman, sitting at a booth in the rear, looked up for one long second, and appeared to recognize her from the plane, but then she returned to her menu.

Chung Pu ordered small rice, one egg roll, and a pot of tea.

The French woman appeared to order many dishes, spice beef, soup, fried rice, chicken with noodles, and tea. Twenty minutes passed. She ordered another pot of tea and two fortune cookies. It seemed she would never leave. Chung Pu had a terrible thought. Perhaps the French woman was meeting someone here. What must she do then? Chung Pu read her fortune cookie again for the sixth time. She hated her prophecy, rolled it into a ball, and threw it into the ashtray. *Be kind to others or ill fortune will come to you.* It was all foolishness. Who would believe a scrap of stupid rice paper? She turned toward the painted windows and peered between the flowers for a sight of the black Lincoln. Where was the man called Hammer? As she turned back to the restaurant, the French woman rose and asked directions to the restroom. The waitress pointed to a long, dark passageway beyond the kitchen area. No other customer had ventured back there since Chung Pu had been sitting at her tiny table. Ah, here was the opportunity! Chung Pu rose and followed quickly down the dark hall. One door said simply *woman*. She opened it and slipped inside to see that one of the doors to the three cubicles was closed. It was too quiet. What if the French woman cried out? Chung Pu turned on the faucet of one of the sinks at full speed and water splashed out of the bowl onto the floor, but she let it run anyway.

The French woman came out of the cubicle, looked curiously at the water running rampant at the sink, hesitated, and then turned to stare at Chung Pu.

"Pardon? Were you not on the plane from Paris? My candy rolled to your feet, no?"

Chung Pu froze. Hammer had not instructed her as to what to do in case she was ever recognized. She looked about nervously, and then shook her head.

"No! You make big mistake, lady. I never see you before!"

The French woman's face went from surprise to icy cold. Holding her shoulder bag close to her side, she began to back slowly to the door, her dark eyes never leaving Chung Pu's face.

"Stop and hand me your bag," ordered the Chinese woman as she drew a long, deadly hatpin from her sleeve. "Or I have to kill you."

The French woman hesitated beside the last sink near the door.

"Poison," Chung Pu hissed as she advanced. "Give me the bag!"

Almost in a slow motion, Nicole stepped to the sink. Her hand reached out and grasped the glass ball that was the soap dispenser. It hung separately from the metal holder attached to the tile over the sink.

The ball came free in Nicole's hand, her arm went back, and the ball flew across the room like a deadly projectile, catching Chung Pu square in the throat. Her eyes wide, her hands pawing helplessly at her neck, the Chinese woman tried to scream, but no sound escaped her lips. The liquid soap poured from the container; the ball rolled across the floor in a cascade of bubbles. Chung Pu took one step forward in her wet, cloth shoes. Her feet flew straight up in the air as she fell backward, and there was an ominous crack as her elbow hit the edge of the sink as she went down. There was another crack as her head crashed hard on the tile floor where she thrashed about in the widening flow of bubbles, then lay still.

Nicole watched in horror. Was the woman dead? There were signs of movement, and she saw the rise and fall of erratic breathing beneath the jacket of the green pantsuit. She listened closely, but the commotion had brought no one running to the restroom. With one last glance at the figure on the floor, she slipped quickly into the dark hall, thankful to see that it was empty, and tried to walk normally to the front of the restaurant. She paid the cashier, left a generous tip, and feeling completely drained from the incident, made it out to the blue, rental car where she sat for a few seconds under the steering wheel before she could turn the key in the ignition. It was the first time since she had been a courier that anyone had attempted to rob her, and it had been an unnerving experience. A hatpin that long? Had it really contained poison? She drove away, taking a route that led through the alleys behind the stores, just in case the Chinese woman had an accomplice waiting for her outside. Her hands were damp with perspiration as she headed toward Washington and her hotel.

*   *   *

The next morning the weather was still unusually hot, and Nicole looked at the red jacket with the brass buttons and the black skirt, which would be too warm for comfort in the Washington heat. Why did she let Rene dictate her clothing for the trip? He had not seen a Washington summer in fifteen years, perhaps more. The Econo Belfair was midtown commercial, strictly for salesmen who wanted to sleep cheap. It had a small, gloomy bar in the foyer but no dining room, snack bar, or gift shop. So, she would have to walk the nearby streets to find a restaurant for a quick breakfast. Reluctantly, she shrugged into the red jacket and black skirt. She checked on the Rene Laurent gift box in her black shoulder bag and wondered whether the Chinese woman had known about the necklace or whether she was just a common thief looking for cash, traveler's checks, or charge cards. Nicole knew that the woman had been on the flight. One could not forget that ugly, green pantsuit or those awful, cloth shoes, and when the woman had blatantly denied seeing her on the plane, Nicole immediately sensed danger and reacted in self-defense. Poison on a hatpin! She recalled the frightening incident of the Israelis, and other incidents with poisoned umbrellas, and sharp instruments, used in bright daylight on busy streets, to stun or disable unsuspecting victims, but she could not imagine anyone attacking her for a necklace worth at the most, a few thousand dollars. Should she have stayed at the restaurant and called the police? The woman may have charged her with assault after that crash landing on the restroom floor in the foaming bubbles because it was she who had become the ultimate victim. One's word against the other.

Hoping for some advice, or at least sympathy for what she had gone through, she called Rene, who sounded as if he had just woken from a deep sleep.

"Yes, who is it?" he muttered, angry at being disturbed.

"It is Nicole. Oh, Rene, I had trouble last night! Someone tried to steal my shoulder bag in a restaurant."

"Mon Dieu! Is the necklace safe?" he shouted, now wide-awake.

"Yes, or you would be hearing from the American police, no? I managed to get away, but Rene, it was a woman from Paris! I know it because I saw her on my flight sitting just down the aisle. She was following me! Who knew I was making this trip, Rene?"

"Only myself, Henri-Paul, and the client, of course. But Henri-Paul is devoted to you and loyal to our business. This woman—she sees you on the plane, and sees that you are so well-dressed, and you must have lots of money—a common thief, Nicole!"

"I was in jeans and an awful big plastic raincoat."

"Oh, how dreadful! But, you are all right, Cherie?"

"Yes, Rene," she assured him. "I am ready to leave the hotel now. I will drive out to the suburbs of Maryland and try to find this house. After I make the delivery, I will go directly to the airport and wait for a flight out."

"Be careful, Nicole," Rene said thoughtfully. "Perhaps I should take out more insurance. This has never happened before."

There was silence and then she asked, "On me, Rene, or the jewels?"

"I will see you tomorrow," he said shortly and hung up.

She made up her face carefully, put on one of her wigs, and dark glasses as she often did. She wondered if she had inherited these dark brows from the father she had never known. Certainly, she did not faintly resemble Yvette or Mimi, two fair and vivacious beauties. She shrugged at her reflection in the mirror, put her travel bag over her arm, and went downstairs to check out of the hotel.

The helpful room clerk was kind enough to give her a map with directions to Bethesda and mark with a yellow highlighter the best route to the address. She had always had problems with space and distances, but she compensated with a photographic memory. If she could see it, she could follow it, to the best of her ability, and with a bit of luck, she would be entering the client's driveway by ten o'clock, the scheduled hour for the delivery. After breakfast, she started out and with only one or two forays into strange neighborhoods, she stayed mainly on track and managed to find the right house only a little after eleven instead of the appointed hour. A brass plaque near the high iron gates held the house number. The lion decorations held a "G" in their mouths, initial of the client, Gazar, so she knew she had found the right place. The fence and gates were solid, no obvious sign of an entrance, and so she sat there with the motor running, looking for a call box. There was none, but a young man, a servant in a white jacket, came out and asked her business, then briefly spoke into a portable phone, and activated the gates. He motioned her inside and closed the gates behind her.

"All the way to the rear, please. Mr. Gazar will receive you shortly. Enter through the door in the far ell of the house and wait there until he joins you."

"Merci," she said automatically, then corrected herself. "Thank you."

She directed the little, blue Escort down the long, white, graveled driveway and found the door at the back wall of the impressive brick mansion. She was surprised to note that despite the heat of the day, a large window stood open, overlooking a lush but tasteful garden area, a jungle of shrubs and flowers. She opened the door and ventured inside to find a beautiful room, a library perhaps, in deep reds. Books lined the walls, and Nicole was completely entranced as she hesitated just inside the door. The open window peaked her curiosity because as she wandered deeper into the room, she noticed a change in temperature. There was definitely air-conditioning at work. Should the window be closed? In front of the window stood a handsome console table of dark cherry and upon its glossy surface sat a basket of dried grass. In the center of the grass sat a large, white, ordinary hen's egg.

Nicole moved further into the room and noticed that some furniture had been recently removed. Markings of two chairs had left dents in the carpet. The only place to sit was the high-backed wing chair in front of the desk, and she eased into it, studying the objects on the desk. There was a newspaper, a date book, and an ashtray with several, cold, cigar butts. She picked up the ashtray, marched to the open window, and tossed the offending butts outside, then returned to the chair to regard the rest of the interesting litter. There was a candle burning right on top of a nice copy of Charles Dickens. As she watched, the wax began to drip on the red morocco binding. Why was a candle burning in daylight and on such a book? This Mr. Gazar must be an eccentric fool! She snuffed it out and gently lifted the dot of warm wax from the book with a letter opener. Then, as she replaced the letter opener, she noticed a thick wad of bills casually stuck under a corner of the desk pad in plain sight. She saw twenties, fifties, more. An ormolu clock next to the money chimed the wrong hour. Twelve o'clock. But it was not yet twelve, it was barely eleven. One drawer, half open, displayed a Smith & Wesson .38, with bullets in the chambers, and the safety off, ready to fire.

A half hour passed, and Nicole waited patiently. She regarded the red morocco bound book and noted that it was *A Tale of Two Cities*, a favorite of hers since childhood. She had picked up the book when she noticed a rippling motion behind the curtain of the open window. She quietly laid the book back on the desk and waited.

A large, black snake slithered along the windowsill, its scales gleaming in the sunlight, jet sequins that moved sensuously toward the basket on the table. It was easily six feet long and as thick around as a large man's wrist. It moved with purpose onto the tabletop, the wide head swaying back and forth. Black eyes glittered as it saw the basket; the jaws stretched wide . . . and in an instant, the white egg disappeared inside the snake. Amazingly, the egg remained whole! Neck muscles rippled. The egg moved down an inch or two as Nicole watched the progress in fascination. Again, the snake's head wavered over the basket and finding nothing more, the big, black body stretched out to full length and dropped off the windowsill out of sight.

Nicole got up and closed the window to keep the air-conditioning inside. Just as she turned around, the door to the interior of the house opened and a small, dark man entered the room. He surveyed the room with a quizzical smile on his face.

"I am Nicole Laurent, from Rene Laurent, the jeweler in Paris," she introduced herself, extending her hand.

He ignored it and pointed to the window. "Why did you close the window?"

"The heat was coming in."

"You saw the snake, didn't you?" he said with a tight smile. "You looked into the drawer. The gun was there. Why didn't you kill it before it attacked you?"

She frowned. "Why should I kill the snake? It was harmless. It only wanted to get the egg from the basket. It took the egg. I closed the window."

He nodded, gave a dry laugh, and unwrapped a fresh cigar. "Do you mind if I smoke?"

"Yes," she answered without hesitation.

He appeared angry but said nothing. His eyes flicked down to the emptied ashtray, over to the wad of money still under the edge of the desk pad, and the now unlit candle lying on its side. He gazed at the ormolu clock, then at his watch, noting the incorrect time on the clock.

"You shut my window, empty my ashtray, why didn't you set the clock?"

"But it would be the wrong time for Americans, would it not? My watch is on European time," she reminded him. "And now, monsieur, if there are no more tricks, we may conduct our business, no?"

"Of course." He put the unlit cigar into the ashtray. "The snake is a pet. It keeps my wife out of my private rooms. Most women and men too, are terrified when they see any snake that large, but you seem very calm."

Nicole unzipped the inner compartment of her shoulder bag and took out the beautifully wrapped package with the brown and gold RL logo on the gift paper and the gold seal on the brown satin ribbon. She placed the package on his desk, and then handed him the certificate of authenticity verifying its value.

Gazar ignored the package but stared intently across the desk at Nicole. She was a beauty, better in person than in Hammer's videos.

"Did you have a nice trip?" he asked. "There were no problems?"

"There was a bit of rain when we left Paris."

"I see," he said. "And my wife's new bracelet got here safely."

"Yes, monsieur, but it is a necklace. You do not wish to open it? You may check the contents, and I will rewrap it for you just as you see it."

"No, don't trouble yourself. My wife will soon open it."

She stood up, ready to leave. "Then I must say good-bye. I will be leaving America this afternoon. Rene Laurent thanks you for your patronage, and we hope you will call us again if you wish something for a special occasion. Bonjour, monsieur."

He scooped up a handful of bills from under the desk pad and tossed them toward her. "Here, take this, a little bonus for your trouble."

"Not necessary, Mr. Gazar," she said as she turned to the door. "And don't forget to set your clock."

"Then perhaps you would like this book, I noticed you admiring it," he offered, extending the copy of Charles Dickens.

Nicole hesitated at the door, turned around, took the lovely first edition, and shoved it deep into the zippered compartment of her shoulder bag. Then she was gone.

He heard the small, blue car drive away and suddenly experienced an emptiness as if the sun had gone under a cloud and the room turned dark. The woman's presence still dominated the room. He looked at the unlit cigar, started to light it, and put it down. A faint expensive perfume hung in the air near his chair where she had been sitting, and he nestled back into it. He felt as if he must remain there as long as the odor clung to the fabric captured by her, her beauty, and the lingering smell of her.

At midafternoon, the telephone shrilled.

"Yes."

"This is Ed. Has she been there?"

"Yes."

"What do you think? Will she make a good agent?"

"Have you seen Chung Pu?" countered Gazar. "Will she be able to travel soon? I want that bungling idiot out of this country as soon as possible."

"Well . . . she has a broken elbow, a slight concussion, and a deep bruise on her clavicle. While I was at the hospital, the owner of the restaurant came and gave her a small amount of money wrapped in red rice paper, and begged her not to sue them for falling on the broken soap dispenser."

"And what did she say?"

"Nothing. For now, she can't speak above a whisper, but she took the money, and the guy began to cry out of gratitude, so I hustled him out of there. I gave her the thousand we had agreed on for the snatch although she royally screwed up, plus a one-way ticket to Hong Kong."

"Take her to the plane yourself and make sure she gets on it," he ordered and abruptly hung up before Hammer could ask any more questions about Nicole Laurent.

The cigar lay nearby on the desk, but he found he had no taste for it. He threw it across the room and pressed back into the high back chair, inhaling deeply, but the tantalizing aroma of her perfume was fading. He stood up and went over to the bookcases next to the fireplace where he searched for a heavy brown-covered tome called The Bookman's Price Guide, thumbed through it until he reached the Ds. There it was. In 1987, the Dickens had been appraised for eight hundred dollars—no, that was his own notation—it had been appraised at six hundred seventy five, and in 1992, he had paid eight hundred, so the value was rising each year. *A Tale of Two Cities*, which had just walked away in Nicole Laurent's handbag, was a worthy bonus indeed.

He wished Hammer had left the videos so that he could play them again and again. He was fascinated by the woman in the couture designed red jacket and smart black skirt who could metamorphose into a dark clad running boy moving like a gazelle through the French countryside in the early hours just after dawn. And about the ormolu clock! The telephone rang again. It would be Hammer, of course, persistent in his quest.

"Yes."

"Have you made a decision about the young woman on the discs?" he asked. "I can be in Paris day after tomorrow."

There was a long silence.

"Gazar, are you there?"

"Yes, don't do anything just yet."

"Why? I have invested seven months on this project, and she is perfect."

Again, there was a long silence and then the mirthless chuckle that Hammer had begun to dread. It was a sound that definitely held incipient evil, and Hammer wished he knew what the man was thinking. For some diabolic reason Gazar was stalling about hiring Nicole Laurent. What else in God's name did he have in mind? She had handled herself exceptionally in the restaurant. Cool, unafraid, and confident. And what was more unexpected, she had told no one, just walked away from it.

"Do nothing at this time," repeated Gazar. "I will tell you when."

"Perhaps we shouldn't pursue this at all," suggested Hammer. He had begun to be apprehensive as nothing was going according to plan.

"Let's see how she runs," Gazar countered, and then chuckled again.

When Gazar added no more to the conversation, Hammer slammed down the telephone in frustration.

Gazar waited until he heard the dial tone return, then punched in the overseas operator in London. He asked for directory assistance.

"The name is Benny Painter," he said. "P-A-I-N-T-E-R. Yes, Benny Painter, just like an artist. Will you ring that number for me? Thanks."

Chapter Two

See How She Runs

Paris was asleep in the dawn of a Sunday morning, but Nicole, used to rising most mornings at five o'clock, was unable to doze off and enjoy the extra leisure, even knowing that the shop was closed on Sundays and Mondays. She wanted to enjoy her usual run, but Sundays she went to Mass. She untangled herself from the weight of Rene's heavy arm across her waist, moved far over to her side of the bed, and eased over onto her stomach. Carefully, she opened the night table drawer, took out the red bound book with its gold touches, and placing it on the floor, began to read one of the most famous lines in world literature.

"It was the best of times, it was the worst of times, it was the age of wisdom, and it was the age of foolishness . . ."

It was like meeting with old friends, for she had first read *A Tale of Two Cities* when she was ten in the convent school she had attended. All classics were encouraged, and Nicole had gobbled them up one by one from the meager library offerings. She grew to love Poe, Du Maurier, and both Brontes, and was hooked on reading everything. She bought paperbacks of contemporary authors such as Ruth Rendall, John Le Carre, and Jonathan Gash.

She read on, savoring the descriptive passages.

"He lowered the window, and looked out at the rising sun. There was a ridge of plowed land with a plough upon it where it had been left." To her annoyance, Rene roused and groggily asked the time. "Very, very early. Go back to sleep, Rene."

"Make the coffee, Cherie. I'm going out to the country. I hear there is a new calf. I hear pages turning. What is that you're reading?"

"Just an old book I picked up while I was in Washington," she answered.

"And was it expensive?"

"Practically a gift," she said as she slid it back in the drawer. "And speaking of expenses, Rene, that hotel, it was in the city. It had no restaurant. For my breakfast, I had to walk three blocks to a place of doughnuts. Next trip, it is the Holiday Inn, no?"

"Was the hotel clean?"

"It smelled of cigarettes and Clorox."

"Clorox. Ahh, then it was clean. Is this the hotel where the man tried to steal your purse? If so, I'll book you elsewhere."

"No! No! Rene, you never pay attention to me. It was a woman in a Chinese restaurant. She was an older Asian person in a terrible green suit and a very long hatpin!"

Rene sat up in bed and stared at her. "She had a hatpin? A long hatpin?"

"Yes, with poison on it . . . at least, that is what she told me."

"I think you have been dreaming the whole thing, Nicole."

Angrily, she pushed his hand away as he reached out to pull her back in the bed. How dare he doubt her word and then try to make love again! She stood up.

"I will make your coffee. Then I leave to take Maman and Mimi to church to early Mass. I tell you, I would have called the police on this person, but she fell into the soap and was possibly hurt. Perhaps the police would detain me, and I had no more money to stay in America for even one more day!"

"Very well, Nicole," he retorted. "Always with you, it is the money."

"You know I have no money, Rene, only what you give me. I work much harder than Henri-Paul, and he gets from you a nice salary."

"What do you need? You have the finest clothes, this beautiful apartment, and you have me."

"You choose my clothes. This is your apartment. You own everything and I, Nicole, have nothing. Not even all of you, Rene!"

"You are being ridiculous. Half the women in Paris would like to be in your shoes. Now, make the coffee!"

He strode into the bathroom with as much dignity as a middle-aged naked man can muster. He was smarting under her reference to his mistress. He had assumed that it was a subject never to be discussed between them, never to be mentioned. Therese was a separate part of his life, and Nicole had no part in it.

Nicole marched into the small kitchen and filled the coffee maker. The black and white tiles were cold to her bare feet as she stood there, listening to the faint drip, drip, drip of the water. She went and got a towel from the linen closet and bathed at the kitchen sink, frustrated because he was showering in the only bathroom in the otherwise luxurious apartment. One of these days, she decided, I will rent a little place with a lovely bath, just for myself. She looked at the kitchen clocks, wishing there was time to go out to the farm where she could run, alone, and free in the crisp morning air, before the heat of the day began. Tomorrow, she promised herself.

The pale gray, linen suit was appropriate for church, but she had no hat. She pinned a small square of white lace over her mop of unruly hair. Maman insisted on a head covering for church. Maman and Mimi would be wearing carefully coordinated outfits, dresses they had made on their Singer machines, and hats chosen to match. My darlings, Nicole sighed, they are everything in the world to me.

She hurried downstairs and out to the parking lot where she found her little, original Volkswagen behind the shop. The paint had faded to an interesting shade or shades, in part light blue and in part faded yellow. It had a rear engine as small as a vacuum cleaner, but on good days, it would race along the autobahn at seventy miles per hour, that is, on any day it chose to run at all. She drove across the city to the rows of decrepit three-story flats that she used to call home, then parked, and trudged up two flights of steep stairs to the third floor. To her horror, there was a man in uniform sitting outside her mother's door.

"Who are you? What are you doing here?" she demanded.

"Well, who are you?" the guard shot back.

At that moment, the door opened and Yvette and Mimi appeared, looking delicious like ice cream sundaes, in strawberry pink, and a shade between mango and peach. Not only their hats, but also shoes and purses matched. Where did they find such things, Nicole often wondered, and all in meticulous taste. Today, they could have had tea with Queen Elizabeth and been in perfect fashion at Buckingham Palace.

"This is Bertrand," they announced. "He is here because of the dress. Bertie, this is our child, Nicole, who is taking us to Mass."

Bertrand tipped his hat and ushered her into the apartment.

"Show her the dress, Yvette," insisted Mimi. "And you'll see why we need Bertie. Everything real . . . no cheating with waxes and plastics on this one!"

As they passed through the living room, Nicole noticed that the hard, old, horsehair sofa, which used to be her own bed, had been nicely slipcovered in rose damask. Along the fireplace mantel were still arranged all her dancing trophies, some twenty or more. Yvette and Mimi took her to ballet school when she was three, but Nicole rebelled and insisted on tap dancing classes, which they thought, were vulgar; but they gave in when they discovered that she had cut all the tutus in pieces and dressed every protesting cat in the neighborhood in pink and blue tulle. They not only gave in, but they also began to take her to the American Classics Theatre, where they would watch the old movies and then would enter Nicole in the talent contests, which were held every Saturday night. Nicole was a natural. She could see a dance routine and memorize all the steps. They dressed her in a little, yellow slicker and hat, and she danced to Gene Kelly's "Singing in the Rain" performance to win her first trophy. Yvette made her a costume straight out of Shirley Temple's movie; *The Little Colonel* and Nicole won another trophy. She won so often that the management asked the ladies to please keep that precocious child at home so that others would have a chance. So they took her to other towns and discovered that some places gave cash awards! But at the age of thirteen, Nicole was nominated as a foreign exchange student to the United States. Yvette and Mimi cried, but she left Paris, only to return during summer vacations, for four long years.

They pushed Nicole along to the bedroom they shared and on one of the twin beds was a cream-colored satin creation of exquisite beauty. Nearby sat bowls of real pearls to be arranged in a design of roses. Yvette uncovered a tray of diamonds and explained in a hushed voice, "They are real. That is why Bertie is here, to guard the dress."

"Oh, Maman, such close work. Your eyes. And your poor fingers."

"But they asked especially for us, Nicole. They wanted the best. What could we do, say no? And we have an invitation to the wedding!"

"She won't let me smoke in my own home because of this dress," complained Mimi. "I must hang out the window like wash on the clothesline!"

Mimi coughed deeply, and Nicole patted her thin back.

"You sound dreadful. You must stop smoking. They are killing you, no?"

"I'll do as I please. It is only a little cold."

"Take her to the doctor, Maman."

"She refuses to go," said Yvette, painfully pulling on her gloves over her arthritic fingers. "Come, we'll be late to Mass."

Bidding Bertrand good-bye, they went down to the parking lot and climbed into Yvette's pretty, blue Citroen, a sort of gift from her long-time lover, Enrico Garibaldi, who bought her a new car every two years but retained the title so that she wouldn't sell it and buy a cheaper model. Nicole drove the Citroen on Sundays, her mother in the passenger seat, and her grandmother in the back seat, her head halfway out of the window, puffing on a cigarette. It was their little Sunday routine and even when quarreling and complaining, they loved being together and adored each other.

After Mass, they always enjoyed breakfast at one of the several cafes, sometimes inside, but in good weather, at one of the street-side outdoor tables. Here, they watched people and made wryly observant and bitingly critical remarks, all in good humor. They had chosen just such a place this Sunday when the incident occurred.

"I would like to slap his face, such a slap as his mother never gave him!" said Mimi, loudly. She bit into a croissant with vicious fury.

The other two women looked up in surprise and gazed around.

"That Englishman!" snarled Mimi, inhaling and expelling a great cloud of blue smoke through her nose. "He has never taken his eyes off our Nicole. Such rudeness! I am insulted. Look, he is drinking tea. I told you he was English, no? Look, now he knows I am on to him. They called us frogs during the big war. We called them limeys."

All three women were now openly staring at the man at a table by the street. He was wiry and thin, with a long, unattractive nose, and he wore a tweed jacket and cap, with baggy trousers. His long fingers closed around his cup, and he hastily looked out into the traffic as if to show he was expecting someone to arrive.

"He is not even looking this way," noted Nicole, reaching for the marmalade.

"Did I not see his face looking at you?" challenged Mimi. "And he was at the church too."

"You imagine this. At the church?"

"Perhaps she is right, Cherie," Yvette put in cautiously. "I noticed a man like that, with a bicycle, waiting outside the church when we came down the steps."

"Didn't I say so?" asked Mimi, triumphantly. "Go, slap his face, Yvette!"

Her voice carried across the sidewalk. The man threw a handful of francs on his table, began to walk away casually, then faster and faster, and turned the corner.

Mimi crushed her cigarette out and stared as the man disappeared out of sight. "I never liked the limeys. Just imagine, he was wearing tweed on a summer's day. It was once a good piece of wool, but now, it is old and worn at the sleeves."

"Yes, a good piece of wool," agreed Yvette.

"He is gone now, no?" shrugged Nicole. "Shall we go by the water and see the children with their little boats?"

"But, look, there is his bicycle," Yvette said. "Chained to a tree just beyond my beautiful new car. Why did he leave his bicycle?"

"Yes, yes," agreed Mimi, quickly. "A red bicycle!"

"A blue bicycle," corrected Yvette. "So curious! Why does he leave it on the tree and walk so quickly away?"

"You are sure this is the same man and the same bicycle?" asked Nicole.

"At the church and then here. I am sure. A tweed cap and coat in the summer? This is not only bad taste but stupid," commented Yvette.

Nicole finished her wine and became silent as the others continued to speculate about the Englishman's abandoned bicycle. She was thinking about the attack in Washington in the Chinese restaurant. No one had ever tried to rob her since she had been a courier although she had always taken precautions in case of such an incident. Sometimes, the jewels were mailed ahead and picked up in the city of delivery. Occasionally, she simply wore the ring or brooch as part of her own clothing and carried an empty box and wrappings in her shoulder bag. The Chinese woman had been on the flight from Paris, followed her from the airport to the little restaurant, and made her attack there. How had she known that Nicole was carrying an expensive necklace unless someone told her? And the restaurant, it was neither a popular spot nor well known in any way, hidden as it was in the shopping center. Someone must have brought her there. Nicole had not mentioned this to her mother or grandmother because it would only distress them, but now . . . this man on a bicycle . . . if he were part of a larger conspiracy to steal jewels, why was he stalking her now when she was carrying nothing of value.

"He is not returning," observed Yvette, peering up the street.

"Oh, forget this mystery man, Maman, let's go see the little boats," suggested Nicole again, "and the little children in their Sunday clothes. So sweet!"

"Rene does not expect you?" asked Mimi. "He does not wish his dinner?"

"He has gone to the country," Nicole informed them. She unpinned the piece of white lace from her hair.

"That woman!" growled Mimi. "He has the most beautiful prize in the world, and he goes to that woman. I never understand men. The only one was your grandfather. He never took a mistress, let me tell you. I would break both his legs!"

"We didn't know about her when we encouraged Nicole to marry."

"Ha! You thought he was rich, and what good does it do us," snapped Mimi, reaching for the last croissant and wrapping it in a napkin.

"Oooh, put that back, Mimi it has butter on it, no?" exclaimed Nicole.

Defiantly, Mimi pushed the croissant into her large straw bag.

As they got up to leave, Nicole reached over, took the cigarette from Mimi's lips, and dropped it into the water in the gutter.

"Stop that! I am your grandmother!"

"Get into the car," said Nicole. "And no smoking in there."

Muttering under her breath, the older woman climbed into the back seat of the Citroen and turned her head away from them angrily.

Out of her hearing, Nicole turned to her mother and murmured softly, "She coughs so deep and gets hoarse quickly. When she coughs, is there blood, Maman?"

Yvette looked down at the sidewalk. "No, but her friend, Gerta, perhaps, Gerta thinks it is . . . oh, Cherie, I cannot say the word."

"Get in the car, Maman," Nicole said gently. "We will think of something. I must check on the rear tires. The car was riding a bit flat today, no?"

"I didn't notice, but you look at them, Nicole. I always leave such car things to Enrico."

As soon as both ladies were seated inside and arguing between themselves, Nicole walked to the rear, casually kicked the tires, and walked back to where the bicycle was chained to the tree. Pretending to shake a pebble from her shoe, she knelt beside the bicycle and let the air out of both tires, then threw the little black caps far over into the grass.

* * *

Monday morning, there was a nice little drizzling rain that washed the dusty streets of the city and freshened the air. Nicole was up, as usual, at 5:00 a.m. She put on a loose T-shirt, skimpy black shorts, white socks and running shoes, and said a prayer that the Volkswagen would start.

Traffic was not heavy at this hour, so she drove quickly across town and out into the countryside about five miles to the LeGrand farm, where she had found the perfect place to run, a sort of four-sided oval totaling exactly seven miles. From the parking area, there was one mile to the stone wall, then three miles along the side where the ruins of the original farmhouse were indicated by crumbling walls that had once been an ancient sod house, now in the last stages of decay. Then around the two miles past the new farmhouse on the far side, and another mile back to where she parked the car. She always ran a little slower as she came to the sod house. How primitive the life within this ruin must have been. A stone sink still stood where the kitchen used to be, a rusted pump handle projecting from its base. The basin was an interesting slate green from the mosses that grew there. And nearby was the old well, dry now except in times of heavy rainfall, the top, with rotted wood slats only partially covered the black hole beneath. Monsieur LeGrand had warned her to stay away from the well, which was unnecessary because she never left the outside path running along the stone wall. And here, on the path, she knew every low hanging branch of the big trees, and where the gnarled roots grew under the wall to trip the unwary runner. It was certainly not the even terrain that the usual runner would pick for himself, so Nicole had this path all to herself.

Some days Monsieur LeGrand would come out and give her fresh, red tomatoes or a piece of fruit, but today, because of the rain, he stayed inside his new farmhouse and waved to her from the window. She waved back and continued to run but when she rounded the turn, she came to an abrupt stop. A huge branch of the tall oak tree stretched some twenty feet or more fell across the path. It was a fresh fall, the leaves still rising and trembling, raindrops spraying from sudden contact with the ground below. Nicole glanced up, and she could see yellowish, white striations where it had fit into the bole, no jagged spikes, but a clean break. Up to the sky, she could see no other damage on this strong tree except for this one, great fallen giant, which stretched across the path.

The limb would be way too heavy for her to move alone. As she stood there, rain running off her head onto her soaking T-shirt, she had the eerie sensation that she was being watched, and in the silence, there came a squeaking sound, as of a turning wheel. It stopped suddenly as if an unseen hand had stilled the wheel. Someone was waiting just beyond, under cover of the fallen branch.

Nicole backed up, ran forward at high speed, and cleared the stone wall in a single leap. She took off, running fast across the fields. Two cows looked up from their grazing, sensed the unusual and began to lumber along behind her, then, seeing a fresh stand of clover near the old well, forgot why they were on the move and stopped to investigate the scent of something tasty. LeGrand's ancient sheepdog struggled to his feet and gave several hoarse barks as she passed the new farmhouse.

"It is only Nicole, Boncoeur," she assured him. "Go back to sleep."

By the time she reached the Volkswagen, the rain had settled into a steady downpour. She jumped inside and reached for an old sweater she kept on the back seat, wiped her wet head and arms as best she could in the confines of the small car. Catching her breath, the wipers swishing back and forth across the windshield, the radio playing softly, she began to laugh at herself.

"You are so silly, Nicole! Of course, the rains weakened the branch or perhaps there was lightning."

She put the car in reverse, turned around and headed for the road that led back to the city. It was still early, and Paris was just beginning to wake to the new day.

* * *

Down on the path near LeGrand's farm, Benny Painter had managed to drag the bicycle out from under the tree branch. Everything had gone wrong. Earlier, he had stood on the seat of the bicycle with a saw he had borrowed from the barn and attacked the oak tree. The branch had come loose sooner than he had planned and crashed down. Taken by surprise, he had managed to jump free, but the bicycle stayed partly under the heavy branch, its back wheel spinning furiously, and making a loud, churning sound just as the woman appeared on the path on the other side of the tree. He had lain down out of sight and attempted to stop the wheel. Now, the spokes were twisted and one fender pressed against a ruptured tire, making it inoperable. Painter swore, lifted his fist at the rain, and thought about the long, long walk back to the main road. He kicked the bike and then dragged it into the underbrush where he covered it with leaves and vines. A rental. He would have to declare it stolen, and Gazar would be angry when he saw this item on the account, but he would pay. "Frighten the girl good," he had instructed, "I want to know how she reacts under pressure. But don't hurt her." Painter shook his head. A minute or two sooner, and the girl would have been under the branch when it crashed to the ground, and then what? A broken neck or back? Perhaps the blow would have killed her. Gazar would have been very angry, and he, poor Benny Painter, would never have escaped the consequences. He would have had to disappear.

Dwelling on his fragile ties to life in this uncertain business, Painter started the long trek back toward the city. At the main road, he managed to get a ride on the back of a chicken farmer's truck, which took him to the market district, not far from the red-light district, where he had a third-floor room over a brothel. Already, he had enjoyed two of the first floor residents, and they seemed to be fond of him. He tried to think of a plan to employ one of the prostitutes to accost Nicole Laurent and beat her up a little, but he couldn't conceive of a likely place where two such opposite ladies would meet. It was up to him. Always Gazar left the hard stuff up to him!

Wearily, he trudged over to the bicycle rental place and with some force, tossed the lock and chain down upon the counter.

"What is wrong, monsieur?" asked the clerk, staring at the lock and chain.

"The bicycle was stolen!" Painter exploded convincingly. He was wet, he was tired, and he smelled strongly of chickens. Feathers clung to his tweed coat and manure smeared the soles of his shoes.

"You are supposed to lock it when not riding. Why do you not do this?"

"I was riding. A big oaf knocked me to the ground and rode away. This Paris is full of thieves, by George! The lock and chain were in my pocket."

"Alors! But you are not hurt, monsieur?" the clerk asked anxiously.

"A bruise here and there. I need another bike right away."

"Perhaps you should rent a car?" suggested the clerk, making copious notes.

"Don't drive. Never have. Let's see what you have in the back room. Something good and sturdy for long rides in the country."

* * *

Rene and Nicole were eating breakfast in the small, but tastefully decorated dining room of the apartment. They felt no need to hurry because the continuing rain was sure to keep most customers away. No need to rush down to the shop.

"A big branch fell from an oak tree on LeGrand's farm where I run," Nicole was trying to tell him. "The leaves still trembled as I approached it."

"I am reading the newspapers, Nicole," grunted Rene.

"Then, I heard the sound of a turning wheel."

"The stock market is down another ten points. Brokers are playing games."

"But I saw no person around." She looked at the back pages of the newspaper, which he held in front of his face. "Yesterday I ate a cat, Rene. And today, I will eat a lizard. Tomorrow . . ."

"I am glad I did not take Henri-Paul's advice. The man is a fool. It is all computers these days. Whatever are you on about, Nicole?"

"Nothing, Rene. Would you like more coffee?"

"No, I am going to the shop now. Come along as soon as you have cleared this up," he said, as he tossed his napkin on the table. He folded the newspaper and stuck it under his arm. He crossed the kitchen, and she could hear his footsteps going down the steps. She stared down into her own empty cup.

"And would you care for more coffee, Nicole?" she asked herself. "Yes, I would. And a bit of jam on that last piece of toast, and my dearest wife, perhaps you would like to work this crossword puzzle in this newspaper before I carry it away?"

She rambled on in a two-way conversation as she gathered the dishes on a large silver tray and took them to the kitchen. She loaded the dishwasher, reached for the telephone, and dialed the number of the LeGrand's farm.

"Madam, this is Nicole. Has the path been cleared of the big tree branch?"

"No, no. My son will come when this rain stops. He has a big saw. Oh, Nicole, Boncoeur is so funny! He knows something is amiss down there. He goes to the stone fence, old feller, and barks at the tree. You would think his bone is hidden there. We call, Boncoeur, Boncoeur! But he stays by the tree. Like old people, he does not like any change. The path will be cleared soon, ma Cherie."

"Thank you, madam. I will see you soon. Bonjour."

Boncoeur. A handsome fellow. He was perhaps ten or twelve. I would like to have a dog. I would love a child. But Rene has made it plain to me that he does not wish to be burdened with encumbrances. How did I ever come to this place?

I want my own life back, Nicole decided.

* * *

Across the ocean, in a small, tidy office within sight of the Smithsonian, G. Edmund Hammer was dreaming of Nicole Laurent. He had an 8 × 10 blowup of her face, taken from the surveillance videos in his top drawer so that each time he reached for a pen or memo pad, he could gaze down at that fascinating image. The eyes were so dark and expressive, and yet, yielding nothing of her inner thoughts. A woman like that, you could never guess what she was thinking, which would be part of the mystery, the enchantment. He desperately wanted her in the game, and he couldn't understand why Gazar was taking so long to call and give final approval to recruit her as a covert agent. Perhaps Gazar was out of the country, he had homes everywhere, but then again, perhaps he was not. With Gazar, one never knew his next move. It was always a waiting game.

* * *

By Thursday, the rains had gone, the big tree branch had been cut into logs, and the path beside the stone fence had been cleared, but still, Nicole had not come to the farm for her early morning run. Benny Painter, however, had been lurking by the big oak tree every day. He would arrive at dawn, hide the bicycle, and wait. The sheep dog was let out of the farmhouse kitchen about 6:00 a.m. and would race down to the fence, sniffing, and letting out the occasional hoarse bark, but the farmer never came down to see if there was trouble. After a while, the dog would lope back to the porch and stay there, but his eyes never left the fence. Damn nuisance, that dog. On Wednesday, it occurred to Painter that maybe Nicole was only running part of the way to avoid the tree, so he ran around the entire seven miles. The pain was excruciating. His long legs were used to pedaling bicycles, and the different set of muscles called into play rebelled half way around. He had to rest near the new farmhouse, and of course, the sheep dog had to make his presence known to the woman in the house. The farmer's wife came out on the porch, eyed him suspiciously, and wiped her hands on her apron.

Painter struggled to his feet, tipped his tweed cap, and kept walking. The woman watched him out of sight, and then called the dog into the house. Tomorrow, Painter vowed, as he unlocked the new bicycle from a tree, if the girl does not come again, I will call Gazar and tell him she left France for Africa, drowned in the Seine, fell from the Eiffel Tower . . . anything! He climbed onto the bike and pedaled slowly back to the main road. Tonight he would pay one of the girls in the brothel to come to his room, massage his legs, and draw him a hot bath. For once, sex was far from his mind. He ached all over. Later in the night, perhaps, but he thought not . . .

* * *

The pink rays of dawn made bars of light on the cream-colored wall as a new day peeped through the slats of the blinds. Rene lay sleeping, but Nicole was wide-awake. Quietly, she slid the drawer of the night table open and brought out the red book. Hanging over the side of the bed, she entered Dickens's world. The latently noble Carton, the horrible Madame Dafarge, and the indomitable Englishwoman, Ms. Pross. As the rising sun illumined the pages, she reluctantly closed the book, and tucked it back in the drawer.

Rene murmured in his sleep, turned over, and ran his hand up the back of her short satin nightshirt; his fingers sought her breast, and he breathed into her neck. She lay very still until he began to snore softly, then slipped out of bed and tiptoed to the bathroom where she showered and dressed.

The black, spandex jogging suit had been on sale. It had wide yellow stripes on the sleeves and down each side of the knee-length pants. She admired the new suit in the door mirror, and then put on her socks and old running shoes.

"What I need is new black shoes, but today, these ugly flops will have to do," she mused.

She went into the kitchen and started the coffee maker, took sweet rolls from the pantry, and set them beside Rene's cup. Quietly, she left the apartment and went down to the Volkswagen where she rolled the windows down to let in the morning breeze. Cool air blew in, ruffling her short, dark hair as she crossed the city.

The leaves and underbrush were still wet from the recent rains on the road to LeGrand's farm and if Nicole had noticed, she would have seen the deep ruts made by a bicycle in the moisture along the shoulder. But her mind was on the trip to Sweden she had to make on the coming Sunday to deliver a three-piece diamond and emerald set to an executive of an international engineering corporation. She had delivered other gems and a few rare coins to the same client in the past, and she looked forward to going again. It was deliciously cool in the mountains and lovely to stay overnight in the guest chalet. Her host always insisted. Could she refuse such kindness?

She parked the Volkswagen in her usual place, got out and limbered up with a few knee bends, a few jumping jacks, then ran in place. When she paused, her ears picked up a sound from a nearby clump of trees—a wheel turning! It stopped. She stood perfectly still. There was silence except for a few birdcalls and the hum of bees in a sweet flowering bush at the side of the road. Looking back warily over her shoulder, she started down the path at a slow pace and gradually increased speed. About a mile ahead, the ruins of the old sod house came into view, the two cows grazed by the stone wall, the fallen limb from the big oak tree had been carried away, and everything up ahead looked normal, so she slackened speed a bit and relaxed.

Abreast of the tree, she glanced back. A tall, thin man had come out of the woods, riding a new red bicycle. He wore a familiar tweed cap and jacket. The Englishman!

Benny Painter pedaled hard until he was just a few yards behind her. He had picked the spot because this area was protected from prying eyes that may be looking from the farmhouse, although he had seen the old farmer's pickup truck leave earlier and believed that no person was at home. As he came face to face with the woman, he drew in his breath. He had not known how pretty she was, having seen her only at a distance. He had never had a really beautiful woman, and he felt an unexpected flush of excitement as she turned to challenge him.

"What do you want? I have nothing to steal!" she shouted at him, holding her empty hands out to show him. "Why are you following me?"

She looked so small and vulnerable. It excited him. Out here, in the woods, who would know? Gazar had said not to hurt her, but she was a married woman. You couldn't rape a married woman, could you? They had to have sex any time their husbands told them to, didn't they? He slowly removed his cap and jacket and tossed them onto the handlebars. He could feel the rapid beating of his heart in anticipation.

Nicole took two steps backward and turned to run, but he was leaping at her, pinioning her arms at her sides. She could feel the gasps of hot breath on her neck and smell his heavy sweat. She gave a sudden twist and came up with her knee into his groin but it glanced off, not strong enough to hurt but hard enough to make him furious and more determined than ever. He grunted, stepped back, and hit her on the side of her head with his hand. She staggered for a second, and then came back with an upward blow under his nose with a force that rocked him. Blood shot from his long, thin nose and tears burst from his eyes at the pain. He clawed away at the blood and half-blinded, rushed at her with both fists upraised, but she jumped out of the way and ran for the stone wall. His fingers reached out as she flew past, but he couldn't find a grip on the shiny spandex of the new running suit. She slipped by him, running faster than she had ever run before. He thundered close behind, guttural noises coming from his throat as he tried to catch her before she reached the stone wall. Like a gazelle, her body lifted up, and she cleared the fence.

Once on the other side, Nicole glanced back. He was struggling to climb over, his long legs straddling the upper stones, grunting, and cursing. With one more effort, he pulled himself up and fell to the other side. He attempted to stand up.

"Holy Mary, Mother of God, help me!" panted Nicole.

The abandoned well lay ahead, but she didn't take time to run around it. She leaped onto one of the decaying boards across the top, heard it fall down into the black water below just as her feet touched ground on the far side, and kept running.

As she neared the LeGrand farmhouse, old Boncoeur came out from under the porch where he had been sleeping and belatedly began his hoarse bark. Nicole ran up on the porch and beat on the door, but nobody answered. Then she noticed that the pickup truck was missing from the driveway. Still she continued to beat on the door just in case Madam LeGrand had not gone with her husband. There was no one at home. After a few minutes, she crept to the edge of the porch and peered toward the path. The cows were moving nervously to the house, their eyes rolling, their plaintive mooing echoing across the pasture. Boncoeur circled them, instinctively watching for danger.

Nicole walked a short way into the yard. A shovel stood near the porch, and she armed herself with it. She circled the house, looked down the steps that led to the basements, and finding nothing, headed for the roads still carrying the shovel.

Looking back and into the woods on either side, she ran all the way back to the clearing where the Volkswagen was parked. The little faded two-toned car started on the first try. With shaking fingers, she made sure the windows were rolled to the top and locked the doors. The shovel lay handy against the passenger's seat.

"Blessed art thou among women," she intoned fervently. "Blessed is the fruit of thy womb, Jesus."

She drove away, alert for any sign of a red bicycle in the rear view mirror, but there was nothing. What is happening to me? Who will help me? She thought distractedly as she headed for the city. Rene pays no attention to me. Yvette and Mimi cannot be troubled with my problems. They would only worry. She drove into Paris, selected a cafe at random, and sat far inside away from the window, ordered a bagel with cream cheese and two cups of hot, strong coffee. That man. He was at the church on Sunday and later at the cafe. Yvette and Mimi saw him and remarked about his woolen cap and jacket. Now he appears at LeGrand's farm and threatens her. Who was he and what did he want from her? Was he a stalker? Nicole had seen that look on men's faces when they looked at her from the time she was a skinny thirteen. If she saw him again, she would go straight and report him to the police. She would do it today, but she knew neither his name nor where he could be found. Her cheek hurt where he had punched her, and she put her hand to her face. I am glad I bloodied his nose, she gloated, clenching her fist, and I would do it again. There would be a bruise. What shall I tell Rene if he notices?

When she reached the apartment, she noted that the sweet rolls and coffee had vanished, dirty dishes were in the sink, and Rene had gone to work downstairs. There was a fluted glass with two white roses in it and beneath the glass was a round trip ticket to Sweden. Her heart softened. Rene was a good man, a tender lover.

She showered, dressed, and carefully covered her cheek with a layer of pancake makeup, then chose one of her wigs, light brown and curly, which effectively pulled forward. Down in the shop below, Rene was busy with a customer, but he looked up and smiled as she passed. She blew him a kiss, walked to the front and began to polish a silver chalice.

* * *

As he sank to the bottom of the well, Benny Painter breathed his last breath. Water gushed into his lungs. The recent heavy rains had filled the deep well to a level of about twelve feet. The long, thin body curled into a fetal position, covered by the last of the rotted boards that had covered the opening.

A week later, Monsieur LeGrand discovered that old wooden cover had finally caved in and arranged to have a new cement top made. In inspecting the damage to the big oak tree, his sheepdog, Boncoeur, had uncovered a broken bicycle hidden by debris nearby and barking his hoarse bark, drew his master's attention to it. And what was more astounding was the discovery of still another bicycle, this one almost new, on the path where the girl, Nicole, always ran, and an old tweed cap and jacket hung over the handlebars. LeGrand looked around for the owner, called out into the woods, but there was no answer. Perhaps a call of nature? Monsieur LeGrand shrugged and left everything as he found it, but later on in the day when he returned, everything was the same. He rolled the new bicycle to his barn and returned to retrieve the broken one. No need for such fine bicycles to stay out in the weather and become rusted. His wife tossed the cap and jacket into the dustbin.

"It is old and stinks of a dirty man's sweat!" she exclaimed, holding her nose.

"But it was once a good piece of wool," observed Monsieur LeGrand.

"Yes, once a good piece of wool," Madam agreed. "But no more."

The two bicycles were a puzzle. He inquired of neighbors but no one claimed them, nor had they noticed anyone strange about the place. Time passed and now and then Monsieur LeGrand regarded the bicycles in his barn. When a suitable period had gone by, he gave the best one, the new red one, to his grandson for his seventh birthday.

* * *

Gazar was angry, and he grew angrier each day that Benny Painter did not report in. He should never have wired him an advance, Gazar thought, just a London to Paris ticket and a few dollars for the low-class rooms that Painter favored. When a week passed, he sent another agent to Paris to locate a place where Painter may be staying.

The third house in the red-light district yielded the information that indeed, Monsieur Painter had stayed there in a room on the third floor, but he had gone away, he owed the madam rent, and a bicycle shop was calling. He called Gazar.

"Go to his room and see what you can find," was the order.

The agent went up to the third floor, knocked, and asked the madam to use her key to open the door. This bit took a quick exchange of cash between them before she wandered off downstairs to leave him to his search. In this place, where Benny Painter had spent his last few days of life, there was little to show that a person had lived here. There was one change of underwear, disposable razors, and one dirty shirt. In a pair of socks was a little less than four hundred dollars tucked into the toe. There was a notice from a bicycle shop threatening civil action if a second bicycle were not returned immediately. The agent called Gazar again.

"Our bird has flown," he reported.

"Close it out," came the terse reply.

The agent paid for the room, settled with the rental shop for the missing bicycle, and returned to Washington on the next flight out from de Gaulle.

Gazar thought about Chung Pu. He thought about Benny Painter. He picked up the telephone and dialed G. Edmund Hammer.

"Ed, get me Nicole Laurent."

Chapter Three

The Interview

Nothing had gone right on the trip to Sweden. When Nicole was met at the airport by Gunther Holm's private limousine, the driver, who introduced himself as Ian, seemed surprised at her lack of luggage. He stowed her tote bag up front and looked around for more, then asked whether there were suit bags containing her dresses for the galas.

Galas? Rene had said nothing about parties. If he had known there would be parties, he probably would have made this trip himself. Was she expected to stay?

"I'm not actually a guest," she explained. "I am just the courier from Rene Laurent, the jeweler. I am delivering Mrs. Nola's anniversary present."

"Nicole Laurent."

"Yes."

"You are listed as a guest," he consulted a chart. "You must be important. You have been given Chalet Ein, nearest the manor, and you are booked as a guest through Wednesday."

"I'm afraid I can't stay that long. I am to deliver the gift to Monsieur Holm on Monday, that's tomorrow, and leave Tuesday morning to go back to Paris. And I did not bring anything formal. I'm afraid there has been a misunderstanding."

Unhappily, she thought about the new Vera Wang that Rene had made for her. It was hanging in the special closet in the apartment and had yet to be worn. If only Rene had guessed that she was expected to stay and attend galas, he would have sent the Wang and a suitable accompanying set of outstanding gems.

"I have nothing appropriate with me. I simply can't stay," she repeated.

"Ms. Honey will find you something. Ms. Honey has two big rooms just for clothes," the driver confided. "As her weight goes up and down, she has sizes from slim to plump and all in between, and she is so generous that she'll open the doors and tell you to pick out anything you want. Such a pleasure working for a real lady."

"And shoes?"

"She has all kinds," Ian assured her. Then gazing down at Nicole's small feet, he suggested that perhaps she would like to stop in town at a little boutique, very stylish, and he knew the manager, who would give her a fair price.

Ms. Honey Bola was a beautiful, buxom blonde, who had had her name changed legally from Charissa May, one week after winning the Ms. Honey contest in Montgomery, Alabama, thirty years ago. Gunther Holms, visiting an engineer friend, agreed to fill in as a judge in the contest, although he knew nothing about beehives or honey. But he recognized a beautiful person when he saw Charissa May. She looked down from the runway, Gunther gazed up, and sparks flew. Two weeks later, they were married, and thirty years later, they were still fascinated by the differences in each other.

Rene had made things for Ms. Honey in the past. She and Gunther dropped by the shop when in Paris and never left empty-handed. Nicole liked them both. She also loved Sweden, the cool, crisp air, and the privacy of the little chalets dotted about the grounds adjacent to the mansion that was home to Gunther and Ms. Honey.

As soon as she was deposited at Chalet Ein, she called Rene and explained the change in plans. Reluctantly, he agreed that she must stay for the galas.

"What Jewelry do you have with you, Nicole?" he asked anxiously.

"Nothing, Rene. Just my wedding band and my silver chain from Mimi."

"What a wasted opportunity!" he fumed. "Half of Europe will be there and the wife of Rene Laurent will be wearing a cheap silver necklace!"

He hung up without saying good-bye.

Nicole touched the silver chain around her neck. She seemed to remember having it for a very long time, since she was three or four. Yvette had not wanted her to have it, but Mimi insisted. It had always been Nicole's favorite piece of jewelry. It was a close-linked chain and from the center hung a tiny swing like a trapeze, and holding the wires was a tiny figure, balanced not on the seat, but above it. Man or woman, one could not tell, just a fragile silver figure, suspended in air.

* * *

On Monday, Nicole gave Gunther Nelm the set of diamonds and emeralds, one ring, one necklace, and one bracelet. There was one gala for charity on Monday afternoon and a second on Tuesday night, which is when he presented Ms. Honey with her gift for their thirtieth anniversary. Everyone exclaimed and admired over it and Ms. Honey immediately took off the diamonds she was wearing and insisted on putting on the new set right away. The jewels sparkled as Gunther and Ms. Honey danced and flirted until the wee hours of the morning. Nicole was pleased that Rene's work had met with such success. The women guests were envious and their husbands were casually checking the wrappings for the name of the designer in case they needed something for a future occasion. Everything appeared to have gone well.

But on Wednesday morning, as Nicole prepared to leave for the airport, Ms. Honey appeared at the door of Chalet Ein, holding the necklace and bracelet in her hand.

"Darling Nicole, if it is not just too much trouble, I want your husband to put in two teensy weensy diamonds in the clasps so that I can sparkle from the back as well as the front," she explained. "And if one goes in the necklace, then one goes in the bracelet or the designs won't match, you do see that, don't you?"

"Of course, Madam, if that would please you," agreed Nicole in an even voice but the older woman felt her tension and saw it in her expression.

"Gunny will make it worth your while, sweetie, and pay for the extra airfare from Paris, and I want you to have those little ole silk things you borrowed for the galas . . . no, no, I insist! They looked darling on you!"

"No, really, I couldn't."

"Ian is putting them in the car. And tell Rene to put in those teensy weensy diamonds as soon as possible because we are leaving for the States in two weeks, and I want to show my mama what a good catch Gunny turned out to be. She still doesn't like him after thirty years. She always liked that ole football coach who was always hanging around when I was a cheerleader, ole Grady Bush, can you imagine?"

"I'll explain to Rene," said Nicole, accepting the jewels reluctantly and putting them deep into the zipper compartment of her shoulder bag. No box! No wrappings!

Ms. Honey kissed her cheek and waved good-bye.

Rene would be furious. Once his designs were complete, he did not want to change a thing. He would be hell to be around. His ego crushed. The shop work schedule halted and a second trip back to Sweden to return the jewels to the Holms. Nicole dreaded the scene when she got back to Paris and had to explain this one. More sparkle, Rene! Oh, the shop would not be a happy place this week until the clasps were done.

* * *

Gazar received a call from Richard Leach, in the Paris office, a few days later with some unexpected news.

"She has booked another flight back to Sweden," he reported. He gave the date, time, and asked if there was anything more Gazar wanted him to do.

"No, thanks, Richard. Good job. My man in Washington will handle it from here and if all goes well, and she agrees to work with us, she will contact you."

"Good luck, sir. She looks damn interesting," said Leach. "I hope it's a go because she looks promising. I look forward to it."

* * *

Nicole stood in the early morning light through the bedroom window, moving quietly so as not to disturb Rene, who was still asleep and gently snoring. She was sorting through her own meager wardrobe. What was appropriate for meeting a total stranger who had opened a mysterious door to a new life? She had not slept well all night and when she did doze off, she must have made troubled sounds because several times Rene had shaken her shoulder and told her to be quiet. Bad dream. The unknown always provoked bad dreams. By 5:00 a.m., she had come to a decision. She would meet the man and simply see what more he had to say but remain noncommittal. She selected a pale beige, linen shirt and black jeans, added a pair of black, leather sandals. In case she arrived too early, she reached into the drawer of the nightstand, took out her copy of *A Tale of Two Cities,* and put it in her shoulder bag to have something to occupy her time. Mr. Hammer had said that he would be taking the eight o'clock flight out of Orly. After that, the man and his offer would be gone, and she would always wonder about it, if she didn't follow through. The attraction, she had to admit, was the money. Real money, money that would be hers alone. Not the plane tickets, nor the designer clothes, and not expensive gems that were always sold to someone else after just one wearing, which is what she had from Rene.

She thought about the man who called himself G. Edmund Hammer. They had met on the plane to Sweden, and he introduced himself, giving her an enigmatic business card, which contained only his name and a telephone number. From his pocket, he had taken a small gift-wrapped box. Chocolates, he explained, Godiva. His friend always gave him the same thing, and he knew he didn't eat chocolates . . . but who can refuse a kind gesture? Would she like to have them, chocolate with a cream praline filling? She told him they were her favorites and accepted the little box. From another pocket, he unrolled a copy of "Elle," the French fashion magazine, and said he had finished reading it and asked would she like to have it to peruse on the flight?

Nicole had considered "Elle" a strange choice for a man who would have looked more at home with "Wall Street Week," but she took it and thanked him.

He seemed very nice. Clean, well shaven. Graying hair. A neat, dark suit and striped tie in good taste. Silver-framed glasses. On the trip over, he spoke to her pleasantly and with obvious intelligence on a variety of subjects. The odd feeling persisted that she had seen him before, perhaps on other flights or in another airport, even another country, but he was in no way, outstanding.

On the return trip, after Nicole had returned the necklace and bracelet to Ms. Honey, Hammer appeared on the same flight to Paris. After carefully checking to identify his seat, he seemed delighted to find himself next to Nicole, and she had almost expected him to produce more chocolates or magazines. Settling into his seat, he immediately began a long conversation about his organization and what interesting, lucrative, and necessary work they were engaged in.

"What do you do?" she had asked. "Is it classified?"

"Oh, no. It is investigative work. It is innovative and exciting, or so my employees tell me, and we're always on the search for qualified recruits."

He went on to tell her that it needed not be full time. His people were assigned a job, sometimes for just a day or two, others may last a week or more, and they were paid very well, a base salary, and a bonus for dangerous situations.

"What would a person have to do?" Nicole had asked cautiously.

"Surveillance, for instance."

"Watch people and report to you?"

"That's it," he said, and as if to give her time to think about it, he turned to his newspaper and read silently for ten or fifteen minutes. Then, as an afterthought, he added, "We start with a thousand up front for any personal incidentals. And our basic cases are paid fifteen hundred a day, care and food are charged, of course."

Nicole had drawn in her breath at the sums he had mentioned so carelessly. Just the day before, Maman had called to tell her that Mimi was staying temporarily with her friend, Cartel, who had a garden apartment on the first floor. It seemed that Maman and Mimi had been shopping and upon returning to their apartment house, Mimi had been taken with such a fit of coughing that she had been too weak to make it up the stairs to their third-floor flat.

"What do people do for so much money?" she had asked him. "Kill someone?"

Hammer had gazed at her as if assessing his answer. His blue eyes behind the silver-framed glasses were cold for a second, and then changed.

"We hope it doesn't come to that," he had replied, and then he laughed.

"Oh, you are making a joke," she had answered.

She had taken her book from her shoulder bag and turning away from him toward the light from the window, snuggled down and began to read, soon immersed in the world of Dickens.

"Is that his child?" said Madam Defarge. Nicole had felt all over again that terrible apprehension that the horrid woman had plans to murder little Lucia. "Yes, Madame," answered Mr. Lorry.

Nicole was aware that Mr. Hammer was watching her as she read, but he remained quiet until they reached the approach to the airport.

As she put away her book, he gently but firmly placed his fingers on her arm and leaned toward her, speaking softly.

"For work with an element of danger, a settlement can be placed in an account of your choice. No one need ever know. Think about it, Nicole."

"I don't recall telling you my name," she had answered.

"I asked the steward," he replied quickly. "My flight back to the States leaves at 8:00 a.m. If you wish to contact me, and I hope you will, please be here by six thirty. And be very discreet about what we have discussed."

"Yes, I will," Nicole had agreed.

They had parted without another word, going their separate ways out of the airport. She had hailed a taxi to take her to Gerta's place.

Mimi and Gerta were outside on the patio, playing cards. Mimi was smoking and Gerta complaining, trying to brush the blue haze away, while dealing the cards. Nearby, on a metal end table lay a portable oxygen mask. Nicole picked it up.

"What is this doing here, Mimi?"

"You know what it is, Cherie," her grandmother had answered hoarsely. "This foolish doctor, he left it there."

"The doctor put it in your nose," screeched Gerta, waving away smoke. "He goes. You take it out!"

"You took it out yourself?" Nicole asked in disbelief. "You are insane. It is there to help you breathe."

"Don't tell me what to do, you ungrateful girl. Didn't I raise you with no father to put bread in your mouth?"

"Jesus! Jesus! Jesus!" wailed Nicole.

She snatched the cigarette from Mimi's mouth, threw it down on the stones and stamped it with both feet.

"Don't blaspheme the Savior, Nicole!"

"I'm praying! Now, put this thing back in your nose."

"You put it in your nose," Mimi had retorted angrily, staring down at the remains of her cigarette. "Wasteful wretch, I had just lit that." She went into a paroxysm of coughing and placed her hand over her chest as if to relieve pain.

"I can do nothing with this one," Gerta said. "Her head is a rock."

Nicole started to pull Mimi up from her chair. "I am taking you to the hospital right now. I cannot stand to hear this."

"Stop! You wicked child. I should have thrown you into the Seine when you were born. Now, shut up and give me that horrid thing," Mimi demanded. She placed the tube up her nose and settled back quietly in her chair, looking very pale.

Nicole sank down on a nearby chaise longue and covered her face with her hands. The flight from Sweden had been turbulent, and the conversation with the man, Hammer, had left her confused and disturbed . . . and now this.

When Mimi started breathing somewhat normally again, Gerta had brought tea for the three of them, a plate of sugar twists, a pint of scotch and three glasses. Later, when Mimi had fallen asleep, Nicole rummaged in the chair cushions and Mimi's handbag, confiscated all cigarettes, and took them with her. She had looked back. My darling Mimi, she thought, she must have the best of everything.

* * *

And now, in the crisp, cool air of the morning, she entered the airport at six thirty, just as he had requested, still unsure why she was meeting this stranger and yet, curious enough to want to pursue his offer more thoroughly. The sums of money were certainly the incentive, but the nature of the work at which he had hinted held an equal intrigue. It had brought up visions of James Bond, Kim Philby, Mata Hari, Nick, and Nora Charles, dear befuddled old Ms. Marple . . . names that spoke of excitement. Nicole laughed at herself—such flights of fancy. To be more realistic, if she did go to work for Hammer, she would most likely be sitting in an unmarked car, snapping pictures of wealthy husbands and wives cheating on each other. That could certainly soon become boring, not to mention, depressing. As she was imagining other scenarios, she heard a deep, familiar voice in her ear.

"You came. I'm so glad. I was hoping you'd consider my offer."

She turned and faced him. "I am not totally committed. I really must know more. One does not rush into the unknown, no?"

They walked together across the expanse of the wide foyer toward the baggage area, his hand gently on her elbow, guiding her along.

"And I need to know more about you," he countered. He thought of the videos, the 8 × 10 blowup in his desk drawer. How fascinating it was to be with the actual subject, smelling her tantalizing perfume, noticing the sensuous movement of her breasts beneath the pale, linen shirt, and seeing her small, perfect, bare feet beneath the straps of her black leather sandals.

They had reached the other side of the baggage area when he stopped before an unmarked door.

"Where are we going?" she asked.

"Here. I have borrowed an office," he said, opening the door.

The room was neat, the furniture sparse. Nicole had the feeling that it may be used to interrogate passengers suspected of bringing in drugs or other contraband, but it was now empty. There were two old leather chairs, a desk, a file cabinet, and two end tables, topped with spindly, tall, brass lamps. Canned music came from speakers high above, monotonous, now high, and now low.

"A little sound diffusion," he noted, glancing upward. He took a notepad from his briefcase and indicated that they sit in the two chairs facing each other. "What is your full name?" He asked, with his pen poised over the notebook.

"Nicole Longet Laurent."

"And your age?"

"Thirty."

He glanced up sharply. Already, she was lying to him! He knows she is not thirty but several years younger according to her birth certificate.

"Somehow I thought you were younger."

She shrugged. "I wish to be thirty," she insisted, as if her age choice was a matter of prerogative rather than simple chronology. "Put that down."

G. Edmund Hammer sighed. This may be tougher than he thought. They went through several more general information questions, and he was never sure whether she was giving him the right answers or telling him what she wanted him to know. Suddenly, he leaned forward and looked her straight in the eye. She stared steadily back at him.

"It may be necessary for you to carry a weapon. Are you familiar with guns?"

"I am excellent with guns and knives," was her surprising answer. "I learned at a private underground shooting range and arena in a mansion in the city where you live."

"How do you know where I live?"

"The area code is Washington, DC."

"Oh, of course, on my card. Where was this private residence?"

"Sorry, monsieur, I will never tell you. It was the home of a relative of my prince, and I will never say anything to bring him trouble."

"Your prince? Are you making this up? If you cannot be straight with me, perhaps we should terminate this interview now," Hammer said testily.

"You don't believe what I am telling you, no? But it is true. In my second year at American University, I fell in love with a prince from the Middle East, and he fell in love with me. I moved into his beautiful apartment, and we lived together. Oh, so happily for more than one year, and then his sister came for a visit and discovered me. What was I to do? She told me that my prince already had been engaged from childhood to marry his cousin, and he could not disobey his family. She was sympathetic to us. She could see we were in love, but she had to tell her family about me. It was so horrible. They sent a private detective to spy upon us, and he went back and told them I was illegitimate and employed as a dishwasher."

"They were lies, of course."

"No, it is true. I am the only child of my mother," she told him frankly, "and I worked as a dishwasher, as well as other menial jobs. I worked in a restaurant. We took big trays and loaded the dirty dishes into the machines, my dear friend, George Archimedes, and me. Then we take out the clean dishes and line them up. Sometimes, there was a little time to study, no? George and me, we got one big meal as part of our pay, so we would eat a very late breakfast and no more 'til we got to work. This way, and my other jobs, I could send money home to my mother."

He stared at her and shook his head.

"What is wrong, you did not have a job when in college, monsieur?"

"I caddied for a while at the local country club. I was thinking that you are the only college student I ever knew who actually sent money home instead of the other way around," he said. "Tell me about this prince."

"At the end of our year, he told them he was not coming home. Some relatives came and drugged him, took him in a small, fast boat to a big yacht in New York harbor, and immediately put out to sea. I know this because Hamid, who was his bodyguard and a real friend to me always, called from New York and told me. Dear Hamid. He took a big risk to call me. He went with us everywhere, of course."

"And you never heard from this prince again?" asked Hammer, wondering if he was being fed a fairy tale or if it could possibly be true.

"Oh yes," Nicole answered. "Over two hundred letters. I still save them. Then, the letters stopped. Hamid wrote me and told me the prince was . . ."

Her expression was so sad. He prompted her gently.

"He told you the prince was dead?"

"Only to me," Nicole murmured. "He finally had agreed to marry his cousin."

"I see. I'm very sorry."

They sat silently for a while and then to change the subject, Hammer looked at her and said, "So you learned self-defense at this firing range?"

"You see, Hamid had to stay in shape, always alert. It was his job. So we went along, and it was fun. We tried guns. Yes, .38s, 9mm, M16s. We threw knives into dummies. We learned to sidestep, elbow back, fist up nose, and chop in throat."

"Please, come to Washington, Nicole. We need you in the game—I mean, I need you in our business, and I can make you rich. I promise you."

She grew very quiet, thinking of Mimi trying to struggle up the steps to the third-floor flat. She needed a new place on the first floor. And Maman, no more sewing beadwork, ruining her hands and her eyes. They could take trips to the seaside, breathe the fresh air, and rest on the beaches any time they liked.

"My husband will send me to the States within the month. I will call you."

They stood and shook hands. Hammer glanced at his watch.

"Time for my flight."

"Au revoir, monsieur! Bon voyage!"

"Merci. I look forward to seeing you soon," he answered.

They paused, and then walked away in opposite directions.

And so it began.

* * *

Within a week, Rene received an order to send twenty-four sterling teaspoons quickly, with his fleur-de-lis design, to the Senate dining room for some special occasion and of course, Nicole was dispatched to Washington sooner than she had planned. Her mind was made up however, and as soon as she reached Dulles, she called G. Edmund Hammer at the number on his card.

They met at a small, private art museum in the heart of the city. In the Impressionist Room, Nicole signed a contract to become a covert agent for one year, with indefinite options. It was then that he told her she would be under control of Gazar, that evil-looking little man she had delivered the necklace to in Bethesda.

No wonder he had not bothered to open the package! The necklace was simply a ploy. He wanted to observe her, and test her reactions with his clock, the snake in the window, and the rest of his bag of tricks. She thought about the Asian woman in the restaurant, then, the horrid man at LeGrand's farm. No, it couldn't be. No one would go so far. And why? It had to be just coincidence—a thief or a stalker—countries apart.

And so, with the contract signed, her new life began. When she had nothing to deliver as Rene's courier, she became adept at inventing excuses to return to the States. There were visits to George Archimedes, her college buddy and fellow dishwasher, and other American friends, mainly fictional. Soon the promised money began to flow in.

She explained to Rene that Enrico Garibaldi, Yvette's longtime lover, paid for the lovely new first-floor apartment for Yvette and Mimi. The two ladies thought that their sudden lavish bank account came from that dear son-in-law, Rene Laurent, who had heretofore been a real scrooge. As to the bank deposits, creative Washington lawyers discovered a dead French relative who had left them a trust.

As to herself, Nicole desired very little. She rented a single-room flat with a tiny kitchenette and bath, in a seedy neighborhood where she could be alone. Even Rene did not know about this hideaway. He had his mistress; she had her secret life.

In her little flat, she finished reading *A Tale of Two Cities*.

"It is a far, far better thing that I do than I have ever done. It is a far, far better rest I go to than I have ever known."

She practiced her juggling, a talent she had fostered since a small child. She perfected her tap-dancing routines, dancing to old American records and a beat-up record player she bought at a flea market. The songs brought back the Saturday nights that Yvette and Mimi would drag her from theatre to theatre, where she did her little act and won prizes. It pleased them so much. They were so proud.

One year passed, then two years.

Chapter Four

St. Augustine Christmas

Through a haze of restless sleep, Nicole heard the telephone. It always sounded loud in the confines of her tiny flat. She opened her eyes and saw the faintest gleam of dawn touching her window through the frost of the December morning. The shrill repetition of the ringing caused her to get up, cross the expanse of thick, pale-blue carpet, and snatch up the telephone.

"Hello?"

"This is Monsieur Delon at the market. The pink grapefruit have come."

"Merci, monsieur."

The tiny crystal clock beside her bed pinged five o'clock. She crossed to the window and closed it down against the icy, fresh air. Through a misty rain, she saw the snakelike winding of the Seine, the faint outline of the Eiffel Tower in the distance.

Will I ever stand here like this again and see this view from my window, she mused. It was always a sobering, recurring thought when the call came in the early morning, and she knew she would be flying to the States on a new mission.

There was always the wild element of danger in the game. The excitement came from the unexpected, and Nicole realized that after two years as a covert agent, the adventure was becoming addictive. She actually looked forward to the messages that took her to the United States. Sometimes, it seemed that the time spent on secret missions became her real life, and the time she shared with Rene, Yvette, and Mimi was merely an interim existence that lasted until the next call. On the job, she had been chased, shot at, and constantly threatened, but it had been worth it. The money had flowed into three separate accounts just as promised by Hammer and Gazar. She hurried to take her shower and dress for the day.

By 6:00 a.m., she was standing at the door of Delon and although the door wore a *closed* sign, there was a faint light in the rear and the sweet odor of hot, baking bread drifted in the air. At her tap, Delon came to the entrance, unlocked the door to his markets, and then locked it again as soon as Nicole entered. She handed him her net bag that she used for groceries.

"Put the pink grapefruit in here, monsieur. I will return shortly."

He nodded and as he wandered over to the produce sections, she continued through the market and into the bright kitchen where Madam Delon was stacking steaming loaves on a long table covered with a white cloth. They nodded to each other, and Nicole left out of the rear door, which led into an alley.

Two blocks away, she entered a crumbling building in a poor business district, walked up the stairs to the second floor, and knocked gently at the solid metal door.

"Come in."

Before entering, Nicole stepped back and looked down the stairwell, then waited a moment, listening for footsteps, but there was no sound from below. She opened the door and then closed it. Still no sound; so, she went in. The room, as always, surprised her by its neatness, and clean, efficient appearance in contrast with the dingy exterior of the old building. This was the Paris office, headed by Richard Leach.

"Good morning, Nicole," Richard greeted her. "Nice to see you again."

"Hello, Richard."

"You know Derek?"

"Of course. Good morning, Monsieur Holland," said Nicole, with a smile.

Derek sat in his own little office by the windows from where he could see all the actions down in the alley, while he counted huge amounts of international currency and sealed them in stacks according to country. Derek Holland was a handsome, well-dressed dwarf taller than most at just under four feet tall. He was seated on a stool and when Nicole walked over to the doorway, he swiveled it around, gave her a long, devilish leer and a lascivious wink. She stared back without expression and then, very slowly, she crossed her eyes and stuck out the tip of her tongue. He laughed so hard that he almost fell off the stool. It was a routine he enjoyed immensely. That little catlike tongue, he marveled! So pink, so cute! He would think of it the rest of the day. Shaking his head, he turned back to his counting, making endless notes on tiny slips of paper, as Nicole turned back to the office, where Richard waited.

"And this is our new travel agent, Giselle. When you leave Paris in two days, she will give you a ride to Charles de Gaulle and further instructions."

Nicole barely acknowledged the young woman with frizzy red hair, who stared at her from a desk in the corner of the room. On the desk were travel brochures, and behind it, on the wall, was a large poster of Hawaii and one of London. A computer sat silently, a fish pattern swimming lazily on the screen in various colors.

"I would like my instructions now," Nicole insisted. "I don't like to go into a new . . ." She stopped and glanced at Giselle. "A new job, cold, Richard."

"Would you like some coffee?" Leach asked, motioning to a small, enclosed area next to Derek Holland's office. "Perhaps there is a Danish left."

The little cubicle was soundproofed. It was like being inside of a space capsule, cramped, airless, and glass enclosed on three sides. And it was quiet, very quiet. As soon as they were seated, almost knee-to-knee at the Formica topped table, Leach poured them each a cup of coffee and noted that the bakery box was empty.

"Sorry about the Danish," he murmured as he pulled a man's photo from his pocket and passed it across the table. "Do you remember Bruce Malcolm Dieter?"

She studied the rather handsome face of a man in his late thirties, brown hair, and blue eyes. Even in the pictures, he looked evasive, as if he held a secret.

"I helped bring him in. He is the agent who went psycho and killed two innocent civilians, said he was directed to do so by a voice. Well, he escaped from the federal sanitarium, I heard—but what does it have to do with me?" asked Nicole. "Richard, it is almost Christmas, and Mimi is expecting Rene and me to help her shop for Maman, take them to church, and get the tree . . ."

"I take it you don't know about Jack McKane?" interrupted Leach.

"What about Jack? He was my partner when we brought in Dieter. In fact, Jack and I worked two other cases together."

"Jack is dead, Nicole. Dieter killed him."

Nicole gasped and covered her face with her hands. In a moment, she seemed to recover, although she seemed shaken by the sudden news. She sat silently, listening.

"Here, the plot gets complicated. He actually had a very young girl along with him when he found Jack and garroted him. That's Dieter's MO, you know. He uses ropes and knives. He convinced the girl that he was an agent doing a job, getting rid of an enemy of the United States. The little idiot bought it but told her parents, who called the FBI. The feds handed it over to Gazar, knowing that Dieter was one of ours. Now, Dieter wants the girl for ratting on him and has been seen in Jacksonville."

"Jacksonville? That's in Florida, isn't it?" Nicole asked. "Is that where the girl lives?"

"Emmalou Shallotte, a teenaged airhead from all reports, lives in St. Augustine, just south of Jacksonville, with her parents, Colt and Dora. And we have agents in place at their home, babysitting the Shallottes. Dieter won't go in as long as they're there, so your job would be to decoy, to draw him out of hiding."

"Decoy?" mused Nicole. "Do I look anything like this . . . Emmalou?"

"Only in general size, about five feet, four inches tall, about one eighteen."

"Thanks. You can add another six pounds or so. Who is babysitting?"

"Beau Jackson is down there with a new guy, Willie Lewis."

Nicole shook her head in indecision. She really did not want to leave Paris at the Christmas season and yet, Jack McKane! Why did he kill Jack? And if Dieter had killed Jack for bringing him in, wouldn't he be also looking for her, the other agent who had aided in his capture? It was a real possibility unless she found him first.

"And here's a picture of Emmalou," said Richard as he slid a photo out of a folder and passed it across the table. "Under the makeup, is a teenager looking for trouble and obviously, she found it."

"But she's half Dieter's age. How did they meet?" asked Nicole, studying the picture carefully, noting the face, clothing, even the posture. She returned it without comment.

"I don't know, but Dieter, at his best, could be a charmer, and he's devious as hell. If he finds this kid alone, you know, he'll kill her in an instant."

Nicole stared down at the floor for a few minutes. "Yes, he would. Give me the plane tickets now, and my thousand in travel money. If I need more, I'll be in touch. How will I identify my pickup man when I get to Florida?"

"Well, it will be Maurice Dupin. You know him, don't you?"

"I thought he was out of the game—retired, or . . ." Her speculation was left unsaid, but Leach understood what she meant.

"He is retired, but he's coming out for this one, and he does live in the area. I believe Beau Jackson said Crescent Beach." Leach flipped back the cuff of his tweed jacket and glanced at his Rolex. "I'll call him and tell him you're on your way. He can pick you up in either Jacksonville or Daytona. Today is Friday. If you leave out of de Gaulle on Monday, you can be in Florida, Tuesday late."

Derek Holland knocked lightly on the door, and Leach motioned him inside the glass cubicle. He put four stacks of American bills in front of Nicole and said in a voice extremely deep for a man of such short stature, "Want to count it?"

Nicole broke the seal on one pack and thumbed rapidly through it, then picked up the other three packs and buried them deep into a zippered compartment in her shoulder bag. They returned to the office area, and Gizelle looked up expectantly.

"Going on a trip? I can drive you to Orly. I can check your luggage. What time shall I pick you up, madam?" she said eagerly, anxious for anything to do.

"Thanks, but I won't need you," said Nicole shortly. She scooped up the plane tickets that were lying on the desk. Richard Leach had been sure she would take the assignment when she heard about Jack McKane's murder and had already set the trip in motion. He had been presumptuous, but he had been right. She was going.

Without saying a quick good-bye, she crossed to the door, and seconds later, they heard her faint footsteps going down to the alley.

"Damn it! I hadn't finished my instructions!" fumed Leach.

"Shall I run after her, monsieur?" asked Giselle, rising from her seat.

"Better not rattle that cage, Giselle. That little lady spells danger," laughed Derek. He strutted over to the window on his bandy legs and gazed out into the alley.

Leach and Giselle joined him and peered below. It was still raining and deep puddles were standing in the worn bricks. Nicole was nowhere in sight. Reluctantly, Derek returned to his desk and made a notation that he had paid out one thousand American to Agent Laurent. Leach stayed at the window, watching the darkening sky, and wondering whether he had done the right thing to send Nicole after Bruce Malcolm Dieter. There was nothing more dangerous than an agent who has slipped over the edge and started freelancing. He had already killed three people, and was looking for Emmalou Shallotte, and if he remembered, in his muddled state, that Nicole Laurent was the other agent who brought him in, she would surely be next on his hit list. He crossed quickly to the telephone and rang Delon's Market, but he was too late.

"She took her pink grapefruit in a big hurry, wished me joyous noel and left. So I guess we will not see her again until after the holidays," reported Delon.

Leach hung up the telephone. He felt a little sick at his stomach. It was too dangerous, putting the Shallotte girl and Nicole together, but he was just following Gazar's orders. The hell with Gazar. He, Richard, would be at the airport on Monday and tell Nicole to abort the mission.

* * *

Nicole returned to her own tiny apartment and threw a few clothes into a carry-on bag, just a couple of sweaters and some jeans, underwears, toothbrush, and cosmetics.

She telephoned to the lovely garden apartment where Yvette and Mimi now lived in comparative splendor to the old third-floor walkup where they had lived for so many years, and where Nicole had grown up poor, but never knew they were poor. The telephone rang and rang and was finally snatched up by a breathless Yvette.

"Yes, yes, who is it? My bath is running, so speak quickly, please!"

"Maman, it is me. I need to go away for a couple of days."

"No! Absolutely no, you may not go! It is Christmas, so much to do! I have ordered our goose. I have spoken to Rene. He is not going to that country sow. He will spend the holiday with us, his family," shouted her mother. "Rene will not send you away to deliver presents so close to Christmas even for a big lot of money!"

"I must go. Yes, it will be a big lot of money, but I will try my best to get home in time, I promise, Maman."

"Oh, I see steam coming from under the door. My bath is ready, Cherie. Do not go, Nicole."

"Good-bye, Maman. And kiss Mimi for me."

She tried the store, but Rene was not there. She tried the apartment and got the answering machine.

"I am going away for a few days. If I don't come back . . ." Nicole hesitated, pondering her choice of words, "I mean, if I don't get back for Christmas, all the presents are wrapped and placed on the table."

For a moment, she sat and held the telephone but could think of nothing else to say. Or perhaps there was too much to say and no clear way to say it. She still loved him, her silver fox, but each day they seemed to be drifting further apart. He tolerated her extra *jobs* in the States. She tried to overlook his mistress.

She called the airport and found out that there was a flight out late that afternoon. So, she cancelled the Monday flight and prepared to leave right away. Final destination would be Daytona, fifty miles south of St. Augustine, where there was no commercial airport.

Oddly enough, she had been to St. Augustine many years ago, on a field trip when she was an exchange student. A teacher had taken a group there to visit the oldest city in the United States over a spring break. Nicole remembered the fabulous glass exhibit at the Lightner Museum, and the old fort, Castillo de San Marcos. She and a girl from her English class had shared a room at the St. Francis Inn, a pale-pink room on the second floor with a large picture on the wall. What was that picture, she mused, a ballerina? She efficiently finished cramming her carry-on bag and stuffed immediate essentials into her shoulder bag.

* * *

Snow was falling as they landed at the big airport near Washington, DC. Across the field, Nicole could see workers deicing a plane which was about to take off into the glowering clouds, probably one of the last flights to take off before the storm forced all planes to be grounded due to the weather. The flight she was on was probably the last from Paris into Dulles, and Nicole was glad she had opted to leave early.

She took a taxi van over to International, which had an immediate flight to Charlotte and on to Daytona. At the layover in Charlotte, she called around until she located Gazar at his place in Georgetown.

"It is Nicole. I am here in the States."

"Where are you? Leach said Monday or Tuesday," Gazar shouted angrily. "Can't you ever follow orders?"

"Put half my fee in my Vienna bank. I will check with Vienna tomorrow. I will call again when I deliver the package," she stated.

She abruptly hung up as he was still sputtering into the telephone and sat in the booth, thinking about Gazar. He was an underhanded, self-serving bastard. He had never mentioned to her, or gotten the message through, that Jack McKane was dead, and he knew that she was the other agent who tracked Dieter and brought him in. She also considered her three separate accounts and knew that within a year or two in the game, there would be sufficient funds to keep Yvette and Mimi comfortable for life if she worked hard and invested wisely. So, Gazar would have to be tolerated, for now.

Her plane to Daytona was due to depart in twenty minutes, so she had no time to try to reach Maurice Dupin in Crescent Beach, and there was a bit of a complication she had not anticipated. She would arrive in the cold hours before dawn, a mean time to arouse an old friend from his warm bed. She pulled the trench coat around her, glad of the wool liner inside, because even here in North Carolina, it was snowing.

It was a short hop to Daytona. Through the stars, the plane circled and banked and as it leveled off for a landing, Nicole could see below the famous oval of the two and a half mile track, where race cars would begin to compete in February. She was glad to see that there was no snow there, but the ground looked wet and chilled. Nicole wandered into the warmth of the terminal and debated calling Maurice Dupin. For Dupin, it would mean about a thirty-mile trip to the airport and then another fifty-mile drive down to St. Augustine, then back home to Crescent Beach. It was 3:00 a.m. Sleep on, Maurice, she decided, and gathering her things, walked outside to Long Term Visitor Parking and gazed down the long rows of cars sitting silently in the pale overhead lights. Not a soul was in sight as she walked slowly along the aisles, pressing the door handles down on each car as she passed. Every one appeared to be locked and some were coded, but that was no problem. There was always a badly hidden magnet stuck somewhere with the code, but she didn't want to dig for it. She took out a nail file, slipped it into the lock of a red Jeep Cherokee and jiggled it until it popped. Glancing inside, she realized it was a salesman's car, full of many boxes of samples or merchandise, carelessly covered with a blanket on the back seat. The ignition was easy to hot-wire. The sleepy cashier paid little attention when she paid the toll and drove away, heading across town to pick up AIA going north.

An hour later, Nicole was on the outskirts of St. Augustine, looking for a motel. Through the darkness, a welcome *vacancy* sign beckoned on the left-hand side of the road, and she noted that it was Best Western. She drove past and farther along on the right side of the road, found a smaller motel, where even the office lay dark. Tired travelers slept behind closed drapes, unmindful of the Jeep Cherokee as it rolled to a stop, lights out, to the farthest corner of the parking lot. Nicole eased the car door open and gathered her bags. Curious, she contemplated the boxes in the back seat, which were marked *cons* and *greets*. Lifting the top of one box, she found neat rows of vendor's condom packages. The larger boxes were crammed with all types of greeting cards. *What an odd combination!* She mused. Carefully, she closed the door, and moved swiftly out of the lot to the road. The *vacancy* sign was still lit at the Best Western, and she hurried across the road toward the motel.

* * *

Nicole slept until ten the next morning, woke up feeling achy with leftover jet lag, and reluctant to face the day. She called Maurice Dupin, who said he would be there in twenty or thirty minutes, then found the number for the Shallotte residence, and called there. Beau Jackson, the chief field agent out of the Alexandria, Virginia office, answered the telephone.

"Beau, it's Nicole. I am here in St. Augustine."

There was a moment of silence and then Jackson's deep voice boomed out. "You mean Gazar sent you? I can't believe it!"

"Yes."

"You know about Jack McKane, don't you?"

"That is why I came."

"You got some kind of guts, girl."

"Dupin will pick me up. See you in a bit, Beau."

"You're in Dieter territory now, baby. He's been sighted. Watch your back."

"Always do."

Maurice Dupin's car was an older model Jaguar, long, black, and well kept. Dupin drove into the motel parking lot, parked, and stood beside his car, letting Nicole check him out from behind the drapes before she opened the door to let him inside.

"Did Gazar pick this place?" he asked.

"No, he doesn't know where I am. I chose it at random."

"How did you get here? Rental from the airport?"

"Don't ask. If you know, you'll be involved in a felony," she laughed.

"Ahhh, Nicole . . . well, I'm your ride as long as you need me."

Dupin was on the edge of sixty, a retired Air Force Colonel, formerly in military intelligence. He was slightly balding, and had the kindest brown eyes that Nicole had ever seen. He seldom took on a case these days, but Nicole had saved his life on one of the two cases they had worked together, and she had his deepest respect. He would do anything for Nicole, and Gazar knew it. And used it.

"Did you bring me a piece? And a knife?"

He handed her a .22, a small thing with a short barrel. The numbers had been shaved off. He rolled the barrel to show it was empty, reached into his coat pocket and handed her some ugly little mercury head bullets and a silencer.

"Sure, this works? It feels funny in my hand. Did you test fire it?"

"Of course. It is very neat. Nice, quiet, little pop," he assured her. "This is a switch blade. Very sharp and opens fast, so be careful. The leg holster."

"Police confiscated junk, isn't it?" she guessed.

"Now it's your turn not to ask questions."

"If we get Dieter, where do we drop him?" she asked casually.

"Gazar says the moat around the Castillo, and the body will wash out to sea on the next tide, but you and I know that that moat hasn't had water in it since the 1930s."

"And Gazar doesn't know that?"

"Oh, hell, yes. His winter place is thirty miles south of here on the road to Ormond Beach. Are you familiar with his place down here?" Dupin asked. "Of course, he and the missus Gazar are in Georgetown for Christmas with all the parties going on among the Washington bigwigs."

Nicole nodded. "And the booze and the bull will flow, things will be said, and they will regret later. That is, if they remember."

"But they are there with the tree and presents, and here we are in a motel room. So, who's crazy, Nicole?"

"We are, monsieur. So what is the agenda? Beau Jackson knows I'm here. We go to meet this girl, Emmalou Shallotte, and we dangle her like bait to flush Dieter out into the open, is that it?"

"Something like that," Dupin muttered, looking away. "All ready to go?"

"I'm starving. I need a good breakfast."

A faint sun struggled to come out though here in the northern end of Florida. It was never as hot as The Keys, but still a welcome change from the ice and snow Nicole had been through on the way south. She unzipped the wool lining from her trench coat, folded it, and stowed it in her carry-on bag. The .22 went into her shoulder bag; the knife went into the leg holster, under her jeans just above her ankle.

In the parking lot, Dupin opened the trunk of the Jaguar and drew out two magnetic signs. He affixed one sign to each door of the car. Dupin Real Estate, and a telephone number in Crescent Beach. Nicole watched curiously.

"Is this a cover, Maurice?"

"No, I have my own real estate business, and I really like it, finding places for folks. Love to work with retirees. We call 'em Snowbirds, you know. They came down here to rent and come back to buy when their kids leave home. I only came out when Gazar called and said you needed me. This one's for you, babe."

She put her arms around him and for a moment lay her head against his cheek. He smelled nice, like a subtle, spicy shaving lotion. His bulky, wool jacket was warm and comforting. He put his hands gently on her shoulders.

"I wish that I had known my father, and he was exactly like you. It's something you miss, you know?" Nicole said. She touched his cheek and backed away.

Moved, Dupin stepped back and opened the passenger side door.

"Okay, Agent Laurent, time to go to work," he said gruffly.

On their way to the city, they stopped at The Oasis and had bacon and eggs, toast, juice, and coffee, then continued to The Bridge of Lions and out to highway 1. They passed the development known as St. Augustine Shores, and Dupin knew that the Shallotte's residence was just down the road.

"Get in the back and lie down. In case Dieter is watching the house, we don't want him to know that you're here. I'm going to slip you in through the carport," directed Dupin, slowing down and pulling to the side of the road.

The Shallotte's place lay in a small clearing surrounded by tall pines, a neat, single story of brick and frame with a long carport, which was shielded by white latticework hung with fragile broom tendrils of dormant climbing roses. Dupin drove into the carport and parked behind a blue Buick sedan, the Shallottes' family car. Behind the house stood a dark blue Chevrolet Caprice, with Maryland tags. Nicole thought she recognized it as Beau Jackson's car.

"I'll go ahead and knock. When the door opens, come in as fast as you can."

The kitchen they entered was cheerfully painted yellow and white, the tile floor was black and white, the curtains white with rows of colorful tulips appliquéd across the bottom, but the bright atmosphere did not extend to the people seated around the polished maple table. Their faces were dark and somber.

"Well, I certainly hope you folks are more effective than those two northerners in there," snapped Dora Shallotte, looking up to see who was invading her kitchen. "This waiting is getting on my nerves. Why can't they find that horrible man?"

Dupin nodded. "We will, Mrs. Shallotte. These things take time. I'd like you to meet my partner, Nicole Laurent."

Dora Shallotte looked over Nicole critically. "A woman. Hmm, honey, who has been cutting your hair? She oughta be sued for malpractice."

"I cut my own," admitted Nicole, startled. She touched her pointed little bangs and ran her fingers through the short mop that tended to curl.

"Oh, sorry, honey. It's just so . . . unique."

"We are shut up here like prisoners in our own home," grumbled the slightly balding fiftyish man, who sat across the table working a crossword puzzle. "My twenty-four-year-old son is in complete charge of my hardware store, and God knows what we're going to find when I get back to work. Probably be looking at bankruptcy."

"Colt Junior is no fool. He showed you how to cut the keys when we got that key-making machine," reminded Dora, still staring at Nicole. "You oughta let it grow out. There's a girl in town that could do wonders."

The telephone was ringing, and in the front of the house, someone went to answer. In seconds, Beau Jackson stood in the doorway of the kitchen.

"It's for Emmalou, a man's voice. The tape is running."

From the front of the house, a young girl's excited voice came. "Hello? Hello? Damn it Bruce, is that you? Please, don't hang up. I won't tell them anything, honest!" There was the sound of the telephone being slammed onto its base, followed by muffled sobs. "I know it is you, Bruce, and why don't you trust me?"

"I cannot stand this. Mama is coming, baby, don't cry."

"Hell!" scowled Colt. "We are living in hell. Does either of you know a four letter word for 'entrance to a mine'?"

Beau Jackson reentered the kitchen with a young, nondescript-looking man in tow.

"Glad to see you guys," he said to Nicole and Dupin. "We're gonna get that son of a bitch. I know, that was him on the phone. Don't say anything when he calls, just asked for Emmalou, then listens to her, making sure she's still here. I really want to nail that bastard."

"We all do, Beau," said Dupin.

"He killed Jack," Nicole added.

"We're gonna get him," Beau repeated angrily. Then, he turned to the young man at his side. "This is Willie Lewis. He's new, a little green, but he's coming along."

"I am Nicole Laurent, Paris office, and this is Maurice Dupin."

"Nicole is the pigeon," explained Jackson, to Nicole's surprise. "We know that Dieter is in the area. We just got to flush him out."

"Dieter will come out of his hiding place if he sees Emmalou," said Nicole. "He may not even recognize me. The only time he saw me was the day we brought him in, and things were pretty hectic. He had to be subdued. Other than trying to kick me and break his restraints—I was holding his arms behind him—I don't think he saw me all that well. I was behind him when we caged him. But he knew Jack." Here she stopped and cleared her throat, waited a few seconds, then continued, "We should walk Emmalou around town during the daylight hours. San Marco? Avenida Menendez. And Willie, here, could go along, as her boyfriend."

"Are you crazy? He goes right for her!" Jackson exclaimed.

"Not in daylight. Not in a public place," insisted Nicole. "Dieter is a coward."

"She's right," put in Dupin. "I never met the guy, but Gazar read me his MO, and he only kills alone and at night."

Beau Jackson rubbed the sweat from his broad, dark face. "Emmalou outside. Man, it scares me to think of it. Dieter is unpredictable now, and he hates Emmalou's guts for testifying against him. Unfortunately, she doesn't buy that. She's still mooning over him after all she has put her family through."

"I'd like to meet her," said Nicole. "That's why I'm here, isn't it?"

They trooped into the living room where the Shallotte's were seated, uneasily, looking at the telephone as if they expected Dieter to call again.

The living room was middle-class traditional with many family pictures on the walls and on the piano. A nativity scene graced the mantel of the fireplace, and a sweet-smelling cedar tree was trimmed with many colored balls and blinking lights. Christmas; Nicole was reminded suddenly, it's almost Christmas! Dora and her daughter were seated against the wall on a soft, rose-colored sofa. Emmalou was much prettier than the picture Richard Leach had shown her in the Paris office. She appeared very immature, but perhaps it was her choice of dress. She wore a pale yellow print with daisies on it, high waisted, and with a small lace collar, more suitable for summer than the cold of December, even here in Florida. Her hair was shoulder-length, light brown, and curly. Nicole walked over and took her hand.

"Hello. I'm Nicole. We're going to help you if we can."

"Hi."

"That is a beautiful dress. Did you buy it in town?" asked Nicole. "I would like one like it, and the sweater too, so nice and warm. Is it handmade?" she continued as Emmalou shrugged.

"Made in China. So, maybe it is. Got it at Belk's."

"Do you wear a hat with it sometimes?"

"Why are you so interested in Emmalou's clothes?" Dora asked suspiciously. "And I would think that a woman of your age would be giving up jeans by now."

"A big, floppy straw hat," said Emmalou.

"Nicole, I know where you're going with this girl, but you don't look like little Ms. Emmalou here," put in Beau Jackson.

"But I could, with a wig and the right clothes."

Dora laughed. "Emmalou is beautiful. You don't even wear makeup. And that hair! Where were you raised, dear?"

"In Paris, madam," Nicole responded shortly. "You know Paris, no?"

Maurice Dupin came further into the room and stood defensively behind Nicole's chair. He had been observing Dora Shallotte and appeared ready to throw her through the picture window if she uttered another sarcastic word.

"Emmalou, would you be willing to go out, say, to lunch, perhaps in a well-populated area, and stroll along the streets, so that Dieter would come out of hiding? Willie Lewis would be at your side all the time, and Mr. Jackson always nearby and there seems to be a local officer cruising this area in an unmarked car. Mr. Dupin and I spotted him about one mile away as we came here."

Maurice tried not to look too surprised. He had missed this one.

"Well, I am going with them!" stated Dora, firmly. "And Daddy too."

"On a date, Mom? Gimme a break!" objected Emmalou fiercely. Her face flushed slightly. "This is just like a movie, I can do this! All I do is go out with Willie and walk around? Oh, this is just too neat."

"And if you see Dieter, that is, Bruce, don't panic and don't look his way. Just give this information to Willie and come straight home, and we will take it from there."

Colt stood up and stared around the room. "It's too damn dangerous. Let Willie stay here, and I'll go along and protect my daughter. I got a .38 in the store, and I know how to use it."

"Daddy, please, it's supposed to be a date! Oooh, this is just too cool."

"He's a damn killer, Emmalou, can't you understand that?" barked Colt.

"She will be fully covered at all times, Mr. Shallotte," Nicole assured him. Turning to Beau Jackson, she asked, "Can we set it up for tomorrow?"

He looked doubtful. "I need to call Gazar. He is the control."

"Tell him what you like. And remind him of Vienna."

"Vienna?"

"He'll know what I mean."

After he left to use the telephone, Nicole turned to Emmalou. "Something has been bothering me. How did a sweet girl like you meet Bruce Malcolm Dieter?"

"Don't you know? We met on the Internet," she answered innocently.

"And he gave you his right name?" Dupin muttered in disbelief.

"Of course."

Nicole and Dupin said good-bye and went out to the Jaguar. Nicole slipped into the backseat and lay down on the worn leather that still smelled new. Surprising how good old cars kept the leathery smell after so many years!

"Let's go shopping. I need a dress, hat, sweater, and wig, no?"

"Do you really cut your hair?" Dupin grinned.

"But, of course, monsieur."

"I love it. It's the real you."

"Thanks, pardner."

"That damn Shallotte dame has no taste," growled Dupin as he sped away.

* * *

Carefully, Beau Jackson and Willie Lewis planned a day's activities on the outside with Emmalou, but of course, the Shallottes insisted on meeting their daughter and Lewis at the Mall for some last minute Christmas shopping. The Mall was crowded with shoppers, which could be either a good thing or a bad thing, depending on what Dieter would do if he saw Emmalou. Then, the Shallottes decided to go to lunch with Emmalou and Lewis. Finally, since there had been no sign of Dieter, they reluctantly headed home, leaving Emmalou and Lewis alone. Early afternoon, they strolled along the waterfront, holding hands, then dropped into the Santa Maria for coffee.

Willie Lewis noted something odd about Emmalou's behavior. Ever since she and her mother had visited the restrooms at the Mall, she had seemed excited, and her eyes were sparkling. She giggled and held on to his arm, looking up into his face.

"I feel like a movie star in a spy story," she confided. Her eyes darted from side to side as if looking for Dieter. "Do you think I can sell my story to the enquirer? Do you know how those people get on talk shows? Are they paid lots?"

Lewis shook his head. "I don't know. I'd suggest a low profile if I were you. There are a lot of nuts out there."

"Well, I mean, after they catch Brucie. You know, the whole thing with Bruce is like a real bad dream. He's really cute and smart, just everything changed when he saw that man, Jack. His eyes got funny, and he seemed to be talking to somebody who wasn't there, maybe like a teensy microphone was in his pocket or something."

"We should be getting you home," Lewis suggested, taking her arm and guiding her back to where the Caprice was parked.

She was a beauty, Lewis thought, but what a fruitcake.

The rain and snow that had pelted the northern states found its way down the coast and made itself felt in the Sunshine State with unusually cold temperatures, even for December. Gray skies hung over the water as they headed out of town and even the radio added to the gloom as Elvis lamented sadly that it would be a blue Christmas. On the way home, Emmalou was quiet. She sat far over to one side, clutching her purse to her chest, with a dreamy smile on her face.

"Are you okay? You got anything to tell me?" Lewis asked.

"Everything is lovely," she sighed and turned away.

When they reached the house, Nicole and Dupin were waiting to hear how the day's outing had gone and make a report of the activities. As Emmalou and Lewis entered the kitchen, Dora was immediately challenging the entire crew. "I don't think you people know what you're doing. My child meets a complete stranger, is involved in a horrible murder, and here you sit, in my kitchen, and I certainly hope all those long distance calls don't show up on my bill, or you will never hear the last of me." She turned to Emmalou. "Are you all right, darling?"

"Of course, Mommy Poo."

Dora looked at her daughter sharply. "You only call me that when you have been up to something, miss!"

"All of our calls are collect, Mrs. Shallotte," Dupin assured her.

Jackson was heard in the carport, parking behind the Caprice.

"And that black man used our car today. He better replace the gas. That's a Buick, top of the line."

"Yes ma'm. It'll be taken care of," Dupin said.

Emmalou threw her soggy hat on the table and hung her damp sweater over the back of a chair but continued to hold on to her purse.

Colt came into the kitchen and looked around. "Well, any sign of that bastard out there after we came home? Do you know what cab fare from the Mall came to? Man, that is robbery. I oughta go out of the hardware business and buy me a cab."

"She didn't recognize anybody," Willie Lewis reported. "There was no unusual movement in the crowd, and no car followed."

They all trooped into the living room, and they arranged themselves on the sofa and various chairs, except for Nicole, who remained standing, observing Emmalou.

Emmalou flopped down on the rug by the fireplace, absentmindedly rearranging the low-hanging balls on the Christmas tree. She kept her purse close to her side and was edging it under the pile of logs in the wood basket, slowly but steadily. Carols were playing, the agents were discussing their next move, and Colt and Dora were arguing over the Buick and whether to charge for insurance as well as the gas used.

Nicole walked over to Emmalou and stood over her until she looked up.

"You saw him. You saw Dieter, didn't you?"

"No, I swear."

"He contacted you then," Nicole insisted.

"Mom," begged Emmalou tearfully. "Make her leave me alone!"

"She's lying," said Nicole, bluntly.

"My daughter doesn't lie, young lady, and you better watch your tongue," protested Colt. "This is my house, and I can throw you out of it anytime, damn it!"

Nicole ignored him and looked straight at Emmalou. "What's in the purse?"

"None of your business!" she blurted out. "Besides, you are all wrong about Brucie. He loves me. That man he had to kill was a wanted serial killer. And I don't care what you say, Daddy . . . and you too, Mom. If he asks me to marry him, I will!"

"Oh god, deliver us!" groaned Colt, throwing up his hands.

"Let's see the purse, Emmalou. If there's nothing there, I will apologize."

"Oh, for heaven's sake!" said Dora. She reached over and snatched the purse from the wood basket, opened it wide and dumped the contents on the coffee table.

Lipsticks rolled, the wallet flew open, dropping change everywhere, powder spewed from a compact, and crumpled Kleenex sat like pink puffballs on the glass top. They crowded around the table, viewing the spilled items individually.

"You see?" challenged Dora. "I guess you owe us all an apology. There is nothing out of place. Our daughter does not lie."

"Does she smoke?" asked Nicole.

"Of course not. Even Colt has quit," Dora answered.

"Then, what is that small paper cylinder about the size of a Virginia Slim cigarette?"

Emmalou started to grab for it, but her mother was faster. Her hand flew out like a striking snake, and she palmed the paper. Carefully, she unrolled it and in silence, read the short, cryptic message written inside. She stared at Emmalou.

"Where did this . . . thing come from, missy?" she almost whispered.

"When we went to the restroom at the Mall, I put my purse on the floor . . . in the . . . you know . . . and maybe then, or when I washed my hands at the sink and went over to get a paper towel, maybe then. But you know, I was wearing my sunglasses, you know, like being a celebrity, even though it was cloudy and when I opened my purse to put them away in the car, I saw this little teensy roll of paper. So I opened it and looked down in my purse and read it."

"And you didn't mention this to Agent Lewis at the time?" asked Jackson.

"It is private. For my eyes only, like in James Bond."

"You don't understand," said Nicole. "This man wants to kill you."

Emmalou looked up at her and actually laughed. "Oh, he would not!"

"This is serious," Nicole attempted to explain. "He killed two innocent people he didn't even know before he killed Jack McKane."

"You're just making that up to scare me."

Frustrated, Nicole shrugged and walked away to the kitchen, where she drew a glass of cold water and stood drinking it slowly, trying to cool down. The little radio on the table was belting out "Jingle Bell Rock" and Colt Shallotte's newspaper still lay there, turned to the crossword. Nicole picked it up and saw the large vacant square at the top. The middle clue said, "Entrance to a mine." She picked up the pen and wrote in the four-letter word "Adit" and threw down the pen just as Beau Jackson entered the kitchen and gave her a reassuring pat on the shoulder. He got himself a cold can of Dr. Pepper from the refrigerator.

"Help yourself to the Peps. Bought these myself. These folks are tight with a buck. Here's the note. Read it and see if it is Dieter's style."

Nicole took the rolled up paper and spread it out on the table. "Well, I can tell you this. Jack McKane worked an espionage case with Dieter back in 1995, and he told me that Dieter would leave these "cigarettes" all over the Middle East for fellow agents to find, so it is definitely part of his MO"

"He is using computer display machines. Types out something, asks to see how it prints out, keeps the sample."

Baby, do not believe what they are saying about me. I was only doing my job. I love you.

Nicole read it and sadly shook her head. He is trying to draw her out. "We got to watch her, in case she decides to fly."

"Why hasn't Dieter tried to reach her on her own computer? That's how she got involved in the first place."

"Because Daddy Colt pulled the plug."

"That was a mistake."

"It is his house, and he shut it down."

Jackson finished the rest of his drink, tossed the can into a nearby trashcan, then guiltily retrieved it, and put it in a plastic container marked *aluminum*.

"Don't want to step on Ms. Dora's toes," he grinned and left the kitchen.

* * *

It was 10:00 p.m., and the Shallottes were sitting in front of the television watching *The Nutcracker*. Beau Jackson had retired to the guest room. Willie Lewis was taking first watch, sitting by himself, reading a magazine, in the hallway.

"Tomorrow is Christmas Eve," reminded Dupin, speaking over his shoulder to Nicole, who was lying on her back in the rear seat of the Jaguar. "Our boy on the street thought he saw someone that looked like Dieter down near St. John's Armory and again near a pawn shop on King Street but was unable to confirm either sighting. I wonder what kind, romantic soul Dieter got to hide that note to Emmalou?"

"Someone who thought she was helping Cupid, no?" guessed Nicole. She was beginning to enjoy her night rides in the back of the Jag. Dupin's voice overhead and the hum of the big engine had a comforting effect. Tomorrow, if all went as planned, she would leave the Shallotte house, disguised as Emmalou, tour the city with Willie Lewis, and hopefully, lure Dieter into the open.

Unexpectedly, the Jag rolled to a stop.

"Come up here with me, Nicole. It's Christmas, and I want you to see The Bridge of Lions. If Dieter shows, I'll shoot his head off," said Dupin.

Nicole climbed over into the passenger seat, carefully avoiding the gun that Dupin had placed between them on the seat. She looked up at the bridge, and the sight was breathtaking. Thousands of tiny white lights decorated the span and reflected down into the water below. Against the black sky, they appeared like clusters of glittering stars. It was very quiet. Few cars traveled over the bridge.

"You know, Nicole, this is a special city, lots of history began here. You should come back sometime when you're not in the game, not on the job . . . just to wander around and get to know this place."

"When my school friends and I visited here years ago when I was a foreign exchange student, we would jog on the beach at Anastasia on the damp sand. There were big rocks offshore, and there were cactus that had something on them like little red apples. Oh, and the trees were bent from the sea wind and bare!"

Dupin chuckled. "Still the same. Well, time to go."

They drove slowly across the magic bridge.

* * *

At 9:00 a.m., on Christmas Eve, St. Augustine was cold and rainy. The "Snowbirds" visiting from States up north, were huddled in their warm condos and motels, waiting for the famous Florida sunshine, which would make no appearance on this gloomy day. The brave ones who had ventured out in shorts and windbreakers soon beat a hasty retreat back to the comfort of central heating.

Nicole had arrived at the Shallottes' house an hour ago, and she now stood in the guest bathroom, gazing at herself in the full-length mirror on the door. Who is that woman, she mused, and where did I go? Her hair was covered with a wig of light brown curly hair. The yellow dress and sweater clung tightly to her shoulders. I'm not wearing that damn hat, she decided, and it is cold. I need my raincoat. Carefully, she applied mascara, eyeliner, blush, and lipstick. That Emmalou really loved cosmetics. Nicole grimaced as she grumbled to herself under layers of foundation. Reluctantly, she strode into the living room, the transformation complete.

The three men who were seated there looked up and stared. Dupin looked away, as if he were amused, and pretended to be interested in the flowers on the coffee table. Lewis grinned in his boyish way and pushed his hair back from his forehead.

"I do believe my date for the prom has arrived," he announced.

Beau Jackson rose and circled Nicole.

"I'm sorry, ma'am, you will have to leave. How did you get in here? Where is security? This is outrageous!" Trying to keep a smile off his broad, dark face, he walked out to the hall and peered around. "What have you done with our Nicole?"

They broke into laughter loud enough to bring the Shallottes from the kitchen where they had been having breakfast. Dora stared at Nicole.

"I must say a little makeup is an improvement. Of course, you won't fool that killer out there. Emmalou's eyes are blue. Yours are almost black. Can't you people get her some contacts?" Dora complained.

Colt seemed spellbound. "I think she looks real nice, honey."

Emmalou stared too, "You won't fool Brucie."

Angrily, the girl flounced from the room, and the Shallottes followed her back to the kitchen, where, from the sounds, an argument had begun immediately. Colt's complimentary remark about Nicole seemed to be drawing heat from Dora and Emmalou.

Ignoring the raised voices from the kitchen, Beau Jackson handed each of the agents a wire. "Here is your communication. Nicole, tape it to your shoulder so that you can simply talk down into it, or pin it to your bra. Lewis will wear one too, in case you are separated. Maurice will be in the vicinity, close enough to pick up anything you say, so you're fully covered. I want you to stay among the crowds but let yourself be seen. I'll be right by the phone here and expect you back before five. Remember, it turns dark by five. Maurice, you got a word?"

"If we can get Dieter to follow Nicole and Lewis, I've got an empty house on 207, the road out near the flea market. The house itself sets way back off the road, but my real estate sign is at the entrance. Here is a map to the place. Lewis, as Emmalou's boyfriend, you are to let her out of the car at the sign. This would mean she will be walking up to the house alone, and if he's on your trail, this is where he'll make his move, and we'll be there. We've got him."

"Still, it might not work. You say a long walk to the house? Why would she be going to an empty house?" asked Willie Lewis, looking doubtfully at Nicole. "What if that son of a bitch moves on her fast? You know, his MO is knives and garrotes, both of them quiet and fast. I want to stay with Nicole all the way."

"We all want to stay with Nicole, Willie, but it won't work," said Jackson.

"There are lights on in the house," explained Dupin. "A radio plays all day and night as if someone lives there. And if Dieter shows, I'll be on your tail like a hungry flea on a dog's back." He passed out the small maps, and then turned to Nicole, who had been silently listening. "Are you okay with this?"

"Let's go to work," she answered.

"I know it's a hell of a way to spend Christmas Eve," grunted Jackson. "I miss my kids. How about you, Nicole? You got family?"

"Somewhere in Paris there is a Christmas goose with my name on it," she said, as she helped Lewis into a heavy, gray plaid jacket.

In turn, he helped her on with her raincoat, and they both tested their concealed wires with Dupin. Nicole's sounded okay as did Lewis's, in that limited range.

"Let's roll," said Lewis. Young, and new to the game, he was experiencing a myriad of feelings, a touch of apprehension tinged with mounting excitement. He brushed his hair back from his forehead and felt for the mike under his shirt.

"Take care," growled Jackson as he turned on his heel and headed for the kitchen, as if he were reluctant to see them leave.

The cold rain was still falling as Lewis and Nicole headed for the city in the blue Chevy Caprice. They had no particular agenda. Dupin followed a few cars behind in the Jaguar.

"This would be a neat place to visit, like a tourist, you know?"

"We may as well have fun," said Nicole. "Find a parking place, if you can, and we'll window shop and see the sights, and let ourselves be seen."

"He may be out there," reminded Lewis. "Keep looking over your shoulder. Either, most folks finished their shopping or the rain is keeping them home. There doesn't seem to be many people on the streets."

"Make it easy to spot Dieter, if he's still around."

Lewis's eyes constantly flitted from one side of the street to the other, then back to the rearview mirror. The Jag did not always stay in sight but appeared sporadically, as if Dupin circled a block here, a block there, seeking Dieter.

"Is this your first big case?" asked Nicole, sensing his nervousness.

"I've been on two drug busts with Beau Jackson, both in New York. We brought in some Columbians."

My life is in the hands of a rookie, thought Nicole, I'm glad Maurice is hanging back there. She touched the wire pinned to her bra.

They managed to find an open space on King St., parked and walked back to the Wax Museum, where there was a lifelike Whoopi Goldberg peering out of the window. Nicole stood in front of the glass pane. In the area behind them, she noted the action. There were two kids running down the street. They had made hats from the St. Augustine Record, to keep off the rain, and their faces were black with newsprint. Their laughter rang through the cold air as they regarded each other. There was a girl with brightly wrapped gifts, which she was trying to shield under clear plastic. A couple hurried to a red Corvette, stopped to lower a white umbrella, then jumped inside. On the other side of the grassy median, an elderly man found shelter under a tree. He sat down to rest on a bench, his cane between his knees. Carols were playing somewhere and colored lights in the store windows reflected in the puddles on the sidewalk.

Nicole and Willie Lewis strolled hand in hand down King St. and turned on St. George. They spent an hour wandering among the shops on the Walking Mall. All of a sudden, they realized they were in an enclosed area where there was no through traffic for vehicles. They had lost Dupin. They turned and hurried back to King St., glancing right and left for the familiar black Jaguar. Nicole reached down and spoke into her mike.

"Maurice? We are heading back to the car. Do you read me?"

"Say again? The battery . . . static . . . static give your loca. Come in."

"His battery is going. Damn. Give him the location of the car," suggested Lewis.

He spoke into his own mike. "King St. There is a statue down there. I think it may be Ponce de Leon. Nicole will wait for you there. Dupin, come in."

Static . . . "Read you," came the reply finally.

Nicole and Lewis parted, going in opposite directions. Lewis went back down to where the car was parked, about two blocks away, as she hurried to meet Maurice Dupin.

The old man, who was still waiting on the bench, got up suddenly and clutching his cane began to move down the street several yards behind Nicole. By the time he had reached the Old Market, he was walking upright, no longer using an old man's forward slump, and tottering gait. He came around the side of the building just as the Jaguar rolled into sight around the corner. He stopped and waited beside the wall. He recognized the car of the real estate man who had been coming to the Shallottes' house. Why was Emmalou meeting the real estate man, he wondered, as the Jag pulled over to the curb. She crossed to the car and began talking to the driver, but they were too far away to make out the words they were saying. As the blue Caprice sped up and stopped just behind the Jag, the old man stepped backward into a nearby doorway out of sight.

"Here, Maurice, I'll give you my mike," said Nicole. She reached into her bra and pulled it loose, then handed it through the window. "Since we are together, we don't need two anyway. And this one works fine, no?"

"I'll try to find the right batteries and fix this damn thing," fumed Dupin, stuffing the faulty wire into the glove compartment. "Any sign of Dieter?"

"Nothing all day, and we're hungry. We're heading across the bridge to eat at the restaurant near the lighthouse. You may as well come with us. There's no use being out in the rain."

"But he was in town yesterday because he got that note to Emmalou. He is devious and clever. You are dealing with a real psycho, so stay alert."

While they talked, a small, gray Geo had come around and was idling, two cars behind the Caprice. The driver was buried deep in a map.

Nicole and Lewis walked back and got into the Caprice. "Lewis here. Do you read?"

"Loud and clear!" answered Dupin. "Let's do lunch." He started his car and drove away toward the bridge, closely followed by the Caprice.

Within seconds, the little Geo pulled out, let a few vehicles get between, and joined the line of cars at the bridge. The driver pulled his old rain hat low over his forehead and tossed the cane into the backseat. She was just ahead in that boy's car, his Emmalou, ungrateful, hateful Emmalou. He began to sing in a high, whispery voice—"Oh, my darling Emmalou, you betrayed me to the police, now I must kill you . . . oh, little stupid bitch woman, how I need to kill you . . . take your skinny little neck and slice it all the way through. Oh yes."

There she was, right there, in the blue car. They couldn't hide her forever.

He rubbed his hand over the stubble of beard on his cheek. He couldn't remember when he had shaved last. His face felt thin. Always running, he thought angrily, no time to eat, no time to sleep. And the voice, always the voice. He had to listen to it. The voice had told him to kill the big, black man at the Shallottes' house, but he couldn't. The black man never came out after dark. He was always with Emmalou, like a black shield, surrounding her. The man smiled. But he wasn't with her today.

The drawbridge went down, and the cars began their steady crawl across the bridge. The Geo stayed in line behind the Caprice, watching to see which way it would turn. Two cars—that could mean a complication. The voice urged, kill them all, everyone. The real estate guy too. Dieter giggled to himself. The Shallottes' were so afraid of him that they were selling their house. Maybe the real estate man was taking them to a new house right now, on the beach side. But no, they turned and drove to a parking lot beside what looked like an old house with a big porch across the front. He waited until the trio went inside, and then circled the drive. It was a restaurant, and heavenly smells of bread and fish and meat wafted on the air. He was furious. He scratched among dirty cartons on the floor, found a dry piece of pizza, and rammed it into his mouth. They were in there eating a nice hot lunch, and he was out here, starving to death. Yes, said the voice, kill them all. Look what they've done to you, Brucie, my boy. Life has never been fair to you. Only his mother ever called him Brucie, and then, Emmalou began to call him Brucie. Mother was dead. Yes, Mother was dead a very long time.

He jumped out of the car suddenly, held his face up to the cold rain, and felt his mother cleansing him, like she did in the tub when he was a boy. Within a few minutes, he was calm and strangely rested. He slid back into the car to continue his vigil and half an hour later, the young man in the gray plaid jacket came out of the restaurant, followed by Emmalou. The real estate man was holding a paper or menu over her head to keep off the rain. They drove away in their cars.

* * *

Nicole glanced at her watch and was surprised to find it was almost four o'clock. Beau Jackson wanted them back at the Shallotte house by five. There had been no sighting of Dieter, and this meant remaining in St. Augustine. Tomorrow would be Christmas Day, and here she was, in the States, while, unaware, Yvette and Mimi would be preparing the goose. She imagined their arthritic fingers at work in the kitchen. Mimi getting in the way, tasting everything and adding wine, tasting again and adding more wine, her cheeks flushed from the heat of the oven, and the spirits consumed until everything tasted exactly right. She thought about last Christmas and how Mimi told the story of the dress they had made for a rich movie star, a beautiful Greek woman who insisted on thousands of hand sewn gold sequins. So, night after night, Maman and Mimi sewed the sequins—ah, such a dress the movie star would have for the Christmas Ball! But alors! It was a thing of great beauty, but too heavy, the poor woman could not stand with it on. They hastily had created a gown of red silk.

"Are you day dreaming, Nicole?" asked Lewis, noticing the smile on her face.

"Remembering another Christmas," she admitted. "You have family, no?"

"You bet: Mom, Dad, one brother, two sisters. They think that I service computers at the military bases for a living. That's why I travel, you know?"

"I am a courier for gems and rare coins," she told him.

"Good cover. I save Bicentennial quarters. Do you think they will increase in value?" he asked, hopefully. "You hardly ever see one these days."

"Oh yes," she assured him. "They already have."

"Gets dark early in winter. Should we head in?"

"Do we have to? See that exotic looking building over there? I've always wanted to go inside. Zorayda Castle. Is it still open?"

"Let me check in with Maurice. His car is so low and black and it's hard to see if he's back there." He pressed the mike. "Going to Zorayda Castle. Read me?"

"Loud and clear," came the confirmation. "Have fun, kids."

Lewis looked up and down the street for a parking space but there was none on this side of the street. "I'll let you out here in front of the Castle and go over behind the college," decided Lewis. "Go ahead. I'll be along in a minute."

He let her out in front of number 83. Zorayda Castle was a smaller replica of The Alhambra, built by a millionaire from Boston in 1883. It was so colorful! Every time they had driven past it, Nicole had an urge to go inside and see what mysteries lay beyond the walls, and all of those odd windows.

The cashier behind the desk offered her the ticket of admission with some reluctance.

"We didn't expect anyone this late, but you go right ahead and look around. There is no one else here except a young boy that I let come in sometimes. He's a neighborhood kid, very sweet and never bothers anything. He's probably upstairs with the cat rug. Seems fascinated by that exhibit."

Nicole wandered about on the first floor, waiting for Willie Lewis to join her, but, as time passed and he didn't come in, she decided that he was just waiting in the car. She made her way up the steps to the second floor. It was very dark, lit only by stained glass hanging lanterns, and on one table toward the front was a dimly lit soapstone lamp. At the rear, was an astonishingly brilliant red glass window as round and fiery as the moon. It shed a long, red gleam the length of the room. She came to the Harem Room, small and sparsely furnished. There was a window, set in such a way that the women of the harem could look out onto the street without being seen. Further along, she became conscious of a slim figure kneeling by an alcove. It seemed to be speaking to something in the alcove, softly and urgently. As Nicole stepped closer, she saw it was the young boy the cashier had mentioned,

"I must go now, but I will pray for you, my princess, that you may enter heaven with both feet!" he whispered, and rose to his feet.

"Hello," said Nicole, softly, not wanting to frighten him.

"I thought there was nobody here," he said, ducking his head shyly. "I was just talking to my princess. I am Luis Domingo. I come here to wait until my mother gets off from work so that I can walk her home and also she is not alone in the dark streets."

"And who is the princess?" asked Nicole.

"She is dead, but here is her little foot."

Nicole glanced into the alcove. On the wall was a rug of some type of animal fur and a sign explained that it had been woven of cat hair over a thousand years ago. Luis Domingo pointed to a small bundle of bones at one side on the floor.

"The princess. Just her little foot."

Nicole went to the balcony and looked down the stairs, but there was still no sign of Willie Lewis. Only a faint light shone from the area of the cashier's desk. "I must go now. It was nice to meet you. Have a very good Christmas!" said the boy and started toward the steps.

"A joyous noel to you too, Luis!" she called after him.

His black curls were momentarily lit by the eerie red glow of the circular window, he stopped and waved up to her, and then he was gone from sight.

Something made her turn and walk back to the front window to look down at the street below and with a start, Nicole saw the blue Chevy Caprice moving slowly along in front of the Castle. It halted to let the boy, Luis Domingo, cross the street, and she looked sharply at the inside of the car. Something was definitely wrong! She saw Lewis's gray, plaid jacket, just the arm of it, on the driver, but in the backseat there was a second coat, a tan one that she knew belonged neither to Lewis, nor to her, and it had not been there before. Something else . . . a stick? No, it was a cane, the crook of it barely visible beneath the coat. Dieter. It was Dieter, out there waiting for Emmalou to appear. She groaned. Where was Willie Lewis?

She turned her head and began to speak desperately into the spot where the mike used to be before she remembered she had given hers to Dupin. And Lewis had the other. Dieter was just outside, circling the block, waiting, expecting to pick up Emmalou and where the hell was Maurice, she wondered.

Nicole flew down the stairs and through the front lobby.

"You exit through our gift shop!" called the cashier, but Nicole had already burst through the front door onto the sidewalk and was looking frantically around for Dupin's black Jaguar. She spotted it at last, on the other side of the street.

The Caprice entered the street again. Nicole looked at the Jaguar and realized the driver's seat was empty. Dupin was nowhere in sight, and Dieter was coming closer.

The Caprice slid to a stop in front of her, with the motor running. The driver reached over and opened the passenger side door without looking at her. His face was turned to the left, watching the oncoming traffic. Without hesitation, Nicole jumped into the car. As she settled into the seat, she reached into her shoulder bag and took the safety off her gun. She withdrew her compact and hopefully held the small mirror to one side as she powdered her nose. In the street behind them, no familiar car followed. Alone. I am in this alone, she realized, and where were Lewis and Dupin?

A peculiar calmness descended. Too often, she had seen other agents panic under fire, and she had determined it would not happen to her. Confronted with depending on her own wits to survive, she began to shed the fear and become alert, aware, and in charge.

"Who are you?" she demanded. "You are not my boyfriend. Did you steal this car? Because my father will kill you if you steal his car! Where are we going?"

To her surprise, the Caprice screamed to a halt so fast it hit the curb. Bruce Malcolm Dieter turned and stared at her, his hands flexing angrily on the wheel.

"Who the hell are you?" he demanded. "You're not Emmalou!"

"I'm . . . her sister, Emmalou's sister . . . Debbie. What have you done with my boyfriend, Willie? I'm going to scream my head off if you don't tell me!"

"That is Emmalou's dress. Emmalou's sweater. I bought them for her. Why are you wearing her clothes?" he demanded, looking around wildly.

"I just borrowed them to wear to town," she began to sob convincingly. "All of our stuff is in such a mess since we moved, I can't find anything to wear and this big old handbag is Mom's. It's just awful with this dress!"

"Moved?" He hit the steering wheel with his fist. "Emmalou moved? You better tell me where she is. You better not be lying to me."

"Where would she be? At our new house, silly."

Dieter sat rigidly, listening to the voice. It had crept in, laughing at him, filling the interior of the car. You are such a fool, Brucie; they tricked you again. Was that his mother behind the windshield wipers? She went back and forth. Back and forth. The raindrops looked like spittle from her lips as she taunted him. Fooled you again. You have to kill them all, you know. Moved. Real estate man. You saw him. Yes. You know what you have to do. Kill them all . . . Yes. You know what you have to do. Kill them all. Click, clack, went the wipers, side to side. Now his mother was opening and shutting her eyes, playing with him.

"I understand," he murmured as he turned his eyes to Nicole and reached into his pocket, bringing out his knife. The switchblade flashed into view. "Now, little miss what did you say your name is? You're going to lead me home."

For one terrifying moment, Nicole couldn't remember the name she had told him. She shrank away from him. "What are you doing with that knife? Please, let me go!"

"What's your name?"

"Debbie. Debbie Shallotte," the name returned suddenly to mind.

His eyes looked crazy, frightened by something she couldn't see. Was he on drugs? He darted glances at the windshield wipers. His teeth were chattering although the heat in the car made it comfortably warm. Whatever happened, she could not let him get anywhere near the Shallottes'. Suddenly, she remembered the little map that Dupin had given them to the empty house that he had for sale and she drew it out, offering it to Dieter, her hand visibly trembling.

"If I give you our new address, will you promise not to hurt me? We can talk this out. Emmalou thinks you're wonderful. I think she's in love with you," Nicole said rapidly. "You would like my dad. You can keep the car, and we'll never tell a soul. You can go up to Jacksonville or any place. Please? Please?"

He snatched the paper out of her hand and looked at the map, studying the directions carefully. "You better not be fooling me!" he warned. He took the knife and thrust it through the material of her skirt, pinioning it deeply into the seat between them. "Touch it, and I'll cut off your hand."

He drove wildly through the dark, exceeding the speed limit, but there were no police cars on the streets on this cold and rainy Christmas Eve. Most of the shops were closed or closing. The shoppers had gone home. Somewhere, far away, a church bell pealed. Would there be a Mass this Christmas Eve in St. Augustine, Nicole wondered. She wished she were safe inside, kneeling, praying to the Virgin.

Dieter began to sing. "I have your little sister, Emmalou . . . and now your darling Brucie is coming to get you . . . why did you turn off your computer? That was so stupid. So stupid, darling Emmalou." He shook his head as if he couldn't believe it. The singing dwindled down and stopped.

Nicole placed her hand inside her handbag and touched her gun. He was driving very fast. If she shot him now, there was a chance they would both die. He made several wrong turns, drove over median strips, stopped once to consult the map, and took off again so suddenly that Nicole's head snapped back onto the seat. Finally, he found his way out of town and careened down the highway. They reached a long, sparsely populated road lined with dense brush and trees on either side.

"Mr. Dupin's sign is still at the entrance to our road, so you'll know where to turn in. You'll see the lights. I bet Mom is stuffing the turkey for tomorrow, and Emmalou makes this delicious cranberry-orange sauce."

Dieter was looking for the sign. He slapped her across the face with one hand to shut her up. "You're messing with my head now. Turkey. Turkey. I'm so hungry: Apple in the pig mouth. Pumpkin pie. No, that's not right. Gumpin pie. God, I'm starving! There's no snow in this place." He shook his head. "No Santa for you, Brucie!"

The car began to slide from side to side, barely missing several large trees. Just ahead was the sign, Dupin Real Estate. Nicole wiggled the knife handle back and forth until it loosened and had almost released her skirt from the seat cushion.

Dieter slammed on the brakes and simultaneously reached for the knife, almost brushing Nicole's hand as she hastily withdrew it. He moved the car into the long driveway, stopped, and flashed the high beams down the road to the house.

"Something not kosher, Ms. Debbie. No cars. Where are the cars?"

Nicole thought quickly. "They have gone to get the tree. We always wait until the last minute because they are really cheap. Sometimes the men just leave them on the lot, and one Christmas we got this great big tree."

"Shut up!" he screamed. He drove on slowly toward the house and began to smile as they heard the music from the radios that Maurice Dupin had placed in the house to make it seem occupied. He reached behind him and retrieved the cane from the backseat. He jabbed Nicole sharply in the ribs as he turned off the ignition.

"Walk ahead of me and no funny tricks, or I'll cut your throat, and I can do it very well because I have had lots of practice and such a pretty neck. Too bad to have to slice it, but I can! Yes. One, two, buckle my shoe," he babbled.

Nicole slipped carefully out of the passenger side and walked around to the front of the car, aware that she was dealing totally with the unknown here, as Dieter seemed to slip back and forth in and out of sanity. The time for her to act was fast running out, and she sensed he would make his move on her between the car and the house. As she moved forward, she dropped her hand into her handbag and closed it around the little

.22 that Maurice Dupin had supplied. Dieter was stumbling along behind her with the cane upraised in his hand. Methodically, he beat her shoulders one at a time, stopping only to poke the center of her back to shove her toward the house. She could feel her eyes smart with tears as the cane found its mark and then, for a fleeting moment, the beating halted, and she realized he had raised it to bring it down on her head. There was a whoosh, and she jumped to one side, feeling it as it barely missed her ear. He rushed forward, furious that he had missed, and she dropped to the ground, rolling to her back, facing him. His laughter was terrible to hear as he drew the knife and stood over her, straddling her legs with his, holding her tightly to the ground.

Nicole raised her gun and fired one shot directly into his groin at close range. His eyes flew wide with shock. The knife fell from his hand, slightly grazing her cheek. He screamed, staggered forward, and for one horrible moment, Nicole thought he was going to fall directly onto her, but he lifted one foot to look down at the blood gushing from the front of his pants, which caused him to teeter sideways, giving her time to pull her legs free. She stood up and thrust him away from her. He fell backward, his eyes staring up at her in disbelief as he lay at her feet.

Nicole reached up and pulled off the wig of light brown curly hair that had covered her own and threw the wig down into the wet grass. She grabbed some tissues from her bag and wiped the heavy makeup from her face, but Dieter showed no sign of recognition. Why didn't he remember her? This would be the last face he saw on this earth, and he didn't even remember who she was.

"My name is Nicole Laurent. I was Jack McKane's partner when we brought you in. Jack was a good man. A good friend and you killed him. The first one was for me. The second one is for Jack," she said slowly as she raised the gun.

She aimed directly at his forehead and pulled the trigger. Dieter gave one grunt and lay still. The silencer had made very little sound in the night, but the woods had become still. Now, the birds began again their nocturnal chirping, and an owl was heard asking, who, who? Somewhere was the sad cry of a mourning dove, and there was a stealthy rustle of some woods creature in the brush at the side of the road.

Nicole walked painfully to the porch and eased herself down on the steps. Her back and shoulders ached where Dieter had beaten her with the cane, and there was a scratch on her cheek from the knife. She wiped away a trickle of blood and vaguely wondered whether there was anything to eat in the house or a drink in the fridge. Perhaps there were crackers or a candy bar. Hot soup, oh, I would love a big bowl of hot soup, she thought miserably, seeing her own breath in the chill country air.

A car turned into the long drive, coming fast, and Nicole recognized Maurice Dupin's Jaguar. He was alive! With a cry of relief, she ran forward and almost threw herself on the hood as he careened to stop just inches short of Dieter's body.

"Thank you, Mary, Mother of Jesus!" she exclaimed as Dupin got out of the car and hurried toward her. "When I saw the Jag on the other side of the street, with no driver, I thought that Dieter had got you too."

She threw her arms around him, burying her face in the warmth of his jacket, and he held her close for a long time.

"I'm an old guy, Nicole," he said apologetically. "I went to the john and when I got back to my car, Zorayda Castle was closed. First, I drove around the area looking for the Caprice, and then headed out to the Shallottes, thinking you were checking back with Jackson. Beau was fit to be tied. He didn't have a clue where any of us were—you, me, Willie—where is Willie?"

"I don't know, but I'm afraid. Dieter was driving the Caprice when I came out of the Castle, and he was wearing Willie's jacket. I knew it wasn't Willie, but I got in the car anyway."

Dupin walked over to the body lying in the driveway. He picked up the knife, and then the discarded wig and the cane.

"You knew it was Dieter, and you got in the car. And you thought he may have killed me, and probably killed Willie Lewis. Are you crazy, Nicole?"

"Well, he had to be stopped!" Nicole muttered angrily.

Dupin stared at the motionless body, stiffening quickly in the cold, damp air, and looked back at Nicole. "Looks like you stopped him. Are you okay?"

"Okay."

"I've got a body bag in the trunk of the Jag. We can't leave him lying out here." He tried to joke. "It could be bad for my real estate business."

"I'll help you."

Together they rolled Dieter's corpse into the body bag, zipped it up, and threw the bundle into the trunk of the Jaguar. Dupin took a hose from the side of the house and hosed down the driveway as Nicole leaned against the hood of the Caprice.

She was listening intently. "What is that sound? Is it . . . tapping?" she motioned Dupin to silence. "Maurice, are you wearing your mike?"

"Of course," he answered, putting it up to his ears.

"It has to be Willie," gasped Nicole. "And it's coming from nearby!"

"The trunk of the Caprice," Dupin guessed. "Where are the keys?"

"Still in the ignition."

She ran to the driver's side, threw the door open and grabbed the keys. They both rushed to the trunk and thrust it open. Coiled in a fetal position, his bloody head in one hand, the other hand was tapping on the steel rim of the spare tire with the tire iron. His mouth was too swollen for him to speak and his nose was broken, but he was still conscious. His eyes gazed up at them, and the tire iron dropped from his hand as he realized he had been rescued. Tears rolled down his cheeks.

"Oh, Willie, you're alive!" said Nicole, reaching out to help him rise to a sitting position. "Maurice, he's hurt very bad. Mon Dieu, he must get to a hospital right away. Hurry, he has lost a lot of blood."

She put the keys to the Caprice into Dupin's hand.

"What about?" Dupin asked, nodding toward his own car where the body of Dieter reposed in the trunk.

"I'll take care of it. Just go, as fast as you can."

"Will you be needing your gun and your knife? The job is done."

She handed them over, and with the other knife, the cane, and wig, he hurried to the house and locked everything inside. The lights went off. The radio stopped playing and an eerie silence descended in the night as Dupin returned.

He came over to the Caprice, and together they gently lifted Willie Lewis into the backseat, where he groaned, and layback, attempting to speak.

"Shhhh . . . ," she told him. "Perhaps one day we will meet again."

Dupin settled into the driver's seat, revved the engine and looked at Nicole solemnly, "And will I see you again, little one?"

"Perhaps. Life is uncertain."

He nodded, understanding. He held out his hand, but she brushed it away, leaned into the car, and kissed his mouth hard, looked into his face as if she were trying to memorize every feature, then abruptly turned and walked away.

The Caprice sped down the driveway, the brake lights blinked briefly at the main road, and they were gone. For a few moments, Nicole gazed at the cloud of dust from the exhaust that lingered on the air, feeling very alone. She got into the Jaguar and followed down the road, then headed south when she reached A1A. Aware that she did not dare be stopped for any violation as long as Dieter's body was in the trunk, she drove carefully, looking for a public telephone. There was one near the Publix grocery store, so she pulled over and called Gazar.

"Gazar, it is Nicole. The package has been delivered. You may deposit the second half in my Paris account."

"Can we talk about that, sweetheart?" he whispered. "I can arrange a nice little bonus if you come to Washington, a little Christmas gift, say?"

"We've had this conversation before. You carry through on our original agreement and forget the bonus."

"Listen, little smart mouth. I own you now. I literally know where the bodies are buried!" he threatened.

"No, as a matter of fact, you don't."

"I can terminate you. You work for me and don't forget it."

Nicole lowered her voice and whispered into the telephone intimately. "And I can terminate you, Gazar. Think it over."

After a moment of tense silence, she hung up the telephone, returned to the Jag, and headed for the Best Western. At the motel, a hot shower and clean clothes gave some relief. She felt weary and exhausted, and a peculiar kind of letdown that came when a mission was completed. She took three aspirins, washed them down with water from the bathroom sink, and regarded the deep scratch on her cheek, which was noticeable. She placed a narrow strip from a Band-Aid over the cut and applied foundation over it. A little powder helped and a touch of rose lipstick. She pulled her short, spiky bangs forward, and the transformation back to her old self was complete. No more Emmalou.

Her few belongings were tossed into her carry-on bag, along with the yellow Emmalou sweater, which she had grown fond of, to her amusement. But not so the frilly dress, with its daisies, and now Dieter's blood, which had sprayed down the front of the skirt as she lay pinioned on the ground beneath his feet. She extricated the plastic liner from the trashcan, pushed the dress down inside and tied a knot at the top of the bag. The dress was quite different from the faded jeans and black turtleneck sweater that she wore now. She shrugged into her raincoat.

The sleepy motel clerk wished her a good trip and went back to watching an old movie on one of the cable channels.

The Jaguar moved smoothly through the darkened streets as she headed down the highway toward Ormond Beach. The radio played the old favorite, "Silent Night" and indeed it was, thought Nicole, as she munched a Rice Krispie bar that Dupin had left on the dashboard. She stopped once for gas and tossed the Emmalou dress into a dumpster behind the service station. The resort community was just ahead, expensive cottages that stayed empty about six months of the year, and in this unexpectedly cold holiday season, the absentee owners must have opted to remain up north because there were very few places with lights. The beach house she was looking for, was white, with distinctive black shutters, a widow's walk around the rooftop, and six palm trees across the front. Several times, Gazar had given her specific directions, urging her to meet him there, but she never had, and never would. The mailbox, in black box letters, said *gazar*.

She was surprised to find no security lights as she drove the Jag far up under the carport to a row of steps, leading up to a kitchen, perhaps. There was one neat thing about Florida. Summer, or winter, there was always sand, and sand was easy to dig. If only she wasn't so beat! Next to the outside shower, under the house, were two oars hanging on the wall. She got out of the car, grabbed one of the oars and began to dig a depression in the sand, approximately six feet long and about three feet deep. After the first few inches, the ground became harder to move, damp, and more solid, and even in the cold, Nicole started to sweat. Tired, and hungry, she felt a strange euphoria come over her, and she dug harder until a sizable area of sand was displaced. Room enough for the bag. Oh yes. She returned to the trunk of the car, carrying both oars. Rigor mortis had set in. Suddenly light-headed, that's why they call them stiffs, she thought crazily. She sank down in the sand. "Get up, Nicole," she could hear Mimi saying, we have saved you a piece of the goose. The beautiful goose, the truffles, the wine, the lovely what was it and the wine, oh, I said that. "Get up, Nicole!"

Nicole stood up and heaved the corpse out of the trunk. With the belt from her raincoat, she tied him to the oars, dragged the bundle to the open pit, and rolled it in. Diligently, carefully, she covered the grave until it was level, and replaced the oars on the wall by the outside shower.

She broke off a huge piece of yucca plant and leaning down, erased all signs of her footprints as she backed to the Jaguar. She got in and sat looking at the hidden grave. "Rest in peace," she finally murmured.

* * *

The airport in Daytona was almost deserted. Those who were going home for Christmas were already there. Those who were not, snuggled in their own beds. Alone, Nicole Laurent sat on a chair in the lobby, watching an all-night news station on television. Ironically, the local weatherman was predicting sunshine tomorrow and a sudden rise to eighty-two degrees for Daytona, St. Augustine, and surrounding areas.

At 3:00 a.m., the announcer called, "Delta Airlines, Flight for Atlanta, leaving at Gate Six, on time. It's Christmas Day, everyone. Have a good trip."

Nicole Laurent rose, gathered her bags, and walked through the empty terminal.

Chapter Five

Little Boy Gone

Beau Jackson sat alone in the motel on Duke St. in Alexandria and pondered the disturbing memo he had received from Gazar. A private messenger had delivered it by hand that morning, rejecting the employment of Agent Nicole Laurent in the rescue of a kidnapped child, Charles Von Braun, the Third. Gazar had not used Nicole in more than two months, possibly three or four, and when Jackson had asked why he could not use her, Gazar had written that she was inept, refused to obey his orders, and when on the job, seldom called in, never completed reports or simply did not turn one in at all. He stated that even other agents assigned to the same mission had no idea what she did when on her own. We cannot, wrote Gazar, have this kind of subordination and disrespect.

However, I need her, Beau Jackson decided. She is the one, the only one who can go in and get that kid. He crumpled the memo, dropped it in the big glass ashtray, set it afire, and smashed the flaming ashes with one huge dark fist. He was still sitting there, contemplating the broken pieces of the ashtray and figuring his next move when a key turned in the lock, and the doorway was filled with the massive bulk of the agent known as Bull Durham, followed by the young, slick new recruit, Jerry Glass. The contrast in the two men, not only in physical appearance, but also manner, demeanor, and attitude was so obvious that they appeared to have sprung from remote planets that had never passed each other in the galaxy. Jackson could not imagine the two men working successfully together, and he questioned Gazar's decision to assign them to the same team.

However, they had been briefed on the kidnapping situation and were aware that the potentially explosive international problem was now deadlocked and because of its sensitive nature, neither nation was admitting even that a problem existed. Durham and Glass greeted Jackson, and Glass draped himself over the sofa. Bull squeezed into a chair.

"You know the problem. If the kid's father, Von Braun, would hand over the formula, then we could set up a meet with these bastards and make an exchange for the boy. I got a kid, my little girl, Vonda. If she were in that embassy, I'd tear it down brick by brick. I'd give 'em any damn thing they wanted. Doesn't Von Braun love that kid?"

Bull shook his head. "What can they do with him hidden in the embassy if the formula don't show up sooner or later? They're messing with the United States. They won't chance killing that boy. We could give them a formula that don't work, maybe?"

Jerry Glass watched the big, black man pacing back and forth. Glass, blond, green-eyed, and good looking in a juvenile way, was already impressed with his part in a covert action. He touched the 9mm Glock in its shoulder holster under his Armani jacket and gave a little world-weary smile as he gazed at the two older men.

"I'm not afraid to go in if you and Durham back me up . . . find a way to get in and I'll hold security at bay while you guys search the damn place. How about it?"

"This is your first case, Glass? For you, there will be no going in anywhere. You'll be along strictly to drive, stay alert, and observe how it goes down," Jackson growled as he stared at Glass, wondering why Gazar had hired him. The kid seemed to believe he was in the movies.

Deke Durham, whom everyone called Bull, had gone into the kitchen and poured a beer for himself in a glass, uncapped another beer in a can, for Glass, and pulled out a cold can of Sprite for Jackson. Durham was heavyset, six foot, three inches, and was built like a truck, an eighteen-wheeler. His features were large and misshapen. Scars made him look permanently angry; one lip drooped to one side, which made drinking from a can sloppy and difficult. In summer, he favored shirts buttoned to the neck, and in winter, always turtleneck sweaters, to cover the huge scar that circled his broad neck where someone had botched the job of cutting his throat. However, appearances were deceptive. Bull Durham was kind, smart, and had proved himself trustworthy in the game.

"We need someone small, yet strong, to go up over that wall like a little black cat," suggested Durham, "and bring that baby down."

"A little black cat," echoed Jackson, nodding his head in agreement.

Glass looked interested. "You know a guy like that?"

"Not a guy. A woman," Jackson answered.

"Oh hell, no. This job is too dangerous to trust to a woman."

"She can take care of herself," Jackson assured him. He looked over at Durham. "You know Nicole Laurent, don't you, Bull? I've asked for Nicole because it just happens that she knows the boy, little Charles Von Braun."

"Nicole," Durham said softly. "Yes, I know Nicole. Me and Maurice Dupin went with her on her very first assignment. It was in New York. A Catholic church had on loan statues of the twelve apostles from another church in Italy. Two of the statues had been stolen, but they didn't want nobody to find out and sure, they didn't want no police, and the news people. Gazar sent the three of us over to babysit the remaining statues in case the thief came back and had a shot at the rest of 'em. Dupin and I were to sit just outside in the van. Nicole, dressed as a nun, she stayed in the church, praying, and lighting candles night after night. Had the habit on, all in black veil, the works. Well, nothing was happening. Whole first week, not a stir, so we was surprised on the end of the second week, out comes Nicole, whippin' on silent little black shoes, down the sidewalk and she gets in the van. Cool as a cucumber."

"It's done. Go in and get the thief, messieurs," is all she said.

"What? What?" me and Dupin was saying. We jump out of the van and run into the church. There was a priest, laying out cold, in front of the altar."

"Man, you're making up this crap, aren't you?" laughed Glass. He shook his head, got up, and walked away to the kitchen to get another beer.

"What did they find?" asked Jackson.

"Well, it seems she was doing her praying thing and a priest comes down the aisle and as he passes she looks to one side and sees he is wearing brown and white shoes with his black robes . . . this don't look kosher, you know? So she slips up to the front there in time to see him secreting one of the statues into a pocket under the robe. He is kneeling down, stuffing the statue into a special sack sewn into the robe. He starts to get up; she drop kicks him in the jaw and lays him out. Me and

Dupin, we run into the church. Guy is out cold, the statue is on him, his jaw has done swelled up like a melon, and he ain't going nowhere."

"Do you believe this, Jackson?" Glass was laughing. "So she screwed up her first job, knocking out a priest?"

"No screw up. He was the thief. They found the other two statues in his room. The shoes? He had been playing golf and forgot to change. Well, Dupin contacts the Monsignor and got a lot of shit about forgiveness, and he just knew that guy was going to get off scot free, so nice as you please, Dupin hangs up, calls 911. Then, we parked the van across the street and waited until NYPD swarmed on that church like bees around a hive."

"Did they lock him up?"

"Nope, just shifted him out of the parish. Case closed."

"Me and Dupin, we never believed in soft stuff like censures and chastises . . . that's just words in the wind. We believe in censure first and then shoot 'em in the foot. Words are forgotten. A bullet in the foot, you remember." Bull Durham's scarred face cracked into what may, or may not have been, a smile.

"Bullet in the foot. You don't mean that literally, do you?" asked Glass.

"There's quite a few mama boys out there walking with a limp, right, Beau?"

Jackson smiled but didn't answer. He was thinking about Nicole. "Bull, did you ever mess up with Gazar and get sent to the Law Office? I had that experience twice."

"Can't say I have."

"That's another Nicole story. She hit a station wagon and arrested seven Mexicans from one family, transporting stolen cigarettes, but only two were actually involved. She was cuffing Grandma, an eighty-five year old blind man, the whole bunch. So Gazar had her put into the Law Office, which is a nicely furnished law office with desks, walls of books, plants, but there are no windows and no bathroom. You're given up to six hours to think about your mistakes. There are no meals. The door is locked and about halfway into your confinement, the rat from hell is let into the office."

"An actual rat," said Glass. He sucked in his breath and looked uneasy.

"He's old, he's big, and he has been without food for hours. He runs around the floor, leaps on the desk, tears at the papers, snatches the plants, and chews on them. You better not have a candy bar on you. I ended up on the third shelf with the books," admitted Jackson, looking grim as he recalled the experience.

"And my—I mean, Gazar put that woman, Nicole, in with the rat?"

"Yes, he did, and he let her stew for at least three hours before he got curious about what was happening in the office. He told another agent to lure the rat back into the cage on the other side of the wall but when the agent looked, the rat was already in its cage, crouching in a corner, all bloody, half dead. Gazar hurries to the door, opens it, and there sits Nicole, reading a book. She looks up at Gazar and says, "Did you know the panda is closer to the raccoon family than the bear family?" Gazar sees a trail of blood across the desk and on the floor leading to the rat hole. Nicole says, "You have a rodent. I stick my chewing gum on the desk, no? The rodent runs to eat it, and I staple his tail to the desk. He chews off his tail and alors, he runs away." She notices the open door behind Gazar and shaking her finger at him she says, "You need a bathroom in here. The philodendron will not need water for two days," and she walks past him and out the door."

"How can we reach Nicole and how soon can she get to Washington?" said Durham.

"A rat! God, I hate those things," muttered Glass, still lost in the story of Nicole in the Law Office.

"I will have to try to reach her through different channels," said Jackson. "Gazar says no, but we need her on this. I'm calling her anyway."

"Go for it," agreed Durham. He looked at his watch. "I gotta go. I'm on surveillance in twenty-five minutes on Embassy Row."

"Any sign of the boy? At the window, maybe?"

"No, but we know he's in there. I'll call you if anything's going down."

Durham left, and Glass crossed to the window that looked down on the motel parking lot, watching as Bull Durham's old gray Mercedes drove away.

"Who is that old fool trying to kid with that shoot-em-in-the foot bit? Is he trying to impress me because I'm kind of new in this job? Listen, I'm Harvard, and he is grade school, borderline illiterate. You hear how he talks. Blooming freak!"

Beau Jackson turned slowly, his fist shot out, and he knocked the can of beer from Glass's hand. It sprayed across the room, soaking a trail into the carpet and lay, spewing foam against the far wall. Glass stood watching, rendered speechless.

"Listen up, you little shit. You don't know Bull and never will. So I'm gonna give you a little background. He was twenty-two years old, putting himself through Georgetown by working as a bank security guard. There was a holdup, a hostage situation, and Bull drew down on the two thieves he could see. A third accomplice, in place in a teller's line behind Bull, attacked him from the back, jumped on him, and slit his throat . . . but Bull got off six shots before he fell. Two dead; the knifer lost most of his face, and instead of going back to college, Bull spent nearly a year with surgeries and rehab. He thought he was unemployable until he was recruited for the game."

Glass, only half listening, was looking at his beer draining into the carpet. His face was flushed with anger as he turned on Jackson.

"And who the hell do you think you are? That was the last beer!"

"Did you hear anything I said?" demanded Jackson.

"Big deal! And don't you ever refer to me as a little shit again. I've got connections like you wouldn't believe," shouted Glass. He moved across the room, shook the beer can and found it empty, then threw it down in disgust.

Jackson stared at the younger man with real curiosity. Gazar had sent him over without a resume or a word about his background. Who the hell was this shitty kid?

"Where did you drop from, little college boy?" Jackson asked.

Glass smiled. "You better be real nice to me, black man. Who knows? I might be your next boss." He strolled slowly over to the door and as he opened it, he turned and said, "And get some more brew in here. None of that domestic crap."

Seething, Jackson watched from the window as Glass ran down the steps and sped away in a white Corvette, dashing into traffic as he entered Duke St. In a few moments, he went to the telephone and dialed a familiar number.

"Charlene, its Beau. I want you to check out a Jerry Glass, about twenty-five, Washington area local probably, hair is light, eyes, green. Height is about five feet nine and weight around one sixty, seventy. Oh, yeah, he said he went to Harvard. Is that enough?"

"Maybe a middle initial. There may be more than one Jerry Glass."

"God forbid," sighed Jackson, "I don't know his middle initial, Charlene."

"Okay. Call you back shortly."

"Thanks."

The telephone rang in twenty minutes, and Charlene was laughing. "Piece of cake, Beau. He has his own page on the web! Jerome Alan Glass, age twenty-seven. He wishes to meet women under twenty-five—oh, and they must be slim. That lets me out, Beau!"

"Be thankful. Anything else?"

"Well, they must have an income exceeding one hundred thou a year or he is not interested. Oh yeah, on the Harvard bit. In his soph year he left with a grade point average of one point eight."

"Anything else on family?"

"Sure. Father is Micah Alan Glass, a retired stockbroker, and his mother's name is Sophie Gazar Glass. She has a fabric import business. They got mucho bucks."

"Run that last part by me again. Did you say Gazar?" He listened as she repeated the names of Glass's parents. Jackson had heard enough.

"Thanks, Charlene."

He hung up the telephone and stared at it in disbelief. Gazar had sent him his own nephew. As control, Gazar had put his own sister's son into the game. He shook his head. There was nothing he could do about Glass, but he could do something about Nicole. He looked up a number in the yellow pages under the odd heading, Hand Written and Illustrated Manuscripts.

"I would like to speak to Mr. Hammer, please."

"Who is calling?" a fragile old male voice asked hesitantly.

"Beauregard Jackson."

"Regarding?"

"Paris. It is about Paris."

In time, G. Edmund Hammer answered the telephone. "You may talk. The brothers don't hear very well. Paris, you say? You refer to Agent Laurent."

"Yes, we need her desperately on the Von Braun case. She knows that boy, sir, and she can do the job of getting him out, but Gazar refuses to let me have her."

"Hmmm. She frustrates him with her refusals to have anything to do with him in a social manner. Do you read me?"

"Perfectly."

"We are all a bit in love with Paris, aren't we?"

"Yes, sir."

"Go ahead with it. I'll go over Gazar and authorize her payment with the others. In confidence, they are losing faith with Gazar. There may be changes. Confidential."

"Of course, sir. And thank you, sir!"

* * *

The dawn's first light crept into the elegantly appointed bedroom and shed a rosy glow across the tangled linen sheets, the lacy pillowcases, and the silk coverlet. It fell on the nude man and woman who lay arms and legs intermingled, breath hot on each other's faces, in satisfied sleep on the tall Victorian tester bed. As the sun reached his cheek, the man stirred, a smile touched his lips, a pleasured smile. He became conscious of the weight of the woman's leg across his hip and tried to lift it off.

"Don't get up yet, Rene," she murmured. "I must kiss you one hundred good mornings. I love you, love you, and love you."

She rubbed her eyes and blinking awake slowly, she stroked his chest. She turned and nuzzled his neck, tasting his sweat on her mouth, making love bites on his eyes and ears and finally coming to rest with her mouth over his. His arms went around her, and they rocked gently together.

"My darling. My angel," he whispered into the warm dampness of her neck.

She pulled away and began to plant kisses the length of his body. She bit his toes until he started to laugh and struggled to sit up. She released him and perched a little distance away on the end of the bed, clutching a pillow to her chest. She regarded him with her dark, almost black eyes. He was looking toward the window.

"What are you thinking, Rene?"

"It need not concern you."

"It does. You have that secret look, and I hate it. I hate it!"

"I did not want to tell you that I am going away for a while to the country," he admitted reluctantly. "I have put Georges in charge of the shop."

"For how long?" Nicole demanded drawing the sheets around her defensively. "You make love to me, and you think about Therese? What kind of love is that?"

He sat silently, trying to think of an answer.

"You were just there, a long time in December!" she reminded him angrily.

"Because you were in America!" he shot back. "You were off on one of those stupid translation jobs, and I had to eat Christmas dinner alone with Yvette and Mimi. We waited until the goose grew cold, and you did not come. Yes! I went to the country after because I knew I could find a good red wine, some fat sausages and most of all, good company."

"I was on the plane, coming home to you, Rene, as fast as I could, but it was so cold in New York. The planes could not fly out with ice on the wings. So very cold!"

Rene wiped his eyes with the back of his hand. Were those tears?

"Therese may be dying, Nicole. It is breast cancer."

"No!" she gasped. She flung herself back on the pillows.

Rene turned and abruptly went into the bathroom. Immediately, she heard the rush of the shower, loud and harsh against the marble tub. She shivered and curled into a ball, thinking about Therese. If one had to have a rival, there could not be a better one than Therese, a sweet-faced older woman, a widow with two grown sons. Nicole had only seen her fleetingly at the markets in town, perhaps four times in the entire five years. Hardly the prototype of a mistress, the older woman had remained in the background, unobtrusive and undemanding, thankful for her times with Rene. Nicole had always been sure that the times they had shared were a quieter, different kind. And now, perhaps Therese was dying, and Nicole found herself praying for her survival.

Rene came back into the bedroom and began to search the armoire for fresh underwear. She sat up and watched him toss things aside.

"Can I help in any way, Rene?" she asked quietly. "Should I tell Maman and Mimi? They know of Therese, of course."

"Just be understanding. No cards! No flowers!" he answered. "She pretends you, and in fact, no one knows about us. This is foolish, of course."

Nicole got up, walked into the still steaming bath and turned on the shower. She stepped under the strong rush of water and lifted her face into the hot stream.

When the telephone shrilled, she did not hear it or Rene's angry voice when he answered.

"Do not bother me about pink grapefruit!" he shouted. "I do not buy the groceries in this house!"

* * *

There was no time for her usual run out at LeGrand's farm this morning. So Nicole dressed and went directly down to the shop. Georges, self-impressed at being in charge, was already at work, briskly placing the trays of less expensive jewels into the display cases at the front of the shop, and lesser prices for the walk-in trade—friendship rings, birthstones, and identification bracelets. The better merchandise was kept far in the back. The best were in safes out of sight altogether, to be shown only in two tiny private rooms. Wealthy, even royal, clients entered from the rear and scurried into the private places to make their selections, separate from the hoi-polloi. They would call in advance so that the alarms at the alley would be temporarily disconnected.

"Any messages for me?" asked Nicole.

"No, madam. Monsieur has no appointments for a week. He says there is illness in the family. Is it your grandmother, madam?"

"No. His cousin, I believe," Nicole answered coldly.

By the time the telephone began to ring, Georges had hastened to the rear of the shop, and Nicole picked it up.

"Rene Laurent. May I help you?"

"Madam! I have been trying to reach you! This is important."

She recognized the voice of Delon, the grocer. "I told you that you must never call me here, or at my mother's place."

"Something has happened. Listen carefully. I will be selling apples on the corner of the Rue B—Come at once."

The front door buzzed just as she hung up the telephone, and she let the other salesman, Henri-Paul, and the accountant, appropriately named Billings, into the shop.

Delon, the grocer, was warning her not to go near the Paris office or to try to contact Richard Leach. Nicole moved to one of the cases, hand-vacuumed the velvet nests where diamonds would glitter, and watched the street. Everything appeared normal. It was spring in Paris, but there was a definite nip in the air. She put on her black beret and a light black jacket, and then called out to Henri-Paul that she was going out for coffee. He hurried to the front as she stepped outside on the pavement.

The awnings on the cafes were down and the sidewalks were filled with small, rickety metal chairs and tables. The delicious smells of morning were everywhere, the aroma of coffee, hot croissants, and crusty bagels was tantalizing on the air. The old men, the regulars, were claiming their observation posts in order to leer at the young women on their way to work. One fellow reached out to pinch Nicole as she passed, but laughing, she nimbly avoided his gnarled fingers and hurried on.

The neighborhood where Delon had directed her was old, with crumbling sidewalks and many small trees lashed into wire enclosures. Still protected, they did not flourish and looked as frail as the elderly, who had come out to sit on the steps in the sun. Down at the end of one block, she spotted Delon. He had opened the back of his station wagon, he leaned against it, and there was a basket of apples at his feet. Their eyes met briefly in recognition, and then she deliberately turned, walked back to a shop on the corner, and pretended to adjust her beret in the window's reflection. Meager traffic passed behind her. Everything appeared normal. She strolled back toward Delon.

"How much, monsieur?" she asked as a man passed behind her. She picked out a few apples. They were firm and damp as if just sprayed in his grocery shop.

"Take more," he directed. "Enough to go in this sack."

She handed him a few francs. He gave her change.

"Merci, madam," Delon said and touched his cap.

Nicole took the sack and wandered down the street, stopped, took out an apple and wiped it on her sleeve. Taking small bites, she continued until she saw an empty bench. When she sat down and glanced back, Delon's station wagon was gone. She hailed a taxi and had the driver drop her off a block from the shop. While in the taxi, she had extracted the short note in the sack, which had been concealed under the apples.

Richard Leach is dead. Perhaps a street mugging. Do not go to the Paris office. It has been closed; Washington has been trying to contact you. Call.

There was a number to call. She memorized the note, tore the note into bits and put the pieces into her jacket pocket. Richard Leach was dead. Why? How? And where was her little friend, the dwarf, Derek . . . and the travel girl, Giselle? Were they all dead?

She went back to work, waiting on customers, answering the telephone, and showing the rings and bracelets as usual and kept memorizing the telephone number repeatedly. At the end of the workday, she was exhausted, and found herself missing Rene. What if Therese died? Although it was an incongruous one, Therese played an important part in Nicole's life. Therese filled the blanks when Nicole went on her missions stateside, occupied Rene when he was feeling sorry for himself.

Therese was always simply there, like a familiar rock on a landscape, not subject to change. Rene had a plush spot to run to when she was called to do her "translation" work in the States.

Instead of going upstairs to the empty flat above the shop that she shared with Rene, Nicole got into her old, faded Volkswagen parked in the alley and drove across town to her own tiny flat. As she let herself in, the telephone number kept running through her head, but she was reluctant to use it for several reasons. For one thing, Rene was gone and Henri-Paul was not always efficient. Customers did not particularly like him, perhaps because of his overt homosexuality, which manifested itself in pink coats and heavy cologne. He also avoided waiting on anyone he didn't like. Another thing, the mystery of how Richard Leach died . . . and again, the whereabouts of Derek and Giselle. A frantic thought raced through her head. Had Richard Leach broken the rules of the game in some way? Disloyalty was lethal. A picture of Bruce Malcolm Dieter rose to mind: Dieter, who was sleeping forever in a sandy grave. Nicole shivered and turned up the thermostat, then turned on all the lights to make the lonely room seem more cheerful.

There was no food in the refrigerator and all she had was half a loaf of hard bread and various boxes of cereal, but no milk to put on them. She flipped on the television, but the pictures flew by in a daze of mediocrity that failed to distract her. She put on her beret and jacket and went out to find a nearby restaurant. There was an Italian cafe on the corner. She had been there several times. The dingy white tablecloths were stained with red wine and the black and white tiles underfoot were sticky with old grease, but the pasta was wonderful and the owners positively affectionate, greeting her with hugs and kisses, wiping off a table with the edges of their aprons. The ravioli was huge, the salad leaves draped over the bowl onto the table. When she left, the Mama pressed bags of peanuts in her pockets, and wrapped some bread, dripping with honey, into a waxed paper cone for her to take along home.

Walking back to her flat, she paused beside a public telephone. The collect call went through to the unfamiliar number without a problem, and Nicole was surprised to hear a child's voice answer.

"This is the Jackson resident. Vonda speaking."

"I think I want to speak to your father, Beau Jackson."

"That is him. He watching the TV and soaking his feet. Want to speak to Mommie?"

"No, no," Nicole said quickly. "Tell your father Paris is calling."

The child's voice drifted off. "Daddy, a lady name Paris is calling you."

"Nicole!" came Jackson's quick reply as he snatched up the telephone. "Glad you got back to me. We need you. How soon can you fly to the States?"

"I can't come, Beau. Have you heard about Richard Leach? The Paris office is down."

There was silence for a minute. "I didn't know that, Nicole. What happened to Leach, and what about the staff, are they okay?" Jackson sounded angry, "And how about you . . . tell me you're all right, Nicole."

"Fine. I'm fine. Delon only mentioned Richard, and he thinks it was a street crime, not a hit. I don't know where the others are."

"Well, I still need you, and there is nothing you can do about the Paris office. They will send in a team to take care of that. We need you here as soon as possible. Do you remember the little boy you told me about once, a kid you called Charlie Brown?"

"Of course. I went to his birthday party. In fact, I ended up being the star of his birthday party when the clown didn't show. He was six years old."

"He has been abducted. Kidnapped. Can you come?" begged Jackson.

"Mon Dieu, Charlie Brown," Nicole sighed, leaning against the cold glass of the telephone booth. Yes, she remembered Charlie Brown, small for his age, big, brown eyes and brown curls. He was living a lonely life with two self-absorbed parents and servants who had barely mastered enough English to understand the little boy, who so desperately needed somebody's attention. Her appetite was gone. She opened the door of the booth, scattered the peanuts for small creatures to find, and tossed the honey-drenched bread into a nearby trashcan. The night breeze was cold against her face.

"Nicole? Are you there?" Jackson's voice came to her faintly.

"Can you pick me up from Dulles? I'm not sure when I can get a flight."

"Thanks, Nicole. God bless you," said Jackson. "Call me from the airport anytime. Days I am in Alexandria. Nights, I'm here. Anytime, Nicole!"

"See you soon, I promise."

She hung up and walked slowly back to her little flat.

* * *

Jackson hung up the telephone and immediately dialed another number to Gazar's residence. Someone answered and walked away. He could hear music, loud conversation and laughter, the sounds of a party in full sway. The interval dragged on until finally, Gazar, sounding slightly drunk, picked up the telephone.

"Gazar here. Who the hell is this?"

"Jackson. Why didn't you tell me the Paris office was down?"

"Happened just yesterday. Why do you want to know?"

"I wanted to contact Agent Laurent!" Jackson began.

Gazar broke in. "I told you to use the new man I sent you. Jerry Glass. He's got to get his feet wet somewhere. That's an order, Jackson."

"There's a child involved and Glass is not . . . ready. What are this guy's qualifications for this type of work anyway?" Jackson demanded angrily.

"Just do what you're told. I'm missing the party."

Gazar had hung up. Jackson stared at the silent telephone, replaced it, and pounded his fist on the table.

"Bastard! Bastard!" he muttered.

"Daddy said a bad word," said a small voice at his elbow. His daughter climbed up into his lap and put her arms tight around his neck.

Jackson thought about Charles Von Braun the Third, somewhere in a strange house among people who spoke another language, and he hugged his daughter to him. "I love you, Vonda. Did I tell you that today?"

"Yes, Daddy," she grinned. "I won't tell Mommie you said a bad word."

"It'll be our secret. Let's get us some strawberry ice cream."

* * *

Nicole managed to get a flight through de Gaulle the next morning early. She called the shop and left a message for Georges that she would also be gone for a few days. She packed a few things to wear, wondering about the weather in Washington, and whether the cherry blossoms would be in bloom. Would the black pea coat with brass buttons be too warm and would three pairs of slacks be enough? Her working wardrobe was always basic but ever changing. Sometimes she bought new clothes in the States and sent the old ones home by mail. Footwear consisted of boots or track shoes.

True to his word, Beau Jackson picked her up at Dulles within two hours of her call. He was driving a brand new Cadillac, black interior and exterior, and she could smell the rich leather of the seats as she got into the passenger's side.

"Glad to see you, Nicole. We are going straight to the office in Alexandria where I'll brief you on what's going down. No one is staying there at this time, so you can pick any bedroom you like. There are two other keys out besides mine. Bull Durham has one, and the new guy, Jerry Glass, has the other one."

"Who is this Glass? He will have a key to where I sleep? No!" Nicole said. "Where is my gun?" she added. "Did you bring one with you?"

Jackson pulled over to the side of the road, reached up over his head behind the visor, and took down an old hand towel. He handed her a shoulder holster that contained a snub-nosed .32 revolver, her preferred weapon, if she had a choice. He laughed.

"You don't plan on shooting Glass, do you?"

"Only if he touches my door."

"Take it easy, Nicole!"

"I'm never easy," she snapped back. She put the extra bullets in her jacket pocket.

"I'm curious. What did you mean when you said that you were the birthday party for the little Braun boy and how did you come to be at the Von Braun's house that day?" asked Jackson. "That's out in Fairfax someplace."

"That's right. I was delivering a necklace for our shop, Rene Laurent. Mr. Von Braun gives his beautiful wife, Claire, a gift on his son's birthday as a sort of thank-you for giving him a son. A nice gesture, no? They are very rich. The necklace was a special order, designed by Rene, and worth thirty thousand dollars."

"Wow!"

"When I arrived at their estate, Mrs. Von Braun was in her bedroom, looking very well but pretending to be sick with the headache because she did not wish to be bothered with the little boys. They were downstairs, having the party beside the tennis courts and the pool. I looked down and saw six little boys, tired of the pool. No one was having any fun because the clown, Mrs. Von Braun informed me, had not come, and there was no entertainment. So, what to do, six bored little boys with no party, no?"

"Should have fed 'em cake and sent 'em home," suggested Jackson.

"I will be the clown, I told Mrs. Von Braun. I found a big red scarf among her things and made a bow on my neck, and took from Mr. VB's closet, a top hat for my head. Then into her makeup for a big smile with a very red lipstick and a touch of red on my nose, and also white gloves. Yes, that was all. I am in the clown business, no?"

Beau Jackson glanced at her to see if she was serious.

"I go down and tell the maid to find a CD player, tapes, or something good with loud music. Okay, she finds music and, it is "Tea for Two"—this song is for tap-dancing, no? I love this song! So, I come in tap dancing, and I dance over to the tennis courts, where I have seen a basket of balls—orange, yellow, and white."

"You dance with tennis balls? Nicole, we haven't been using all your talents, gal. I'll make a note of that," Jackson chuckled as he glanced at her sideways.

"I juggle with the tennis balls. I do tricks like the waterfall. Oh, they are watching me now, their eyes are big, and I toss the balls higher and higher and when an orange one comes down, I dropkick it into my little audience. Then, I am dropping and kicking the balls everywhere, and the boys are screaming and running to catch them. Balls on the patio, balls in the pool. Then the maid, she is playing 'March of the Wooden Soldiers,' so I put the boys in line, and we march, kicking out, out, out goose step to the music, and they are laughing. Everybody is having a good time, and I see Mrs. Von Braun looking down from her bedroom window."

"Damn, I wish I had been at that party."

"You are too big and old, only we kids and clowns allowed. Then the maid brings out the cake, and the party is soon over."

Nicole sat silently, looking out the window as they sped down the highway. After a few minutes, she spoke again, hesitantly. "After the boys went home, I went upstairs to remove the clothes and makeup. Mrs. Von Braun tried to pay me. I was . . . humiliated. I refused, of course. Charlie Brown came in, in his pajamas. "Read to me," he said. "Mommie has a headache, darling, all those noisy boys," she said to him. I took his hand, and we went down to the library. I read that wonderful Sendak book, "*Where the Wild Things Are*" and gave him a kiss. I love you, Clown Lady," he said.

"So, that is why you came."

"Could I say no?"

"I've arranged a meeting for you with the father at ten in the morning. He has been uncooperative. I want you to break him, Nicole. I want that goddamned formula."

"If it exists, I'll get it," she promised grimly.

Nicole found out that it was definitely cold enough in Washington to wear her black pea coat. She buttoned the brass buttons to the top as she walked toward DuPont Circle at nine thirty, and pulled her black beret over her ears. Precisely at ten to ten, she was sitting in the anteroom of Von Braun's office, watching a very young receptionist play games on a computer. At ten minutes after ten, she stood up and approached the desk, which was empty except for a telephone and a copy of *people* magazine.

"My appointment was for ten o'clock. Tell him Nicole Laurent is here, and I am leaving if I don't get in to see him in the next two minutes. Now, call him!"

The startled receptionist erased her game from the computer, stood up, and went over to the closed door to Von Braun's office, where she knocked tentatively.

"Come in!" ordered the voice from beyond the door.

Nicole brushed past her and opened the door. Once inside, she turned and locked the door behind her, which immediately drew Von Braun's attention. "Why did you lock that door?" he demanded.

"We want privacy, don't we, Mr. Von Braun? I'm here to help you get your son back."

"I suppose Jackson sent you to try to worm the formula out of me, but I made it clear to him that I don't have it. When I realized what I had created, I destroyed my notes, my experiments, everything. Can you imagine something deadlier than anthrax?"

She watched his face, a slight flush of pride as he spoke about his experiments, and she knew that he was lying. He wouldn't have so easily given up all the years of work and final success on a formula, which had been his lifetime obsession. Somewhere, a bit of that knowledge still existed, and Von Braun knew where it was.

He rose from his desk to face her, and she was surprised to see he was shorter than she expected. His hair was short and gray, his face florid and strong featured. His eyes darted about, looking everywhere except into hers.

She gauged him silently, and then said, "It still exists. You know it."

"I do want my son back. My wife is absolutely ill, and I have brought in a nurse to be with her . . . she has these terrible migraines," Von Braun was saying, as Nicole circled the desk, pulled out the telephone line and snapped off the plug. Her hand probed the lamp for a possible bug or direct recorder, but there was nothing. The corners of the room were clear of cameras. There were no pictures on the walls.

"Don't want to be interrupted, sir, while we conduct our business," Nicole said as she pulled out the connection to the intercom. "It's kind of warm in here, don't you think, Mr. Von Braun?"

She took off the black pea coat and hung it over a chair, exposing the shoulder holster. She took out the gun and fitted a silencer onto the end of the barrel.

Von Braun's face was bright red. "What do you think you're doing?" He sat back down at the desk and reached down to open a drawer.

Nicole was around the desk in a second and pulled the drawer all the way out. There was no weapon inside, just a bottle of Jack Daniels.

"Go ahead," she said. "You look like you need a drink, and we may be here for a very long time. I intend to stay until you tell me where the formula is."

"I'll have you fired."

"Can't do that, Mr. Von Braun. I'm self-employed."

There was a timid knock on the door and the receptionist said, "Oh sir, there's something wrong with the intercom."

"It's an electrical problem," coached Nicole.

"It's an electrical problem," echoed Von Braun. Then he added, "You may take the rest of the day off, Ms. Dudley."

"Gee, thanks!"

They heard drawers open and shut, the office door slam, and she was gone. Von Braun sat slumped in his chair, trying to decide what to do. If his work on the formula became public, the whole world would panic. That's why there was no paper trail to follow, no diaries, no legal pads full of notes, no computer files. He rubbed his eyes and taking the bottle of Jack Daniels, poured himself a paper cup half full. He drank it down in one gulp and poured another, which he held in his hand.

Nicole, in a chair across from him, reached into her pocket and pulled out a Trix bar, which she unwrapped and began to eat.

He motioned to the bottle, and she shook her head.

Von Braun rested his head against the back of his chair and thought about the two microdots, just two microdots in a most unlikely hiding place. He took another drink and gazed across the desk at the young woman casually eating a candy bar. He would have to trust her. There was no other way out. He wanted his formula back and if she were successful in finding young Charles . . .

Nicole waited. The tension in the room was very strong. Von Braun looked miserable. His eyes were puffy from lack of sleep. Sweat ringed his forehead, and one hand beat a nervous tattoo while the other clutched the bottle. He was ready to break.

"I can't give you the formula but it does exist," he admitted, not looking at her. "It is concealed under two microdots, but I can't give them the formula to get Charles back."

"Mon Dieu, he is your son! Have you no feelings!" Nicole cried out.

Tears appeared in Von Braun's eyes. "I love that boy. He is our life. If he doesn't come home, Claire will surely leave me."

"Confide in me, and I'll do everything I can to bring him home. He is a precious little boy and as to your experiments, I'll try to find them too, but if they are as lethal as you say, then I leave it to your conscience to destroy them."

"It is my life work, you know. And it will be our secret?"

She nodded.

He reached into the desk and took out his checkbook, picked up his pen and scribbled furiously. She could recognize a line of zeroes.

"How do you spell your name?" he asked. She spelled it for him.

"Put away your checkbook, Mr. Von Braun,"

"Half a million on delivery of my formula. This is an incentive bonus just for you. You look like a smart girl, and I'm betting half a million that you can retrieve that formula. Caution! Not a word to the rest of your team. This is just for you."

Anger began to churn inside of Nicole's gut. Not a word about his son. No money offered for the return of Charlie Brown. She tried to stay calm.

"Tell me where it is."

"Well, they kidnapped Charles from our library downstairs where he had fallen asleep on the sofa, watching TV, I guess. Nobody knew he was there. Claire and I had retired and the servants must have overlooked him. He wasn't in his room all night. The bed had not been slept in, or so the maid reported the next morning when she went up to do the rooms. That's when we discovered he was gone."

"No bedtime stories? No kisses goodnight?"

For a moment he looked confused, "You can't get good help these days. Of course, the maid should have taken the boy upstairs. The kidnappers came in through the open French doors, and there was a smell of ether on the sofa. Charles was drugged and carried away."

"Yes. But where is the formula?" persisted Nicole.

"He has it. Charles has it."

"You gave it to a child?" Unconsciously, she placed her hand on her gun.

"It's not like you think! Charles has what they call a sleep pillow. It looks like the head of Smokey the Bear, with the ranger's hat. He keeps his pajamas in a zippered compartment in the back and when they took Charles, they took the pillow."

"Go on," she thumbed the revolver, and it made a rattling sound in the sudden quiet of the office.

Von Braun, startled at the noise, jumped, and the check on his desk fluttered to the floor but neither bent to pick it up. She pointed the gun.

"Microdots under the bear's eyes!" he blurted, "Now put that thing away!"

"Thank you, Mr. Von Braun. I'll see myself out," Nicole said. She holstered the gun, put on her jacket, and strode to the door, accidentally stepping on the check on the way out.

Weak from the ordeal, Von Braun lay his head down on the desk. "My formula," he groaned into the desk blotter. "Find my formula!"

* * *

Nicole walked around the streets of Washington, familiar to her from the four years she spent at American University, four years of concentration on languages and foreign relations, a place where she lived and breathed academics. The old, three-story brick home where she rented an attic room for an astronomical six hundred a month still looked the same. She wondered whether the angry old woman, and her equally shrewish daughters still lived there. They liked the rent; despised the students, and Nicole had no desire to see them again. She wandered along the streets where she did odd jobs, the corner where she had relieved the hot dog vendor on Wednesdays, and the corner where she sold flowers for another vendor every weekend. And then, there was her main job. The restaurant was still in business where she washed dishes every night from eleven until 2:00 a.m. She smiled, thinking of her fellow student and dishwasher, George Archimedes, who still sent cards at Christmas and birthdays. The alley where they entered through the back door was the same. The ugly red door had lost a little more paint.

Had it actually been five years?

Nicole stepped out into the street and hailed a taxi. It was driven by a Sikh in a pale blue silk turban. When he realized he had a trip to Alexandria, a white grin broke out in his tan face, and he careened out into traffic at a high rate of speed, leaving frightened drivers stomping on brakes and screaming obscenities.

When she reached the motel, she realized she had no American money and was forced to call out to Beau Jackson to come and pay the taxi driver.

As the taxi sped away, Jackson looked down at her and growled, "Why didn't you rob him and take his cab?" Then, he laughed to show he was kidding.

"He may have family," Nicole answered seriously.

Jackson looked at her and shrugged. Was she kidding him? He could never tell with Nicole. Everything was right or wrong, no shades of gray. That strangely serene, lovely face showed few emotions at all, and he could never fathom when she was serious or quietly having a personal laugh at the naïveté of those around her.

"I'll issue you your money," he assured her. "And you'll get to meet the team."

When they entered the motel rooms, Jerry Glass remained sprawled on the sofa, but Bull Durham came forward to give her a great bear hug as soon as he saw her.

"You remember me, dontcha, Nicole?"

"Of course. Deke Durham, one of my first missions."

Durham turned to Glass. "Meet the Kicking Nun I told you about."

Jerry Glass stood up, and turning on the charm, took both of her hands in his. "You guys didn't warn me she was such a babe! It'll be a pleasure working with you."

"Thank you. I hope so." Nicole smiled and withdrew her hands, then turned to Jackson. "What do you have so far?"

"We have made the house but of course, because of diplomatic status, we can't just go in. If you were able to get the formula from Von Braun, we'll run an ad in the *Post* classified in such a way that they will understand we are prepared to make an exchange. Otherwise, we'll have to wing it the best we can."

"Von Braun told me that he didn't have the formula. That it was destroyed, and there were no copies, no files, no tapes," she reported. "How did you find the house?"

Durham took out a large, wrinkled grocery bag and dumped its contents on the table. "You can tell a hell of a lot from garbage, and this is from that house. Frosted Cheerios, one empty box, four M and M wrappers. They must give him one a day as a treat, and today is day five. And the piece de resistance . . . you're going to love this, Nicole . . . here are four pages of a newspaper and each day, next to the comics, is a large picture for kids to color. So here are four pages, neatly—see how he stays in the lines in crayon—colored in bright colors."

"But how do you know it was done by Charlie Brown?" asked Nicole.

"Here's the clincher. Nobody in that house noticed, but like every good artist, proud of his work, he has signed it!" Durham gloated and tossed her the newspaper pages he had salvaged from the dumpster behind the house.

"There it was. Small, but carefully printed in red crayon—Charles."

Nicole gave out a cry of relief and pressed the four pages to her chest. Here was proof that Charles Von Braun the Third was still alive, hidden in that embassy. She touched the picture softly as if by doing this she could make personal contact. It was a red car and a blue truck, waiting at a red stoplight, but on his own, he had also put in the yellow and green lights and added a big yellow sun. Nicole held the picture close. Van Gogh had nothing on Von Braun at that precious moment.

"I'll find him," she swore. "Deke, I want to see that house!"

Durham ducked his big head shyly. "You call me Deke, Nicole, and you're the only one besides my mom that calls me by my name. You can call me Bull, if you want to. Everybody else does."

"I want to call you Deke," she said simply. "He will be my pickup man, no?"

Jackson stirred uncomfortably, "We are to assign that to Glass."

The room went quiet. Both Bull and Nicole had assumed that since they had successfully worked together before, they would be partners again.

"Glass? Why not me?" growled Bull.

"He . . ." Jackson floundered for a reason and picked up Gazar's phrase. "He has to get his feet wet sometime, so he will drive Nicole. Since we have nothing to negotiate with, she will have to find a way to get into the house and contact the boy."

Glass was surprised and thrilled at his assignment as Nicole's driver. He patted the Glock under his coat and grinned. "You got nothing to worry about, sweetheart."

"And we can call backup on our cells," Glass added, bringing out the thinnest cell phone they had ever seen. "Everybody got their cells?"

"Good god!" Jackson exploded. "We can't use that stuff. We don't even use a hard-wired telephone except in emergency. No cells, you gotta leave that shit home. No PCs."

"Hey, man, this is my lifeline to the real world."

"There's the catch, Glass. Think about it. And ditch the 'phone,'" Jackson ordered. "You will drive and only do backup if she needs you. No heroics. We don't take any unnecessary chances in this game. Let's walk through this. No formula, right, Nicole?"

She shook her head. He continued to look at her hard.

"He incinerated everything, including the animals."

"Animals? There were animals?"

"Mice, rats, monkeys," Jackson pushed.

"I don't know, but they would have died anyway if it was successful, no?"

"Point taken," admitted Jackson.

"I need to see the place!" insisted Nicole.

"You just cool it, lady," warned Jackson. He had the distinct impression that Nicole was not telling him everything she knew. "I'll say when to move. We've done some groundwork here, and you'd better shut up and listen up. Bull, fill her in."

Durham cleared his throat, took out a pair of reading glasses, and a small notebook and began to read. "In the house, there are the principals, one man, and one woman. There is a maid, I think, Spanish or Philipino, and a cook, who lives off premises. The cook arrives about seven and leaves around four. There are two security guards and a man, who seems to be a chauffeur, and maybe works in the house. In the day, others come and go. And the dogs, black Dobermans, two are all I've seen, loose after ten, or earlier depending on when the guy lets them out."

"And they have no M and M eating kids?" asked Jackson.

"No kids, but of course, adults eat 'em too," put in Glass.

"But they don't color the children's page in the newspaper," reminded Durham.

"Or sign their work Charles," smiled Nicole. "Oh, it is him. I know it!"

Durham looked over at her and smiled back. He continued to read from his notes. "They will be going to dinner and to the Kennedy Center on Friday night, with a delegation from Hong Kong. For this occasion, they rented a super stretch limo so the chauffeur will have the night off, so he may be at the house or not. Probably will. He's doing the maid, and she slips over to his place after dark and stays 'til dawn."

"Man, don't you ever sleep?" asked Glass, in amazement.

"Doing what? With the maid?" Nicole asked seriously.

The men stared at her. Was she kidding?

Beau Jackson finally grinned. "Making whoopee, getting it on, sex, Nicole."

Nicole sighed and threw up her hands. "These strange American expressions. I must watch more of your stupid, decadent, television-called sitcoms, no?"

"Don't waste your time. So, could you get into the house?"

"I must see the house."

"You're going to be sick of looking at it over the next two days. Here are some photos. There are lots of trees and bushes. Focus is not too good," apologized Durham.

She spread them out on the table. Twenty-four prints, front, sides, back, some of the yard, driveway, high iron fence all around, garage on right far behind the house, with living quarters overhead. Jackson handed her a magnifying glass, and she peered closely at the brick walls, covered in dense ivy, and at the drainpipes.

"What's your guess on where they're keeping the boy?" she asked.

"The attic light, up there, stays on all night."

"Get some sleep," Nicole told Glass. "We pull surveillance tonight."

Glass looked startled. "All night? I had a computer date for tonight."

"If you can't handle the hours, Glass, you're in the wrong job," Jackson said, half hoping that Glass would quit and flounce out of the motel.

"Okay, okay! I'll work something out! See you, maybe nine or ten?"

"Make it eight" Nicole suggested. "It should be dark by then. And is that white Corvette out there in the parking lot your car? You might borrow something that is less conspicuous."

"Ditch my 'Vette'? No way, babe. See you guys later," said Glass, sounding upset. "I gotta rearrange my love life. Damn, she sounded *so* hot."

He slammed the motel door behind him as he left and seconds later, the sharp white car barreled out of the parking lot.

"What am I going to do with him!" said Jackson, throwing up his hands.

"Dig a hole. Put him in," suggested Durham, laughing.

Out of the blue, Nicole looked suddenly wary. "Sand," she murmured. "Sand is very easy to dig. I guess I better get some sleep if I have to spend the night in a sports car with that person, no?"

She went to her bedroom and closed the door.

Bull Durham and Beau Jackson sat across from each other at the kitchen table. Jackson was fixing a pot of coffee for tonight. Three thermos bottles stood in a row on the sink. Like old warhorses, they had begun to feel the tingle of excitement when the game was beginning to go down.

"I will be behind the house and you take the backup position about a block behind Glass in the Corvette. The Corvette will be in a private driveway, which belongs to a house that is up for sale. We have removed the sign. It has been arranged. Stay in sight of the Corvette. If, for any reason, Glass pulls out alone, we'll just go in and cover Nicole—I don't trust the guy. My priority is Nicole and the boy."

"Our little black cat," nodded Durham, "will go up the wall."

Jackson filled the bottles, made a second pot and left it on the back burner so that Nicole would see it when she woke from her nap, and then the two men left the motel.

At six o'clock, Nicole woke, took a shower and put on a dark sweat suit and black track shoes over the heavy black socks. The gun fit under her arm in its leather holster, and she reached under the sweat top, pulled it out, took off the safety, and then tucked it back in place. She looked in the mirror to see if the gun showed.

The refrigerator was well stocked with ham, chicken, cheese, yogurt, soft drinks in cans, and other fresh looking food. Bagels and rye bread stood on the counter. She made a huge sandwich and felt the coffeepot. Still warm. She poured a cup and turned on the television, punching the remote until she found a nature channel showing the migration of turtles. Their large, clawed feet made patterns in the sand of some island as they traveled down to the sea. I wonder if Charlie Brown is watching this channel, she mused, if they let him have a television. He would like the turtles. Be brave, my little man, Clown Lady is coming to get you soon.

There was a knock at the motel door, then the sound of a key and Glass bounced into the room. He was wearing a sports shirt, Dockers, and a heavy cable knit sweater, with a logo on the pocket. On his feet were reasonably old white Reeboks.

"Do not worry, Super Jerry is here, and on time."

She smiled. "Something to eat? A cup of coffee?"

"Got a beer in that thing, babe?"

"I'm afraid there is only Coke and Sprite."

"Oh, hell yeah, there would be Sprite, Jackson's pleasure." Nicole poured him a cup of coffee and added sugar.

"Au lait?" she asked, indicating a bottle of milk.

"Sure, I lay, babe. Do you think we got time?" He laughed at his own joke.

This is going to be one long night, Nicole thought, unhappily. She took the plastic cups down, put two at each thermos, and added napkins. Then they sat and watched the turtles clawing their way to the sea until they heard the very faint toot of a horn just below the window. Looking down, she recognized Jackson's shiny black Olds and on the far side of the parking lot, Durham's old gray Mercedes idled, the exhaust trailing pale smoke in the chill of the evening air. She flipped the lights on, then off.

"Get the coffee. One for Deke and one for Beau. Let's go."

Glass looked suddenly apprehensive. "We're really gonna do this thing?"

"Of course."

"Are you packing a rod too?"

"A rod. What kind of rod? Oh, you mean a gun, a gangster's weapon?"

"A gun. Can you tell I'm packing, under this loose sweater?" he worried.

"You look dressed for anything," she reassured him. Tennis, golf maybe.

They locked the door, went down, and Glass handed the coffee through the windows of the Olds and Mercedes while Nicole got into the white Corvette, putting the thermos between them. The three cars pulled out onto Duke St., putting some distance between.

"Embassy Row, is that right?" asked Glass, nervously.

As they left Alexandria, the Cad fell in behind and stayed with them all the way into Washington. The Mercedes was now nowhere in sight. Durham had taken another route and may already be casing the streets ahead into the target neighborhood.

The old mansions were individual and beautiful. So pretty on the outside, thought Nicole, but on the inside were people ever plotting, planning, and conniving. Diplomats. One face for the public, the other was anyone's guess. Entering this territory of the rich and powerful was treading in deep water indeed.

"Is this the house? It looks like the pictures?" said Glass, in a whisper. "Where do I park?"

Beau Jackson pulled alongside. "Pull into the driveway of the second house from the corner. Back in the drive and face the street."

The black Cad slithered away, and its lights flashed as it turned the corner. They would not see Jackson for the rest of the night. Glass did as he had been instructed. The house behind the drive was nearly dark, with one light on the second floor and a single light beside the garage at the rear.

"Doughnuts. I would like the Krispy Kreme," murmured Nicole. "Too bad."

Jerry Glass, very quiet, sat staring at the house across the street. It appeared unusually tall, the ivy giving it an eerie facade. The fence was black iron, about six feet high, with little spikes along the tops of the posts. Somewhere a cat howled at the pale half moon. Two sleek black figures, the Dobermans, raced to the fence and began to sniff excitedly as if trying to locate the cat for a midnight snack.

"Look, there are the Dobermans," whispered Glass. "They don't know you, they tear you apart in a New York minute."

"Pretty dogs. Many in Germany."

"Jackson says you're going up the wall. How will you get past them?"

"Meat. I'll prepare it myself. I don't want to kill them, just make them sleep."

"Why do you do this stuff? I mean, take a chance on getting killed."

"We help people," she answered simply, looking at him as if this was something he should have already figured out for himself.

"You ever had to kill anybody?"

Deliberately dodging the question, she distracted him by pointing up to the top floor where a light was burning. "That is the attic where Deke thinks the boy is being kept. I'll be back in ten minutes, so I must get closer to the house. Stay here."

Nicole walked to the corner, crossed the street, and walked slowly down the other side. She was barely visible in the dark clothes but several alert dogs began to bark. They quieted as she spoke softly to them in a high crooning sound.

She returned to the Corvette. "So many trees, so many bushes. The place is a jungle. Good cover, but I can't see ten feet in any direction in that yard."

"Are you thinking about, maybe scratching this mission?" suggested Glass. He stared around into the dark and reassured himself by touching the Glock.

"No, Charlie Brown is in that house, a wonderful little boy."

The night dragged on. At ten o'clock, the light in the garage apartment went on in the front room. The door opened, shedding light on the steps going down to the driveway. Someone entered, the door closed and the front light went off. Just as Durham had reported, the maid had joined her lover. Nicole checked her watch.

"When do those entertainments at the Kennedy Center usually end? We must look in the newspaper, no?"

"Depends on what's playing, I suppose. I don't dig that stuff."

"Would you care for coffee?" she asked, leaning toward him to retrieve the thermos and cups.

Glass leaned toward her, so closely that their foreheads were almost touching, and held out his hand. His fingers brushed hers as he accepted his cup.

"You smell wonderful," he murmured. "What is that scent you're wearing?"

Nicole drew back. "Soap," she snapped shortly. "Are you familiar with it?"

Glass shrugged, put the coffee cup between his knees and reached down on the floorboard to pick up a brown paper bag. He unscrewed a bottle of rum and tipped it into his coffee cup.

"You seem tense. Let me sweeten that coffee for you, babe," he offered.

"You need to stay alert. You should never drink when the game is on."

"God's sake! We're just sitting here doing nothing. We could make out for all anybody would know."

Disgusted, Nicole opened the door, got out of the Corvette and stood, propped against the hood, until she saw a dark car with a pale blue light on top moving slowly around the corner. It progressed toward them. She beat on the car window to attract Glass's attention.

"Get down! It's a police security check!"

Glass dived down across the front seats out of sight as Nicole leaped into a tall clump of azaleas beside the driveway and crouched there. The police car continued its crawl along the deserted street. It was a little bit past twelve. They had not seen a security patrol since they had arrived just past eight o' clock. A four-hour cycle. This meant the game had to go down between eleven and twelve midnight.

* * *

She woke at noon on Friday in her room at the motel. Her first thought was of Charlie Brown up in the attic room. Had he eaten his bowl of Frosted Cheerios this morning? Had he colored the page in the newspaper? As the time grew near to the rescue, she felt very close to the little boy and longed to see him once again.

There was much to prepare. Meat for the dogs, those Dobermans on watch in the yard. She needed a fine length of cable, a grapple strong enough to hold her weight, plus about forty, maybe forty-five pounds duct tape to hold her knife to her ankle, in case they were using restraints on the boy. And her shoes, the shoes worried her. Great for running, they were heavy for climbing, and what's more, the soles had a distinctive pattern that would impress if the ground were damp. She would have to climb up the wall with bare feet, a job she didn't relish because she had had to do it twice before, once for a small art piece and once for some papers needed in an investigation. At those times, the objects had been light in weight, this time she would, hopefully, have the boy. At the thought of actually holding Charlie Brown, she told herself, I can do it, I can!

She made a direct call to Paris and spoke to her mother, who reported that Mimi was not feeling well—one of her colds. Always they said, one of her colds, but they both knew it was more than that, and it frightened them too much to say the truth. She hung up and checked with Georges, who was minding the store and enjoying his importance. Georges informed her that Rene was still in the country with his ailing "Cousin" and would call again on Monday. All of them assumed that she was at her own tiny flat in Paris, not miles away in another country. When she hung up, she crossed herself and said a prayer for Mimi, and another, that she, Nicole, would come home safe, for them.

Bull Durham was in the kitchen, cooking lunch. It would be very elaborate because cooking was one of Bull's talents. He was preparing broiled chicken breasts with a special sauce, green beans almandine, a fresh fruit salad, some type of little puffs constructed of potatoes and cheese and hot rolls. Coffee perked in a pot on the counter.

Beau Jackson sat at one end of the conference table, which also doubled as the dining room table. He was plotting the rescue minute by minute and every now and then, a picture of his own Vonda appeared in his mind, and he wiped sweat from his forehead. What if it were Vonda up in that strange attic, and he had to trust Nicole Laurent to bring her down safely? He glanced over to the window where Nicole sat, one small, strong hand on the telephone. Her face was calm and serene as if she had come to terms with whatever danger lay ahead, Yes, he thought to himself, I would trust Nicole anytime. As if she knew his thoughts, Nicole turned and smiled at him.

"Doesn't the food smell delicious?"

"Bull could open his own restaurant," Jackson declared.

"And I could wash the dishes. I have the experience, no?" she laughed.

"Where is Glass? Doesn't he know the routine? I've tried to brief him but I'm never sure when he is taking this all in. This will be the last meal until after the snatch goes down."

Unconsciously, they all consulted their watches, very aware of the passage of time. Nicole rose and set the table for four. They waited almost an hour for Glass.

"My chicken is getting too dry," growled Durham angrily, "and look at my beans! My beans are going limp."

Jackson glanced out into the parking lot, but there was no sign of the white Corvette "This is ridiculous. Let's eat. Son of a bitch."

Around five o'clock, the Vette roared into the parking lot and minutes later, Jerry Glass used his key at the door.

Durham was unloading the dishwasher and putting the dishes away. He didn't look up when Glass breezed in and flopped on the sofa, grabbing for the TV remote. A basketball game was in progress, and Glass turned to Bull.

"Hey, where is everybody? You got a brew in that fridge?"

"No," grunted Bull, hanging up the damp dishtowel.

Beau Jackson had gone home and would take up his position at the rear of the house on Embassy Row precisely at two minutes after eight. Nicole had gone to her room and was putting on her cat suit, a sleek black outfit that fit like an extra skin when zipped up to her neck. The sleeves were long and when they left for the mission, she would put on thin black leather gloves. Reluctantly, she left off her shoes and already her feet felt cold, but she didn't worry about a little physical discomfort because she knew from past experience that once the game began, she would enter a sort of out-of-body suspension of senses that had carried her through many dangerous situations. It was this emotional detachment that enabled her to do whatever became necessary.

Nicole came into the room and nodded at Glass. "You missed a wonderful meal. That lingering aroma is Deke's chicken. Delicious!"

Glass sat forward, "Hey, babe, you're looking cool. Dig that crazy Spiderman outfit! Did I miss Halloween or something?" He stood up and stretched so that she could see what he was wearing. His jeans were tight. There was a T-shirt, and jacket, all with the little CK of Calvin Klein. His Timberlands worn without socks were fashionably scuffed. His fashion statement seemed to say, my daddy has money, and I'm wearing it.

He seemed disappointed when Nicole walked past him without comment, opened the refrigerator, got out the doctored meat for the Dobermans and placed it in a plastic bag. She put it beside the cable, the grapple, and the duct tape that already lay together on the coffee table. She unzipped the right leg of her suit and taped a knife, in its sheath, just above her ankle.

Glass watched it all apprehensively. "What's with the knife, babe?"

"You got a problem, Glass? You look kind of pale. Maybe you getting sick or something." growled Durham. His face twitched in a smile of sorts. "Did you think we were just fooling around? We're going in to get that kid tonight and if you not feeling up to it, I'll drive Nicole, and you can take backup."

"No, no," Glass stammered. "I'm cool."

"It ain't right," muttered Durham, shaking his head. "No job for a rookie."

Nicole changed the channel to the local news then watched the national news, as the two men paced around the room, ignoring each other, suppressing their nervousness. At the stroke of seven, she rose and gathered her equipment from the table, hoisting the cable over her shoulder.

Durham came over and gave her a bear hug.

"Your shoes?" said Glass. "It is cold outside."

"Coldest spring I can remember," murmured Durham.

Both men glanced down at Nicole's small bare feet.

"No shoes," she said.

"Then let's get this show on the road. Good luck, sweetheart, and if things get rough, get the hell outta there," advised Durham. He turned to Glass. "When she gets back to your car with the kid, pull out, pop your lights, and I'll fall in right behind."

"Right. Then we head back here to the motel."

Silently, they moved out to the parking lot. The white Vette led the way and the old Mercedes kept in sight just a few cars behind. Despite, the chill of the night, Glass wiped his forehead, which was beaded with nervous perspiration. On Duke St., he nearly ran a red light but managed to brake in time.

Nicole sat quietly, trying to recall the topography of the extensive lawn with the many trees and bushes between the street and the house. Oddly enough, the big driveway gates opened electronically but the old front gate was still manual. A single iron bar on the inside held it closed. As soon as the dogs were subdued, her plan was to climb the fence, lift the bar, and leave the gate ajar so she could run through it quickly with Charlie Brown. Then, they would race back to the car.

Suddenly, Glass grasped the front of his jacket and turned to her with a stricken expression. "My gun! I forgot my gun! I couldn't get it to fit right under my Klein jacket, then I tried the Armani, but it didn't go with the jeans, so I put the Klein back on, and then I was in a rush and left the Glock on the bed."

"You forgot your gun?" gasped Nicole, in disbelief.

"Beau Jackson will kill me," Glass groaned. "Can I go home and get it?"

"Mon Dieu, it is almost eight! There is no time!"

"You give me yours, Nicole. Think about it, I'll be sitting out here in the dark, all alone. Anything could happen. Someone could try to steal the Vette."

"No."

"Look, this is confidential. You don't know who I am. Give me the gun!"

"No," she repeated.

His face was pale as he leaned toward her. "My uncle is Gazar!" He hissed as he pulled into the driveway of the house where they had parked the night before. He carefully backed the sleek white car between the azaleas and cut the engine.

Almost immediately, the police security patrol passed on the eight o'clock rounds. It was on time. The pale blue light faded from sight. It would return at midnight. In the dark inside the car, Nicole and Glass huddled out of sight.

"I don't care if your uncle is the Pope. Forgive me, Mother Mary, I mean no blasphemy," said Nicole, her eyes cast heavenward. "You are not having my gun, stupid!"

She gathered her equipment and got out of the car. The grass was cold and damp to her feet, and she ran to the patio area beside the empty house where they were parked. Here, she crouched against the warmth of the bricks and checked her watch by the dim light that shone next to the front door as she surveilled the target house across the street. The usual light was on up in the attic room, but the rest of the house was dark. Tonight, the maid left early to go over to her lover above the garage. While the cat is away, thought Nicole, knowing that the owners were on their way to the Kennedy Center, the help will play . . . The door over the garage was flung open, the lovers went into a clinch, he dragged the maid inside . . . there was laughter, the door closed. They appeared to dance by the lighted window, and then the lights went out. Nicole waited.

Fifteen, twenty minutes passed before she returned to Glass's car, where he sat, still fuming from her last remark. He refused to turn and look at her when she spoke.

"I'm going in now. Watch for me."

Nicole took off, running across the street, keeping in the shadows until she arrived at the high fence. She hesitated. Where were the Dobermans? There was no rush of slick, black bodies clamoring at the fence. She scaled the fence with the package of meat in her hand and dropped to the inside. No dogs appeared. The yard was eerily quiet. She went to the gate, lifted the heavy iron bar, pushed the gate open, and waited.

Cautiously, she crept toward the house but froze in place when her bare foot touched a warm, furry body lying in a clump of leaves. A nasal whine whistled up at her. She peered closer. The dog twitched, his eyes moved, but he made no attempt to get up. A few feet further on, she found the second dog, in a state of semiconsciousness. His legs trembled, but he did not try to rise as she stroked his coat and whispered comforting sounds. Both animals were definitely drugged and coming around with difficulty. Who would have done such a thing? She took out her own package of meat and strewed it between where the dogs lay and the corner of the house in case they suddenly recovered and became active at the moment she tried to reach the gate with Charlie Brown. The Dobermans raised their heads at the smell of the fresh meat, then lay back down, panting heavily. Could the maid be dosing the dogs so that she could cross to the garage without their barking alerting anyone in the household? That was one possibility. The other was that there was already a stranger on the property, someone else who didn't belong there.

Nicole backed up to the nearest tree and scanned as much of the grounds as she could see. She listened, but there was no sound except for a slight breeze high in the trees overhead and no movement nearby. There was a faint light in the downstairs hall, or foyer, and one on the second floor—a bathroom? And the attic light was on. Stepping carefully, she circled to the rear where the kitchen was well lit. Inside, were two guards. One slept in a chair in front of a television set, the other read a newspaper. The table contained the remains of a heavy meal, a standing rib roast, and bowls of something, cake, and several beer bottles, eight, nine, by count. No one was taking guard duty seriously.

Pressing hard against the house to avoid tripping any security lights that could come on automatically, Nicole returned to the front of the building. A large oak tree reached to the second floor and beside it ran a drainpipe, all the way to the roof, and passing close beside the attic window. She looked at the wires that hung loosely beside the drainpipe. No wonder the security lights hadn't come on. The wires were cut! Neatly severed near the ground line. A sign that a professional was at work here.

As she paused at the base of the big oak tree, a tall figure, dressed in a black outfit, not unlike her own, dropped from above, and landed right in front of her. Her heart leaped, and she fell back against the bole of the tree.

The man in black peeled off the cap that had hugged his forehead, revealing a mop of short dark curls. Laughing, he held up a small sack in his hand. His dark eyes twinkled in the dim light from the hall as he almost whispered, close to her face.

"You can go home now, little guy! I got every damn thing of value except what the old broad wore to the Kennedy Center. Better luck next time." He started to leave and then turned around to come back to where Nicole still stood, completely speechless. He reached into the sack, took out a piece of . . . what? Jewelry?

"Just so the night isn't a complete loss. Honor among thieves, right?"

He reached over and unzipped her cat suit, then stepped back and apologized.

"Hey, sorry! Didn't guess you were a girl," he exclaimed hoarsely as he touched the top of her brassiere in surprise. He dropped the trinket inside.

He ran off a few feet, stopped abruptly, and came back. He took Nicole's face in his hands and stared at her fiercely, tracing her features with his fingers. Still, she had not uttered a word until he asked, "Who are you? What is your name?"

"Nicole. My name is Nicole," she managed to whisper. She felt the cold gems fall against the warmth of her breast, and she shivered as she stared up at the thief.

With one longer look, the stranger in black turned and ran toward the open gate, and then he was gone into the darkness of the street. Somewhere a car started up, then another. His accomplices had been waiting, just as her team was waiting for her.

Nicole quickly grasped the lowest limb of the tree and pulled herself upward. Branch by branch she climbed, sometimes steadying herself on the drainpipe, sometimes clinging to the dense ivy that covered the brick walls. She had to hurry now. The chance meeting with the thief had taken precious minutes. The dogs could be rousing from the effect of the drugged meat. The guards could get ambitious and decide to patrol.

Beyond the second floor, it was necessary to attempt to set the grapple onto the edge of the roof. The cable went up twice, three times before the grapple settled deeply enough into place. She pulled down on it hard, and it held her weight, so she continued to climb. Up she went, one gloved hand holding the drainpipe until she finally reached the attic window. From the wide outside sill, she gazed into the room.

There were twin beds, a chest, some worn rugs, a table . . . on one wall was a fireplace where flames flickered beyond a mesh like screen, andirons, and coalscuttle. She leaned to one side and then she saw him, looking little and fragile, cheeks slightly flushed, his fists tucked under his chin, fast asleep in one of the beds. The covers were pushed back, and he was wearing wrinkled pajamas, possibly the same ones he was wearing the night he was kidnapped. Charlie Brown! Her heart throbbed at the sight of him so near.

The window was old, the type that pushed outward rather than raised, and there was a hook holding it to the sill on the inside. She managed to get her knife out and ran it back and forth until the hook lifted aside. Bringing the cable with her, she climbed in under the dirty pane.

Quickly, she crossed the room and locked the door to the hall. If they came up to check on the boy, it would give her a few seconds as they struggled to break the door in. To her horror, she saw an automatic in a holster, carelessly left hanging under a smock, on the wall next to the door. It was loaded. A loaded gun left with a six-year-old child. Nicole removed the clip, and then stood holding the gun, wondering what to do with it. The boy stirred in his sleep, and she hastily wrapped the gun and clip in the smock.

Time was fleeting by. She had to get Charlie Brown out as soon as she could. Going over to the bed, she knelt down and began to sing in a soft voice, an old French lullaby that was familiar to children all over the world . . . "Brother John, brother John" . . . She stroked his hair. He came suddenly awake and stared at her in alarm.

"Who are you? Where is Carla?" he whimpered, tears forming in his eyes.

"Don't you remember me, Charlie Brown? I am Clown Lady. I came to your birthday party, and we played games and tossed the balls in the air. We read a book together."

He sat up and stared in disbelief. "My Clown Lady? You are my Clown Lady. Am I dreaming or are you real?"

"It is not a dream. I've come to take you home, but you must be very brave and be very quiet and do exactly what I tell you."

Charlie Brown grinned. "You wore my daddy's hat. And, the balls went up and up and up and some went in the swimming pool. Mario had to fish them out with a net."

"You know the story of Peter Pan," Nicole began. "You must trust me. So the bad guys don't get us. We have to fly out of that window like Peter Pan and Wendy, down to the ground on this magic rope. It will be fun, no? I'll hold you so tight!"

His eyes grew big, as he looked at the window, then at the cable, which she still had circled over her shoulder. "I be Peter Pan 'cause I'm the boy," he decided.

"Right!" she agreed, as she slowly scanned the room. "Charlie Brown, where is your Smokey the Bear pillow that you brought with you?"

He started guiltily and his eyes looked down. "I was bad," Carla said. "I was bad but I couldn't help it. They gave me a bunch of horbull old medicine, and I threw up. I was so sick that I threw up all over Smokey, and it made a big stink and Carla, she grabbed him up and threw him away. I've never seen Smokey again."

"Where did she throw Smokey?"

"I don't know. I ran to my bathroom, threw it all up, and went to sleep," he related in a breathless voice. At the mention of the bathroom, he wiggled and looked toward a door in the far wall where a nightlight burned feebly. "Before we jump out the window, Clown Lady, I gotta wee wee one more time. It'll take just a little minute."

"Sure, go ahead. Take your time."

He scuttled over to the bathroom and closed the door modestly behind him.

Nicole quickly scanned the room again and spotted a flip-top trashcan near the door. She hesitated. Even the unseen Carla wouldn't leave a soiled pillow for five days or would she? She flipped the lid. It was a big stink all right. With the edge of her gloved finger, she picked up the Smokey pillow. It was a mess, matted, and stained just as the boy had said, but the big black plastic eyes were intact, still hiding the evil secret of Von Braun's formula.

She picked up the gun hidden in the smock and crossing to the fireplace, knelt down, and looked up into the fireplace. There was a shelf above the firebox that extended about a foot back. The thin smoke of the hot embers drifted up, past the shelf, and was vented to the outside through the chimney. She shoved the gun and smock back on the shelf with the poker. A shower of soot fell, scattering in the fireplace and on the rug in front of it. She took one last look at Smokey. His eyes glittered back at her.

"Good-bye, Smokey," she muttered as she thrust him deep into the embers and covered him with coal from the scuttle just as a small voice from the bathroom called softly.

"Clown Lady, can you help me with this back part?"

He came out holding up the flap of the pajamas, and she quickly snapped the two buttons in place, turning him sharply away from the fire screen in case some part of his old pillow became visible. The embers caught and flared in a puff of black smoke.

"Hold me tight around my neck and put your legs around my waist," she directed.

Trustingly, he held up his arms.

She settled him on her hips, grasped the cable, and worked her way through the window. She pulled on the grapple, and it held. Going down the wall was swifter than she had planned it would be. The boy was heavier than he appeared, and they twirled out from the ivy, the cable ripping into the leather of her gloves as they jolted to the ground,

"Stand still!" she cautioned him as she tried to get the grapple to release from the roof but it held its points dug into some hard substance. "The hell with it!" she muttered. Let the thing go and run, she commanded herself. She scooped up the little boy and raced across the lawn to the open gate. Her bare feet tromped on twigs, sharp rocks, and millions of acorns scattered from the oak tree. She flew out of the gate, her heart pounding, and bent over from the weight of Charlie Brown, she dashed as fast as she could toward the second driveway from the corner where she assumed the Corvette was hidden between the azaleas. She stopped. The driveway was empty! Glass, and the white Corvette were gone. Her side hurt, her feet were bleeding. She put the boy down and sank down beside him on the asphalt of the driveway. Why had Glass left her? Was this his sick idea of revenge because she wouldn't give him her gun? Even an untrained agent wouldn't desert another agent when the game was going down, would they?

"Are we lost?" asked Charlie Brown. "What's the matter, Clown Lady?" He reached over and held on tightly to her leg as he snuggled closer.

"We are resting," Nicole assured him, holding him close. She considered her next move. Bull Durham should be one or two blocks behind them in the Mercedes, and Beau Jackson was in place behind the house and would be there until midnight. She breathed deeply and got to her feet, pulling the little boy up into her arms again.

A search of the next two blocks told her that Durham and the backup car were not there. Glass may take off—but Durham never! He would never let her down. Beau Jackson was her last hope. She felt a stitch in her side and had to put the boy down.

"Blessed Mary," she prayed aloud, "Mother of God, help me!" She wiped the blood off her feet on the cold grass and began to run to the end of the block, pulling Charlie Brown behind her as fast as his little feet would move. His pajamas were falling down, and he began to cry, picking up on her own fear.

They turned the corner. The Cadillac was there.

"Beau, Beau, help me!" she cried as she beat on the closed window.

Startled, Jackson placed his hand on his gun, and then recognizing Nicole in the dark, he leaped out of the car and snatched up the boy, thrusting him quickly into the backseat, and covering him with a soft blanket. Nicole swayed against the hood, trying to get her breath. Jackson pushed her into the passenger seat, climbed in, and took off, the big black sedan careening through the night streets like a rocket.

Nicole glanced down at her watch. Two minutes to twelve. In another two minutes, Beau Jackson would have been gone, and she would have been on the street alone.

"Where is Glass? Where the hell is Bull?" Jackson demanded as they headed out of Washington.

"I don't know. They were gone. Both cars are gone."

"You mean they left you?" he said, shaking his head in total disbelief. He beat his fist against the steering wheel. "I'll kill 'em. Sonsa bitches. I'll kill 'em!"

"The boy can hear you," she cautioned, looking over at the backseat, where Charlie Brown sat up, wrapped to his ears, in the blanket. He appeared in a daze.

"This has never happened on my teams before. It's incomprehensible," growled Jackson angrily. His rage was so palpable it filled the car.

Nicole lay back against the seat and tried to relax. A trickle of blood ran down her cheek, and she vaguely remembered hitting a limb on the way down the wall. Her hand came away from her forehead covered with blood, and Jackson glanced around.

"You look like hell for an angel," he commented. "Did you fall?"

"I'm okay. Just a scratch."

He thrust a rumpled handkerchief at her and watched her wipe her face, then try to mop at her torn feet. He looked up into the rearview mirror.

"You okay back there, little buddy?"

"Yes, sir. Am I going home now?"

"First you get some sleep. Then, first thing in the morning," he promised.

At the motel, Nicole gave Charlie Brown a much-needed bath and reluctantly had to put his dirty underwear and pajamas back on. He had nothing else. The kidnappers had not brought any extra clothing nor bought any while he was in the attic room. She put him to sleep beside her on the queen-sized bed in her room where he fell into a deep sleep, clutching a pillow, exhausted. Being Peter Pan, even for one night, was a very tiring experience when you are only six years old.

She went into the bathroom, washed up, and put tape over the gash over her eyebrow. She soaked her feet, dried them, and put on a pair of heavy socks. Every muscle in her body was screaming, but she was too keyed up to fall asleep. She went into the living room where Beau Jackson was pacing the floor, a can of Sprite in his hand. His anger filled the room as he cursed Glass, then Durham, damning them both to a fiery hell.

Nicole sank down on the sofa and turned on the television, surfing with the remote, but the events of the night were still so strongly with her that she really was not paying attention to any of the programs that flickered across the screen. At 2:00 a.m., there was the rattle of a key at the motel door.

Durham stalked into the room and looked around, his eyes falling on Nicole.

"Nicole?" he said hoarsely. "The boy, did you get the boy?"

"He's asleep in the other room. The question is, what the hell happened to Glass, and where the hell were you when she was out there in the street with the boy?" barked Jackson. "We've been buddies a long time but I want your resignation right now!"

"You got it," answered Durham. He put his large head down on the table and wept.

"Oh god, I'm so sorry, so sorry. Nicole . . . ?"

"I'm waiting for an explanation, and it better be good. Start talking." Jackson grabbed Durham's shoulder and pulled him upright. One big fist drew back, and then he seemed to reconsider and dropped his hand at his side. "Let's hear it."

"Well, it went down like this. Nicole had hardly been in the yard of the house maybe ten, fifteen minutes tops when he sees her come back out of the gate, empty handed, and she starts to run down the opposite side of the street. She don't come nowhere near the car so he waits to see if somebody is chasing her, but she keeps running and disappears in the dark. She's bent over, no kid, and going like hell away from the car."

"If he thought she was being chased, why didn't he get out of the car and cover her. He has a gun. That's the time to use it."

"I don't think he had a gun."

"Sure he does. I issued him a Glock when he came on the case."

Nicole remained silent.

"I saw the white Vette pull outa the driveway, so I think that the game is over. Nicole is in the Vette with the kid, right? I pull out seconds later, following Glass. I never saw nobody running. I'm just doing backup. Glass is driving crazy, up on the curbs, flashing his high beams here and there, like he's looking for something. First, he speeds up, and then he slows down. I don't know what to do, but I'm behind him all the way. That's my job, right? He goes up on people's lawns, stops in the middle of the street, and then takes off fast and at the corner, he crashes into a tree, knocking out one headlight and the fender just kind of peels off and lays in the street. I pull alongside, and I see that Nicole is not in the seat, so I tell Glass I gotta go back. He begs me to call a wrecker. He is holding the fender and staring at it like he's about to bawl. So I says I will, but I gotta go back. I note the location, stop at a booth, and call the wrecker."

"Was Glass hurt?" Jackson asked with an almost hopeful note in his voice.

"No, but he's upset about the car. I questioned him, and he told me about Nicole running away. Ran past his car and kept going. Something is wrong. I went back to Embassy Row and took up my position, but Nicole never showed. I went around the block and to the driveway where the Vette had been parked before. Nothing. I cruised and I waited. Finally, I give up and head on back here. I don't know where Glass is."

"There was someone else at the house, and he was dressed in black, like me, but it was a man, much taller. He did leave approximately the time that Glass said he saw the figure running past," Nicole told them. "He mistook that man for me."

"What was the man doing at the house? And did he see you?" Jackson asked.

"He saw me. He was a thief. He knew about the people going to the Kennedy Center and that the place would be less guarded. He had already fed the dogs some meat that put them in a stupor by the time I arrived and cut the outside security lights. He laughed at me because he had got there first. He told me to go home because he thought I had come there to steal. Obviously, he didn't know about the boy in the attic."

"What exactly did he say to you?"

"He said, go home, I got it all. Then he ran very fast. I did hear two cars, but I thought they were his accomplices, waiting for the . . . uh, the loot."

"And Glass, thinking it was you, chased the guy, and Bull followed."

"Damn," said Jackson softly after a few minutes of contemplation. He sank down beside Nicole on the sofa. "I sure am glad I stuck around to the last minute."

"Me, too," she smiled. "But I am very tired. I must go to bed."

"Good job, Agent Laurent," Jackson smiled back. "You're the best."

Bull Durham didn't look up as she passed. His ugly face was buried in his hands, and he felt that he had let her down when she needed him most. No matter what the circumstances were, he felt himself a failure, his first in a long career.

Nicole went into her room and lay down beside the little boy. She gazed in awe at the delicacy of his face, the curls, the long lashes swept against his cheek. "I wish I had a little boy who looked exactly like you," she murmured softly, as she pulled the bedspread up around his shoulders. He moved over and snuggled close, his head pressed against her arm. She lay quietly, and in minutes, she too was fast asleep.

* * *

In the early morning, Beau Jackson came to get him.

"I want Clown Lady to come too!" insisted a plaintive little voice. "She can drive the car. She knows where my house is!"

"Let her sleep. She is very tired," argued Jackson, picking the boy up in his arms. He looked around the room. "Did you have any toys or anything?"

"No, my Smokey died."

"I'm sorry to hear that. I bet your mom and dad will be so happy to see you. They will buy you just about anything you want. Maybe a bike or something."

"There were dogs outside that house. Can I get a puppy?"

Their voices faded. The door closed and Nicole heard the purr as the Cadillac started up. It left the parking lot. She felt desolate, more alone than she had ever felt. She rolled over and put her face into Charlie Brown's pillow. It was still warm. After a while, she got up, walked out to the living room, and looked down into the parking lot. Bull Durham's car was gone. Charlie Brown was on his way home. She stumbled back to the bathroom, took a long, hot shower, and brushed her teeth. She found clean jeans, a sweatshirt, looked into the mirror over the dresser, and gasped. She stared at her own dark straight brows, the funny hair that tended to curl, and her straight nose. My Holy Mother, she breathed, he looks just like me? The stranger, who came back to stare at her, to touch her face, to ask her name. He looks like me! No wonder Glass thought he was seeing me when the man ran past. Holy Mother, he looked enough like me to be my own father. Her thoughts raced back to the words on her birth certificate that had always seemed so cruel, even when she was very small—father unknown—every child had a father somewhere, but she had never known her own. Could her father have been an American?

All of a sudden, she remembered the trinket he had tossed into the front of her cat suit, a kind of consolation prize for getting there too late. She snatched the suit out of her travel bag and shook it, but nothing fell out. Frantic, she ran her hand in the suit until on a seam under the arm she found the bracelet. It was beautiful. A tennis bracelet of finest platinum, set with square-cut emeralds, interspersed with diamonds. She put it on under the sleeve of her sweatshirt, and then pulled the sleeve back to gaze at it. Tentatively, she thought, a gift from my father? Maybe. Maybe. Stop kidding yourself, Nicole, she admonished herself sternly. Stop dreaming.

She finished dressing, took the knife and the gun and placed them in the drawer. The mission was accomplished. It was time to return home. She picked up the telephone and dialed the number for a transatlantic airline.

"Reservation for one on the next flight to Paris, please."

Chapter Six

Bringing Derek in from the Cold

It was cold in the vault of the shop, but the inventory had to be done and Rene was not at work, in fact, had not been in the shop for a week. From time to time, their insurance coverers wanted an estimate of the value of loose gems and coins held in the safes on the premises. Nicole counted an unusual amount of emeralds, two hundred seventy six. There were seven hundred small rubies and two hundred sapphires. She noted the amounts, placed the gems in velvet bags, and placed them in a safe. Why were there so many emeralds? The demand for diamonds was constant, the emeralds were not so much in favor.

"Excuse me, madam, your grandmother, Madame Mimi, says to tell you that she has a cold and you should be with her because Madam Yvette is taking a trip with Monsieur Garibaldi," reported Henri-Paul. He adored gossip. "She added that Monsieur Garibaldi had a wife and seven children in Rome. She appears to be angry with Madame Yvette."

"It is nothing! Henri-Paul, why do we have extra emeralds?"

"Mrs. Castle, the American, had a design ordered, with emeralds."

"Hmmm . . . I will call Mimi when I get a moment, anything else?"

"One other call. There was a gentleman, very cultured, by his voice, a luscious baritone," began Henri-Paul, pausing to raise his eyes upward in appreciation. "But I did not wish to bother you. He asks for you, and then he says the silly thing, Zirconium, indeed! He should know that we, at Rene Laurent, do not deal in costume pieces."

"What does this man say, exactly?" she asked, pausing with her hand on the telephone to return Mimi's call.

"Tell Madam Laurent that I wish to buy a present for my wife . . . oh, that lovely voice to say such a silly thing! A pink grapefruit!"

Nicole became suddenly alert. "What did you say?"

"He wishes a pink zircon as big as a grapefruit." Henri-Paul looked at her, rolled his eyes and gave his high, penetrating giggle.

"And did this caller leave a number where he can be reached?"

"But, madam, surely this is a big joke!"

"Yes, it is a prank, but it sounds like a friend who loves to tease me, and I wish to hear from him."

"He did say he would call back. A joke, of course!" Henri-Paul looked relieved.

Nicole put her call to her grandmother on hold and sat waiting beside the telephone. Was this Washington's way of letting her know that a new Paris office was to be opened, or that she was needed on another mission? She was curious, Richard Leach was dead. Derek Holland, and the travel girl, Giselle, had completely disappeared . . . when she had driven past the alley entrance of the Paris office, the travel agency sign was gone and a new sign had appeared that of an independent broker of real estate.

Thirty minutes passed, an hour, two. The telephone began to ring, and she picked it up. "Rene Laurent. How can I help you?" she asked.

"Nicole?" the deep baritone voice breathed into the telephone. "Is anyone listening? Are you on a secure line?"

"Yes," she assured him.

"It's Derek. I must see you as soon as possible. Can you meet me?"

The dapper dwarf. Richard Leach's moneyman. She hesitated.

"Please, Nicole, I want to come in. I only worked through Richard. I have no other connections. You must help me," he pleaded desperately. "I have the money."

"Name a place, not crowded. When the shop closes, I will try to find you."

He named a small cafe in a section of town that she had heard of but was not really familiar with, a place about half a mile beyond the business district. He said that his silver blue Renault would be parked in front, and he would wait inside the cafe. He hung up abruptly just as Henri-Paul, ever curious, sidled up to her.

"That was my friend," she laughed, "Always joking with me."

"Excuse me, madam, do you know when Monsieur Rene will return? Mrs. Castle called about her custom-designed emerald bracelet he promised her today."

Nicole's face clouded. "I have no idea. I will close the shop. Tell Georges and Billings they may also leave early. There are no customers in the shop, and I have other things to do. Go on, now!"

She dismissed him with a wave of her hand, and he hastened to the closet where he kept his cashmere overcoat and the English bowler hat he thought made him look rich and highborn. The others picked up their coats and bid her goodnight.

She followed them to the front door and locked it behind them. She finished covering the cases, left a single light near the rear and set all the alarms. As she went about the necessary moves of closing the shop, she became more and more angry with Rene. Damn Rene! The dramatic announcement that Therese had breast cancer had turned into a lesser scare. She had had a simple lumpectomy and no chemotherapy or radiation was needed, and yet, Rene had taken this opportunity to stay in the country, spending time with Therese instead of coming back to Paris and attending to his business and his wife! Nicole was running the business. She took care of the apartment over the shop and her own tiny flat across town. She was there for Yvette and Mimi when they needed her. Where was the real Nicole? As she stood there in the darkness of the empty shop, she realized that the only time she felt like someone was when she was involved in a mission. *When they call me from America, I become the real me, the evil sprite, Nicole. I know myself.*

As she began to walk toward the neighborhood where the cafe was located, the weather became misty. The streets were narrow, ugly, and poorly lit, with seedy buildings that appeared largely unoccupied. Two women, dressed in tight satin shorts, T-tops and nylon wigs, stood on the corner. They eyed her angrily as she hurried past. In the following blocks, she saw women in the windows. A pitiful gay man, dressed as a bride, stood by a wall, trying to keep warm as he pulled his ragged veil and dirty lace shawl around his fragile shoulders. His pocked face was ravaged with disease, but he smiled at her.

"Keep moving, pretty girl, or these ugly bats will get you for invading their territory. They're jealous of real beauty like yours, you know. Hurry, pretty girl."

She stopped and asked the location of the cafe.

"You're almost there. Sweetheart, could you spare just a sou?"

Nicole opened her shoulder bag and without looking at the amount, crushed a handful of notes into his trembling hand. "Please, get a hot meal, some wine. Go home."

He dropped his eyes and turned away. He had almost forgotten kindness.

A few feet further on, two figures emerged stealthily from behind a wall, one tall and black, the other small and hunched. She could smell them as they approached her, the stench of cheap beer, old clothes, urine, and garlic . . . such garlic. They began to walk closely behind her, bumping at her heels. She walked faster, but they kept up and just as she recognized a sign at the end of the next block as the cafe where Derek Holland was waiting, the tall one grabbed at the back of her jacket.

"Both of us, same time, come on inna alley, little pig."

Nicole turned to face them, and she could see that he held some type of weapon in his hand, something with a bar like a razor. She tried to remember what she had in her shoulder bag. If she had known she had to come through a red-light district, she would have brought a switchblade, but now it was too late. Some heavy object lay in the bottom of her bag, and it took a moment to recall what it was. Her spray cologne! A wonderful black plastic case, trimmed in gold, Chanel No. 5.

The smaller man, his eyes wild with excitement, reached out for her, but she sidestepped and ended up behind him. As one hand sought the spray, her arm wrapped around his waist from the rear, holding him tight. The heavy black and gold case pulled free, she flipped off the top and sprayed in his eyes at close range. The alcohol stung and the man screamed. The case went down on the bridge of his nose and blood spurted forward, spraying on the taller man. The taller man backed up, looking down at the front of his filthy jacket in surprise. He held up his hands and stepped away toward the street.

"What is it? What she hit you with?" he called out. He wiped at the blood.

"Gun. She got a gun!" cried the smaller man.

The tall man's weapon dropped into the gutter, and they ran for the alley; the smaller one lagging behind, running drunkenly as he clawed at his eyes. The towering odor of Chanel No. 5 was fast overcoming the rancid smell of garlic in the street, and it would only be a matter of time before they figured out what had really happened. She found the weapon where he had tossed it. It was an afro-pick with long metal teeth. She kicked it into the gutter where it rattled down into the sewer, and ran as fast as she could toward the cafe.

The silver blue Renault was parked in front, and Nicole peered inside. There were eight-inch blocks under the gas and brake pedals so she knew it had been custom made to fit the short legs of the dwarf. The episode with the two aspiring rapists had taken time, so she hurried inside. Derek Holland was seated at a rear booth, nervously nursing a cup of thick black coffee. His face lit up as she came through the door.

"Thank God, you came. I was afraid you wouldn't help me."

"Sorry I'm late. I bumped into some people."

"You'll have something? Some wine?" he offered. He raised one small but heavily muscled hand to summon the man behind the counter.

The man sauntered over with a handwritten card, a soiled piece of cardboard that was the menu. The man was the owner of the cafe, also the cook, bus boy, and bartender.

To Derek's obvious alarm, Nicole accepted the card and studied it seriously.

Derek could not remember ever having seen anyone order from the menu in this place where stale chips, dusty baskets of crackers, and petrified croissants were the only food in sight. He cleared his throat, but it was too late. To his chagrin, Nicole smiled up at the cafe owner and cheerfully began to order a large meal.

"I'll have the house wine, the red. Bring the bottle. And a green salad with croutons, and the small steak, medium well done. Oh, and a fresh pot of coffee. And what shall he bring you, Derek?"

"I have eaten earlier, thank you. Just coffee, please."

"Perhaps a hot croissant with butter, to keep me company?"

"That would be nice," Derek murmured uncertainly.

The owner appeared stunned. He turned toward the small cold, greasy grill behind the counter with a worried expression. Several minutes passed and then he turned to Nicole with a grateful smile, the menu trembling in his hands.

"Yes, madam, I can do that. I can do it for you. I have this piece of beef, so tender, a filet. And lettuce for the salad!" He was becoming enthusiastic. "But, of course, first the wine, a lovely red. And I have a tablecloth, yes!"

"A white one," suggested Nicole.

The man's face fell. "Oh, how sorry I do not have a white one. But I have red, with white checks."

"Even better. We spill a bit of wine, who knows?" shrugged Nicole.

Derek stared in amazement. Two elderly men, cafe regulars, had stopped drinking their wine to turn around, stare, and mutter quietly to each other in disbelief.

The grill was lit. The checked tablecloth appeared and a candle in a tin holder was placed in the center of the table. Soon the smell of sizzling beef filled the small cafe and the sound of frantic chopping came from behind the counter. The chef was now singing. Croissants were split and thrown on the edge of the grill to toast.

Derek took out a packet of thin tissues, the kind that used to be used to roll cigarettes. He wrote on one paper and passed it over to Nicole. She read, "I have all of the currency from the office, as well as the books all encoded."

She put it into the ashtray and reached for a second message. "I want to go to the United States. Can you help me, please?"

He lit the two messages and they silently watched them burn.

The house wine appeared.

"Do you have family, a wife, or close friend, to leave behind in Paris?"

"My parents are alive, but I have not seen them for but a few occasions since I was seventeen. I embarrass them being as I am. So, I am now alone and unemployed and I am still young so I want to start a new life in a new country, but I have the burden of this money which belongs to the United States."

Nicole studied the face of this worried young man who sat across from her. Derek was indeed attractive even though his head was large in proportion to his body. His features were actually handsome, kind brown eyes, a strong jaw. His clothes were custom and always impeccable, the voice, as Henri-Paul had noticed, was melodious and warm. She could not fathom that any parents could turn away from a child and man who had so much to give. A chance remark by Richard Leach had made her suspect that royalty was involved.

The steak and salad arrived with a basket of hot croissants. The chef made a quick trip and returned with a pot of steaming coffee. He stood, smiling broadly, admiring his own cuisine.

"Perfect," said Derek.

"Yes, it is perfect. My compliments to your staff, monsieur," said Nicole.

"I am the staff, madam!" laughed the man, flipping out two linen napkins.

"Then you need no other."

After the man left to go behind his counter, Derek scribbled another message and passed it across as he reached for one of the croissants. He had written, "I cannot go through normal channels. Bags of currency raise suspicions in customs."

"Of course. When can you be ready to leave Paris?"

"I am ready. I have been ready since the office went down."

"Call me tomorrow at the shop. I will try to arrange something."

"How can I ever thank you, my darling Nicole? I knew you would help me."

The steak was delicious; brown on the outside, just slightly pink in the center. Nicole raised her fork in appreciation and blew a kiss to the man behind the counter.

He pretended to catch it and pressed his fingers to his lips.

They finished their meal and went outside to the silver blue Renault. The streets were dark. The prostitutes were mere blurs of light colors against the lampposts, waiting in the mists for men who seldom came to this pathetic blight of a neighborhood.

"I'd like a ride back to the shop if it's not out of your way?" Nicole asked. "I walked here so I don't have my car."

"You walked here!" exclaimed Derek. "Through this neighborhood?" He quickly unlocked the car door and motioned her inside. "My god!"

"I was not familiar with it. I've never been here before."

"I picked it because nobody we knew would be likely to see us together. You walked here! I can't believe it. Oh, my dear Nicole, you are lucky to be alive."

She laughed, "People keep saying that to me. Isn't that funny?"

* * *

The voice on the direct line to Washington had a strange message to deliver after she had identified herself.

"I'm sorry, but Mr. Gazar is on indefinite leave and cannot be reached."

"This is Paris, and I have an emergency situation. Who is in control?"

"Major Kelvin Whitt, Paris."

"Can you patch me through to Beau Jackson in the Alexandria office?"

"I'm sorry. You must call that number direct."

She hesitated. She did not like bypassing the man who had hired her, who had always been in charge. Beau Jackson was only her section chief, but she trusted him more than a man whom she had never met. Who was Major Kelvin Whitt? She rang the telephone number in Alexandria, and Beau Jackson answered immediately.

"This is Paris."

"I've been trying to reach you at your apartment but no answer. I've got a really big job for you. How soon can you come to the States?"

"Wait a minute, Beau. I have my own problem. I want to bring in Derek Holland, Richard Leach's cashier and bookkeeper. He has luggage that cannot come through customs, and he wishes to make a permanent move to the States. Can you possibly arrange that?"

Jackson acted as if he had not heard her. "Do you speak Romany?" he asked.

"What does that have to do with bringing Derek in from the cold?"

"What it means is that if you help me, I'll help you," Beau laughed.

She thought about it. Romany, the language of the gypsies. "Well, perhaps I can manage enough to be understood, but there are so many dialects. Frequently, the Roms can't even understand each other unless they go to another shared language. But Beau, what is wrong with Gazar? And who is this new head of operations?"

"Gazar is in the Betty Ford Clinic. He likes his drinks, you know, so they'll dry him out and then it's good-bye time. He will be retired. I ain't cryin' over it. About Major Whitt, he's a different horse. Air force, just retired. Big man in Desert Storm. You want statistics? He's got blue eyes, and he's forty-nine years old."

"Enough! I didn't ask for a bio. How can I bring Derek in?" she demanded.

"I'll have the major call you. Where are you now?"

"My own apartment in Paris."

"And promise me that you will come with Holland because I need you for a very big job." Unexpectedly, Jackson erupted into laughter. "A very big job."

"Beau, Beau, what is so funny?"

"Stay put and wait for Whitt's call." Jackson hung up.

Nicole also hung up the telephone and then immediately called her grandmother. Mimi started berating Yvette for leaving her alone when she was sick. "She only goes with that Garibaldi because he gives her beautiful cars to drive. He has seven children!"

"She loves him, my darling Grandmere. Are you very ill?"

"Always I have this cough and this terrible machine with me."

"The oxygen is to help you breathe, Mimi. Shall I come to see you?"

"Gerta is here, and she cooks. She can also work my VCR very good. We have movies of Maurice Chevalier and Simone Signoret. She smokes more than me, that Simone!"

"You have a nice time with Gerta. I love you, Grandmere." Nicole started to hang up but Mimi called out anxiously for her to wait. It was most important!

"Nicole, when I die, I want you to have my beautiful wooden trunk with the brass. We have always used it as a coffee table, first in our old apartment and here at this new apartment. I am putting this in my will. I have a lawyer, Nicole, and I do not want your mother to have my trunk. It is for you when I die."

"Stop! I don't want to hear about dying."

"My wedding dress is in there. Family pictures, many things, Nicole, and when I die, it is yours."

"Not for many years, Mimi. You are making me cry. Goodnight, my darling."

The conversation with her grandmother had been disturbing, and she knew she would not be able to sleep, so she thumbed through some magazines while waiting for the call from Major Whitt. Finally, she curled up on the bed and nodded off. About 3:00 a.m., the telephone rang, and she sleepily picked up the receiver.

"Paris? This is Major Whitt, your new control. Listen carefully. Are you fully awake? I can put you on a Lear jet, C21A, out of Paris, bound for RAF Mildenhall at sixteen hundred hours—four o'clock civilian time. A driver will pick you up at your place of business one hour prior to departure. Be ready to move."

"Tomorrow? Mildenhall?" she said groggily. "That is in England. We want to go to the States."

"That will be arranged, Agent Laurent. Looking forward to meeting you. Goodbye."

The call terminated and as she struggled into her Mickey Mouse sleep shirt, she remembered that she had no way to get in touch with Derek. It was all happening so fast. The desperate dwarf was to call her at the shop. Would he call in time to arrange to get to the shop before three o'clock? She lay back on the bed and toward dawn drifted into an uneasy sleep.

* * *

As soon as Nicole entered the shop the next morning, Georges rushed to her with anguished wails. "Mrs. Castle called again about her emerald bracelet. Is it hidden somewhere in the safe, madam?"

"No, it is not in the safe. It is nowhere; I don't think Rene ever made it. If you want to know, you must call Rene in the country. I suggest you do that."

Georges drew back. "Oh, madam, he forbids it. He specifically ordered us not to disturb him when he is in the country. He said to refer all calls to madam."

"Really? Who signs your checks, Georges?" Nicole fished in a desk drawer and took out the forbidden number to Therese's farm. "He is here. Call him!"

Reluctantly, the clerk took the piece of paper and dialed the number. The conversation was swift and unsettling. Monsieur Laurent was having his breakfast on the terrace and did not wish to be bothered. He sent the message that he would return to the city the following Wednesday. Georges literally wrung his hands.

"Mrs. Castle is a very good customer. I cannot face the woman. She will have to return to the States on Sunday and without the bracelet. So bad for our reputation, madam. What shall I say if she calls us again?"

"You will say nothing. You, and Henri-Paul, and Billings, are on paid vacation as of this minute. Go and inform the others. I am closing the shop."

Georges looked around frantically. "Friday is often our best day, madam."

Nicole lowered her head like an angry bull, and the air around her seemed to crackle like the atmosphere before a thunderstorm. "If Monsieur Rene does not wish to care about his business, then why should we? And now, you may leave!"

Georges wisely hurried away to tell the others. They grabbed their coats and filed past her as she held the front door open. Only Henri-Paul hesitated.

"When shall we return from our vacation?"

"I suggest you take the full week," she told him.

Nicole, the evil sprite, had surfaced, and she felt a deep satisfaction on the thought of Rene returning to his place of business to find them all gone. All of his hard-working little puppets, playing his own game, letting the business go to hell while they took vacations. Rene would be shocked, unbelieving at such audacity. Then he would get furious. Nicole didn't care what he felt. She simply didn't care.

At noon, the telephone rang loudly in the silence of the empty shop.

"It is Derek," the dwarf said. "What shall I do?"

"It has been arranged. They are sending a car to take us to the airport. You must be here by three o'clock with the money and all of your personal belongings."

"I have been ready a long time, but I must use my car to get to the shop. What shall I do about my car?"

"Park in the alley. Dismantle something inside and remove it. Tie a distress flag to the aerial. If it is not stolen, it will take a while to be discovered. You are absolutely sure this is what you want to do?"

"Yes, I am sure."

"Then be here by three."

"I will," he promised. His words were sure but his tone was uncertain.

It would not be an easy move for one of a normal size, but if you were a dwarf, this life choice was a monumental decision, Nicole mused. Derek was very brave.

Derek arrived at two o'clock, nervous and afraid that if he did not come to the shop and leave the trappings of his former life behind, he might change his mind and miss this opportunity. His car was full, and he preferred to stay in it until the very last minute, guarding the full suitcases of various currencies he had saved from the Paris office. At three o'clock Nicole set the alarms, gathered her carry-on bag and her large shoulder bag, and joined Derek by his car in the alley. Right on time, a large dark limousine drove into the alley behind the Renault. Without a word, the driver climbed out and helped them load the contents of Derek's car into the limousine. There were three leather bags bulging with Derek's wardrobe plus the moneybags.

As soon as they were loaded, Nicole and Derek climbed into the rear seat and the driver pulled away. They noted the small bar and television, mints, and tissues.

"We ride in style," noted Nicole, talking to distract Derek's nervousness. "Would you like a drink?"

"No," he muttered, his eyes on the Paris streets he was leaving behind forever.

"It will be okay. A new life, possibly an even better one," she suggested. He didn't reply.

They arrived at a private landing strip adjacent to Orly and the driver pulled up closely, almost under the Lear jet, which sat on an apron of asphalt near a grove of trees. Airports had always impressed Nicole as Mecca's of intrigue. It was on a plane that she first met G. Edmund Hammer, in an airport that she agreed to work for the organization that changed her own life, and now, here she was . . . Derek Holland was about to change his life, and they were waiting in an airport.

She thought about Major Whitt, who had so efficiently arranged the flight out of Paris and put wheels in motion to bring Derek to the States. What about a green card and Immigration? Could he fix those too? What a change he was from Gazar, who tended to leave his teams hanging out on a limb, to solve problems on their own, when often he could have rallied support and bailed them out of danger. Some agents died, others strangely disappeared, but the lucky ones, like Maurice Dupin, were smart enough to get out of the game alive and direct their own futures. But survivors in the field were few.

Nicole turned to Derek who had been very quiet, "Are you having regrets?"

"No," he sighed. "This is my destiny. I am born Dutch, I have lived as a Frenchman, and now I will be an American." He brushed a speck of dust from his camel hair coat and gazed down at the matching cap he held in his hand. A gold ring, with some kind of crest, sparkled on the middle finger of his left hand.

"If you're having second thoughts, I can take the money in, and you can take your personal bags and turn back at this point."

"I have nothing to go back to. I called my parents and told them I was going to America. I lied. I said I had a job there. They wished me good luck. They are good people. They couldn't adjust to me being the way I am. When I completed my elementary education at the age of nine, my parents—it was father actually—put me in the circus."

Nicole drew in her breath sharply.

"I was apprenticed to a clown, a wonderfully kind man whose stage name was Beez-Bol. Perhaps you remember him. He had me tutored to the college level over the next eight years. Beez-Bol and I had an act together. I was a human wheelbarrow, which kept running away. Another time I was his big turban that fell off and ran away when he made a bow at the end of his act. Oh, how the children laughed!"

"And were there other little people?"

"Of course. Dwarves and a family of midgets, who stayed mostly to themselves."

"I left the circus to study accounting. I always liked numbers, and Richard Leach hired me," Derek continued. "For a while I believed that it was a genuine travel agency. Code names related to countries and agents were frequent flyers. In fact, the temp girls never caught on to the real use of the Paris office."

"Where is Giselle?"

"Back home in Germany," he turned sharply and looked out of the limo window.

"Oh, oh, it's party time," said Nicole.

A civilian pilot and a woman in an Air Force uniform were heading for the Lear jet, laughing and drinking coffee from paper cups as they strode toward the plane.

The limo driver loaded the bags onto the plane, waved off the tip, which Derek offered, got back into the long car and sped away. There was an odd little clam-shaped door on the left side with steps built into the lower half and Nicole and Derek boarded the plane, which only had seats for six or seven people.

"Fasten your seat belts, please. Would you care for something to drink? This is a short hop," said the woman in uniform.

They shook their heads and fastened their seat belts. As they climbed into the clouds, they looked down and watched Paris disappear. Suddenly, Derek turned away and covered his face with his hands, visibly shaken, as he realized what he was doing,

"Bon jour, bonsoir, bon nuit, Paris," he murmured, his voice breaking.

"You will return," Nicole comforted him. She reached for his small, strong hand and held tightly as the plane burst out of the clouds into sunshine.

RAF Mildenhall was only one of several British air bases that shared space with the USAF North of London they lay, with names like Sculthorpe, Lakenheath, Woodbridge, Bentwaters, and Mildenhall. Some were now closed, others still operating, allies within allies, Old Glory and Union Jack, history mainly forgotten except for a few Brits who loved to refer to "the colonies" as if they were bad stepchildren.

The Lear landed and taxied to a far end of the field where a much larger plane was waiting. To Nicole, it appeared to be one of the old

"Air Force One" types, a VC 137, like the presidents flew on, and she wondered what VIPs were lucky enough to be flying home to the States on this one. To her surprise, the Lear cut its engines and rolled to a stop adjacent to the larger plane. This would be their ride. She began to have a great respect for the expertise of Major Whitt in making classy arrangements.

Nicole and Derek rose and stretched, already feeling a touch of jet lag from the short flight from Paris. They stumbled down the steps as a tall, blond haired man came across the field toward them. He wore a flight jacket without insignia, starched Dockers, and shiny black combat boots.

"Agent Laurent? I'm Kel Whitt. I flew in to escort you home," he announced. He glanced down at Derek, barely masking his surprise.

"This is Agent Holland of the Paris office. He is the one who has all the answers about the currency, and the books, so guard him well, Major," Nicole said, "Our records are all encoded, and we can do nothing without Agent Holland because he is the only one who knows the code."

Whitt bent and shook Derek's hand, then looked up at Nicole. He had the most magnificent blue eyes she had ever seen.

"I guess you know I am replacing Gazar, so we will probably be working together quite a bit in the future," he said, shaking her hand and holding it for just a few seconds longer than necessary.

"Gazar never involved himself in the game directly with the field agents. He kept in touch from one of his many homes. Do you plan to work in the field?"

"Let us just say that from now on, it's an entirely new ballgame. You will find my methods somewhat different, Agent Laurent. Now, if you'll climb aboard."

Two young airmen loaded the baggage, entered the body of the plane, checked it out and reported back to Major Whitt. "All clear, sir. Come aboard," one said.

Nicole smiled to herself as she viewed the luxury of the larger plane, thinking back to less elegant modes of travel in her five-year career. There were the spitting camels, leaking wooden dugouts, many cheap rental cars, long commercial flights, and trains, bicycles, and endless walking, walking, walking, walking. She could get used to planes like this one. But could she get used to Major Whitt? He was an enigma so far.

They sat down in their seats and waited for more than thirty minutes. Finally, Nicole turned toward Whitt and asked, "What are we waiting for?"

"Our pay load," he answered gruffly. "You don't think this plane was just for us, do you? I only got us on this ride because some retired politicians needed a hop stateside, and there happened to be extra seats available."

"I thought it was too good to be true," muttered Nicole.

"There is plenty of room, Nicole. I counted twenty-two seats," Derek informed her.

"Here they come now," announced Whitt. "Be courteous, Agent Laurent."

A silver limousine pulled up alongside the plane and out jumped a short fat man in a white jacket, white cap, and green and gold plaid knickers. Two elderly men, similarly attired in sports outfits, followed him toward the plane. The limo driver was helping a woman from the car. As she stood and thanked him, Nicole saw that she was very tall and thin, dressed in a pink silk jumpsuit and a matching wide-brimmed hat. To Nicole's amusement, they all wore dark glasses, despite the lateness of the evening.

"That woman looks like a horse," Derek observed, seriously. "Note the long face, the long nose, and very skinny legs. She must be a thoroughbred."

"A horse in pink pajamas—isn't that a song—something like that?" asked Nicole.

The Captain had come forward and was waiting at the doorway, hand outstretched to greet his passengers, with a welcoming smile on his face.

"Welcome aboard, Mr. Secretary," he gushed, pumping the fat man's hand. Then he turned to the other two men. "And Senator . . . and Senator." He reached for the horse lady and reeled her in. "Nice weather for the flight, ma'am."

The woman paused just inside the door and stared at Nicole and Derek, especially at Derek, whose short legs stuck out before him on the seat.

"And just who are these people?" she demanded, flicking her hand in their direction.

Major Whitt came forward quickly. "Special security," he explained.

To his amazement, Nicole opened her shoulder bag, flipped back the inside flap, and displayed an official-looking silver badge. The horse lady seemed impressed, turned away, and followed the men to their seats. Nicole slapped the flap shut. Derek and Whitt still had their mouths open in surprise. Once the passengers were out of hearing, Whitt leaned down across Derek and hissed at Nicole.

"What the hell is that badge? You know agents carry no badges and no form of identification except what we allot to you."

She turned back the flap, and he stared at the badge. "Jesus!" he exploded, and then sat down across the aisle. He covered his face with a newspaper as if to disassociate himself from them as much as possible and pretended to try to sleep.

"What does it say, Nicole?" muttered Derek.

"It says Deputy Sheriff, Waco, Texas."

"Looks impressive. Does it work?"

"Every time."

Dinner was served as soon as they were aloft. There was chicken cordon bleu, slim asparagus, and fruit salads. There were flutes of champagne, and later, strong tiny cups of coffee and crème brulee.

Derek ate heartily and then said, "In America, I will have a Whopper and curly fries. I want to be like Americans and that's what they consume on the telly."

Nicole laughed and settled back to get some sleep while Derek, in the seat beside her, covered his face with his cap, and tried to do the same. Across the aisle, Major Whitt removed the newspaper and regarded the strange duo, gently snoring their way across the Atlantic. Nicole Laurent—he had never been so fascinated by anyone before.

The flight was uneventful. They landed at Andrews Air Force Base, gathered the moneybags, and Derek's personal possessions, and were met by an Air Force sergeant who then transferred everything into the back of a Jeep Cherokee. Major Whitt chose the seat by the driver; Nicole and Derek arranged themselves uncomfortably among the luggage.

* * *

In the Alexandria office in the motel, Beau Jackson had tried not to show his surprise when he met Derek Holland. Nicole had never mentioned that he was a dwarf. The little man was all she said he was, above average intelligence, neat in appearance, and quick to catch on to things that were bound to be new to him. But she had omitted the obvious as if it were of no importance and perhaps it wasn't. If he worked out, Holland was here to keep records, decode, give out funds, and arrange travel, all things in which he had become proficient in the Paris office. Nowhere in his job description was he required to play basketball.

Beau showed Derek around the complex of adjoining rooms and told him he could stay in one of the bedrooms until he located an apartment and acquired some transportation. As they talked to each other, the tall gruff black man and the short dapper French agent seemed to find an area of common interests. Both loved to work and took it very seriously, both loved kids, played chess, and on rare occasions smoked a cigar. They liked nice cars and expensive clothing.

"Can you start tomorrow?" asked Beau. "I'm shorthanded here because I have put one agent on leave and another I fired. You may have to do some fieldwork if necessary, but mainly, you'll be here in the office. You drive, don't you?"

"Yes, with adjustments. I'll start looking for a car tomorrow," Derek said sadly. He was thinking of the special silver blue Renault he had to leave behind. "And Nicole, will she be working here in the office?"

"Afraid not. She is a field agent. If I can persuade her, she'll soon be out of here and on her way down south, taking care of a very big problem. Where is she anyway?"

"Major Whitt has taken her out for a drink. He is acting like a schoolboy, Mr. Jackson. I think he is falling in love," confided Derek anxiously.

"He will have to get in line," observed Beau.

"Yes, she has that effect, even on me, Mr. Jackson," admitted Derek.

"Call me Beau."

Derek smiled. He had the job. Now he had a possible friend. He thought he was going to like it here in America.

Beau Jackson looked down at the little man and decided that there was something that needed to be said to set the record straight, something important to keep in mind. "About Nicole, the field agents are not like you and me. They are made of different stuff. While guys like us are happy to play in left field, the field agents are always up to bat, and they will kill to win. Never underestimate them. They are dangerous."

Derek nodded. *He is describing Nicole.* He gazed thoughtfully down into the parking lot below. The cars, vans, and taxis came and went across the lot, but he saw nothing.

He was thinking back to his earliest days with the circus. He had been just a child, but he recalled the flighty, frantic blonde Frenchwoman who attended every performance in the environs of Paris and surrounding cities, always carrying a tiny dark-haired baby girl with eyes so black, and sometimes there was an older woman with them. The woman was petite, blue-eyed, and fragile as a broken butterfly seeking a safe flower on which to light. The older woman was different, strong and stern, wearing an unhappy expression as if she resented each moment of being at the circus. Still, she came.

For many years now, Derek had held the secret within him. His clown, his mentor, that kind, gray-haired father figure whose stage name was Beez-Bol, had cautioned him repeatedly, "That baby must never know her father." It was kind of a silent code among the circus people. The circus moved from city to city and after a while, the two women with the baby stopped coming. Derek had solemnly promised Beez-Bol that the secret was safe with him but that had been more than twenty years ago. He thought of the shock he had experienced when Nicole had first walked into the Paris office. He thought he was suffering from some crazy illusion, for here was a female so exactly like Nicolas Campion, the high-wire performer known simply as Spider, and he felt for a moment that he was hallucinating. Even her body was like his, the tough, small, yet broad hands, the muscled legs, the short, dark curly hair and nearly black eyes under straight brows, and that beautiful face! Nicolas Campion had been a startlingly handsome man. What the woman was wearing could have even been his clothes—fitted black pants, a turtleneck sweater, and short black boots! He had not a second's doubt who she was. On that day, he had become so confused that he had walked out of the office without his coat and stumbled through the alleys for miles, not returning to the Paris office until he was certain that the apparition would be gone. But Nicole had come back . . .

And so now, here in Beau Jackson's office in America, he felt bursting to relieve himself of the secret he had carried for so long. He turned away from the window.

"I knew Nicole's father, many years ago," he blurted out suddenly.

"Beg pardon?" asked Jackson, looking up from a mass of papers on his desk. "Can you get started on some of this today?"

"Of course." Derek hurried to the desk and climbed up onto a chair.

"Whose father?"

"Nicole's father," said Derek, already regretting his decision.

"I think you are mistaken. She doesn't know her father and the birth certificate states, *unknown*. I've seen it. She is sensitive about the subject when it comes up. Once when she was assigned to a job she didn't want to do, she said to me, "Don't worry, this little bastard will take care of it." and now, you're telling me that our Nicole actually had a real father! Somehow I thought she may have catapulted into this world all by herself."

They both laughed.

"I am sure. I never saw such an eerie resemblance, and I saw Spider every day until the trouble." She has his vitality. Things crackled when Nicolas appeared. He had no fear but everyone feared him. On the lot, no one ever challenged Nicolas, not even Monstro, the four hundred pound strong man. Nicolas, who could be fast and as invisible as a black cat, would slip up behind Monstro and handcuff him to a tent pole, just for fun. The guy lines would sway. The tent would flap. We clowns would shout, "Monstro has awaken. Nicolas would uncuff him, dance away, and disappear until show time."

"He worked on the high-wires, right?"

"Yes. He was the Spider, in a black suit with silver strands that expanded like wings, when he spread his arms to fly. Sometimes he balanced on the middle and juggled silver, fluorescent balls high in the air."

"Nicole is a juggler," Jackson mused. "Why didn't you tell her? She married that older man, Rene Laurent, and you know what a psychologist would make of that, looking for her father."

"I made a promise to Beez-Bol, my clown. You see, all the time that Nicolas was in the circus, he had been living a life of crime we knew nothing about. He was a thief, with a bad reputation. He was strong and clever, and he had amassed a fortune in jewels by the time he was caught, but they were never found. Some think he had an accomplice in America, who would take the pieces apart and make new ones that could not be traced. He was taken to Fleury-Merogis, but he climbed the wall and escaped. He stole again and was caught. He went to the prison on St. Martin, on the Ile de Re, and again, he is gone!"

"I'm afraid I'm not that familiar with France," admitted Jackson.

"It is off the coast near La Rochelle. Ha! Did they think that Spider could not easily swim three miles, dry himself off, and then find a lady willing to hide him from the police? He had the charm to do anything. After his last escape, he was never seen again and many in the circus believed that he had left France and returned to America."

"So Nicole's father is an American?"

"Oh yes, Monsieur Jackson. But also a common thief."

"That was a long time ago. Perhaps he has changed."

"I hope so. Now that I have confided the truth about Nicole's father, do you feel that you must tell her?" Derek asked anxiously.

"You just unloaded a heavy burden on me, man," growled Jackson, rubbing his head in indecision. He stood up and began to pace the floor, back and forth, back and forth. He crossed to the refrigerator and took out a can of Sprite. He went back and sat down at the desk. He finished the drink in three gulps and crushed the can in his fist. He had no heart to tell Nicole that her father was a thief, an escaped convict, and a man who would probably be in hiding for the rest of his life.

"I'm not going to tell her," he finally said, "You've been living with this knowledge all these years and the responsibility rests with you. Do what you will."

"I will never hurt Nicole, Mr. Jackson," declared Derek. "If I have to carry the secret forever."

"Call me Beau," Jackson repeated.

Chapter Seven

Travels with Tanya

"Nicole, if you'll step over here to the window you can see a blue van in the far corner of the motel parking lot," said Beau Jackson. "That will, more or less, be your home for the next couple of days."

Nicole picked up her bagel and coffee and crossed the room to glance down in the direction he was indicating. The van was large, teal blue, square-shaped, and the word *safari* stood out. There were heavy, steel running boards affixed under the doors, new and shiny, as if recently installed. Otherwise, it appeared ordinary.

"The lady that you will drive to her brother's farm in South Carolina, just north of Charleston, is in that motel room behind the van. That's all you gotta do. Get her home safely. There have been some threats against her life, but we're not taking them too seriously because the people who made those threats have every reason to get as far away as possible, as quickly as possible, so your job should be simple. Get the lady home."

"Is that a policeman in the chair outside her door?"

"Yes, he's just there as a precaution."

"She seems to be well protected. I hope we don't run into trouble," she said.

"We don't think you will have trouble, but you never know."

"I would like my gun."

Jackson unlocked a bottom file drawer and drew out a small revolver and a shoulder holster. He paused. "You want a knife too?"

"Yes."

Nicole placed the gun and holster on a nearby table, raised the left pants leg of her jeans, and strapped the sheath with the knife in it above her ankle. She took off her jacket and shrugged into the holster, thumbed the revolver, took note of the bullets and safety, then shoved the gun into the holster.

Jackson handed her a thousand dollars in cash, mixed denominations. She folded the bills and placed them in six separate spots, most in the shoulder bag.

"Here is a charge card, van registration, and a driver's license in the name of Nicole Tzoffke. That is T Z 0 F F K E, learn to spell it! For this trip, you are the daughter of Madam Tanya Tzoffke."

"I am the daughter of a gypsy? You will give me the background, no?"

Her face showed no emotion other than a mild curiosity. Jackson never failed to be amazed at her acceptance of any job and whatever it took to get the job done. She listened as if he were telling her how much oil to use to make French fries at McDonalds. He glanced down at the small, tough hands that cradled her coffee cup.

"A troupe of gypsies from Middle Europe, three men and two women, came to the States, purportedly to begin a musical tour which would begin in DC, and travel cross country to California. Madam Tanya, who has some family ties to one of the group, was asked to travel with them as a companion and translator. She's been in the States for ten years, but she's still proficient in Romany and other languages, and, oh yes, she plays the tambourine," Jackson began.

Nicole smiled, crossed to the sink and rinsed out her coffee cup. "So they have a tambourine artiste already so they send her home. How very rude!"

"It was all a scam. Their plan was to get into the States, disperse and disappear into one of the larger cities. There's a vast underground of these people. They take menial jobs, get their wages in cash, and if things get tough, they resort to crime. Well, this bunch didn't count on Madam Tanya's fierce allegiance to her adopted country. When she discovered their scheme, she raised unholy hell. That lady loves America! She threatened them with immigration, jail, possibly the firing squad, and she was ready to turn in the whole troupe to the Feds."

"I love America too," said Nicole, somewhat wistfully. "I may come here to live one day but for now, I cannot leave my mother and grandmother. They will never leave Paris and until . . ." She gave a sigh and left the rest unspoken.

She crossed to the window and looked down at the big blue van. It looked very wide, even at this distance, and she had never driven a van before. She wondered why Beau Jackson had not chosen a car. But *I must adapt*, she decided, *it is my job.*

Jackson was continuing with the story. "In the middle of the night, two men grabbed Madam Tanya, taped her hands together and stuffed her into the bathtub, but before they could tape her mouth shut she screamed out at them. She put a gypsy curse on each one, calling them by name. That curse must have been potent stuff because it scared the hell outa them. They were getting ready to off her right then, but a motel security car cruised by, blue lights on top. They thought it was cops and so they waited 'til it passed, got their stuff together, and high-tailed it out in the middle of the night."

Nicole looked thoughtful, "A gypsy curse can be very strong if Madam is an Ababina. An Ababina can go either way. She can bless you or make your life miserable. No wonder they are terrified. No Rom would be unkind to an Ababina because she has the power to make them all sick, even to die, if she so chooses." Beau Jackson laughed, his white teeth standing out in his dark face. "You believe that stuff, girl?" He shook his head in disbelief. Going over to the kitchen counter, he picked out the biggest sugar doughnut in the box, shoving aside Nicole's bagels. "How do you eat those ole hard donut-wannabes? Already taste day-old when you buy 'em. So, you really believe in that gypsy curse, Nicole?"

"Seen it work."

"That lady might put a curse on you. Ain't you scared?" he teased.

"I've got a few tricks of my own," said Nicole seriously.

Jackson polished off the rest of his doughnut and licked the sugar from his fingers. He contemplated Nicole. "I just bet you do, baby, just bet you do."

Agent Laurent was the only member of his team who truly made him nervous. In more than half her cases, the disposition of the perpetrator was unknown. She found, them and they were never seen again. Her case report read *deceased*, and it was understood that it was not wise to pursue the why, the how, and the where. The new director of operations could be trouble. Major Kelvin Whitt, USAF, recently retired, seemed to be fascinated by Nicole. He had volunteered to accompany Madam Tanya and Nicole on their trip south and was disappointed when he was told that there was no room for him in the van.

"So I am to take this lady to South Carolina. That is all you wish to tell me?"

"Get her safely to her brother's home." Jackson glanced at his watch. "The van is ready. You can leave anytime but I warn you, Miz Tanya likes to sleep days and prowl by night. Her light, over there, stays on until dawn."

"That could be a problem. It is my habit to rise at six and run seven miles before breakfast. Why don't you drive us to International and put us on a plane to Charleston? It would be simpler than driving so far, no?"

"Sorry. In this case, that is not possible."

Nicole shrugged. "I don't understand why not, but . . . go tell this lady to be ready to move as soon as I call Paris and check on my grandmother."

"Mimi doing okay?" asked Jackson, noting her worried expression.

"Just one of her colds."

Nicole was already dialing long distance as Jackson left to cross the parking lot. Her mother's maid answered the telephone and informed her that Madam Yvette was now in Sicily with her friend, Monsieur Garibaldi, and Madam Mimi had felt well enough to go shopping with her friend, Gerta. Nicole thanked her and was about to hang up when the maid spoke again, this time sounding very anxious.

"Oh, Madame, it is not my place, but I feel that I must tell you! Monsieur Rene has been calling here, and he is very angry. I could not help but overhear. He told Madam Mimi he is getting a divorce from you. He said you are ruining his business. Why does he say such a dreadful thing? Oh, Madame, what will you do without a husband?"

"He said divorce?" Nicole hesitated. "Don't worry about it, Marie. Good-bye."

She hung up and sat quietly, thinking about Rene. She knew how angry he would be when he came home and found the shop closed, but divorce? Looking back, it was not entirely unexpected. He could always run for comfort to his old mistress, Therese, and his sanctuary in the country, but he would never marry her because she could never fit into his larger world. One day in the future, he would seek out another Nicole and introduce this creature into the excitement of parties, high fashion, beautiful gems, rare coins, and the company of the rich and famous that Rene so enjoyed. And he would wear her, just as he wore Nicole on his arm, as much a decoration as the large diamond he wore on his little finger of his left hand. Sadness washed over her. It was a good life and a part of her would always love Rene. Then she got angry.

How dare he tell Mimi before he even mentions divorce to me? Mon Dieu, even the maid knows! How could he be so insensitive!

Jackson slammed back into the room. "Okay, I told her to get ready," he announced. "Anytime you're free to go."

Free to go anytime. I'm free to go anytime, Nicole realized, wrestling with an unfamiliar sensation. To her surprise, it was a sense of relief.

"I'll go over and introduce myself to Madam Tanya," she said.

When he saw Nicole coming toward him across the parking lot, the policeman rose and stretched, then walked over to her side as she stopped and contemplated the big blue *safari* van. He smiled at her and produced a key.

"Like to have a look inside?" he offered. "It's really nice, fixed up special," Mr. Jackson said "you'd be doing the driving."

"Yes, thanks," she said, thinking of her ancient Volkswagen.

He unlocked one of the big sliding doors and let her peer inside. She climbed on the new, shiny running board and exclaimed at the remarkable conversion that had created a comfortable looking bed-sitting room. He demonstrated how the bed folded up to make a sofa by day, and how the passenger side-seat in the front had been replaced with a neat table tray, with indentions for cups or glasses.

"All of this was done just for the comfort of one gypsy lady?" Nicole asked.

"Nope. Just did these running boards, actually. This van is for the FBI on long surveillance, but they loaned it to Mr. Jackson for this trip. That lady is going to be a lot more comfortable in this van going back than she was coming up here riding in the back of her brother's truck."

"In the back of a truck?" Nicole repeated. Something sounded wrong. Beau Jackson was hiding something important from her. Why would anyone choose to make a four or perhaps five hundred mile journey in the back of a truck?

"Open the motel room door," Nicole demanded.

"Madam Tanya probably has gone back to sleep," the guard said uneasily.

"Well, she's on my time now, and I say open it."

He took out another key, turned the lock and stepped aside.

Nicole entered a room of almost total darkness. The blinds and drapes were both drawn and the only light, a dim one, came from the adjoining bath. Even after her eyes adjusted to the shadowy interior, she saw no person anywhere in the room. An empty chair stood at one side of a cluttered chest of drawers. A bed, pushed against one side of the wall, was covered with heaps of clothing, colorful masses of materials several feet high. Nicole peeked into the bathroom. It was empty. She switched on a little lamp on the vanity table and upon looking down was amazed to see two rather small feet protruding from the pile of material on the bed. She advanced further and discovered that something within the heap appeared to be breathing heavily, or perhaps snoring.

"Madam Tanya? I am Agent Nicole Laurent, and I've come to take you back to South Carolina. If you are packed and ready to leave, we could make it to Richmond tonight."

"I take my nap!" came an angry growl from the pile. Materials rose and trembled. The bedsprings squeaked in protest.

"I wish to leave while it is daylight," said Nicole firmly.

The giant heap rose suddenly. Colorful materials fell into layers of scarves, blouses, tunics, and multiple skirts. Atop it all, was a woman's head. Mimi and Yvette had taken Nicole to many circuses during her childhood, sometimes they went twice in a single week, and she had seen the alligator skin man, the thin man, assorted midgets, and dwarves . . . but here was the fattest woman that she had ever seen. And she was wearing the most clothing! Nicole stood, transfixed with fascination, at the apparition.

The woman's head appeared small above the bulk of her body. She had narrow, flashing black eyes, and black hair pulled severely back into a knot at the nape of a wide, mobile neck. She was short and had a way of holding her head back, looking down her nose when she spoke, as if she were superior in every way. Madam Tanya put one small, jeweled hand on her bulging hip. "I finish my nap!" she insisted imperiously. "I will be ready to leave at midnight!"

"I need to drive during the day. I do not know these American roads, and I have never driven anything as big as this van before," Nicole insisted. "Besides, I need you to show me the way to South Carolina."

"I leave at midnight!" bellowed the gypsy, and flopped down on the bed.

Nicole felt her temper rising. She clenched her fists and started to count to ten but her patience evaporated. There would be no eight, nine, or ten. She exploded, "Listen to me, Fatso, we are leaving now. I'm the driver, and I say we go now, so get your stuff together and get your butt out there into that van!"

"Who you call Fatso, you skinny little nothing?" roared Madam Tanya.

"You've got just twenty minutes. I am going across to get my bags and if you are not in that van when I return, you're on your own, Fatso!" Nicole snapped back.

"You can't leave without me, you skinny thing, because people are trying to kill me," the big woman cried. "Why can't that big black man drive me?"

"Mr. Jackson has to stay here. You will be safe with me," Nicole assured her. She slightly moved her jacket aside so that Madam Tanya could glimpse the gun holster. Madam Tanya was no stranger to guns, and it was not the weapon that impressed her. She stared steadily at Nicole. There was something in the face of the young woman who stood before her that convinced her not to argue. She began to gather her belongings and toss them into a number of shopping bags and hand-woven baskets.

Nicole knocked on the door, and the policeman let her out. She turned to him and asked,

"Which way do you go to get to Richmond from here?"

"Aww, it's easy. Just go on down this road here in front of the motel and hook up with 95 and head on south. Can't miss it. You not from around here, are you?"

"No," she answered, looking at the big blue van. Surely, there would be road maps in the glove compartment, so all she would have to do is look on the map, find Charleston, and head in that direction. I can do that, she thought to herself, of course I can. Anyone who can survive the autobahn in a Volkswagen can drive anywhere.

Nicole told Beau Jackson that she was ready to leave. As she picked up her tote bag, she asked him if there were maps in the van.

"I think so. It's not our van. Where do you want your money sent?"

"My Swiss account."

"Little nest egg, right? I gotcha. Have a good trip."

"Sure."

When Nicole returned to the van, she found to her surprise that Madam Tanya was already seated in the middle of the sofa bed, her shopping bags and many bundles crowded around her feet. She climbed up into the driver's seat and turned to her passenger.

"Major Whitt wants us to keep a journal of our trip so I'm giving that job to you since I'm driving. You do write English, don't you?"

"Of course! I am in America ten years, and I am no dummy! I write very good."

"And here is a walkie-talkie with a range of about twenty yards. Push this button and it beeps; the light will come on, on my unit, and I push this button to hear you."

Madam Tanya accepted the unit, and placed it on the seat next to her. She had a pen in one hand and the notebook in the other.

Carefully, Nicole put the van in reverse and backed out of the parking space, crossed the lot and made a left turn into Duke St., joining the traffic headed mainly for Washington. After two blocks, she glanced up into the rearview mirror to check out the cars immediately behind her. In the right lane was a blue sedan with two men in it, followed by a red sports car driven by a woman alone. Beyond the red car, she could see an old black pickup truck, then an open jeep with two soldiers, other cars further behind. The blue car had an unmarked car look about it but the men inside were talking to each other and paying no attention to the van. After a couple of miles, the red car turned off to the right and the old truck moved up. The jeep fell in behind, and they all held the same positions as they sped toward Washington. Nicole glimpsed a sign that said 395, but hadn't the policeman said just 95? To add to the confusion, there was 495!

Recklessly, she hurdled off onto 495, and almost immediately had the feeling that she was heading north, not south, or perhaps west, but the traffic was going so fast that it was all she could do to move along with it at about eighty miles an hour. I must watch for signs. This is worse than the autobahn, she thought grimly. She glanced into the rearview mirror. Blue car was gone, red car had reappeared! The old truck and the jeep were still coming. Holy Mary, Mother of God, send me a map, she begged.

"Madam Tanya, do you see a glove compartment anywhere in this van?"

"No, this vardo don't have no glove compartments."

They both stared at the usual spot under the right hand side of the dashboard, but there was nothing there. A flip-open compartment in the front seat contained nothing.

"We are lost. You make us lost, Skinny! And I am getting hungry back here. You start looking for golden arches!" demanded the big woman.

The red sports car passed doing eighty-five miles an hour, and Nicole noted that the woman had picked up a passenger at some time during the time she had dropped from sight because a dark man, in some sort of cap or hat, was seated on the passenger side. The jeep was directly behind the van, and much further back, the old truck had merged into traffic traveling at a slower pace.

There was the sound of cellophane crackling. Madam Tanya was unwrapping a giant-sized Mounds bar.

"I'm getting off at the next exit, and I don't care where the hell it goes," muttered Nicole, as she swung the van sharply to the left lane and careened off the maddening circle with a sigh of relief.

It was getting dark, and she found the lights, switched them on and discovered that the dense foliage along the lesser road obscured the signs. They were mere white flashes with unreadable names. And the gas gauge was now showing a quarter tank! What else? In answer, her walkie-talkie lit up and beeped loudly in the confines of the van. With irritation, she reached over and punched in *talk*.

"I am starving to death, Skinny, and I need the bathroom," came the message.

"I'm right in front of you! Why are you using the machine?"

"See how it works. Maybe this machine be nicer to me than you, Skinny," said Madam Tanya. "Hello, nice machine. I got to go."

Nicole felt that sanity had left the van a long time ago. Why, oh, why, Mother Mary, am I flying down a strange American highway with a three hundred pound gypsy talking to a machine? Mon Dieu! She began to pray earnestly and suddenly a brightly lit convenience store appeared out of the darkness just ahead. And there were gas pumps out front. Oh, merci, merci, Mon Dieu! There were a few cars in the parking lot, and she could see people inside. A sign in the window said, *Restroom. Ask for key*. God was listening to Nicole, and she was grateful.

There were sounds from the backseat. Shopping bags rustled and the gypsy's multiple skirts began tinkling, banging, and clinking. What did she carry in there? Madam Tanya was on the move, ready to rise. Even the tambourine was jostled into song.

Nicole jumped down and ran around to the right side of the van where she slid back the big door toward the rear. Madam Tanya nodded toward the restroom, which was at the backside of the store and reached only by an outside door.

"You get the key and meet me back there, okay?"

"Yes," agreed Nicole, peering into the lighted interior. "I see a deli in there. I'll get some food and fill the tank."

When Nicole entered the store, a man and woman were cleaning up, getting ready to close, but they stopped and took her order for the food, and gave her the key to the restroom. She went out back to find a disconsolate Madam Tanya contemplating the narrow door to the restroom, concealed from the road by a lattice. Nicole fitted the key into the lock, pushed the door aside, and turned on the light. There was a tiny sink with a paper towel rack over it and beyond the sink was the toilet. Nicole had seen broom closets larger than this American . . . what did they call them? Johns? Or maybe johnnies?

Madam Tanya shook her head woefully. "I no make it in there. You go, Skinny, and don't worry. I'm a country girl. I know where to go."

She gathered her long skirts and crossed the concrete strip that led to the deep woods. In seconds, she disappeared among a dense growth of trees.

Several minutes passed. Nicole took out her walkie-talkie and pressed the button, but there was no response. She went in and used the restroom, came out and waited beside the lattice, pressing the button again, but there was still no response. As she debated whether to go into the woods and look for her charge, a tall, red-haired woman in fringed jeans and a matching fringed leather jacket came around the corner of the store. Even in the dim glow of the light by the restroom door, Nicole could see that the woman was coarse-looking and had a badly pockmarked complexion. A stranger and yet, she was vaguely familiar. Was it the woman in the red sports car? Nicole wasn't sure.

"Man inside said you got the key?" the woman breathed through fumes of beer.

Nicole silently handed her the key as the woman looked her over with an ugly suspicion. She pushed herself close into Nicole's face.

"You one a them Lesbos? Think you can hang around decent ladies restrooms and pick up a few bucks?"

"I'm waiting for my mother," said Nicole, quietly unbuttoning her jacket. She kept the holster out of view but placed her hand on the gun.

"She in the crapper?"

"No," answered Nicole, glancing toward the woods.

"Well, where the hell is she?" growled the woman. "You full of bull. I betcha don't even have a mother. All by your little self, ain't you? My, that's a pretty jacket you got on. I'd sure like to have that jacket. Look, I'll give you twenty bucks for it. Now, ain't that reasonable?"

"My jacket is not for sale."

"Look, bitch, my man will get it off you, and he won't give you nothin' but a hard time. If I didn't have to pee so bad, I'd get it off you myself."

Uncertainly, the woman stood, chafing her legs together, eying the jacket in indecision, and trying to decide what action to take next. Suddenly, one long thin arm darted out and tried to wrench Nicole's jacket from her shoulders. Nicole stepped back.

With a single motion, she reached down to her ankle, snapped the knife from the sheath strapped to her ankle. The switchblade slid forward, but she held it loosely at her side. The woman stared at it, gleaming in the dim light, and backed off.

"Holy shit! I was just kiddin', you crazy lesbo bitch!" the woman screamed. She grabbed her crotch, but it was too late. Dampness spread over the leather-fringed jeans. She slammed into the tiny restroom, and Nicole could hear her jamming down the hook that held the flimsy lock on the other side.

Madam Tanya finally emerged from the woods and moved across the high grass like a clipper ship under full sail, scarves flying, and skirts picking up bits of debris.

"You okay, Skinny? I hear loud voices."

"Where is your walkie-talkie? I need to know where you were at all times."

"You worry too much, Skinny. Who going to get me in the woods? A big squirrel?" Madam Tanya laughed heartily at her own joke. "Oh, maybe a bunny rabbit?"

There was not a sound from behind the restroom door. Madam Tanya brushed past, still laughing as she headed for the van. She had not noticed the knife and behind her, Nicole bent and slipped it back into the sheath under the leg of her jeans. Together they walked to the front of the building.

Madam Tanya walked directly to the van and climbed up into the rear seat. Nicole moved to the gas pumps and put eighteen gallons into the tank. It indicated more, but she was anxious to leave. The red-haired woman could make trouble.

"Lock the doors, Fatso," she ordered. "And stay put. I'll be back with the food."

Madam Tanya called down casually. "I do like HoHos." She rummaged around, found the walkie-talkie and like an obedient child, held it up for Nicole to see. "Machine say, Tanya loves HoHos . . . ha ha ha . . . oh, oh, forgot to turn button!"

As Nicole entered the store, a tall, rangy man shoved past her coming out.

He wore a fringed jacket and jeans like the woman in the restroom. He strode angrily over to the red sports car, looked inside for the woman, kicked the tires viciously, and finally flung himself into the passenger's seat. He picked up a cap and slammed it onto his head. Man and woman in a red sports car. Were they following her? Probably just a coincidence. There were many red cars.

Her food was ready and even the big greasy bag smelled good. She paid for the food, the gas, and added several boxes of HoHos.

"I need directions," Nicole said to the store clerk. "I'm not even sure what state I'm in."

"You are in York, in the state of Pennsylvania. Yes, ma'am, this is Amish country. Everybody works hard and goes to bed at sundown. No TVs, you know. My wife and I are Methodists, spend too much time watching foolishness. If you're looking for a place to spend the night, there are some nice towns just on down the road."

"What would you recommend?"

"Well, I'd spend the night in intercourse."

"Pardon?" said Nicole, in disbelief.

"Oughta try it. For a good nights rest you can't do better than to spend it in intercourse," he insisted.

"That is not an option," snapped Nicole. "I am traveling with my mother!" Who would have dreamed that such a kindly old storekeeper would suggest such a thing. Mon Dieu, just when she thought she had begun to understand Americans, now this!

When she came out of the store, she noticed that the red car was gone from the parking lot. Nicole breathed a sigh of relief, but it was temporary, for as she walked toward the van, which was now the only vehicle in the lot, an unexpected thing occurred. Down the road came the old, black pickup truck that had been behind them all the way from Alexandria. This one was too distinctive by age and condition to be just a similar model. It slowed abruptly at the sight of the van, and she could see the driver plainly now. He was very dark and young. He was wearing a red shirt and a straw hat, shaped like a cowboy's hat. The driver applied his squeaking brakes, then sped on past, going fast. He ducked his head down, but Nicole had seen him clearly.

Inside the van, Madam Tanya had missed this little happening. She was opening the door for Nicole and the food, and had not seen the old black truck as it passed. She had placed paper towels as placemats on the table that replaced the seat on the passenger's side and for a touch of elegance had laid a single exquisite rose at each place.

"Where did you get the roses? They are beautiful!" Nicole exclaimed.

"I make them myself out of very thin paper, covered with my secret mixture, a thin coating of my special wax," said Madam Tanya proudly.

"They couldn't be paper. You found them in the woods."

Madam Tanya uncovered a large basket at her feet. Inside, there must have been several hundred roses, packed so tightly together that their heads of pink, red, yellow, and white appeared to be the pattern of an oriental rug of exceptional beauty.

Nicole put the bag of food on the table and ran her hand over the tops of the flowers, which felt as damp and fresh as those recently picked from a garden.

"I sell them on the highway on Friday and Saturday. I also make handmade baskets. I make good business, lady, you be surprised."

Nicole examined the basket, an intricate design in two shades of blue. "I would like to buy this basket when we reach South Carolina."

"Sorry, Skinny, this basket not for sale," said Madam Tanya, covering the roses with a silk scarf. "I am so starving to death. Let us eat."

Nicole brought out the food. There was barbecue on thick rolls, baked beans, macaroni salad, cheese, ham slices, chips, cheesecake, and a bottle of wine, and two pints of coffee. And three boxes of HoHos.

When the big gypsy woman spied the HoHos, her sharp black eyes lit up, her habitually stern face softened, and she looked shyly away from Nicole. "You not such a bad egg, Skinny."

"You either, Mom, here, try some of these beans."

They dug into the food hungrily, periodically wiping their greasy fingers. Finally, they shared the wine and cheesecake, passing a single plastic fork between them. Nicole did not mention seeing the old truck, but she limited herself to a single glass of wine, keeping her head clear in case of trouble.

"I bring my flowers with me to throw to our audiences at each place we do our show," said Madam Tanya sadly. "We practice wonderful Romany music. The girls would twirl in their dances. Beautiful costumes.

Eelie play the drums, and Micah, the flute, Bela, he play violin, the notes so high and sweet, make a dog run away. Susie and Magda would dance. We sing old songs. I shake my tambourine to the drum beat, all very good . . ." Suddenly, she was weeping in her private pain, thinking of promises not kept.

Nicole glanced away and stared into the darkness of the night. There were no stars in the sky; it was turning cold. Perhaps it would rain. She was wondering where the old black truck had gone with the dark, young man in the red shirt. Which of that merry, little band of musicians had been chosen to hunt, find, and kill Madam Tanya, to rid them of the Ababina's curse? She was sure he was out there, waiting his chance.

The miles dragged past and the wine had put Madam Tanya to sleep, sitting straight up in the center of the sofa bed. Now and then, she would slump over, her elbow would hit the tambourine, and it would tinkle its tiny cymbals in protest. They appeared to be alone on this road, but Nicole watched ahead for the truck. A slight, misting rain began and the headlights of the big blue van cut a wet swathe across the asphalt. The hum of the motor, plus the murmur of a talk show on the radio, was having a lethargic effect. Somehow, she had gotten on a bypass road. A sign said 462, approaching the Susquehanna River . . . Hundreds of miles from Alexandria, going in the wrong direction, Nicole thought crazily. I am so tired. So tired. Euphoric. Her eyes closed for one second, and the van hit the edge of the road. Gravel scattered, sounding like hail against the hubcaps. The sound jerked her upright, and shaking, she edged the van back on the road. The back tires wobbled as if she had run over sharp branches, or perhaps rocks, on the shoulder.

Suddenly, on the opposite side of the road, the high beams of a vehicle shone out of the darkness and an old engine revved at its highest speed. The old black truck pulled into the center of the two lanes and rushed directly at the van, attempting to run it off the road. For one fleeting moment, Nicole stared into the wild eyes of the young man in the red shirt through the windshield. She hung onto the steering wheel and swerved to the left, missing the truck by inches. Brakes on both vehicles screamed. The worn tires of the old truck left streaks of rubber for several yards until it stopped, the motor still racing. The driver put it in reverse, looking around for a spot in the road wide enough so that he could turn the truck and try again, but it was knocking loudly now and refusing to start.

Nicole was wide-awake, and the adrenalin was rushing. She grabbed her gun out of its holster and laid it on the compartment between her seat and the little table.

"What has happened?" screamed Madam Tanya. "Why we are stopping?"

"Someone tried to run us off the road and kill us, and I think you know who it is. Tell me quick, what kind of weapons do they have?"

"I don't know! I never see no weapons."

"Hang on," ordered Nicole as she swung the big van in a tight arc, backed up and moved slowly toward the sputtering truck. Leaving the motor running, she stopped close behind the truck and got out with the gun in her hand. She turned once and called out, "Stay inside and lock the doors."

The young man at the wheel of the truck kept jabbing at the ignition, but it kept gasping and periodically cutting off. He turned his head to see her approaching and his eyes glittered red in the headlights of the van. Now he leapt down into the road to face her, and in his hand, he was holding a machete, ready to strike. He waved it about, first up in the air, then swooping down to his feet. The wicked blade was slightly curved and reached almost to the toes of an elegant pair of black and white snakeskin boots. The toes of the boots pointed upward as if they were two sizes too large.

"Stand away," the man shouted, searching hard for the right English words. "I got to kill that woman. She told the American peoples on us. They got Micah. Maybe Bela too. She ruin all our plan to be free in this country. You, you stand away, or I kill you too."

Two cars passed, going fast. Perhaps it was the misty rain, or the darkness, or maybe, they sensed trouble and didn't want to get involved with a small, determined woman with a gun and a crazy cowboy with a machete. They flew by into the night, heads turned away.

The lights of the vehicles faded into the night, and Nicole and the cowboy stepped toward each other. To their surprise, something else clattered down the road. There was the sound of horse's hooves, going at a fast clip. Nicole lowered her gun. The man held his machete down beside his leg. A black buggy appeared, a stern-faced man in a black hat holding the reins. It rolled past and continued down the road, flashing an orange fluorescent triangular caution sign on the back.

To her consternation, Nicole heard the van door slide back and the running board creaking from the weight of three hundred solid pounds of gypsy descending to the road.

"No, no, no, Eelie!" Madam Tanya cried out.

The young man jumped forward and shook the machete at Nicole. "You stand away! Or I kill you too." He held the machete aloft. "You going to die, old woman!"

Nicole held her ground between the two gypsies. She didn't want to kill this crazy man, but his threat was definitely sincere, and she was responsible for Madam Tanya. The words of *Bull Durham* came to her clearly shoot 'em in the foot. She lowered the gun and aimed at his feet. The shot tore the first two toes from the nearest boot. Black and white snakeskin sprayed outward like confetti caught in a whirlwind, and blood gushed red, small rivulets draining onto the damp road.

For one long moment, there was silence; they stood frozen like a tableau of actors who had forgotten their lines. Then the young man screamed and clutched at his bleeding foot. The machete skittered to the ground and slid through the widening pool of gore. Nicole stepped over and picked up the big knife, went past Madam Tanya to the van, and threw it under the driver's seat. She returned to face the wounded man . . . and stopped . . .

A small-bore gun was pressing into her back.

"Please don't kill him," begged Madam Tanya. "He is my son."

Nicole turned around and Madam Tanya dropped her own weapon back into the many folds of her colorful skirts. It had been merely one of the things hidden in the multiple layers of clothing, along with scissors, pens, mirrors—even a small silver flask came in view, as the big woman pocketed the small but lethal Derringer.

"He hurt bad. You got the big knife now. Let him go!"

"You gotta die, old woman! You put the curse and already it is working on us. They got Micah. And where is Bela and Susie, I don't know. Maybe they dead. Poor Magda, she every day sick, throw up and throw up. Maybe she die too because you make her food poison!"

Madam Tanya tossed her head back and stared at him through narrowed eyes. "You are a fool, Eelie. Magda is pregnant by you. It will be a boy, born early October. Go to Magda Give yourselves to the police. Nothing will happen to you, but you be deported from this country. You go home, Eelie. Get a job."

He stood defiantly in the road, holding his bleeding foot. "You take off the curse!" he insisted. "It will follow where we go."

The Ababina held up one hand. "It is gone."

Madam Tanya walked over to Nicole and put her arm through hers. Leaning heavily, as if exhausted from what she had just gone through, she made her way slowly to the van and climbed inside. Nicole stepped up into the driver's seat and together they watched as Eelie limped painfully back to the old black truck. After several tries, the truck came to life, took off down the road, and disappeared from sight.

"I need to sleep," said Nicole.

"You could have killed him."

"And you could have killed me. Haven't seen a Derringer in a very long time."

Madam Tanya gave a little laugh and opened her hand for Nicole to see inside. Nestled in her palm were the bullets from the gun. "I would not kill my daughter, Ms. Nicole Tzoffke. I see that credit card. Nicole Tzoffke, I wish was true—you my daughter."

"Thank you."

* * *

The faint lights of the sign on the Harvest Home Motel beckoned from down a side road. *Vacancy*. Nicole eagerly turned in at the long white building and looked for the office. She noticed that there was a restaurant at one side, now closed for the night.

The room was clean, with two double beds. And there was a sizable bath with plenty of hot water and fluffy, pink towels. At first, Madam Tanya appeared set to spend the night in the van but after carefully testing one of the beds and considering the bath, she opted to stay in the room with Nicole.

"I snore," she told Nicole.

"I know," Nicole answered.

They slept deeply and by the time they woke the next morning it was almost nine o' clock. Nicole had noticed the long, country roads that stretched out beyond the farms and regretted that she could not have her usual run. The weather stayed chill and a good run would have been invigorating. She thought wistfully of LeGrand's farm outside of Paris and the seven-mile loop around the edge of the outskirts of the property, and the dear old dog, Boncoeur, who sometimes came out to meet her.

They jockeyed around each other in the motel room, taking turns brushing teeth and taking baths, finding clean clothes, and repacking their bags. Finally, they emerged into the brisk Pennsylvania morning. In the acreage beyond the motel, three men were preparing a field for planting. They were bearded, and wore purple shirts and black trousers held up by suspenders. Their horses were large and strong; their wagons were of wood. They were turning the rich soil the same way their fathers and grandfathers had done before them for centuries. The mounds of upturned earth smelled sweet. Nicole and Madam Tanya stood watching them at work.

"My brother has tractor. Not so hard work," remarked Madam Tanya. "The Amish have no tractors. They are called the Plain People. Ha! Not so plain, Skinny. My brother never wear a purple shirt!"

Nicole laughed. "There's a restaurant over there. You go ahead. Just order me anything. I've got to call in."

Madam Tanya's eyes lit up, and she moved off swiftly, following the scent of food like a hound on the trail of a fox, her homemade cape billowing behind her.

Nicole watched Madam Tanya safely across the parking lot, then entered the outside telephone booth, where she called Alexandria collect to Beau Jackson. "Where the hell have you been?" he exploded as soon as he heard her voice.

Oh, oh, what happened to the nice, friendly, "Hello, Nicole," she mused as she pondered exactly how much to tell him.

"Where are you?" he insisted.

"I think it is Pennsylvania."

There was silence, and then Jackson sighed deeply.

"How come you are way up north when you are supposed to be heading south? I had two of my best men riding shotgun right behind you when you left Alexandria, and they lost you somewhere off 495. They circled The Beltway twice and came in, and if you think I'm pissed off, you oughta see them!"

Nicole thought back. "Two men in a blue sedan?" she asked.

"Yeah, you made them? And then you lost them?"

"Not on purpose. You didn't mention we had a cover."

Jackson groaned. "For god's sake, Nicole, think south. And call in!"

"I am calling in, no?" she laughed. "Bon jour."

He seemed to be shouting something, but she quietly hung up.

At the restaurant, she found Madam Tanya seated at a large table in the rear that was covered with a dozen plates of food. There were the usual pancakes, eggs, sausages, fried apples, biscuits, jellies, and things Nicole didn't recognize.

Nicole sat down. "What is all this? Who else is coming to breakfast, Fatso?"

"For you and me, Skinny. We hungry. Travel all night."

Madam Tanya snared a piece of bacon and chewed pensively. "My Eelie will be caught soon. Those were not Eelie's clothes he was wearing. He never a cowboy, and that was not his truck. He was always, always the thief, that one."

Nicole drew up a platter of pancakes and covered them in maple syrup. "So somewhere there is a naked cowboy, trying to thumb a ride, no?"

"Yes, Eelie was born a thief. As a little boy, he would steal clothes from people's clothesline, and I not know where these peoples live. He sell clothes in the next town and buy candy. He carry corn in his pocket, steal the chicken. Here, try the sausages."

Nicole was trying to remember what Beau Jackson was screaming about when she hung up the telephone: something about keeping a journal and Major Whitt.

"Fatso, have you been writing in the notebook about what we do?"

"Sure, I write very good. Hmmm, try these good apples."

Nicole spooned apples onto her plate. "What have you written so far?"

"I write, me and Skinny in the vardo ride a long time and eat barbecue."

"That is it?"

"Well," answered Madam Tanya thoughtfully. "That is what we do."

Nicole stared at her in disbelief. Not a word about her machete-waving son who had come to kill his own mother, to remove the Ababina's curse from the gypsy troupe. Madam was proving to be more than discreet. She could be creatively evasive. Eat barbecue! Today, she would probably describe this massive breakfast in detail; Beau Jackson would love that. And what was he saying about Major Whitt? Mon Dieu, he had such sharp blue eyes! And his hands were broad and appeared to be . . .

"You dreaming about your husband, Skinny?" said Madam Tanya slyly. She forked over a glob of honey-glazed ribs onto her plate and smiled at Nicole's sudden uneasy expression. So it was some other man. Better to change that touchy subject. "You got any children, Skinny?"

"No, but I would like some. Children are to love, no?"

"You better hurry up. Clock ticking, like people say." Madam Tanya sipped her coffee. "I was married at fourteen first time. Real Romany wedding lasted three days with much dancing and foods. I no like this man. I never see him before, but he have plenty money so, for my family, I go to him. One year later, I have my son, Bashar, but then, I have the chicken pox and his family, they think I am diseased, so they take my Bashar and travel far away, to Russia. They say they will send for me when I am well, but they never send, and I never see my Bashar again."

"That is terrible! But you had Eelie. You said he is your son."

"I don't got Eelie. My boyfriend don't want to be married, so when Eelie come, his mother take the baby. I got nothing because they take my heart when they take my baby. I so lonely, so I marry one more time to a good old man, and I have my Damon. We come to America after my husband die ten years ago. Me and Damon live with my brother, William, and his family. Life here is like a good dream, plenty to eat. Good school for Damon."

The food on the table had diminished considerably, and Madam Tanya was carefully wrapping the rest of the biscuits in paper napkins as she talked, a little something later, for the road. They pushed themselves heavily away from the table and rose.

When Nicole handed the check to the cashier, who was also the owner, she asked to buy a map of the southeastern states. He indicated a display by the cash register.

"Take one. For any of my customers who can eat thirty-six dollars worth of breakfast food, the map is free." He whistled in disbelief. "Here, a match book. And for each of you, a nice pen with our name, Harvest Home Restaurant and Motel."

Madam Tanya threw back her head and regarded him kindly. "You make very good cooking."

He laughed. "And you do very good eating."

She laughed along with him, her chins in motion, and her bosom rising and falling. She took the bag he offered in which she put the biscuits.

In the parking lot, Nicole hesitated beside the telephone booth. "I guess I should call my husband."

The Ababina continued to walk toward the van. She waved her hands about the area where the Amish were working the fields. "He not home. He in the country, I think."

Nicole stopped. "How do you know where he is? Are you reading my mind? If you are picking up my thoughts, old woman, you stop that right now." After a moment, she followed the billowing, homemade cape that Madam wore against the chill morning.

The big woman waited by the van and regarded her with sadness. "You are beautiful and strong, but I see turmoil all around you. You are a Leo, am I not right? I will read the cards for you."

"Yes, Leo. August the ninth," admitted Nicole. She was positive she had not mentioned her birthday previously.

"Who is the dark man who is ever standing just beyond your shoulder? His spirit guards you but his heart has been always with you . . ."

"What are you babbling about, old woman?" Nicole said angrily. "Don't try any of that mumbo-jumbo on me again, do you understand? I don't buy it!"

"You got older brother, look just like you?" Madam Tanya insisted, gazing just beyond Nicole's shoulder as if she could see someone standing there.

"No brother and no sister. Now, get the hell in that van. No more crazy talk."

They climbed up into the van and as Nicole sat in the driver's seat looking at the map, she could hear the slap, slap, slap of cards hitting the seat of the sofa bed. Madam Tanya was quietly singing a gypsy lullaby, haunting and very sad.

I will go around Washington and take 301 south, she decided. Mon Dieu, Nicole, all you must do is keep going south, Mother Mary, guide my hand, she prayed.

* * *

Nicole had not intended to go to Wilmington, Delaware, but she neglected to mention that to Madam Tanya, who appeared to be getting increasingly depressed as she dealt the cards over and over in an attempt to get a better reading for Nicole's future.

"Do you want lunch?" Nicole asked. "There is a log building ahead and the sign says—Dinning. Fambly dinning—bad spelling. Sounds not so good, no?"

"I no hungry," was the unexpected reply from the backseat.

Nicole turned around. "Are you sick? Let's get out and get some air."

"Are we lost again, Skinny? Where are we?"

"I think that water is the Chesapeake Bay." She noticed that Madam Tanya was lying down on the sofa bed. The tambourine lay on top of the last box of HoHos, which were, as yet, unopened. A giant sigh shook the bed.

"What is the matter, Fatso? I know I am not a good driver, but I will bring you home safely. I heard on the news report on the radio that the police picked up Eelie at a hospital. The doctors removed two toes. I am sorry I had to shoot him, but you know that he intended to use that big knife." Her foot touched the blade under the seat, and she pushed it further back out of sight.

"I know. Eelie was never no good, but it is you worries me. I see in the cards, death all around you, coming soon. I see fire."

"I am not going to die."

"No, not you, but within your aura. I so scare I am sick!"

"Come on, get out. If you walk in the fresh air you will feel better."

Madam Tanya gathered her cape about her, and clinking and clanking from the arsenal of hidden treasures beneath her skirts, climbed down onto the side of the road. Spotting a stand of woods on one side, she waved in that direction and wandered off across a grassy field. Nicole waited beside the van.

A small, very dirty little girl came hurrying down the road from the log building and paused a few feet away. She had tousled yellow hair. An oversized sweater, used as a coat, hung to her knees, and she wore tennis shoes with no socks. A boy, a bit older and thinner, wearing overalls, a wool cap with ear flaps, and no shoes, had followed the girl down the road and stood protectively nearby.

"Would you like to see our zoo? It's only one buck," the girl said.

"That is one buck each," the boy added. "I seen your mom go into the woods. Our Grannie used to do that, but she is dead. We got a real nice possum."

"And sort of a monkcy," mumbled the girl hesitantly.

Madam Tanya came back across the grasses, her cape standing out in the breeze like giant wings. The children watched her in fascination.

"Boy, I bet she eats a lot. Our Mom can make sammiches. We got drinks. Did you see our sign? I made the sign, but we don't get too many folks," said the boy.

"We're not hungry but thanks," said Nicole. As Madam Tanya came up to the van, she said to her, "These children have a zoo. Would you like to see it?"

"Only one buck each," reminded the boy.

"You got a bear?" growled Madam Tanya, in a deep voice.

The children looked at each other and shook their heads.

"Possum," relayed Nicole, solemnly.

To her surprise, Madam Tanya took a child by each hand and started off down the road toward the log building, speaking in a low serious voice.

"When I am little like you, my papa had a brown bear, we call Toby. My mama, she play the concertina, I play my tambourine, and Toby would dance, all over Europe, and that is how we make our living with the dancing bear."

"How did the bear learn to dance?" asked the little girl.

"When he is a cub, very little, we throw down embers under his feet and . . ."

"What is embers?"

"Coals of fire. We play the music and when the bear feet burn, he jump all around and that is how he learn to dance when he hear the music."

"Oh, Mon Dieu! Shut up about the poor bear," muttered Nicole.

"Soon, he learn very good. No more burn his feet. He starts dancing whenever he hears the music."

"Thank God," muttered Nicole. "That was cruel."

Madam Tanya twirled around defensively. "We love Toby. He sleeps with us right in the vardo on a nice pile of hay."

They reached the log building, and the boy led them to a long, attached wooden shed, where he held out his hand. "That'll be two bucks, please."

Madam Tanya retrieved a soft leather pouch from inside of one of her many pockets and gravely counted out two one-dollar bills. The boy jammed the money under his hat and flipped on an overhead light in the shed to reveal a beautiful little spotted pony. The pony was brown and white, with a white mane and tail. He was clean and cared for and stabled in his own little area. The boy lovingly stroked the pony's head.

"This is Champ. He is a gen-u-wine Chincoteague pony, which is famous the world over. And now he will do a trick. Champ, say "Hi" to these ladies," instructed the boy. He pointed to the pony's feet.

The pony shook his mane, bowed his head, and stomped one white hoof.

"Well done, Champ!" the boy grinned. He took a lump of sugar from his overalls and Champ nuzzled it from his hand and looked around for more.

"This is our possum," said the girl. "He don't do nothing, but we think he is pretty except his tail do look like a rat. Don't pet him. He bites."

They admired the possum from a distance.

"This is my hawk. He's chained, but he can pick your eyes out if he breaks loose. We had some wild birds but Pirate here got to 'em one night and in the morning there was nothing left but a bunch of feathers so don't stand too close."

The hawk wore a black hood over his eyes, but he sensed the presence of strangers, raised his wings in warning and his powerful legs traversed the length of his perch. This seemed to be the extent of his act. He cocked his head expectantly.

"Very good, Pirate," said the boy, carefully handing him a bit of meat. The treat appeared to be part of a recent mouse, but they didn't inquire.

There was a tree propped up by feedbags. The branches were bare but green paper leaves had been pasted at intervals. On the top of the farthest limb, sat a glassy-eyed monkey. It wore a red collar. Its fur was missing in patches. Madam Tanya and Nicole stared at the monkey for several minutes, but it didn't move.

"You monkey is dead," decided Madam Tanya. "He be dead a long time."

The children looked embarrassed. The boy fished in his pocket and came up with two coins. "Tell you what, I'll give each of you ladies a quarter back. We don't mean to cheat nobody, but nobody ever looks at him as hard as you ladies."

"Never mind the money," said Nicole quickly, "What else do you have?"

"The snakes," said the boy. "We just got five things."

"No snakes!" bellowed Madam Tanya. "I don't want to see no snakes!" She moved hurriedly away from the wire enclosure where there were signs of slithering movement. She picked up her long skirts and waddled at great speed for the door.

The boy was obviously disappointed. He wanted to show his snakes, which he considered the next best thing to his pony. Nicole looked down into the cage. Smaller ones crawled on the wire, looking for escape from the larger ones. The biggest formed knots of writhing menace, individual heads rising medusa-like from the masses.

The little girl sidled up to Nicole. "You can have your dollar back. Our monkey died last winter."

"Oh no, Cherie, you have a wonderful zoo here," Nicole assured her. She looked down at the old sweater that served as a coat. She noted the boy's bare feet. She reached down into her right boot and withdrew a hundred dollar bill, gazed at the children's faces and extracted another hundred. She handed one to the boy and the other to the girl.

"Buy yourself a new monkey."

"Is this real? We never seen a bill this big before," whispered the boy, holding the money to his chest as if she might decide to take it away.

"Yes, it is real. Use it well."

The children seemed glued to the floor, neither moving nor speaking as she slipped out of the door and made her way quickly back to where the van was parked.

"I've been thinking about you, lady, and I decide you French," stated Madam Tanya. "You French all right. Ha-ha-ha. The children say they got five things. You think I no understand French? Listen! Une, deux, trois, quatre, cinq—is that not right?"

"Yek, dui, trin, star, panch," Nicole shot back in Romany. "Does that sound like French to you?"

Madam Tanya tossed back her head and laughed. "You not Rom, Skinny, you just a gorgio. Ha-ha-ha. Maybe later, I be hungry. Spaghetti would be very good."

Nicole had no idea what happened to 301. It was supposed to go straight south, but somewhere it disappeared. The next town was Fredericksburg, according to a road sign that said Rt 1. She saw no place that might have spaghetti, so they settled for Kentucky Fried Chicken. When they came out of the restaurant, Nicole noticed that the two back tires on the van appeared to be going flat, and she recalled running over something sharp on the side of the road when she fell asleep at the wheel, but then they had the encounter with Eelie. She had forgotten to check later for leaks. Sure enough, on inspection, there was glass in the tires. She drove carefully down the highway, looking for that rarity, a full service station. These days you could buy a quart of milk, a carton of Cokes or six kinds of bread, but you couldn't get your oil changed. You could buy fish bait, but you couldn't get water for a steaming radiator. Somewhere in time, someone had taken the service out of service stations.

Finally, they found one. They had to sit in a cramped waiting room while the owner located two tires of the right size but after three hours, they were on their way.

In the backseat, Madam Tanya was dutifully writing in the journal. Me and Skinny eat fried chicken. Pretty pony and poor dead monkey. Tires gone bust. She tucked the notebook under her seat, satisfied with her entry.

Nicole headed down a long, well-lit corridor, which led out of Fredericksburg, and more signs indicated they were at last on their way to Richmond. No more north, east, or west. They were headed south and Nicole breathed a sigh of relief. Keep on this highway, she told herself, or you will be stuck with that oversized medium forever. She was now snoring loudly in the backseat. The rains came just as they entered the city of Richmond and night made an early descent. Streetlights gleamed on nearly empty streets. Buses, with only one or two passengers, passed on their way to residential neighborhoods. On Broad Street, vacancy signs abounded on dark storefronts. The occasional restaurant cast a dim glow on wet sidewalks from windows misted over from the warmth inside. A few people, like silhouettes against the walls, scurried close to the buildings to get out of the rain.

Nicole drove slowly, looking for a motel. After crossing Main Street, she found herself on a bridge going out of town into an even darker urban neighborhood. She recrossed the bridge, and then took a left, which went straight downhill on cobble-stoned streets. Now she was in a section of what appeared to be abandoned warehouses and old, crumbling brick buildings with many broken windows. Tall, narrow row housing had yellow condemned signs on nearly every listing front porch but some of the forbidden property must have attracted squatters, for Nicole saw flickers of candles through doorless hallways.

Madam Tanya looked around uncasily. She pulled a large silver cross out of her bosom and appeared to be ready to start praying if trouble erupted. "This is a bad place, Skinny, where is the motels?" She touched the Derringer to reassure herself.

"I am going back up the hill to the stoplights," decided Nicole.

At that moment, an apparition dressed in red sequins ran in front of the van. The headlights picked up the figure of a light-skinned black woman in a glittering dress and silver high heels. Nicole hit the brakes, praying that the van would not skid on the wet street. The woman pounded on the hood, crying hysterically.

"You gots to help me! He gonna kill de baby!"

Nicole cautiously lowered the window. "Who is going to kill your baby? Go call 911 and ask the police to help you."

"Up there. He on crack, he don't know what he doing. Oh, Lordy, he gots the baby hanging out the window," cried the woman.

"I see him!" shouted Madam Tanya. She slid the big door back. "Stop, Mr!"

Despite the screams of both women, the street remained eerily empty. The furtive creatures who dwelled behind these condemned walls stayed out of sight, and as Nicole watched, candles were doused as if to deny that any human resided inside. *What kind of people are these?* Nicole jumped down into the street and gazed upward through the rain to see, on the second floor, a half naked black man with long, greasy dreadlocks hanging over the rotting sill of a glassless window and in his hands he was holding a baby, gently swinging a baby back and forth over the street below as he spoke in a high voice.

"Not my bassard." He cackled maniacally. "He not my bassard going to hell. Jus' maybe, girl, you bring you money up here I give him you. Or maybe I jus' crack he head open on that pav-mint. Go rockaby, lil baby, for de las' time, yeah."

The young black woman fell down into the gutter and beat her fists on the cobblestones on the street until they were bloody. For a moment, she seemed to lose consciousness, collapsing in a heap of red sequins in a puddle of water.

Nicole gauged the distance from the window to the street, and then turned to Madam Tanya.

"Can you catch that baby?"

"I can catch him."

"I'm going in. Keep watching that window."

Madam Tanya moved directly under the window and raised her arms as Nicole drew her gun and stumbled up the broken steps that led to a shallow porch. Through the open doorway, Nicole crept into the lower hall, and picking her way through broken bottles, old newspapers, and fast-food trash, she moved forward until she located the steps that led to the second floor. The faint gleam of a candle overhead guided her to the upper hall. She had to cover her face to shut out the overwhelming stench of urine-soaked walls, and heaps of feces, both human and animal, that littered the floors. From far off, the pungent odor of kerosene was welcome. Someone had a heater to counter the chill.

Halfway down the hall, a sleeping woman was lying under some rags, her face hidden from sight, turned to the wall. She wore a large, vary-colored knit beret. Wisps of long gray hair escaped down her back. The legs and feet were encased in torn stockings and patent leather shoes covered with dust. She lay very quiet, seemingly unaware of the screams in the street below or the ranting of the mad man in the window.

Nicole entered the room adjacent to the one where the man held the baby and looked down in the street to judge Madam Tanya's position. The young woman in red sequins had recovered and had staggered several yards away to stand beside a rusting iron fence, but as Nicole watched, the woman moved away from the fence into the shadows and disappeared into the darkness. Madam Tanya stayed below the window, poised on the balls of her feet, moving like a basketball player, despite her size. Left to right she went as the crazy man dangled the baby, swinging it back and forth, all the while grunting his constant threats. Any moment, he could lose his grip and the baby would plummet below.

Nicole slipped silently into the room. To the left, was a makeshift bed of tangled covers and beyond it burned a candle on an overturned crate. There was an incredible pile of trash everywhere, half-eaten meals, plastic cups and paper plates, pizza boxes, and mountains of fast-food garbage littered every inch of the floor.

If I can catch him unaware and pull him backward into the room, she decided, I can grab the baby and run for the stairs. She held the gun in her left hand and moved toward the man, but at the last minute, he seemed to sense her approach and started to turn his head. Knowing that she had to act fast, with all of her strength, she reached out and grabbed a handful of the long greasy hair and jerked backward, catapulting him off his feet. At the same moment, the baby flew out of his hands, up into the air and out of the window. There was a loud searing crack that echoed in the room. Nicole dropped the hunk of hair, jumped back against the wall, and fanned the room with her gun. What was that sound? It sounded like the crack of a rifle but nothing moved in the shadows. She waited, and stared at the man lying on the floor. He neither moved nor made any noise. For the first time, she noted his odd clothing. Bare-chested, he wore leopard skin briefs and on his feet was a pair of gold-colored clogs. The woman's shoes? When she ventured closer to the twisted body, she realized what had made the loud, cracking sound, not a shot from another gun as she had expected, but the snapping of the bones of the man's neck. The massive dreadlocks lay at a strange angle, a white bone protruded from behind one ear. He must have died instantly when he turned his head, she surmised. Nicole hesitated, then made the sign of the cross over the body and tiptoed into the hall.

The old woman still lay against the wall in the hall, her face to the wall. I had better warn her to wake up and get far away from this place, she thought.

"Wake up, Grannie," she hissed, gently pushing the old woman's shoulder under the pile of rags. "Come on now. You must leave this house!" She pushed again, a bit harder. "Please, madam?"

The vary-colored beret fell away from the long gray hair, the head fell sideways, and Nicole found herself gazing into empty eye sockets. Bones were visible beneath the dark parchment of dried skin and in the jaw were a few yellowed teeth, bared in an expression of ultimate despair. Nicole estimated that the woman had been dead for several weeks, long enough for the skin to lose all moisture and turn it to leather. And people had come and gone through this hall, ate pizza, made love, made a baby, and all the while, a corpse lay decomposing in the hall. Again, Nicole made the sign of the cross.

"May God take you, old mother," she prayed in a whisper.

Shaken at the horrible discovery, she scrambled down the stairs and checked out the two rooms below. There was no one there, just more trash and broken pieces that once were furniture. She retraced her steps up the stairs, passed the remains of the corpse without looking at it and went into the room that held the body of the man. She knelt down beside him and pressed her fingers deep into his neck but found no pulse. Satisfied that he was dead, she crossed to the crate, picked up the burning candle, dropped it into the pile of dirty rags, and torn blankets that covered the bed. The flames spread quickly, igniting a greasy carton of half-eaten food, and flickered up the wall. Nicole stayed and watched until the flames reached the man's body, licked at the leopard skin briefs, and sizzled in the mass of dreadlocks. Then she turned away and raced down the stairs, dashed across the rain-drenched street to the van where she found Madam Tanya inside, seated on the sofa bed, with a triumphant smile on her broad face.

"I catch her like you tell me. Fly through air. Baby is very good okay?"

"Good, good," Nicole repeated, as she thrust the key into the ignition with trembling fingers. She laid the gun at her feet and took off through the dark, unfamiliar streets as fast as she could, wavering erratically up the hill toward the lights. Her heart was pounding, and she could not rid herself of the sight of the decomposing woman in the hall. Perhaps she was someone's mother, somebody's wife. It was not right! How had the woman come to this inglorious end in a condemned building? Nicole felt the urge to run back to Paris, hold her beautiful mother, and grandmother, and promise them that they would not die alone . . . never, never, never!

"Skinny, I am hungry. We did not have no supper," came a plaintive whine from the backseat. "And I need to go shopping. Need to find a grocery store."

"Yes, I had forgotten. We need to eat," agreed Nicole. "I think I see the lights of a shopping center up there ahead."

As they paused at a stoplight, the faint sounds of fire engines came closer, and then the swirling arc of red lights cut through the darkness as the trucks passed, their bells clanging in the quiet of the wet streets. Nicole watched them breathlessly.

"The lights are changed, Skinny. We can go."

"Yes, yes. It is just that I am so tired."

The light turned red again, and they had to wait.

"I see golden arches, and oh, here is grocery and pharmacy, everything I need, right here." Madam Tanya gathered her cape and got ready to leap from the van.

"There is a Holiday Inn across the street," Nicole pointed out. "I really need some rest." She was still seeing the dead woman's empty eyes, feeling the tension.

They pulled into the brightly lit parking lot of the shopping center and stopped near McDonald's. Madam Tanya clutched her cape together and quickly climbed out.

"You get food for me, please. I go to grocery store now. Oh, I take two Big Mac, big soda, double fries," she called back over her shoulder as she hurried off.

The rain had slowed down, but the parking lot was full of red, green, yellow, and white puddles, rainwater reflecting the lights from the stores. Nicole splashed through to the welcome warmth of the restaurant and stood in a very short line. The hour was late and customers few. She chose a spot near the window where she could watch for Madam Tanya to come out of the grocery store. As she was finishing her cheeseburger, the big woman appeared, carrying a large bag that she took into the van. Madam Tanya stayed in the van for quite a while, long enough to make Nicole curious. It is not like the galloping gourmet to stay away from food this long, thought Nicole. She finished the last of her Coke just as Madam Tanya breezed in and settled down to eat.

"I'm afraid it is cold, no?" asked Nicole. "You were gone so long."

"Oh, tastes very good," said Madam Tanya, without further explanation.

"I need to call in and I see a public phone booth over there. Have you got your walkie-talkie with you?"

"No. Why I need walkie-talkie? Nobody be after me. Eelie in the jail."

As Nicole got up to leave, Madam Tanya clutched at her jacket sleeve and looked her straight in the eye. "Something bother me about that black man. He in the window, then sudden, he gone! Baby fly out. Did you shoot the black man, Skinny?"

Nicole stared back. "I did not shoot the black man," she answered truthfully. She pulled away, crossed to the door and made her way to the telephone booth.

No one answered in the Alexandria office, and she left a message on the answering machine for Beau Jackson. "I'm on my way to North Carolina. The package is secure. I had to put two new tires on the van. I will call in again tomorrow." For one long moment, she laid her head against the cold glass of the telephone booth and recalled the sharp sound of the man's neck breaking. It had sounded like a shot. Had Madam Tanya possibly have heard that loud crack, all the way down in the street? Wearily, she made her way back to McDonald's but the booth was now empty so she returned to the van.

"Is Holiday Inn okay with you, Fatso? They have a full breakfast," she suggested as she climbed into the driver's seat.

"I think I stay in the van."

"I pay for a double anyway. May as well be comfortable."

"I will stay in the van," insisted Madam Tanya. "I got plenty blankets."

"Only if you keep the walkie-talkie on your pillow and promise to call me if anyone comes near the van or acts in a suspicious manner," Nicole said. Privately, she was looking forward to a snore-free night in a queen-sized bed with four pillows.

When they checked into the motel, Madam Tanya came into the room, used the bathroom and then ran the hot water until it steamed. She took a brand new half-gallon thermos and filled it partly with the hot water. When she noticed Nicole eying her curiously, she said, "Make a little tea later maybe." Then she brushed her teeth, hurried to the door and called out a goodnight.

"Lock the van!" ordered Nicole, watching until the gypsy was safely inside.

The local news came on the television at eleven. There were pictures of two tenement houses that had been completely destroyed by fire, and firemen, combing the wreckage, had uncovered two unidentified bodies, which were burned beyond recognition. The cameras panned the neighborhood but there was not a person in sight. No onlookers had come out to watch. No cars passed. Nicole turned off the light and fell to sleep.

* * *

North Carolina was several degrees warmer and the sun pouring through the window of the van from the east felt good on Nicole's shoulders as they headed south. Due to the free breakfast and Madam Tanya's second trip to the buffet, it was ten o'clock by the time they got on the road, and they were making good road time until Madam Tanya indicated it was necessary to find a place for a pit stop. Due to three cups of coffee, she began to search for a secluded area, but there was nary a bush nor a tree on the superhighway within walking distance.

Along 95, signs pointed off to small towns at various exits, so Nicole veered off, and they found themselves on lesser roads. Pretty soon, Madam Tanya spied a deserted service station and a small forested area just beyond and called out to Nicole to stop. As she hurried off past the station, Nicole turned to a nearby sign, which read 64, east, and threw up her hands in desperation. What had happened to south? She turned on the radio and caught the news; there was a brief mention of the fire in Richmond and the bodies had only been identified as transients. Her thoughts turned to Madam Tanya, who had been acting even stranger than usual, singing her Romany songs in a loud voice and shaking the tambourine in a monotonous rhythm, and wearing her cape in the van, although it was warm. But I kind of like her, Nicole decided, just look how quickly she agreed to try to catch that poor baby. The large object of her musings came nimbly around the side of the van and slid back the door. At the sound of the door opening, there was a high, wailing cry, and Nicole turned around quickly.

"Oooh, my poor finger," whined Madam Tanya, "caught in the big door!"

"Are you hurt? I have a Band-Aid in my tote bag."

"No, no, I be fine. You just drive. Go! Go!"

As soon as she was seated in the backseat, zinga, zinga, zinga went the tambourine, and the sofa bed began to bounce in time to the music. The Romany songs began again.

Holy Mary, Mother of God, prayed Nicole fervently, please send me a place on this road where I can get ten aspirins, a gallon of Coke, and perhaps a decent lunch that doesn't come from a paper sack! My poor head, Mother Mary, is not going to be able to stand this musical marathon much longer. Within a few miles, she saw ahead "The Happy Wayside," a combination hardware, grocery, and diner, with gas pumps. Thank you, Mary, she intoned silently as she pulled into the graveled area near the telephone booth.

"Why don't you go inside and get some food?" Nicole suggested. "I need to call in and put some gas in the van."

"You go get food. I stay here."

"Well . . . can you pump the gas then?"

"I no pump gas."

"At least, get out and walk around. Get some fresh air."

"Country people look at me funny. I stay here."

Nicole held her temper. "Suit yourself then."

Beau Jackson answered on the first ring and she could tell he was still angry with her. "Agent Laurent, where the hell is your location?"

"We are in North Carolina."

"Whereabouts in North Carolina, Laurent? That's a big state. Major Whitt is going ballistic not knowing where you are. He's flying to Charleston, and William Bonny, who is Tzoffke's brother, is going to pick him up and bring him to the farm, so you better quit messing around and get down there today!"

Nicole stopped a passing teenager and asked, "Could you tell me where we are?"

"The Happy Wayside," said the boy, with a shrug at the obvious.

"No, I mean, this road, where does it go?"

"On down here a piece and over the bridge, and you hit a town called Manteo. It's real pretty, and there's a place there what has Christmas all year round, the trees all lit up, even in summer. And there's the Aquarium," he added enthusiastically, looking for a moment, as if he might jump in the van and go along, but instead, he just grinned and headed on down the road.

"Thanks!" she called after him and turned back to the telephone. "We are in Manteo, almost. Why is Major Whitt checking up on me?"

"Just maybe, Agent Laurent, because you are turning a two-day trip into a tour of the eastern United States. Now, girl, get your butt down to South Carolina."

She hung up and crossed to the store, where she ordered lunch from the diner area. As she waited, she noticed that Madam Tanya got out of the van carrying a large bag of trash which she heaved into a dumpster at the rear. It appeared to be a lot for just HoHo boxes and candy wrappers. Wrapped in the cape, the big woman then walked around the van several times, her lips moving as if she were talking to herself, then climbed back inside. Nicole opted to eat inside the diner and took her time with a delicious chicken salad plate, a large Dr. Pepper, three aspirins, homemade pie and vanilla ice cream. As she ate, she thought about the phone call. Major Whitt was flying down to South Carolina. He may be already there. What a different sort he was from the old control, Gazar! Gazar never left any of his residences in and around Washington, or his place in Florida, to go into the field, so why was Whitt involving himself? Pondering this little bit of information, she finished her meal, and ordered for Madam Tanya, a hot barbecue plate, a quart of hot coffee and half of a lemon pie to go.

Nicole put the tray on the small table in the van, "Here's your lunch."

"Hmmm . . . everything looks very good, Skinny."

"And how is your sore finger?"

"Finger? Oh no, hurts."

Within a few miles, they reached the bridge, crossed it, and found themselves in Manteo, a town surrounded by water on every side. They passed through the streets and came to another longer bridge, which ended in an intersection of several merging roads. Nicole bore to the left, and beyond row after row of nearly empty beach cottages; she saw the wild, white-capped waves of a gray Atlantic Ocean. Above the sound of the waves pulsing at the shoreline, she heard the thin, wailing cry she had heard before. Madam Tanya began to slap the tambourine against her knee and croon softly. Nicole swerved the van into the nearest empty driveway and cut the motor.

She swung around angrily. "Fatso, I heard that! You have picked up a cat from somewhere. I want that cat out of this van right now."

"No," said Madam Tanya, looking around wildly. "I got no cat in here."

Nicole jumped down from the driver's seat, ran around to the right side, and slid the door aside. "Okay, Fatso, where is it?" she demanded.

Madam Tanya's eyes filled with tears as she reached far back on the sofa bed and brought out what appeared to be a bundle of her skirts and scarves. She turned back a corner of the material. A tiny pink face emerged; two dimpled hands flailed the air. It was a baby with soft dark hair, blue eyes, and skin so pure that it was almost translucent. The mouth, damp as a morning rose, blew a bubble, and smiled.

Nicole was speechless, her throat closed with emotion. It was the most beautiful baby she had ever seen. She finally slid the big door back in place and walked several yards away from the van. How could she cope with this situation? Nothing had prepared her how to handle the responsibility of a kidnapped baby—the woman's baby.

Holy Mother, why had the gypsy taken the woman's baby? The old wives tales of gypsies stealing babies had always circulated throughout Europe when she was small. Her grandmother, Mimi, would say, "Hide the child, Yvette, the gypsies are camped outside Paris." But as Nicole grew older and began to know gypsies, she understood that most were so poor that they could barely feed their own children. No one she knew had ever actually heard of a Rom kidnapping a gorgio child, and yet, here was Madam Tanya, and there was the baby!

Nicole heard footsteps behind her, and Madam Tanya descended to where she was standing, overlooking the ocean. She came up and stood beside Nicole, holding the baby in her massive arms. Nicole looked at the baby, who stared back through a tangle of skirts.

"Let us sit down by the dunes. It will be warmer there."

Reluctantly, Nicole took the baby as Madam Tanya lowered herself to the sand. Sea oats waved over their heads. Near the shoreline, a man walked his dog, and several cottages away, an elderly couple, bundled in blankets, sat on their deck drinking something hot. Nicole could see the steam rising from their cups.

"Why didn't you give the baby over to its mother as soon as you caught him? The poor woman must be out of her mind with worry!"

"I was stand under the window like you told me. You say, catch the baby, and I do catch her," argued Madam Tanya, defensively.

"Damn it, I didn't tell you to keep it!"

"You don't need call her it. She got a name. I call her Angel because she fall to me out of heaven, and I gonna keep her. I never have daughter, just three sons, and God say, here, Tanya, and drop her down on me."

Nicole looked at the baby curiously. "I thought it was a boy, and the man in the window thought it was a boy. Mon Dieu, I do not want to go all the way back!"

"Listen to what I say, I am in the rain and watch crazy man in the window. The woman she pull hard on my arm and she say to me, let her fall, she don't have no chance in life anyway. Then, one minute, she stand by the fence. She don't look back. She walk away in the rain. I don't know where she gone. I catch baby. You not come a long time. Mother never come back. I put baby in the vardo in a warm bed."

Let her fall. Let her fall. The terrible words hung in the air between them.

"Let me hold her," said Nicole softly. She took the baby and buried her face into the baby's neck, breathing in the unbelievable sweetness.

For most of an hour, they sat in the shelter of the dune until the baby became restless and thrust one small fist into her mouth, sucking fiercely.

"She hungry. And my legs go to sleep in the sand."

"You have to give her up. In the eyes of the law, what we have done is kidnapping because we have crossed state lines with a baby not our own," explained Nicole.

"Oh, she mine now," declared Madam Tanya.

"You have no birth certificate and no adoption papers, and what do you plan to tell your brother when you show up at his place with someone else's child?"

Madam Tanya's confidence wavered. "William, he take me and my son, Damon, for ten years. He and wife, Nancy, they got one boy, Billy, and one girl, Karen. You think he gonna throw away one more baby?"

"Kidnapping is a federal offense. We could go to jail for a long time, and then, Damon would have to grow up without a mother, no?"

"You say federal?" Madam Tanya asked in alarm. "The U.S. government?"

Prison held no fear but the threat of possible deportation was traumatic. Her life, and possibly Damon's too, would be over. Would they be sent back to Europe?

"But I got papers. I can sing 'Star Spandled Banner all the way through,' cried the big woman, rocking back and forth in anguish. She began to weep.

"Oh, Fatso!" Nicole put her hands over her face to keep from crying. Her heart was breaking but one of them had to stay strong and figure out what course to take. If only we could just take Angel and run away, just run away forever, she mused.

The baby gave her long, unhappy cry and shook them back to the reality of the moment. Nicole rose and held out her hand to Madam Tanya to help her rise from the sand. The baby began to fret in earnest.

"There is milk in the vardo. I mix while you sleep in Holiday Inn. She no trouble. She a good eater, like me."

When they reached the van, Nicole held out the baby to Madam Tanya. "Here, feed this starving child. I need to think this through. I am going for a short run. It always helps to clear my head. And Angel definitely needs changing!"

"I buy little Huggies. See how small?"

Madam Tanya reached behind the sofa bed and pulled out a big pink box. Angel lay patiently. A tiny pink bottom came into view as two little feet kicked in the air. They both admired such perfection. Was that a smile? Oh yes, a smile!

Nicole found her running shoes and put them on. "Lock the doors and keep your walkie-talkie next to you. I will run just down this road a bit, no?"

"We okay. We be fine," agreed Madam Tanya. She began to sing as she poured a bottle of milk from the new thermos.

Nicole turned away from the van and began to jog slowly. She was out of practice and it took a full mile before her legs responded to the old cadence. The past days had been full of too much driving and too much food, and now, there was a baby! That woman is going to kill me if I don't get her home soon, she thought dourly, I always do—seven miles, and here I am, already winded at three. She loped toward a bench at the side of the road, flopped down and rubbed her tingling muscles, thinking of Angel. She thought about the hellhole the baby had come from, the corpse rotting in the hallway and the mother who said, "Let her fall." Would that woman recall a big blue van? And would she remember Madam Tanya in the street? Would she go to the police? Somehow, Nicole felt she wouldn't involve the police. The baby was obviously not related to the man in the window. He didn't even know it was female.

A long, sleek Lincoln approached, pulled up beside the bench, and an elderly woman, looking chic in a flowered straw hat, rolled down the window.

"Could you tell us where to find the Angel of the Sea Church? We're here for the wedding tomorrow and want to make sure we are in the right place so that we won't arrive too late. You know how short the services are these days. You hardly get to see the dress."

"I'm sorry," Nicole answered. "I'm a visitor here myself."

"Thanks anyway, dear, we'll find it!"

The big car continued down the road, and Nicole watched its progress until it halted a half-mile away, turned right into a parking lot, and disappeared from sight. Angel of the Sea Church. Curious, she began to jog in that direction.

The church sat back several yards from the sandy road with a large parking area in front. It was an old, attractive building of gray cedar shakes, with an aqua trim. To one side was a longer, newer building, possibly a Sunday school. The front doors were open. A florist was delivering flowers, and the lady from the Lincoln and her elderly gentleman companion were peering into the dark interior of the church. They all went inside, returned shortly, laughing and talking. The florist closed the doors, and they all drove away as Nicole watched from behind the screened porch of the house next door.

As soon as they were out of sight, Nicole ran across the parking lot and tried the doors, which were locked. She unscrewed the antenna from her walkie-talkie, picked the lock, and went inside. The darkness smelled cloyingly sweet from the masses of blossoms that banked the altar, and were attached to springy, white sheer bows, on every post of every pew down the center aisle.

Nicole stood in the foyer, genuflected to the statue of Jesus over the altar and repeated her Hail Marys over several times. She looked around for a statue of the Virgin, and seeing none, raised her eyes up to the ceiling and prayed for guidance.

The message came loud and clear. "Suffer the little children to come unto me," she quoted. Nicole shivered. "Holy Mother, guide me."

When she returned to the van, she found it empty and for a moment, she felt panic as the thought occurred that Madam Tanya may have taken Angel and tried to run away, but then, behind the dune she saw the flurry of colorful skirts blowing in the wind from the ocean. Madam Tanya held the precious bundle against her breast. When Nicole approached them, she could tell that Madam Tanya had been crying. Her eyes were half-closed and puffy, and Nicole didn't have the heart to upbraid her for leaving the van.

"You realize we must give her up."

"I know."

"Let me hold her," said Nicole, and gently took the baby.

"I have put a lifetime blessing on this child," announced the Ababina, seriously. "She will suffer no more the hard life. She will live in a mansion with grass all around and have many pretty dresses. My heart is lighter now that I have done this."

"She can have pretty dresses now," promised Nicole. "I saw a big K-Mart store on the other road as we came in. I'll buy her everything she needs. We will dress little Angel up like a princess." She gazed down at the baby in her arms, with her fair skin, blue eyes, and soft dark hair. Again came the suspicion, who was this angel child who had fallen from the sky?

* * *

According to the announcement on the outside bulletin board of the church, the wedding would take place at 10:00 a.m., so Nicole and Madam Tanya left their motel by seven, ate a quick breakfast and were in the driveway of a vacant cottage several yards down the road by eight. They watched as a man, possibly the church janitor, let himself in, came out front with a broom, and tackled the sandy walkway. He got into his truck and drove away a few moments later. Then, the Minister—he was wearing the collar—came and unlocked the doors for any early-comers, glanced inside, got back in his car and left.

"You have fed and changed her? She has not kicked out of her new socks, has she? I think they are too big, no?" asked Nicole, anxiously inspecting Angel.

"Did you write her name on the paper? Put her name Angel on the paper?" insisted Madame Tanya, half sick with worry. "Did you put she a poor orphan and need a good family?"

"Oh, shut up! You know I did! If you love that baby, give her to me!"

Madam Tanya kissed the sweet pink forehead, handed Angel to Nicole, and turned her face away, unable to see her go.

Nicole looked carefully down the road, crossed swiftly to the church parking lot, and holding the new carrier close to her chest, dashed inside the church. The flowers smelled sweet, the white bows on each pew seemed to stand at attention, as if waiting for something special to happen. Nicole placed Angel, in her carrier, in front of the altar and tucked the note with the name, Angel, and instructions for the formula for the milk, into the soft, new blanket. She could not look at the baby. She turned and fled down the aisle without looking back.

It was risky, but they stayed in the van across the road until they could be sure that Angel had been discovered. A long, white van arrived at the church at nine o' clock, and four young girls in pastel dresses alighted. They stopped in the parking lot and helped each other pin wreaths of flowers into their hair. A second white van arrived and four young men in white tuxedos jumped out and joined the girls. They were all talking and laughing excitedly when the Minister arrived, in full clerical robes and indicated that the church was open, and they were to go inside.

The doors opened, and Nicole and Madam Tanya both leaned forward anxiously.

"I hear her crying!" said Madam Tanya. "What they do to my Angel?"

"She is fine."

Other wedding guests arrived; the parking lot filled with cars. The sheriff's car pulled up to the church doors, and a station wagon, with some sort of seal on the side, parked behind the sheriff. Social services, thought Nicole. It was time to leave.

Nicole slowly pulled the van into the sandy road and drove away in the opposite direction from the church. In the back of the van, Madam Tanya was sobbing, the skirts and scarves that had cradled the baby held close to her face.

Miles flew by on the highway and, eventually, Nicole heard the rhythm of deep sleep. Exhausted from the ordeal, Madam Tanya was snoring. Route 17 ran down the Atlantic coastline through New Bern, Jacksonville, and Wilmington. Still, she headed south; she could hear Madam Tanya, now awake, moving about on the sofa bed. She glanced over her shoulder and could see that the gypsy was writing on the notepad, keeping the journal.

"Fatso, I really need to eat," she said.

"If you hungry, we stop. Is okay. Where are we?"

"According to the map, this is Cherry Point. Near Myrtle Beach," answered Nicole, in surprise. She had no idea when they had crossed the state line into South Carolina.

"Oh, we not far from my home! There be a good cafeteria at Myrtle Beach and don't take too much money!" exclaimed Madam Tanya, brightening up at the idea of food.

"Don't worry about money, Fatso. Have anything you like."

"I know where I am now. This is all familiar, very good to me. My brother, William, his farm is near the big swamp, not so far now. Soon, I see my Damon."

"Big swamp?" Nicole said, glancing down at the map again. "Do you mean Francis Marion National Forest? Is that it?"

"You got it, Skinny. Big swamp."

Within the next few miles, they sighted the cafeteria and this time, Madam Tanya eagerly elected to go inside. Sometimes, the big woman seemed secure about entering public places and others she refused. It became obvious that she had been to this cafeteria many times before. Several of the employees spoke to her and smiled as she took a tray and waltzed down the food aisle, choosing a small but gourmet selection.

Nicole wanted a bottle of wine but settled for coffee to go with her pasta and salad. They ate quietly, thinking of Angel, wondering who was holding her now.

"What were you writing in the journal?" asked Nicole.

"Our journey, like you say. Here, you can read." Madam Tanya handed the notebook across the table.

Nicole scanned it. There were short paragraphs, some mentioning towns they had passed through, and what food they had eaten, but not a word about the encounter with Eelie, or the machete that lay under the driver's seat. There was nothing about a baby, their Angel. They looked at each other. Some things were best left unsaid.

"Thank you, Fatso. I'll give this to Major Whitt, he will be at the farm."

They left the cafeteria and got into the van. The last forty miles seemed to pass like a dream, knowing that their time together was almost over. Soon, they were turning off into the long, dirt road that led to William Bonny's farm. It was a road of tall pines and dense with the green shiny branches of magnolias; the air was sweet with the smell of fragrant southernwoods. Suddenly, they reached a large clearing, and there was the farmhouse, a rambling old two-storied colonial, surrounded on three sides by wide porches.

Three children were playing on a swing set, but they stopped as the van rolled into the yard and one, a handsome, chubby boy, ran forward, laughing and jumping. At that same moment, Major Whitt came out of the house, followed by an older man, who, even at a distance appeared familiar, and as they approached, Nicole recognized her old friend, Bull Durham. Behind them came a younger, taller version of Madam Tanya, her brother William, with his wife. Their two children came across the yard from the swings.

"My Damon!" shouted Madam Tanya, scrambling heavily down from the van as soon as it rolled to a stop. She clutched the chubby boy into her arms and turned proudly to Nicole. "My son. He big for twelve years old, don't you think? And these childrens is Billy, and the girl, she is Karen. Oh, I miss you all!"

Major Whitt, looking as sharp as usual in his flight jacket and neatly creased chinos, came over and shook Nicole's hand and made some remark about a long trip. Bull Durham gave her a bear hug and pulled her out of hearing of the others.

"Got to brief you on what's going down at this end. The last two of that gypsy musical troupe, Bela and Susie, have been seen around Charleston, asking about the location of the farm but the Feds are on it, the INSs, but I'm here until they're picked up," Durham confided. "William is wise but there's no need to worry the kids and ladies."

"I can stay if there is danger," offered Nicole, looking anxiously at Madam Tanya. She had brought her all this way, and she wouldn't leave her now if there were trouble.

"We got it covered," Durham assured her.

"Any news about the other gypsy girl, Magda?"

"She was picked up at a clinic. She was having bad morning sickness. She's being held for deportation along with her nutty boyfriend, Eli or something like that, as soon as he gets out of the hospital. He claims he got into a bar fight and got half his toes shot off. You don't know nothing about that, do you, Nicole?"

"Me?" she answered vaguely. "Poor fellow." It was unlikely that Eelie would admit he had been stalking his own mother with intent to kill when he got shot on that lonely road in Amish country. She remembered what Madam Tanya had said about Magda's pregnancy. So it had been true. Maybe I should have paid more attention to the Ababina's mumbo-jumbo, thought Nicole. She did seem able to tap into something otherworldly.

"It happened in Pennsylvania," probed Durham, eying her suspiciously. "Weren't you in Pennsylvania, Nicole?"

"It's a big state," shot back Nicole as she walked away.

Major Whitt approached her. "Would you like to stay here tonight or get on the road? I expect you're pretty tired from the trip." He waited for an answer. "Or we could head north and stop at a motel."

"What do you mean, we?"

"I'll be driving back to Washington with you. The Feds are anxious to get their surveillance van back, and the sooner we get started, the sooner they can have it."

Nicole shrugged wearily. "Whatever you say. You are the boss now, no?" She walked a few feet away. "I must say good-bye to Madam Tanya before we go."

William and Madam Tanya were resting on the porch steps and as they watched Nicole come toward them across the wide, grassy lawn, William shook his head and looked at his sister.

"You trusted that little gorgio woman with your life? She doesn't look like she could be of much help in time of big trouble."

"Oh yes, I could trust her very good. You be surprised about that little gorgio woman." Madam Tanya turned to her brother and changed into the Rom language. "Do you remember this, William? Shuk chi hal pe la royasa."

He grinned. "I remember. Things are not always as they seem. Beauty cannot be eaten with a spoon. Well, she brings you home okay, so all be well."

Nicole approached the porch.

"I'll be going now."

"I'll get your things from the vardo, I mean van, Tanya," William offered.

He called out to Damon. "Come on, boy, help me get your mother's things."

Major Whitt went into the house to retrieve his flight bag while they were unloading the many shopping bags and baskets full of Madam Tanya's possessions. Damon stepped inside and was busily handing things down to William as Madam Tanya supervised, but when Damon attempted to lift the heavy blue basket full of roses, she called out to him sharply to put it down and leave it in the van.

"Not that one, my darling!" She turned to Nicole. "These are for you, Skinny, the roses and the basket, for you remember me and what we do together."

"Oh no, it is too much!" exclaimed Nicole. "How could I ever forget you?"

They put their arms around each other and held on tight. Together, they walked off a little way under the trees, thinking of Eelie, thinking of Angel.

"Tell me something, Fatso," Nicole said lightly. "That stranger that stands behind my shoulder, can you see him now? Is it Major Whitt?"

Madam Tanya broke into her hearty laugh. "So you believe in the Ababina now?" She roared as if it were a big joke. "No, it is not Major Whitt, Skinny!"

They strolled back to the van, and Nicole climbed into the driver's seat from habit as Major Whitt threw his bag into the backseat.

"I'll drive if you like," he offered, but she had switched on the ignition. He climbed into the rear seat and looked around for a seat belt.

They waved good-bye and as Nicole turned the van around, the machete slid out and landed under the table on the passenger's side. Major Whitt stared at it.

"Just what is that machete doing in here, Agent Laurent?" he demanded.

"It's a souvenir," Nicole answered, and kicked it back under the driver's seat.

"Now, Agent Laurent, remember. Go north!" Whitt said, as he settled back on the sofa bed. "I'll take a little nap and spell you at the wheel later."

"Okay," Nicole agreed slowly driving out of the long, dirt road to Rt. 17 and turned south.

Chapter Eight

A Door Closes

Starting half asleep, with sweet little kisses, his passion mounted as his hands caressed Nicole's body like a gentle, tingling massage over the shoulders, down her upper arms, tilting her breasts toward his chest. Then, kneading her back, with wonderfully strong strokes, drawing her closer and closer into him, his breathing became deeper. Perspiration dampened his, as yet unshaven beard, and trickled down her cheeks and neck.

Nicole, eyes shut, mouth slightly open, pushed against him, her arms around his waist.

"Now, Rene," she whispered, and thrust against him.

Despite the heat of the July sun pouring through the open bedroom window, she flipped the pale blue linen sheet over their bodies, making a cocoon, in which they moved together, the salty sweat blending them so tightly that they did not know, or care, where one body stopped and the other began.

He groaned, "Don't stop!" His fingers dug into her back.

The room tilted. They gasped and fell apart. The sheet bound their legs and they kicked it to the bottom of the bed, and then lay naked and unmoving. After a while, Rene turned and kissed her. "I want you to look especially beautiful tonight and wear the Vera Wang, and I'll pick out something from the safe, diamonds?"

"I want to wear the flowered thing that Ms. Honey Holm gave me," Nicole said. "It's pale yellow and aqua on white silk. Maybe some aquamarines would go well."

"But, you know it is a custom original! What if someone sees you and recognizes that it is a hand-me-down from the Holm woman?"

"You get all my designer clothes from Encore, Encore. They all belonged to someone else."

"The originals would bankrupt me," said Rene gruffly. "You will wear the Wang, Nicole."

"No."

"You must look exquisite. This is a party of my peers. They only have the jewelry designer awards fete every ten years, and it is very important to me. I expect to be first. I want that award. I want to be number one!"

"Which design did you submit?"

"Mrs. Castle's emerald bracelet."

"But," Nicole stared at him. "You never made that bracelet, Rene! The whole staff hunted and hunted for it, and we were all upset because she had to leave Paris without it."

"We do not submit the object, just the design. No one need know I never made it!"

"It seems deceptive," argued Nicole, getting up from the bed and walking to the window, where she closed it firmly. She set the thermostat for the air conditioning. "What if you win? And they want a photograph?"

Rene at first appeared alarmed, and then merely looked annoyed. "They wouldn't do that! They have my design. They can photograph that." He threw the sheet aside and stomped to the bathroom. "You will wear the Wang, diamonds, the crescent brooch, and matching earrings." He slammed the bathroom door, and the water began to run furiously into the marble shower.

"No," repeated Nicole, to the closed door. She crossed to the closet, opened the plastic storage bag and inspected Mrs. Honey's lovely gift dress. "We're going to a party tonight," she told it, and put it back into the closet.

Naked, she strolled into the kitchen and began to prepare the coffee. She cradled her breasts and leaned against the cool tile of the countertop, waiting for the coffee. And thought about Major Whitt. He had called her tiny apartment twice in the last month, saying she was needed on special assignments in the States, but she had refused to go. Mimi had not made the effort to dress for church last Sunday but had insisted that

Yvette and Nicole go without her. Her beloved Mimi was failing. Mimi's friend, Gerta, came over to the apartment and stayed while Yvette and Nicole went to Mass and prayed.

* * *

The prestigious Association of Jewelers and Custom Designers had out done themselves in preparation for this decade's honors event and although there were less than two hundred members, these men, and a few women, were the elite of their trade. Some worked independently and others like Rene, had shops, or arrangements with shop outlets, which carried one artist's name exclusively.

The smaller, but most elegant ballroom of the Monarch Hotel, had been decorated with a thousand tiny lights in clear and gem colors, cascading on invisible wires from the ceiling, and more tiny lights lay in trails among the floral arrangements on the white linen tablecloths. The effect was as if diamonds, rubies, emeralds, and sapphires were falling like a gentle summer shower, and as the guests entered the room, each paused and gazed up in delight at the dazzling display.

There would be dinner, followed by a speech and finally the award ceremony, which would honor the ten most talented. The design entries, sixty were accepted this year, were framed in identical narrow black frames and hung on the wall behind the speaker's dais.

As the guests entered, they moved slowly to the back wall, allowing themselves to be admired and greeted by friends, the men in formal black, the women in gowns carefully chosen to compliment a selection of jewelry that would be the source of conversation and speculation for months to come. There were diamonds on black, or red, emeralds on white silk, topaz on gold satin—the chosen gown must be of top quality but must never, never, outshine the jewels. They stopped at each of the selected entries, analyzing the execution, the originality—the jewelers estimated sheer weight of the gems and projected enormous sums if the finished product found its way to Saudi, or America, even Switzerland.

Rene dawdled in the parking lot, greeting friends as they arrived, while Nicole leaned against the new BMW they had rented that morning. She wore the Ms. Honey dress, the diamond crescent brooch with matching earrings and short light brown wig with highlights. This early in the evening, her dark eyes were already glazing over with boredom. She was thinking about a refreshing run around LeGrand's farm in the cool of dawn and was not aware that anything was happening until she heard Rene's strangled gasp and felt his fingers tighten about her upper arm as if he would wring it off.

Coming directly toward them was Gunther Holm and Ms. Honey, with Rene's archrival in the jewelry game, Marcel Charme. They were waving! Rene looked as if he was ready to thrust Nicole and the dress under the car, but she shook him off and stepped forward with a welcoming smile.

"Hello, Hello, it's so good to see you. What a surprise!" said Nicole.

"Nicole, darling, you're so lovely!" Ms. Honey gave her a hug, turned and embraced Rene. "You see what I'm wearing—the yellow diamonds—a Rene Laurent! Of course, Marcel was terribly upset, so I had to wear his earrings!" She touched two simple coils of gold almost buried in her blond hair.

"Good fortune on your entry, Rene," said Marcel. "I have a piece accepted also, just a little . . ."

"Yes, yes," nodded Rene. "Shall we go in?" He grabbed Nicole's elbow and pulled her forward and the others followed them into the hotel. "I'll never forgive you for embarrassing me like this!" he hissed under his breath. "I told you to wear the Wang!"

"Poor, poor Rene!" laughed Nicole. "I don't think she even recognized it."

They all exclaimed over the lighting, and the flowers in abundance, their fragrance competing with the heavy perfumes of the women.

Rene, stiff with apprehension and yet curious, guided them to the designs on the rear wall. There they hung, the best of the best, sixty exceptionally beautiful creations. Marcel proudly pointed to his entry, and Nicole heard Rene give an involuntary little grunt of dismay. The Charme entry was a bracelet of emeralds. Rene's entry was a bracelet of emeralds. There were bound to be comments and comparisons. The two men graciously admired each other's work and moved quickly on through the line and on into the ballroom to find their place cards at the dining tables. The Holms and their host were at a table across the room near the dais. Rene and Nicole found their seats at the rear near the door where Rene flung himself down angrily.

"I think he knew what I submitted to the committee."

"How, Rene? The design was in the safe."

"Somehow he knew. Perhaps Henri-Paul in one of his moods . . ."

"Only you and I have the keys."

"My god, what will happen to me next?" he fumed. He turned to signal one of the many white-coated waiters. "Some wine here, a decent white, very dry—."

"Perhaps we should wait for dinner?" suggested Nicole, knowing he had had two drinks before they left home.

"I'm nervous. This is the most important night of my life. I see Jean Claude, and who is that fairy he is with? And there is Madame Grieg—she is a contender—did you see that mound of pearls in her necklace design? I must mingle."

Rene leaped up and began to greet old friends, shaking hands and joking as he went from table to table.

Nicole sipped the wine and regarded the menu. Caviar, tiny crab quiche, a fish dish, lamb, asparagus, everything with its own sauce, of course. Halfway through the list, her thoughts turned back to Madam Tanya and breakfast at the Harvest Home Motel restaurant. She looked at the painfully created small French portions and laughed aloud. Where were the barbecued ribs in a honey glaze? Ah, Madam Tanya, you really know how to eat, she sighed.

Rene returned to their table when the first courses arrived, his face flushed and looking more confident.

"Many of them raved about my design. They begged to see the creation itself."

"I bet Mrs. Castle would too," murmured Nicole, chasing a morsel of crab hiding beneath the garnish in her soup.

Rene sipped his wine and pretended not to hear. He toyed with his soup. He wished the evening were over, and he was standing in his store, wondering where the most visible spot for the award would be. As his customers entered the door, the award must be immediately conspicuous, yet not obviously so. It should be in line with the door and to the back, and with a special subtle lighting to draw the eye. First prize was a sterling cup. The other nine awards were engraved bronze plaques.

"Excuse me, Madam Laurent?" said a voice behind their chairs.

Nicole turned. "Yes?"

"I am sorry, but there is an urgent telephone call from a Sister Mary Celeste. Would you take it in the manager's office? It is private there."

"The hospital," said Nicole. She dropped the fork under the table. Her napkin floated to the floor as she stood up.

"Rene, it is Mimi! We have to go!"

"Are you insane?" Rene answered angrily. "We will leave when the affair is over, and not a moment before. Mimi is always having her little spells."

"It is the hospital, Rene. They would not call me here if it were not serious, no? Maman must have told them where we were."

"We're not leaving."

"You stay, but I have to go."

"You will not go either," insisted Rene, pulling Nicole down into her chair. He turned to the hotel clerk. "Tell Sister that you could not locate Madam Laurent." He grasped Nicole by the wrist to prevent her from rising again.

"Let me go, Rene," Nicole said, in a voice so cold that he slowly released her arm. She stood and turned to the clerk. "Show me to the telephone, please."

"If you go, Nicole, do not come back to my apartment, ever! We are through. It is over!" his voice rose, and people were staring in their direction.

Across, Ms. Honey Holm, sensing trouble, had begun to push back her chair as if to come to Nicole's aid, while Gunther and Marcel appeared to try to talk her out of interfering.

Nicole rushed out of the room and hurried the clerk through the lobby. He indicated the manager's office, and happy to be out of a hostile situation, disappeared into the nearest elevator.

"Hello, this is Nicole Laurent."

"Dear, we have your grandmother in intensive care. She is very ill, and you must come at once. It is a matter of time, dear. You must prepare yourself for this eventuality," warned Sister Mary Celeste. "When God calls one of his children . . ."

The Nun's voice droned into empty air. The telephone dangled over the desk and fell to the floor as the office door swung shut behind Nicole. She ran through the lobby, her long gown billowing behind, and out into the street. There was not a taxi in sight. Rene had the keys to the rented BMW in his pocket. The hospital was four blocks away through the narrow, crowded city streets. Nicole tore off her shoes and failing to fit them into her tiny formal purse, threw them into the first trashcan she passed. She wrenched the wig from her head and tossed it in as well. The sidewalk picked at the soles of her stocking feet, and the gown swirled around her legs, but she ran faster than she had ever run before. People stopped, stared, and stepped aside at the ethereal apparition flying by.

She took the three steps of the hospital with a single leap and fell into the broad arms of Sister Mary Celeste, who had been waiting just inside the door.

"Come with me to the chapel, dear. We need to pray when the end is near," said the nun in a doleful voice.

"Where is Mimi?" demanded Nicole.

"Come to the chapel . . ."

"If you don't take me, I'll scream this place down until someone answers. I'm starting on this floor! Where is my mother? Is she with Mimi?"

"Calm yourself, child. Remember the sick and dying," cautioned the nun, as she resigned herself to leading the way to Mimi Longet's small room. "Your mother has been with her all day and without a bite to eat or a drop to drink, with such devotion!"

Mimi lay like a broken doll, her thin face a waxen mask, but she turned her head as Nicole entered the room. Her eyes found Nicole and a smile touched her lips.

Yvette half lay on the end of the bed, seated in a wooden straight chair, her head resting on her arm. She looked barely able to breathe. And to Nicole's surprise, Enrico Garibaldi sat silently in a dim corner of the room, his dark expressive eyes full of tears, and a crumpled handkerchief in his hand.

"Maman, I am here."

"Nicole," acknowledged Yvette. She tried to sit up straight in the chair.

Nicole crossed to the bed and kissed Mimi's cheek, which was cold to the touch, and reached for her grandmother's hands.

"Nicole, you have no shoes," said Yvette.

"No shoes?" echoed Enrico, leaning forward to gaze at Nicole's torn stockings. "Yvette, should I go and buy your daughter some shoes?"

"Don't worry about it," said Nicole. She sat down on the other side of the bed. "Why didn't you call me sooner?"

"I did. Rene did not tell you?"

"No."

"He must have forgotten in the excitement of his big dinner. He said it was important. At the Monarch Hotel."

"That is a fine hotel," nodded Enrico.

Nicole turned to Mimi. "How are you, my darling?"

"She can no longer speak," whispered Enrico. "She does not speak all day."

Yvette began to cry and put her head again down on the bed.

"I am here now," said Nicole. "Please Enrico, take Maman and get her to eat a little and have a glass of wine."

"There is a place just across the street."

"I cannot leave my mother," protested Yvette.

"I'll be with her. I promise to be right here, and Sister is in the hall."

"Yvette, mi amore, listen to Nicole. I could stand some coffee myself."

"Oh, Enrico, I was not thinking of you!" cried Yvette. "You must be hungry."

"It is nothing!" Enrico spread his hands. "I am too fat anyway."

"Promise you will stay, Nicole," said Yvette, rising shakily from the chair. "Enrico must have something to eat."

"We will be just there," Enrico pointed. "If there is a change."

Mimi did not turn her head to watch them leave. Her faded blue eyes gazed at the ceiling. Her lips moved but no sound escaped her lips. She seemed to be praying, looking directly into the eyes of God.

It won't be long, Nicole realized. In a way, she has already left us. She went to the door and looked in the hall.

"Sister, will you come pray with us?" Nicole asked. "We can say the words of the twenty-third psalm. It is her favorite. I think it would comfort her."

Sister Mary Celeste entered the room, her rosary clinking beneath her black robe, and together they knelt beside the bed.

Nicole held Mimi's hands as the familiar words drifted over the bed and when the prayer was done, Sister rose heavily from her knees and trod back to her place in the hall.

After a while, Nicole realized that Mimi's hands had grown icily still. She covered them with the bedspread. Mimi stared at the ceiling, unblinking. Nicole placed her fingers to the side of Mimi's neck, then to the wrists. There was no pulse, no beat of life. Mimi had passed away at some time during the saying of the prayer.

Still, Nicole sat by the side of the bed. Ten, fifteen minutes, then twenty. She was reluctant to let go. Then an odd thing occurred. As Nicole watched, a puff, like smoke, a pale blue haze, hovered over Mimi's body and just hung there like a cloud for several minutes, and as Nicole stared, the haze lifted slowly, rose to the ceiling, and dissolved. Nicole was so astonished that she was unable to move, unable to speak.

A clock somewhere struck twelve. Jolted into reality, Nicole staggered to the door, shaken by the experience.

"Sister, call the priest. It is time," she managed to say.

She sank down in the chair and began to sob. Life, as she had known it, would never be the same. Her beloved Mimi was gone.

*   *   *

At 2:00 a.m., having rejected a ride with Yvette and Enrico, Nicole stood in the street looking for a taxi. Her short dark hair dangled in damp curls, her eyes were puffed from crying. She had shed her dirty, torn panty hose in the hospital restroom and stood barefooted in the gutter. Two drivers, noticing her appearance, suspected an angry boyfriend lurking nearby and had hastily sped away. Finally, a third driver took a chance. Nicole climbed into the backseat and gave him the address of her own small flat just a few miles away.

The first thing she noticed was the blinking light on the telephone signaling a message. She ignored it, supposing it would be Rene, and she was not able to deal with him yet. He would find out soon enough that Mimi had died. Perhaps Yvette had already called him. Nicole stripped out of the gown and carefully unpinned the diamond crescent brooch, then removed the earrings, which she would return to the shop or send back by bonded messenger. She did not want to see him. She took a shower, put on her Mickey Mouse sleep shirt and lay on the bed, exhausted, yet unable to fall asleep. The light on the telephone blinked on, distracting all efforts at sleep. She got up and pressed the message bar.

"Paris, we have a problem. Get in touch."

It was Beau Jackson's voice. What time was it in America? Should she use the home number he had given her? She wanted to tell him about Mimi. She needed someone to say, "I'm sorry. I do share your pain." Beau would understand. She dialed the home number.

"Beau—," she could hear the tears rising in her throat. "Beau?"

For a moment, there was silence.

"Nicole, is that you? Your voice sounds funny—are you okay?"

"It's Mimi."

"She sick? Bad this time, right? Anything I can do?"

"Mimi died tonight. I can't take an assignment. I can't do anything. The funeral is day after tomorrow."

Nicole began to sob into the silent telephone. She couldn't seem to stop.

"Hold on, baby, hold on," Beau finally said. "She has no more pain, baby. God's taking care of her now. You hold yourself together. Now get some rest. Mimi would want you to take care of your mama at a time like this, so you gotta be strong!"

"I will," she promised. "I must take care of Maman, no?"

"You got it, baby. Be strong!"

"I'll try. I really will. Good night Beau."

Nicole hung up. There were no other messages to answer. The blinking light lay dark. She lay back on the bed. I was only thinking of myself, she thought as her eyes closed. Maman will need me.

* * *

The next day was remote and fuzzy like a bad dream in slow motion. Nicole had to pick out a burial dress for Mimi. She chose a blue silk with a high lace collar and cuffs in an off-white color. The death notice, old friends from the old apartment house where they used to live and new ones, people at church. All had to be notified. Ready the burial plot next to Grandfather and the two babies who died, one stillborn the other just three months old.

Nicole stood in front of the clothes closet, wondering, in her grief, why she was standing and staring at her clothes. Something black, she finally realized, as she pushed aside her jeans and reached to the back. There was a linen suit with a long skirt and jackets, and a plain shift, sleeveless.

She sat down on the bed. "Mimi, if you were here, we'd smoke a pack together, drink a bottle of wine, and jump out of the window. That's the way to go. Have a good time and bam! No more worries. No more pain." She looked at the little snapshot she carried in her purse. My darling Mimi.

The telephone rang loudly. It was Yvette. "Nicole, Rene is trying to reach you. He thought you were with me. He read the notice in the paper and is very upset."

"In the paper—already?"

"Enrico took care of it."

"Enrico has not returned to Italy?"

"He will stay with me for the funeral."

"Well—," Nicole hesitated, hearing something in her mother's voice that was totally unexpected. A sudden independence? And Enrico, what was the future of Enrico? "Should I come over right away? Do you need me Maman?"

"Of course! I want you with me, Cherie."

"I'm coming, Maman."

* * *

The day of the funeral, Rene arrived early at Yvette's flat, dressed in his only black suit. It was silk, and must have been very hot in the July weather. His silver hair was shining, and he had acquired a flattering tan. His shirt was white, his tie blue.

When Nicole walked in, she looked at Rene and saw one of the most handsome men in Paris. Then he spoke.

"I was reading the review of the jeweler's association awards dinner," he said, looking over the silver-rimmed half glasses that he wore only to read.

"A very prestigious occasion," Enrico commented. He always seemed impressed by Rene, his openness with people, his sort of personal assurance and perfection, although Enrico himself was successful in his own right. "Many important people."

"Hello, Rene."

"Hello, Nicole. I'm sorry about Mimi. A sad occasion."

"Yes."

"We must go to the church," said Yvette. "We must be first, as a family. And Gerta and her daughters will sit with us as she was Mimi's friend all of her life. She took her to her own lawyer to write a will, although there was not much."

"Maman, I don't want to hear this. Rene, am I to ride with you?"

They all looked at her in surprise. Obviously, they had not heard about the altercation at the award's dinner and Rene's threat to her, not to come back to the apartment, if she left him at the table.

"Of course. You are still my wife."

"What do you mean, Rene?" asked Yvette anxiously looking from one to the other.

"Rene wants a divorce," stated Nicole. "He has wanted one for quite a while. He even expressed his wishes to Marie."

Yvette looked baffled. "To our maid?"

"Shut up, Nicole, this is not the time," warned Rene, his face flushing angrily.

"Nor the place," agreed Nicole. She pinned a black lace headpiece to her hair and buttoned the black linen jacket. "Shall we go?"

The ride to the church was in chilly silence.

The ceremony was surprisingly well attended, with even the store merchants from their old neighborhood arriving in a van together and so many people from the garment district, who had worked with Mimi, and Yvette.

Mimi was to be buried in the churchyard next to her husband and the babies. As the family lined up on the grass next to the open pit, something drew Nicole's glance to a mausoleum about thirty feet away. Before the ornate door stood two men. Nicole blinked, looked down at the grave, then back at the men, one large and black, the other tall and blond. Beau Jackson and Major Whitt had come to pay their last respects. Nicole saw the flowers they held awkwardly in their hands. When the service ended, the mourners filed by placing their floral tributes beside the grave. Jackson and Whitt joined the line and placed flowers with the others, passing just inches away.

"Thank you," Yvette was saying. "Thank you for coming. How lovely—how kind."

"Thank you," echoed Nicole. She raised her eyes and looked directly at Major Whitt. He turned slightly toward her, paused, and then followed Jackson up a small hill.

"Nicole, who are those people?" asked Yvette, her gaze following the two strange men as they disappeared behind the stonewall that led out of the cemetery to the street.

"I don't know, Maman."

After the graveside ceremony, the mourners returned to Yvette's apartment for wine and petit fours. The family rested quietly as Gerta and her daughters served the line of guests. Rene sat staidly next to Nicole, his arm resting lightly across the back of her chair.

Nicole took a sip of wine. "And so, Rene, did you win the silver cup?"

"It went to Madame Grieg. Jean Claude took second, and I received the third place."

"It is still an honor."

"It is nothing! I deserved that cup," Rene insisted. "And you did nothing to improve the evening by running out and leaving me when I needed my wife at my side!"

Nicole picked up her glass. "So you intend to divorce me?"

"I will see my lawyer in the morning," he said, and then added hastily, "But I expect you will still work in the store, and as a courier, when I need you. I'll put you on salary, of course. You could never live on that pittance you make doing translations in the States."

"Oh, Rene!" she exclaimed. She laughed, rose, and went to help Gerta with the cakes.

"Gerta, what is the name of the lawyer who drew up Mimi's will?"

"Monsieur Stein, Michael Stein," Gerta answered. She nodded across the room toward Rene. "So, at last you have decided not to put up any longer with his foolishness? You will not be sorry."

Chapter Nine

Another Door Opens

All day on Wednesday, Nicole stayed huddled in her bed with the blinds drawn against the sun. Her body felt too heavy with grief to move. She cradled the little picture of Mimi in her palm and held it against her cheek, half listening as the telephone rang and rang. Then thankfully it stopped and she slept away the afternoon and dreamed.

"Get up, Nicole," came Mimi's voice in the dark room.

Nicole jerked awake and looked wildly around the room. Night had come, and it was raining hard against the window.

"Mimi?" she whispered.

"Get up, Nicole," it came again, clearly. Nicole put her feet over the side of the bed and immediately felt dizzy. She had not eaten for more than a day. She stood unsteadily, went into the tiny kitchen area, put on the kettle, found the bottle of aspirin and took three with a glass of water.

"It's raining into the grave," Nicole said aloud. "Oh god." She began to sob.

"I am not there," Mimi said. "I have risen. You must go on, my darling one."

"I'm hallucinating," Nicole reasoned. Her head felt hot, she felt nauseated.

She made a strong cup of tea, took a handful of crackers, and sat by the window. The vision of the rain beating into the soft muddy earth of Mimi's grave disturbed her. It was too much to bear alone. She went to the telephone and called Yvette but when Enrico answered, she hung up. She dialed Rene's number. It rang and rang, but he did not answer. She had never felt so alone, so isolated, in her life.

* * *

On Friday morning, Nicole took a taxi to the alley behind the shop, picked up her old Volkswagen, and drove to Yvette's apartment.

Yvette was already dressed and waiting. Enrico was nowhere to be seen.

"Please, Cherie, take my beautiful car. It will make a better impression on the lawyer," insisted Yvette, thrusting her keys in Nicole's hand. "Why don't you buy a new car?"

"Why? The Volkswagen started on the first try, Maman. It just looks a little—."

"It is dreadful," stated Yvette as she settled into the passenger side of her own car.

"I hardly slept a wink last night. I must tell you what happened. The last thing I did when we left for the funeral was to close the door to Mimi's bedroom. I did not wish to return and see her lovely old bed and be reminded it would be empty forever, but when Enrico and I walked into my apartment, the bedroom door was open! We smelled smoke, like those thin little brown cigarettes Mimi sometimes smoked—and then we heard it, both of us!"

"Heard what, Mama?"

Even in the bright sunlight, Yvette's face was pale and her hands shook. "A cough. Then another cough. I fell on the sofa! Enrico went to Mimi's bedroom but saw nothing but a faint blue haze near the window, which immediately disappeared. My hair stood up, Nicole!"

Nicole thought about her own experience, of hearing Mimi's voice, but decided to remain silent. Yvette was already obviously frightened. "Enrico stayed by me all night. Early this morning, I drove him to Orly. I want to sell Mimi's furniture and make a sewing room. I can do alterations and special costumes, unless you wish to have Mimi's furniture?"

"No, Maman, I have no place for it."

"The office is just down here. Look for a place to park, there, on the corner."

Michael Stern was young, perhaps thirty to thirty-five, but had a shrewd manner beyond his years. His forte was accident cases, but he did a little bit of everything.

Yvette looked annoyed because Stern's shirt was unbuttoned at the neck and his tie dangled halfway down his shirtfront.

"We're here for the will of Mimi Longet," she said coldly, crossing her lovely legs and hanging on tightly to her purse.

"Have it right here," Stern said, picking up a single sheet of paper from his desk and scanning it briefly. "Only two heirs are mentioned, but a discretionary gift is designated to her friend—."

"Gerta?"

"Yes, that's the name—," he began. "Madam Mimi Longet has left everything to her daughter Yvette entirely with the exception of . . ." Here, he read verbatim, "My brass bound trunk, which, with all contents, I bequeath to my granddaughter, Nicole Laurent." He stopped and gazed at Nicole with interest. "You called and asked whether I handled divorce cases, didn't you?"

"Yes, I did."

"Oh, Cherie, surely Rene is only teasing you!"

Michael Stern leaned across the desk and waited for Nicole's reply, but she said nothing. He buttoned his shirt and pulled his tie up into place.

"You wish to make an appointment to discuss it? Who is representing your husband?" he urged, noting she still wore her wedding ring. The first thing some clients did was to take off the ring as a symbol of independence.

"I don't know his lawyer. I will call you," said Nicole.

"He is also Catholic? There may be problems."

"No, he is not religious. We were not married in the church. We were married in a chapel."

"I see . . ." Stern's pen rolled off the desk unnoticed.

"We are here for the will of Mimi Longet, Monsieur!" said Yvette sharply, irritated at Nicole. "What does she say of Gerta?"

"At your discretion, she would like her gold ring from Madrid to go to Gerta and two pairs of pearl earrings to go to Helga and Marta—."

"Gerta's daughters," explained Yvette. "I am happy to carry out her wishes. They were very heavy girls, but sweet, always wonderful to my mother. Perhaps they would like to have the furniture also, although they are well to do. Marta plays the piano and Helga the flute. Perhaps I could introduce you, Monsieur?" said Yvette rapidly. "They are young and unmarried."

Stern looked astonished. Nicole stared into a corner of the office trying hard not to laugh. It would seem inappropriate, but she was amused at Yvette's perception.

"That's about it then, ladies. Here is a copy of the will for each of you."

"Thank you, monsieur. Is there a fee?" asked Yvette, opening her purse.

"It has been paid," Stern noted. "If I can be of more help, please call me." He reached across the desk and shook their hands, clinging on to Nicole's. "I am so sorry to hear of your grandmother's death"

"Thank you," said Nicole.

Yvette was already hurrying through the door, the will clutched to her chest as she made her way to the elevator. Nicole followed behind in time to leap into the elevator.

"He could not keep his eyes from you! He hardly explained the will." Yvette fumed, jamming the papers into her purse. "I don't like that—ambulance chaser!"

Nicole drove to the cemetery, and they walked to the gravesite hand in hand, drawing strength from each other. To Nicole's relief, the torrential shower had not disturbed the grave, and the flowers remained fresh, their petals dimpled with raindrops. She thought about Beau Jackson and Major Whitt. They had flown all this way on such short notice to show her they cared. Major Whitt must have arranged a military hop. He seemed to be good at things like that.

Yvette had begun to cry.

"Come, Maman, I will buy you a good lunch," offered Nicole, leading Yvette away from the grave.

"I cannot eat."

"I know a place that makes the very lightest crepes, they float from the plate."

"Crepes? Yes, perhaps one or two."

After lunch, they returned to Yvette's apartment to decide what to do about the trunk. Nicole had decided to take it to her own small place where there was room against one wall for it to fit nicely. Too big for the Volkswagen, too tall for Yvette's car trunk, it would have to be moved by truck at a later date, but in the meanwhile, they were both anxious to open it and see what lay inside. Yvette could not remember seeing it open since Mimi came to live with her—had it been twenty years?—since her father died? Mon Dieu, more than twenty years!

An ordinary skeleton key hung by the lock, but Nicole looked at it and began to have a queer feeling that something was not exactly right. Yvette waited nearby anxiously, feeling somewhat invasive at prying into

Mimi's things, even now that she was dead. Nicole slipped the skeleton key into the projecting metal lock, and it slid aside. Another keyhole, very small, appeared. Of course, a smaller key!

Nicole and Yvette looked at each other in horror, realizing what was wrong.

"The little key! She always wore it on a fine chain around her neck," gasped Yvette, putting her hand to her throat.

"Where is it now, Maman?"

Yvette seemed frozen. "It didn't come back with her things from the hospital." They stared at the tiny keyhole, a single black eye, which seemed to be slyly mocking them.

"She's still wearing it," said Nicole very slowly, placing her hand over the hole. "She took it with her."

"We can look in antique shops for another key," suggested Yvette. "The trunk is very old."

"Or perhaps a dental tool, no?" Mused Nicole, replacing the big sham lock that covered the secret keyhole. "Are you in a hurry for me to move it, Maman? I can call the Belvoir Brothers, their trucks are all over town."

"No hurry. Have you spoken with Rene?"

"Briefly. His lawyer is Henry Schermer. Rene is pushing ahead with the divorce, but he seemed shocked that I hired Michael Stern. Perhaps he assumed I would not choose to be represented—I would just walk away, quietly."

"I must work," said Yvette worriedly. "Rene will no longer pay for this lovely garden apartment if you are divorced."

"Don't worry about it, Maman," Nicole assured her. "The rent will be paid." She had always let Mimi and Yvette believe that Rene was their benefactor.

"Stay with me, Cherie?" begged Yvette. "This place is so quiet now."

"I have to check the telephone in my flat for messages and tomorrow I must go pick up my things from the apartment over the shop. I need my clothes."

"Stay with me this weekend and on Sunday after church, we can take my big beautiful car and go get your things. I want to go with you in case Rene makes trouble. He has been acting odd. Are you sure there is not another young woman? Had he been—attentive to you lately?"

"Oh, Maman, the sex was fine!" laughed Nicole. "Just everything else was wrong. I'll go check my messages and be back for dinner."

She gave Yvette a kiss, went out to the Volkswagen and drove across town to her own flat. It had a closed, dusty smell, and she threw open the windows while she picked out a sleep shirt and clothes for the next day. Lastly, she pushed the bar on the answering machine and listened carefully.

"Paris, get in touch," Beau Jackson.

"Madam Laurent, we must talk. Henry Schermer has been in touch. He's tough, and he's unwilling to give you one franc. We're going to have to fight this one. I can see you Monday afternoon at four. Confirm? Stern."

"Paris, get in touch." Major Whitt.

"I will be in the country this weekend. Do not contact me there." Rene.

Nicole erased the messages and sank down on the bed. I'm going to need money, she thought. If necessary, I can tap my numbered account, but that would be a last solution. And I am curious, she admitted. What was the next assignment? Like a racehorse, which had been idling away the days grazing in a pasture, she was ready to go back to the track—eager for the fast pace, the unknown dangers.

She closed the flat, went down to the street, passed the Volkswagen at the curb, and continued to the telephone booth on the corner. She called the Alexandria office.

"This is Paris."

"Got a puzzler for you," said Beau Jackson. "You got any nursing experience?"

"No."

"You can fake it. A nice, old, crazy lady seems to need some close supervision. Can you book a flight tomorrow?"

"So soon?"

"I know you just buried your grandmother, but it may be what you need, a break to cope with it, and get on with your own life, girl."

"Rene is divorcing me."

"What? What?" Jackson said. He turned away from the telephone and spoke rapidly to someone in the office.

"Who are you speaking to?" demanded Nicole.

"Major Whitt. He has a proposition to discuss."

"Give me two days. I'll call from Dulles."

"Nicole, are you there?"

She hung up and hurried back to the Volkswagen.

* * *

After the service on Sunday, they went and stood by Mimi's grave in the churchyard for a long time. They removed the dead flowers and carried them to cans near the street. Many wreaths and sprays bore the simple word *friend* or *neighbor* on net banners, and they felt somewhat guilty as they pressed them down among the debris—but what would one do with such reminders?

"Shall we go to that café near the river?" asked Nicole. "We can see the little children."

"Their croissants are fresh," commented Yvette. "You should have had a baby, Nicole."

"Yes," Nicole agreed. "I don't know why it never happened. Oh, I would even settle for a dog, Maman! You should see Boncoeur, the sheepdog at LeGrand's farm where I go to run, he is wonderful."

"All this running, Cherie, it makes muscles in your legs. It is not feminine. Come; let's go away from this place. I am reminded of Mimi and the small key."

They left the churchyard and joined the Sunday crowd at the café. Both were conspicuous in their somber black on this warm July morning. Yvette had set six weeks as a suitable time for mourning and seemed to have an endless supply of black clothing, whereas Nicole was pairing white linen blouses with the long black skirt, and the plain black shift was worn for casual wear. Six weeks of this to please Maman she thought unhappily, Mon Dieu, I will need more black clothing. There were one or two things in the apartment she shared with Rene that would do.

Over coffee, Yvette looked searchingly, across the small table and asked the question she had been avoiding.

"I know you are not at fault, Cherie, but is there something which has made Rene unhappy with you?"

Nicole laughed. "Many things, Maman. I will not go as a courier to Saudi. He has to send Georges when there is a delivery."

"You're afraid you may see your prince after all these years," said Yvette wisely.

"Yes," Nicole admitted. "I went once. I called the Prince's bodyguard, Hamid, and asked whether the Prince was well and happy. Hamid said he is well, yes, happy, never. I cried and cried. And the rest of the trip was a disaster. The Sheik, who had bought the stomacher for one of his dancing girls, was in the desert at a Wadi. I had to take a Rover, which broke down, and then I rode a camel, a very mean camel, to the Wadi. It spit on my back!"

Yvette looked puzzled. "A stomacher?"

"It is a thing that goes around one's middle. The gems were actually paste but the little bells were pure gold. The girl was quite happy with it."

"And with Rene there were other problems?"

"He told me exactly what to wear, and oh! Those wigs! I was sick and tired of it, no? On the night Mimi died, I wore a gown of my own choice—he was furious—then I got the call, and I walked out of the award's dinner. Rene knew he was losing control of me, and I guess he just snapped."

"I am very sorry, Nicole."

"Don't be, Maman."

"What will you do now that you are also leaving your position in the store?"

"I will do very well, no?"

"Of course. Shall we go get your things? I hope there will not be trouble."

"He's not there. He is in the country with Therese. He always runs to her for comfort."

Nicole drove skillfully through the city streets in the Citroen. She was enjoying the smoothness of the big car and the automatic features that were totally lacking on her own car. *Perhaps I should give up my Volkswagen, with its peculiar two-tone colors, both faded, and the little engine in the rear that started on most, but not all days,* she admitted. Then she felt a sensation of disloyalty—*but I love that little car!* Her thoughts turned to the Paris office closing, the unexpected death of Richard Leach by a mugger, Derek gone—and Mimi—*everything changes. Everything. Why dwell on a silly little old Volkswagen?*

They arrived at the alley entrance behind the shop to find the parking area partially blocked by a large, white American car. Nicole pulled in beside it, and she and Yvette got out.

"Whose car is that?"

Nicole looked at it closely and then glanced up the stairs that led to the flat above. The door was shut.

"It is Dr. Gumbullah's car, Rene's doctor. I recognize it because when Rene hurt his knee a couple of years ago trying to learn to play tennis, I took him to the doctor for treatments, and she would drive him home."

"It's a Cadillac," Yvette observed, "but old. My car is newer. A woman doctor, Nicole?"

"Oh, Maman, there are many women doctors."

"And she is your doctor too?"

"I am never sick," Nicole shrugged.

"You once threw up at the circus."

"Maman, I was three, and had too much caramel popcorn!"

"Mimi always fed you too much."

They made their way up the stairs and found the door locked. Nicole drew out her own keys and let them into the kitchen. They could see through to the living room. No lights were on but somewhere a radio played very softly. Nicole put her fingers to her lips to caution Yvette to keep quiet and moved silently through the hall toward the music, which was coming from the bedroom.

The bedroom door was slightly open, and Nicole shoved it aside with a bang.

It was hard to tell who was the most surprised, Nicole and Yvette, or the nude, dark-skinned woman who stood with her back to them.

"Dr. Gumbullah?" Nicole asked in disbelief. She looked around at the disarray in the bedroom. The designer gowns were pulled from the closet, and tossed on the bed. Nicole's personal chest of drawers stood open, with lingerie and stockings hanging half in and half out. On the bed, was a large cerise-colored raffia tote bag, and Nicole could see her own best silk underpants and some new lace half-slips.

The woman turned and grabbed for a red and gold sari, holding it in front of her. She was attractive of face, with large dark eyes and a ruby of good quality glinted from one side of her nose. Sleek black hair fell to her waist.

Incredulously, she screamed at Nicole. "Who are you? What are you doing here?"

Nicole brushed past her and opened the bathroom door, looked into the shower. The place was empty.

"How did you get in here?" Nicole demanded. "And who in hell are you? You're not Dr. Gumbullah, but you're driving her car."

"I'm Kim, and Monsieur Rene Laurent gave me his key, and the key to the special closet for the most beautiful gowns."

The woman pouted. "They are too long for me and small in the chest. He said if they fit me, we would go to parties, and I would meet important people."

"You're Dr. Gumbullah's niece, aren't you? You work sometimes for your aunt in the office, no?" said Nicole, as she walked to the bed, picked up the raffia tote bag and emptied it on the bed. To her dismay, an antique silver hand mirror, comb, and brush fell out among the lingerie. "And you are nothing more than a common thief. Maman, call the police."

"Monsieur Rene gave me the keys!" The woman shouted but her eyes darted back and forth guiltily, looking for a way to escape. The sari fell away giving a view of young, but already pendulous breasts, a thick waistline, and short thin legs.

How could Rene dream that this pig would fit into my clothes, Nicole mused, her anger rising, even as she remained calm.

"Just throw her out, Cherie," suggested Yvette, snatching the sari and throwing it to the floor. "Throw her naked into the street, Cherie."

"Yes, Maman," said Nicole, but first she rummaged among the clothes on the bed and located Rene's set of keys, which she dropped into her skirt pocket. She turned to the woman who was edging toward the door. "Never come here again, do you understand? I'll have you arrested."

"Monsieur Rene said you were never coming back. He hates you!"

"Maybe he does," agreed Nicole coldly. "But we are not divorced yet."

She grabbed the woman by her upper arm in a grip that pressed into the flesh, and marched her rapidly through the flat.

"Stop! Stop! I need my clothes. You are breaking my arm!" Kim Gumballah protested, clinging to the kitchen door.

"Hand me that little red purse. That is your purse, no? And the sari, Maman. We do not want to give the neighborhood a bad name, no?" Nicole pushed the woman through the door. Yvette handed her the sari, and Nicole tossed it over the railing, where it floated like a red and gold parachute through the air, landing on top of the white Cadillac. The red purse fell into the alley, spilling car keys and few francs.

Yvette shut the door, and they stood inside the kitchen silently waiting. A minute later, they heard the smooth roar of the Cadillac starting up, the grinding of gears as Kim Gumbullah put it into reverse, and gravel flew against the tires as the cars sped away.

Nicole and Yvette went back to the bedroom and began to restore order to the chairs, Nicole putting aside the things she would take with her. All of a sudden, she paused and went to the chest of drawers. She pulled out the false bottom of the middle drawer, removed the top, and took out a tray of outstanding jewels, ten pieces in all. "She didn't find these. They were my gifts from Rene. Five birthdays and five anniversaries. I . . . I . . ." Nicole paused, unable to go on as her fingers touched each piece.

"What are all these papers? Should they be in with these valuable gems?" asked Yvette.

"Cards and letters from Rene from the day we met. See this pale blue stationery with tiny letters, just his name in gold?"

"Elegant. Always Rene is elegant."

"But here, Maman, the last two years—see, he has written on the back of our business card—'Love' and 'Happy birthday.'"

Yvette put her arms around her. "Remember the happiness, Cherie. And he was a good lover, no? Frenchmen have that reputation. As for myself, Frenchmen had little appeal—my first love—" She stopped abruptly and glanced at Nicole, then laughed, "Now I love Enrico."

"What were you about to say about your first love, Maman?"

"Oh nothing! A silly boy from school," said Yvette quickly. "Come help me with this big suitcase. I will not make it down the steps."

"Kim Gumbullah left her tote bag. What shall I do with it?"

"Leave it. Leave it for Rene," suggested Yvette slyly, turning it with the tips of her fingers. "Shoddy workmanship, deplorable color—Just the thing for a fussy man of impeccable taste."

Chapter Ten

Moving On

Michael Stern was not in his office at four o'clock, five minutes after, or ten minutes past, and Nicole grew weary of standing in the dusty hall behind his locked door. There was not a note or notice stuck to the pebbled glass of the opaque pane. She took out a nail file, ran it up and down until she heard a click and pushed the door open. The inside smelled like stale pizza and some kind of medicine, nose spray? She found the light switch, cleared a wooden bench and sat down.

When Michael Stern pushed his way carefully, hesitantly, into his open office, suspecting some deranged client, intent on revenge, he found, instead, Nicole reading a magazine.

"This magazine is four years old and a Christmas issue," she complained as she glanced at her watch. "And you are thirty minutes late."

"How did you—."

"Let's get started. I'm leaving Paris at midnight for the States."

He hustled over behind his desk and tossed a bulging briefcase on the floor beside his chair. "I've had my beavers at work on your case, and we've got plenty to work with, Rene Lauren's financial records, his real property, and his health records."

"Beavers?"

"Two hacker kids, aces with digging up information."

"Why go for his health records?"

"Sometimes an older man with a young wife conceals a heart condition, or even sexually transmitted diseases, in order to keep his . . ."

"Rene is perfectly healthy!"

"Seems so. A few allergies—hell, I have those myself—got my little inhaler right here, and he had a broken bone in the patella—that's the knee, coupla years ago. No surgeries unless you count the vasectomy fifteen years ago."

Nicole froze. The magazine slid to the floor. "Vasectomy?" She echoed faintly.

"Yes, I guess that takes care of the issue of children in the marriage. No little bambinos to share custody or demand support payments from dear old dad, right?"

When Nicole continued to look down at the floor and remain silent, Stern glanced up to see her stricken expression.

"Madame Laurent, are you ill? Divorce is never easy. Shall we meet another time if you're not feeling well?"

"No," she managed, "continue, please."

"You knew his finances. You went on the mortgage to buy the building. If he keeps that property, the shop and apartment, you can ask for one half, or if you want continued partnership in the business and building . . ."

"No, he had the business long before we married," Nicole said. "I'll settle for an equivalent sum."

Stern made copious notes to that effect, "And the investment property, a small working farm, rented at a ridiculously low amount to a widow and her two sons—and this is ludicrous! Schermer tells me Laurent wants your clothes! He claims them as business expenses. How cheap can a man get?"

"The farm," Nicole queried. "This is free and clear and in Rene's name only—no other name on the deed?"

"Absolutely, and there was a terrace and small pool added about five years ago. It's a nice place, isn't it?"

"I've never seen it," she admitted. "If I were not leaving tonight, I certainly would go to see it." She stood up and began to pace around the confines of the small office. Stern's "beavers" had uncovered more secrets in one day than she had even suspected in five years. I loved Rene, therefore I trusted him, she realized. I really loved him! Now I know he denied me children when he knew how much I waited for the baby that never came, year after year.

"I want half of that farm!" She declared viciously, hitting the desk so hard that she could feel the top crack. "And, as for my clothes, he will rot in hell before he gets one sequin, one button, one dangling piece of thread! I want you to go for it, Michael Stern, and if he doesn't agree to the terms, I will make his life miserable!"

"You didn't know, did you, about the vasectomy?" Stern figured. Nothing else could have unearthed this much anger.

"No," she whispered, her head lowered so that he couldn't see the tears. "I'll call you when I get back from the States."

She looped her shoulder bag over her arm. It felt heavy, as if her whole body were weighted down.

"Can I take you home?" Stern asked, coming out from behind the desk. "Or call a taxi?"

"No, thank you. I have my car," she murmured as she crossed the office, went out of the door and closed it softly.

Stern went to the window and looked down into the street. In a few minutes, he saw Nicole Laurent emerge from the building, cross the street, and get into the weirdest little Volkswagen—was it blue, or yellow?—he had ever seen.

"We'll take him to the cleaners, baby," he muttered. As he watched the little car sputter away, he mused aloud, "I wonder how soon she'll start dating?" He looked at his reflection in the window glass, smoothed back his short, curly, black hair, and straightened his tie.

Chapter Eleven

Secrets of the Mind

The midnight departure was delayed by hours as an electrical storm raged outside of deGaulle, lightning split the black sky, and the rumble of thunder vibrated the glass in the windows that overlooked the field. Grounded flights sat in staggered rows like ghost planes.

Nicole turned away from the black rain pelted windows and into the lighted body of the airport. A few disgruntled passengers milled about the gift shop, buying things they didn't need, just to be filling time, and she joined them at the confectioner's where she purchased a box of four Godiva Chocolates. Godiva was her weakness. She justified the chocolate as a quick energy source. She chose one to munch on as she wandered over to the souvenirs. There was a display of chunky little metal paperweights, which, when one was turned over, also concealed a pencil sharpener. They were touristy and tacky, so she bought two and shoved them into her shoulder bag.

She glanced outside and saw that lightning still circled the field. She looked around the terminal for an empty bench, and curled into a ball, half asleep, like a little black cat, her head on her shoulder bag, one hand clutching her suit bag and tote bag. Thieves were everywhere. She had seen one lifting a bag of candy from a sleeping child. Another attempted to brush close enough to the back pocket of a young American tourist to lift her passport, but just in time, friends approached the girl and the pickpocket drifted away into the crowd.

Nicole's flight did not take off until 5:00 a.m. and then it was directed to Greenland. When she arrived, she called the Alexandria office and left a message, noting that it was now Derek Holland's voice on the tape instead of Beau Jackson's. She was happy that the dapper dwarf was doing well in America. She called Yvette, who was very excited because Enrico had arrived and was taking Polaroid pictures of Mimi's heavy antique bedroom furniture to send to Sotheby's in London because he felt it would bring Yvette a considerable sum at auction. Nicole felt a sharp pang of regret. Those tall, carved headboards on the twin beds had been there most of her life they had been in the old house until Pere Longet died. Then Mimi moved the big, heavy bedroom suite to the old apartment on the third floor, the movers groaning under the marble tops, and for a third time, to the new ground floor apartment and now, perhaps, they would go to strangers.

"But, Maman—must they be sold?"

"You don't want them, and I can never sleep in my own twin bed again without Mimi in the other one. I have been sleeping on the sofa since . . . When I go in that room I feel she is still there, Nicole!"

"Then, do what you must, Maman. I'll be home in a few days."

"Be safe, my darling. Good-bye."

She wanted to ask if Rene had called, had asked about her, but Yvette had volunteered nothing about Rene. Could five years have meant so little to him? She felt cold and damp from the rain, and emptiness, a sadness that had nothing to do with the weather.

* * *

It was late afternoon of the following day when the long delayed and rerouted flight finally taxied down the runway to Dulles. Nicole had a severe headache from lack of sleep and an aching back from sitting up on the plane, watching an especially bad movie, which had no plot or comprehensible dialogue, but attempted to compensate with special effects. Where was Cary Grant when you needed him, she had thought dismally, comparing the sad flick to "North by Northwest."

She was plodding slowly through the terminal, actually dragging the suit bag, when she passed a pair of very shiny boots that looked familiar. The knife-creased chinos cinched it. She peered around into the row of seats, and there, fast asleep was Major Whitt, yesterday's newspaper crumpled in one hand and a hand lettered square of white cardboard lying on his chest. The sign said *laurent*. Had he been here at Dulles for two whole days? She dropped into the seat next to him, gently removed the sign, and for some reason, sat gazing at his face while he slept. After several minutes, she reached out and shook his arm.

"Major? Are you waiting for me?"

Those startling blue eyes flew open and a trace of a smile brushed his face.

"You finally . . ." he stammered. "I mean, the storms? Was it bad? I waited."

"Thank you."

He rubbed his eyes and stretched out his legs. The newspaper fell to the floor. "You must be completely . . ." He flexed his shoulders, groaned, and stood up. "How long have you been here?"

"A few minutes."

"Luggage? Can I get your luggage?"

"This is it."

He scooped up the suit bag and her carry-on bag, and she followed him through the terminal to the parking lot. He put her things into the rear of a navy blue Jeep Cherokee, and they pulled out of the lot onto the highway.

"It's late," Nicole said. "There will be no one at the office in Alexandria. Do you have a key?"

"We're not going to the office. I'm taking you home with me."

When she didn't answer, he glanced around. "It's a big house. Everything is very private. I think you'll like it."

"I am very tired, no?" she answered, turning away and looking out the window.

"Of course!" he agreed. "I've got some important issues to discuss with you, but they can wait until tomorrow. Beau Jackson is anxious to see you too."

"It was kind of you to attend my grandmother's funeral."

"We arranged a military hop. Beau knew how much she meant to you."

The highway flew by. He flipped on the headlights as night descended on the Virginia countryside and in the sudden light she glimpsed a road sign—*back lick road*. What an odd name she thought, I wonder what it means. They were turning off now on a narrow private road between tall trees, and immediately gravel stung the sides of the jeep as they approached a cleared area along a single-story old brick house sitting at the end of the road. Azaleas, taller than the windows, crowded the house walls and spread down one side of the drive. Ivy crept rampant on the stones of the porch and clustered on the chimneys.

"It needs a lot of work," Major Whitt apologized. "It was tied up in an estate until I bought it six months ago. I've always lived in military base housing, but the organization ordered me to find a place, remote, and yet easy to secure. I see the road has been graveled since I was here last."

"You live here alone?"

"Yes, I have a son, but he's in premed at Duke. He has an apartment in Durham. No military for him." Whitt laughed. "You can see he's already smarter than I am."

The jeep crunched around to the right side of the house, around an extended ell at the rear, and under an open roof of latticework, that reached to a matching ell on the left side. The only light beamed down from a door in the center.

"This house is so long and wide, no?"

"It was built about 1918, by an eccentric couple who couldn't stand each other. That, over there in that ell, was her territory. His was here. They shared the middle for sixty years."

"Mon Dieu!" exclaimed Nicole.

"They must have met in the middle at some time," shrugged Whitt. "They had three children, who inherited their parent's anger as well as this place. None wished to share it, so it stood empty until the last heir died, very sad!"

"Not to love family—I do not understand," murmured Nicole, thinking of Mimi.

"Yes," agreed Whitt. He got out of the jeep, stepped up the single stone step and unlocked the door to the lighted hall. To the left was the kitchen. Hesitantly, as Nicole ventured into the open door, the smell of fresh paint assailed her nose. Cabinets were glossy white, the walls, a gentle daffodil yellow, and the floor had been tiled in black and white, but there was no stove or refrigerator in the empty spaces where they once stood. No table, no chairs, and no pets or dishes.

She tentatively stepped into a very long passageway that seemed to lead straight through to the front door. Here, too, was the fresh paint smell and a sea of tall off-white walls sprang into view as she located the switch that illumined four small chandeliers placed at intervals down the hall ceiling. She walked slowly through the hall, glancing into rooms on either side that were swept clean, but were empty. They seem to go on and on and on.

Whitt came in with her suit bag and carry-on, and saw her hesitating at the front door, unsure where to go next.

"Keep around to your right through the parlor and sun room and down the far hall to the last two rooms."

"I shall drop bread crumbs to find my way back," decided Nicole, flipping on light switches as she followed his directions through the vast empty spaces. At the next to last room, at last she discovered some furniture, a modern natural oak queen-sized bed, an armoire, and a triple dresser, a matched set straight from the show room. Yes, she thought, a man would do that—most men—but not Rene, with his carefully selected antiques. Ahhh, Rene! I do miss him! I even miss the smell of him, she admitted feeling angry with herself.

"New carpet," Whitt was saying as he hung her suit bag in the armoire next to his clothes, "and venetian blinds."

"Wait! This is your bedroom, no?"

"It's the only bedroom furnished."

"Take my bag out from that armoire!"

"You will sleep here. I will stay on the sofa in the library. Look, here is your private bath."

"And where is the library?"

"The next room, down the hall. I'll show you. I think you'll be surprised."

Nicole dropped her shoulder bag on the bed and followed him down the hall.

When the lamps flared, she drew in a deep breath. A crazy sense of *déjà vu* washed over her, and she stared at the desk in the center of the room, the two chairs facing it, the books lining every wall, even a fireplace at the far end—where was it? Where was it? Suddenly, some things clicked into place. The walls and carpets were not the right color, but everything else was the same. Gazar's entire library had been moved into this house.

"Everything but the snake," Nicole said, moving to the desk. She opened the drawer. The gun was there in its place.

"A snake?"

She touched the console. "Here is his basket where the egg is kept for him to find."

"A snake?" repeated Whitt.

"Never mind. I hope he is safe in his garden. How did you get these things?"

"Gazar is divorced. His wife arranged for us to move these from the Bethesda house. He has retired to Florida," Whitt told her. "Gazar had been acting erratic for almost a year. I heard that now he is wandering about his neighborhood in Florida telling people he couldn't sleep because his house is haunted."

Nicole stood very still. "Why does he say that?" she asked.

Whitt thumped his forehead. "Getting a bit senile, I guess. Care for a bite to heat?" He reached into a Mimi refrigerator, which hummed in the corner, and brought out French bread, some apples and peaches, a bottle of wine, and a plastic bag of sliced roast beef.

Nicole cleared some papers from the desk and found glasses in a cabinet under the bookcase, suddenly feeling ravenous.

"A new stove and refrigerator is on order for the kitchen."

"It's like a picnic, no?" She decided as she covered the desktop with newspaper. She expertly split the bread with a letter opener and poured wine into the glasses. "Ah, this wine! I like a bit sweet, sometimes."

They ate the quickly put together meal and finished the wine, both feeling slightly heady from fatigue and the wine.

"No dessert?" she asked as he gazed across the desk. A bit of breadcrumb stuck to his cheek, and she longed to take it off but instead she went into the bedroom and took the last two Godiva chocolates from her bag. Her hand touched something of hard metal, and she drew out one of the paperweights, the *Arc de Triomphe*. She came back to the library and placed the melting chocolates on the table, one on each side.

"I know you didn't have time to pick up a souvenir on your trip to Paris, so I brought you this."

Whitt took it and held it in his hand without saying a word. He cleared his throat.

"I am sorry. It is too tacky, no?"

He turned it over and noted the pencil sharpener. He traced the square little chunk of pot metal with his fingertip carefully, as it were a treasure from the *Louvre*, still remaining silent.

"I will take it back, Major. It was just a silly whim," she apologized as she reached across the desk, "to remember Paris."

He drew his hand out of reach and pocketed the paperweight. "I've been needing a pencil sharpener. Thank you, Laurent."

She stood up. "I would like to go to bed now." In the doorway, she paused. He had taken the paperweight out of his pocket and was looking at it.

"Good night, Laurent."
"Good night, Major."

* * *

The sun was up, filtering through the Venetian blinds—Nicole forgot where she was, and out of habit, reached across to the other pillow to touch Rene. The pillow was cool and smooth to the touch, and suddenly remembering where she was, she sat up in bed and glanced at a clock on the triple dresser. It was 11:00 a.m.! In the mirror over the dresser, she caught sight of herself. Her hair, now grown longer, stood out in dark curly masses, and there were smudges of fatigue under her eyes. Mon Dieu, I will scare the pants off the major looking so spooky, she thought, and then she paused, thinking of the powerful legs under those starched chinos. Mon Dieu! Nicole was mentally undressing Major Whitt and had removed his shiny shoes and socks. What kind of socks? His shirt peeled away when all of a sudden she became aware of the sound of muffled voices from the library. One or more other people had come into this house while she lay sleeping. She jumped out of bed, snatched jeans and a black T-shirt from her carry-on, and hurried into the bathroom. She threw water on her hair and brushed it into a messy French twist in the back, bangs and tendrils escaping as soon as it began to dry.

A huge pounding began on the bedroom door, and a familiar voice boomed out.

"Sleepy head? I'm not waiting for you all day, girl! We got business to attend to!"

Nicole threw open the door.

"Beau!"

"In person. Get a move on. I brought breakfast. I know major. He won't feed you. He doesn't even keep a dog."

Jackson gave her a bear hug, and she hugged him back. He stood back and looked at her. "What's the matter with your head?"

She tried to push her hair into place. "Oh, shut up. At least I have hair."

"Touche," he grinned, running his hand over the receding edges of his hairline.

She went over to her shoulder bag and took out the other paperweight, which she handed to him. "For you, from Paris with love."

Beau was looking down at the paperweight, a replica of the Eiffel Tower, when Whitt came up behind him in the hall and glanced over Beau's shoulder.

"What do you do, buy those things by the gross?" he said to Nicole, a note of anger in his voice.

Nicole stared at him, confused by the chill in his tone. "Two, I only bought two."

Beau Jackson turned and looked at Whitt, then down at the Eiffel Tower. He turned it over and noticed the pencil sharpener in the bottom. "Neat. This is neat, Nicole. What's your problem, Major?"

Whitt turned and walked back down the hall to the library. "Can't we get to work?"

Nicole looked at Beau and shrugged, and then followed Whitt as Beau walked close behind, leaning over, whispering in her ear, "Got cold orange juice, big old greasy bacon, egg and cheese biscuits. Donuts and coffee with double sugar too. Love ya, baby."

"Love you, Beau," she whispered back.

Major Whitt was already seated behind the desk that formerly belonged to Gazar. There was a large television exposed behind open cabinet doors. Food was laid out on the console, but nobody moved to touch it.

"Well, go ahead, Boss," began Jackson, dropping into one of the wingback chairs that faced the desk. "You can lay your proposition on the table first, so we can see how the wind blows and proceed from there."

"You sound so mysterious," said Nicole, glancing back at the console. She could smell the coffee and hot sugar doughnuts.

"As you're aware, the Paris office hasn't existed since the death of Richard Leach. We want to reestablish a base. Delon has indicated he will continue as liaison, and we have one or two who might make the move—agents ready to settle in one place. My idea, Nicole—Agent Laurent," he quickly corrected himself, "is to put you in charge of the new French division."

Nicole looked completely surprised. Beau Jackson was watching her shrewdly. No expression crossed his face as they waited for her answer.

Major Whitt shifted in his chair. "No more assignments. Regular payroll and short hours. Still an element of danger, but . . ."

"No thank you. I do not want the job!" said Nicole firmly. "I am hungry. The coffee is hot, no?" She crossed to the console, poured a cup from a giant thermos, and selected a biscuit.

"Goddamn it, you would be safe! At least as safe as anybody in this business! You'd report to me, just as Leach reported to Gazar."

"Richard Leach is dead. He was not safe in the office," Nicole pointed out.

"It was a mugger!" Whitt exploded. "It was not part of the game!"

Nicole looked thoughtful as she chewed the biscuit, holding the bulging contents inside of a large greasy napkin. "Perhaps Derek Holland would consider your offer. He is smart and knows every part of the Paris operation."

"You mean the dwarf?" asked Whitt.

"He won't go," put in Jackson. "He likes it here, and he's doing great with us in the Alexandria office."

Major Whitt turned away, drummed his fingers on the desk, obviously frustrated. "In the meantime, we'll have to depend on Interpol." He whipped around to face Nicole. "Would you mind telling me why you don't want this job—no guns, no knives, no crazy people taking pot shots at you?"

Nicole wiped her mouth and reached for a doughnut. "Maybe I like what I do. I like the uncertainty. I like the game."

"Well, hell!" growled Whitt. "Okay, Jackson, I gave it my best shot. She's all yours."

"Where is the disc?"

Whitt went over to the endless line of bookcases, reached to the fourth shelf, and took down a copy of *Jungle Book*. He pressed each side of the cover, the spine lifted away, and a disc slid out into his hand.

"The inventory is not complete. The sham books are all here, but Gazar took some rare first editions." He slipped the tape into the DVD.

There is one book he didn't take, Nicole thought, *A Tale of Two Cities,* which was locked in the safety deposit of a Paris bank, along with the jewels Rene had given her on various special occasions.

"This interview was bumped over to us from the Feds. They take no stock in it because the woman this young lady is describing has been certified by two doctors as being in the first stage of Alzheimer's disease, but we decided to check it out. She seems genuinely concerned," Whitt explained. He pushed the *play* button.

The image of a very pretty, very agitated, young woman appeared on the screen. She was a light cocoa color, with large expressive eyes, and neat braided hair that was tied in some way in the back.

"My name is Saucy La Shaundra Dodd. I work at Meadowlea Manor..."

A murmur from an unseen source prompted an answer.

"Nineteen years old. I've been at Meadowlea since last year when I graduated high school. I want to be a nurse, and I'm saving up for nurse's school"

Again, the off-screen voice prompted.

The girl turned toward the voice. "I am getting to it. You said give you some—some personal background—okay? You want me to say about Ms. Ann now?" She appeared to sulk. "You don't believe me anyway. The other man didn't, the one with the badge on his belt."

"We believe you, Ms. Dodd. We're going to follow up on it and keep you informed," promised the voice clearly. "Go ahead."

Saucy La Shaundra Dodd looked down at the floor, seemed to compose herself, and gazed straight into the camera.

"Three months ago, Ms. Ann Hemphill came to Meadowlea, brought by her niece, Marilyn Hewitt, because a big fire destroyed one whole end of her mansion. It was in all the papers, Richmond Times Dispatch, and even the Washington Post, because of who she was, her dead husband being once the Secretary of Defense. Yeah, she's the one—really rich but really nice. Eat anything on her tray. Takes her shower and puts pretty clothes on herself every day. She takes care of herself really nice, not like some of 'em out there. One day, she felt well enough, not so—out of it, you know, and we went on the Meadowlea Van that goes to the mall, and I go with her and she buys me perfume or candy, and I carry her bags."

The murmur prompted her to continue.

"You mean, about the funny stuff? Well, she's old, but I think they are telling her she's off her head—that woman is not crazy. I been at Meadowlea for eleven months and I know crazy when I hear it. Ms. Ann got something terrible on her mind about that fire."

"Where was she at the time of the fire?"

"In her bed, in the farthest wing away from the kitchen. There was a big gas explosion. The fire people said it was a little old broke place in the gas line to the hot water heater in the utility room, but it been hissing into that big old kitchen all night. The cook's helper, and a handy man come in about 6:00 a.m., that woman lights a match to the tea kettle, and the whole thing went up in flame!"

Again, the off-screen voice prompted.

"Dead. They burned up. It was on TV and next day, my mom and I drove over there and looked at it. The day after that, Ms. Ann came to Meadowlea because there was no way to cook, the kitchen, the pantry, and a sun room on the front was gone."

Saucy Dodd paused, looking off into a corner of the room, listening to the voice.

"No sir, Ms. Ann is not talking about exactly the fire. She is talking her daughter being in the fire, but it couldn't be so because her daughter ran off years ago when they lived in Washington with Mr. Secretary."

Another aside.

"No sir, that child never came home. Ms. Ann said one time she got a phone call and her daughter was alive, and she had got married and was in big trouble. Ms. Ann told her, you come straight home, and Lily Ann said she would, but she never did. What—? Yes sir, when she got that call they had left Washington and was living back here near Charlottesville."

"How does the Alzheimer's affect Mrs. Hemphill? Is she lucid most of the time?" The voice, nearer the microphone came in clearly.

"Lucy? Lucy? Ms. Ann knows who she is." Saucy Dodd looked indignant.

"I mean does she think straight?"

"Most times, I guess. We humor her. She calls an aide by her daughter's name, then catches herself and apologizes to Diana. They both have long kind of brown hair. She has seven pictures of her daughter at Meadowlea, one even in the bathroom."

"Any other incident?"

"Forgetful. All of our people are like that. They lose their teeth and their glasses and don't remember names. It is sad. They put on hats and try to go home sometimes. Of course, Ms. Ann will go home as soon as her house is fixed from the fire."

"We will look into this. Thank you for coming to us with this information."

Saucy Dodd hurriedly left the room. The disc continued to run against a blank wall.

"Interview terminated," said the voice and the screen went black.

Major Whitt slipped the disc into "Jungle Book" and replaced it on the shelf.

"The telephone call that Mrs. Hemphill said was from her daughter. Did anyone trace that with the phone records?" asked Jackson.

"There was a call, from a shelter in Richmond, a collect call that lasted approximately twenty minutes," answered Whitt.

"Could the daughter be one of the victims?" Nicole speculated. "Perhaps she came home that night. Somehow Mrs. Hemphill heard her voice and woke up—."

"We know who the burn victims are," interrupted Whitt. He consulted a file on his desk.

"The woman was white, sixty-five, about 175 pounds and gave her name as Alma Patty. The man was black, no age given, had a heart condition, a med bracelet gave his name as Ezekial Williams."

"Old family retainers can be loved and missed just like family. I had an uncle who stayed in service to one family for almost fifty years," commented Jackson. "He spoke of those folks with respect and admiration. He called them his people."

"Patty and Williams hardly fit that description. The Hamphill's house manager, Frank Gantry, hired them off the streets three weeks before the fire!"

"Mon Dieu!" exclaimed Nicole.

"Homeless people," guessed Jackson.

"Expendable," nodded Major Whitt. No one came forward to claim their bodies.

* * *

Finding employment at Meadowlea Manor did not prove to be a problem. Meadowlea was not only too far away for easy commuting from the nearest cities, they paid minimum wage to all help except staff, despite the high rates paid by what Meadowlea termed their guests. The woman behind the desk was fiftiesh, with a red-blonde bouffant hairstyle, lovely skin, and a piercing gaze in her green eyes as she scrutinized Nicole, who sat in a chair across from her desk.

"We don't have uniforms as such but a lovely selection of tunic-length, washable smocks to be worn with solid colored pants, white socks, and gym shoes," instructed Ms. Brown. "And remember, neatness is not only a virtue, but at Meadowlea, it is a necessity. No baggy pants and if a guest throws up on your smock, change it immediately. Too bad you have no nursing experience, so it shall be kitchen or laundry."

"Excuse me," Nicole said quietly. "I have experience washing dishes." She adjusted her clear-lens glasses with gold frames and peered at Mrs.

Brown. She had also snipped off her hair again, and it was in spiky bangs and choppy curls just to her ears, the total gamin look.

"If you had pursued your education, you wouldn't be washing dishes at age thirty, my dear." Brown peered at Nicole. "You certainly don't look thirty, you look about eighteen, but a girl wouldn't lie upward about her age, would she?"

"No, ma'am," answered Nicole, thinking that she had been thirty, her chosen age, since she was twenty-four, and at last her chronological age was catching up with her.

"Education! I excelled at Blair and here I am, Vice Director at Meadowlea! But I'm afraid it's the scullery for you, dear, so report to the kitchens at 5:00 a.m."

"Yes, ma'am."

She left the green lawns of the home in the old blue Ford Tempo Whitt had provided. The car had a key scratch across the rear and was missing a side-view mirror, appropriate for her role as a kitchen worker, but the car ran like wild fire, having been a confiscated drug vehicle purchased from the Feds for one dollar. At the nearest service station, she pulled into the spot beside the public telephone and dialed the Alexandria office. The answering machine came on. "This is Paris. I'm in," she reported and hung up. She drove down the road to a motel made up of log cabins in a half circle and turned into number six. She did not like the motel. Last night, something had been gnawing inside the walls; maybe she could find something better.

She lay down on the chenille bedspread, kicked off her shoes, and turned on the television, which was suspended on a metal strap from the ceiling deep in the corner by the door. Some kind of name talk show was on. An overweight host tried to introduce a sexual reference into everything the guests said. Caught on camera was a man who held an applause sign, which he waved frantically and often, and the obedient audience laughed and cheered.

"Entertainment is dead," decided Nicole, snapping the television into silence.

There was a knock on the door, and glancing out the tiny side window, she saw the elderly manager waiting outside. She opened the door, but he remained on the stoop.

"My wife and I wondered if you'd like to share supper since we don't have an eating place on our property? We don't ask just anybody,"—here he gave a chuckle, "but my wife said you being a girl alone, and you don't look like no serial killer, it would be the neighborly thing to do."

"That is so kind, no?" Nicole exclaimed. "What time shall I come?"

"About six. Bring a good appetite!"

The manager trotted on back to the office to tell his wife to set another place, and Nicole sat down on the bed. She stared at the blank screen of the television, and then crossed the room to get her shoulder bag. She unzipped a bottom compartment, took out a snub-noosed .38 revolver, dropped the bullets out of the cylinder, rubbed it clean with a linen handkerchief and reloaded. She shined the switchblade, flipping it in and out for speed and accuracy and pushed both weapons down in the bag.

At a quarter to six, she went down to the manager's cabin, which was just behind the office. A small table was laid with nice china. There was glazed ham and sweet potatoes, biscuits from scratch, and later, cake with ice cream.

As she ate the dessert, Nicole was almost prompted to tell them that tomorrow will be her birthday, August 9. Here, in a backwoods motel, was her party, vanilla ice cream and chocolate cake.

* * *

Some of the guests had breakfast in bed, others ate in the breakfast room, and while the warm weather prevailed, still others enjoyed being served on the terrace just off the breakfast room, so the kitchen girls ran from place to place with trays. At eleven, there was a snack in the large gathering room where all guests were required to attend, because this was cleaning and bed-making time when they had to be out of their rooms so that this work could be done without interruption.

Nicole had to figure a way to attract Mrs. Hemphill's attention, but she had not been assigned Mrs. Hemphill's breakfast tray. She knew which of the ladies "Ms. Ann" was, however, because Saucy Dodd, the young woman on the tape, was her personal companion. Each Alzheimer patient was assigned one of these aides.

When Nicole passed the two women on their way to the terrace, she observed Mrs. Hemphill. Here was a woman of patrician beauty, grown old too soon, rather tall and with hair already silver, she emanated an aura of sadness. At sixty, already widowed, and her only-child missing, life had written these tragedies on her face and in the droop of her shoulders.

"Good morning," Nicole ventured as she came abreast of them in the hall.

"Good morning," Saucy Dodd answered. "You're the new girl, aren't you?"

"Are you Sylvia?" asked Mrs. Hemphill. "I believe you used to be my secretary or . . ." she hesitated, her eyes distant. "Did you know my husband? He was a fine man."

"My name is Nicole."

"Glad to meet you," said Saucy. "You're kitchen, aren't you? Here's some advice. Stay far away from Big Em. She's horrible!"

"Do you know my daughter?" Mrs. Hemphill probed. "Her name is Lily Ann."

"No, Ma'am. See you at eleven in the gathering room."

As they walked slowly away, Mrs. Hemphill looked back over her shoulder. "Has she seen my daughter?" she murmured.

"No, ma'am. Let's get your breakfast now," Saucy Dodd said, guiding her charge to the terrace.

Nicole returned to the kitchen and began setting up the refreshment trays, which consisted of bowls of fruit and two kinds of cookies. She was getting oranges and apples from the open refrigerator when she was brutally shoved against the metal shelves and pinioned there by two massive black arms. Someone had come up behind her back and was crushing her against the open refrigerator.

"What you doing in there, white girl?" boomed a deep voice into the back of Nicole's head.

"Getting fruit for the elevens," gasped Nicole as the apples and oranges pressed into her chest and arms. "I'm the new girl."

The pressure eased, the arms fell away, and Nicole managed to turn around. The woman was very black, very tall. Flabby fat hung from her inside arms, and giant feet were encased in men's sneakers. Her head, with its short, nubby cut, appeared much too small for the gross body.

"This is my kitchen," the apparition told her. "You get orange when I say get orange. You put the cookies on the plates."

"But I already have the fruit."

"Put it back."

"Why? We just have to get it out again."

"'Cause I say why, bitch. Get onto the cookies."

Janna and Alice, the other two girls, the cook, and the pastry chef busied themselves at their tasks, not looking in the direction of the exchange.

Nicole turned back to the open refrigerator and dropped the fruit back into the bins, thinking to herself, I could have gut-punched that tub of suet, but I need to keep this job. There will be a next time, I'm sure of that. When Nicole turned around, the big black woman was leaving the kitchen, both hands clutching cookies, which she was cramming into her mouth.

One of the other girls scrambled to Nicole's side. "I saw how hard she pushed you. Are you hurt?"

"Nothing serious, I will live, no?"

"That was Big Em. She is so mean! She hurts the little guest ladies that can't talk back. She threw one down on her bed so hard that the lady bounced off and broke her arm. We all knew it, but Brown said it was an accident."

"And she eats the guest's desserts," put in Alice. "Especially chocolate. She takes it off the trays and eats it in the halls."

"Mon Dieu! Why is she not fired?" exclaimed Nicole.

"She can turn a mattress all by herself."

"She is Brown's pet. We think she has something on Brown."

Nicole looked at them. "We could kill her."

They giggled nervously. "Don't we wish!"

Nicole went to the refrigerator, took out the apples and oranges and began to arrange them in the fruit bowls as the girls watched while keeping one eye on the kitchen door.

"Big Em said for you to do the cookies," Janna said nervously.

Nicole finished the fruit bowls and put them on the rolling trolleys. She wheeled them to the hallway door. "I'll be in the gathering room."

Janna and Alice hastily began placing the cookies on the trays, anxiously watching the door in case Big Em returned.

In the gathering room, a young porter was covering the long buffet table with a white cloth. He placed fresh flowers in the center, the coffee urn at one end, and teapot at the other.

"Hey, I'm Jason." He looked up, smiling.

"Nicole," she said. "Where do you want these?"

He looked suspiciously at the fruit. "Janna and Alice do the fruit."

"Not today. Today Nicole does the fruit."

"Are they sick?"

"No."

They placed the bowls next to the flowers.

"Did you hurt yourself? You've got a red mark across your forehead."

"Walked into a refrigerator."

"Sorry."

"Somebody is going to be sorrier than you," said Nicole, flashing him a look.

He had never seen such dark eyes as the ones peering through the clear, gold-rimmed glasses, or such straight dark brows. I think I'm in love, decided Jason. "Do you date? I'm available."

"Sorry, I'm just on loan from the convent."

Janna and Alice raced breathlessly into the room and started unloading cookies from their trolley as Nicole pushed her trolley back to the kitchen.

Nicole stopped by the pastry chef and watched him folding apples into a graham cracker crust.

"Tonight, the apple tart. Tomorrow the chocolate mousse, Wednesday the raspberry crème brulee! We feed them often, so they don't get too bored."

"Just like the cruise liners, always eating."

He started to hand her a leftover cookie, but a dark shadow appeared behind him, and either sensing or smelling Big Em, the chef replaced the cookie on the plate.

"That food is for the guests," Big Em grunted. "And you—you get back in there and pour the tea."

"Yes, your royal highness," and Nicole snatched up the proffered cookie, and went out the door to the hallway, walking swiftly.

"That smart mouth will get you fired. I'm reporting you to Brown," growled Big Em, puffing along behind. "You'll be out of here!"

Nicole burst into the gathering room, which was filling rapidly. The guests filed along in single file down the buffet, took their selections to small tables around the edges of the room or out to the terrace. When the demand for tea waned, she went over to the fruit bowls and picked up five oranges.

Gasps of surprise and delighted laughter filled the room as Nicole began to juggle the oranges. She added a banana, dropped off one orange and added two red apples. The myriad of colors sailed higher and higher. The guests applauded, spellbound at the flying fruit. Nicole put down the apples, then the banana, and rolled the remaining oranges from her shoulder to her wrist in a waterfall. Calmly, she walked back to the teapot and began to stack the cups and saucers as if nothing had happened. From the corner of her eyes, she noticed that Brown, summoned by Big Em, was watching her from the doorway.

"That was fascinating!" called Mrs. Dupont across the room. "Encore! You're wonderful."

A stately guest, a Mrs. Pritchard from her nametag, came across the open floor to the beautiful white Steinway by the French doors, and produced sheet music. She seated herself, flexed her fingers, and ruffling through the pages, made her selection.

Brown and Big Em were heading purposefully toward Nicole and the teapot but before they could reach the table, Nicole slipped out and hurried over to the piano. "Do you play 'Tea For Two?'" she asked Mrs. Pritchard, who stared at her curiously.

"Do you sing?" Mrs. Pritchard asked.

"No, but I can dance if you can play it."

"I played at La Scala, dear," the pianist informed her. "I believe I can manage 'Tea For Two.'"

Powerful fingers embraced the keys and the jaunty tune poured forth effortlessly as Nicole removed her smock and her glasses and moved to the center of the floor. It was hard to even soft tap in sneakers, but she danced around the room. She picked up a handful of sand from a large cactus plant and tossed it to the floor.

The guests sat like statues. Coffee grew cold, cookies were forgotten, as the piano pounded and Nicole danced on the sand making long dragging noises with her shoes.

Mrs. Pritchard, nodding and smiling, segued into "Entrance of the Gladiators" and Nicole went to the far end of the room and executed six neat forward flyers until she stood once more beside the piano.

"We got us a gawd damn acca-bat," decided Big Em. "I guess you seen that."

"And they loved it," said Brown, peering at the guests with narrowed eyes. "This is the most excitement we've had in ages."

"You're gonna fire that bitch, aren't you?"

"Not in a million years," snapped Brown.

"But she sassed me! She did the fruit!"

Without answering, Brown turned and left the room.

Nicole saw Big Em standing in the hallway to the kitchen and knew that that way would only lead to trouble, so she made her way toward the terrace where Saucy Dodd and Mrs. Hemphill had been sitting. As she passed by the tables in the gathering room, old hands adorned with many diamond rings reached out to touch her. One old gentleman kissed her hand.

"Will you come and dance again?" one begged. "Maybe you can teach us."

"We enjoyed it. My husband would have liked the juggling, God rest him."

"Are you in show business?"

And the hands, just touching, making contact with something magic that may, somehow, transfer the spirit to themselves and bring back youth and times past.

Nicole pressed each hand as she passed giving each a moment, and a thank-you, so that by the time she reached the terrace her quarry had disappeared. A glance back at the door told her Big Em was biding her time, waiting for her to return to the kitchen.

Nicole left by the terrace, ran around the house, and entered the kitchen by the back door. The help was supposed to be given two meals, and she had not yet had breakfast. So she filled a thermos with hot coffee, threw in two sugars, and grabbed a handful of cookies, beating it out the back door just as she heard the heavy tread of Big Em coming down the hall.

Mrs. Hemphill's room was on the second floor, and ignoring the elevator, Nicole took the stairs two steps at a time, arriving just as Saucy Dodd came out of the room.

"Hey, could you sit my lady for a few minutes? She'll be no trouble. She's going to sleep until one or later. I want to call my boyfriend and tell him I gotta work tonight," begged Saucy.

"Sure. I'm on my break. Can you get back in twenty minutes?" Nicole agreed.

Saucy started to rush down the hall, and then turned. "You couldn't work five to nine for me, could you? The relief girl says she's sick and can't show up."

"Maybe. What do I have to do?"

"Supper and bed. Miss is a doll!"

"I can do that."

Mon Dieu, there was a God, and he was listening to Nicole, she breathed. Given four hours, she could count Mrs. Hemphill's teeth and find out the name of her second grade teacher, if she could only get her to talk.

The tall, silver-haired lady lay across the bed, dressed except for her shoes, and the light steady breathing indicated sleep.

Nicole sat down on the far side of the room under the window and placed her thermos on the small table there as she surveyed the surroundings. The furniture was French provincial, the carpet off-white. The daughter's pictures were everywhere, on the desk, on the wall, the bedside table. Lily Ann Hemphill, only child of Ann and William De Haviland Hemphill, vanished, stolen, run away—never to return. On the bedside table was a prescription bottle, and Nicole picked it up and looked at the label. Immediately, an alarm bill went off. She had never seen a prescription printed by hand, in ink, rather than typewritten. The information was scant, Hemphill, twice a day at nine and three, Dr. Wardlaw, and no indication what the medication was, or what it was prescribed for. She shook out the tablets into her hand and to her amazement the small letters DZ were imprinted in the center of each tablet. She knew these tablets! Beau Jackson had a bottle in the medicine cabinet in the Alexandria office, but they were in a nonprescription bottle that in no way resembled this container.

Mrs. Hemphill stirred and looked up.

"Saucy? Are you Sylvia?"

"No, ma'am. I'm Nicole. Saucy has gone to make a telephone call. Can I get you anything?"

"I smell coffee. They give me decaf, but it is so watered down, its just hot water."

"I have coffee," confided Nicole, "and it's the good stuff. Two sugars. I was just about to have some when you woke."

"You won't tell?"

"Never."

She found a plastic glass in the bathroom, and poured Mr. Hemphill a steaming cup. She poured herself one in the metal cap of the thermos.

"Cheers," Nicole said.

"Bottom's up!" giggled Mrs. Hemphill, sitting up slowly and reaching for the glass. "I'm a little dizzy. I sleep so much."

"Have a cookie."

"Oh god, is this real?" exclaimed Mrs. Hemphill, sucking up the coffee like a person dying from thirst. "Is there more?"

"Sure, take your time."

"William liked his coffee very hot. Is he here, dear? No, no, he is gone. All of them are gone. Mother, Father. Is my old nanny in the cemetery too?"

"I expect so."

"Is there enough for another cup? Oh, I am rude to be drinking your coffee."

Saucy knocked gently and walked into the room, instantly smelling the coffee.

"Is that decaf, Nancy?" she asked suspiciously. "She can only have decaf."

"My name is not Nancy. It's Nicole."

"Saucy, you will not mention this," declared Mrs. Hemphill, finishing her second cup.

"Yes, ma'am," agreed Saucy reluctantly, and turned to Nicole, "But if you sub for me tonight, you better not try no more diet changes."

Nicole stuffed the last cookie in her pocket and picked up the thermos. "See you at five."

Walking down the hall to the stairs, she took out the tablet she had palmed from the bedside bottle. That little DZ stood for Doz, a sleeping pill. There was only one reason a sleeping pill would be given twice in the daylight hours, to affect that slow, dazed appearance that mimicked a more dangerous disease.

She went down to the nurse's station and asked for something for a headache. The medicine cabinet was opened, and Nicole quickly scanned the shelves for Doz, but there was none. Mrs. Hemphill's medication had come from another source. "I wonder if I could have Tylenol instead of Aspirin."

"Excuse me a sec. I believe one of the other nurses took the Tylenol down to Mr. Taylor's room," the nurse said as she hurried out. "That's a definite no-no!"

Nicole perused the medicine cabinet, and she took a bottle of generic aspirin. Then her eyes lit on a large box of chocolate-flavored laxative. On impulse, she snatched a handful and shoved them into her pocket, replacing the box just in time.

"Here you go. There're cups by the sink," the nurse said, handing out two tablets.

"Thanks so much."

* * *

Mrs. Hemphill, at five o'clock, was her old drowsing self, picking listlessly at her supper, which she had had sent up to her room. Nicole ate with her, a sandwich she had brought from the kitchen, with a cold Sprite. It reminded her of Beau Jackson, who always drank Sprite. There were cans of Sprite in the office refrigerator when there was nothing else to drink. She needed to call Beau. Or should she report to Major Whitt? His number would not be listed at that new house, and he had not given it to her.

"My house was on fire," said Mrs. Hemphill.

"Yes."

"I heard my daughter's voice, and I thought it was a dream, then I smelled the smoke. I know it was Lily Ann."

"And then," said Nicole, treading carefully, "you found out the kitchen was afire, no?"

"No," said Mrs. Hemphill, moving a piece of lettuce around her plate, "another fire."

Nicole waited.

"I heard Lily Ann. She was talking and crying from a long way off and then, there was another voice—I thought maybe it was the TV. William was sleeping soundly. A stranger was talking and crying. I thought I was dreaming, you see. I went back to sleep. Later, I woke and smelled the fire. I told this to Saucy. Did I tell you?"

"No, ma'am, but I'd like to hear more."

"That was the first fire, not the kitchen."

"There were two fires?"

"I looked outside that night. My windows were open and smoke came up past my window. It was just Mr. Gantry burning trash—how strange . . ."

"Mr. Gantry burning trash?" prompted Nicole.

"Three o'clock in the morning," said Mrs. Hemphill. We left to go to the White House as guests of honor just two hours later. See, I do remember. "My husband received the highest honor that can be bestowed on a civilian for his work during time of the war. I don't think I'm crazy, do you?"

"Absolutely not."

"I am so tired."

"Let me help you get ready for bed. I think you'll be feeling better tomorrow."

"You're very kind, Sylvia."

Nicole helped her into her nightgown and sat by the bed until Mrs. Hemphill slept. She must have been a beautiful young woman, Nicole mused, smoothing the silver hair. But someone is playing dirty tricks. She reached over, picked up the bottle of DZ tablets, and emptied them into a compartment of her shoulder bag. She replaced them with the generic aspirins on which she had copied DZ, the two small letters in black ink with a ballpoint pen.

* * *

The kitchen crew was fixing the lunch trays. Big Em was moving about putting bits and pieces into her mouth, pushing her guest's trays together, ready to put them on her trolleys. Nicole was doing salads, and Janna was doing desserts. Alice was handling special needs, diabetes, allergies, etc.

Nicole worked her way over to Janna. "Mrs. Cogbill and Broaddus are diabetic and take no sweets, but I see chocolate mousse on their trays."

"They are for Big Em," Janna whispered. "She puts whipped cream on top and a tiny garnish of chocolate shavings over the cream."

Nicole went to the telephone in the gathering room and dialed the Meadowlea Manor switchboard. When she got through, she asked for Kitchen. "Big Em to the front office, please," she said and immediately hung up. She raced out of the French door, rounded the house, and entered the back door of the kitchen.

Janna had loaded her trolleys. Big Em was going down the hall. The two cooks were standing outside, one smoking, and the other talking, until dinnertime, as their work was done.

Nicole opened the napkin she had brought in her pocket, crossed to the Cogbill and Broaddus trays, pushed the mousse apart and dumped in the contents. She pushed the mousse back together, smoothed the cream, and sprinkled the rest of the chocolate shavings lavishly on the top.

"Bon appetit."

She loaded her trolley and headed for the second floor. She quickly distributed her trays, saving Mrs. Hemphill to the last. She knocked lightly and pushed the door open, surprised to find two other people in the room, a tall man with black, very slick hair, and the bearing of a military man, and a short-haired woman, stuffed into a light green pantsuit like a sausage. Saucy hovered in the corner, leaning against a chest of drawers.

"Come in, dear," said Mrs. Hemphill, looking lovely in a haired suit, "This is my house manager, Mr. Gantry, and our cook, Olla Rhodes. Frank and Olla have been with me—how long, Frank?" She was speaking clearly.

"Eighteen years. Ms. Ann, that is, with Mr. William."

"We'll be taking her home Sunday. Gantry had them working night and day, and the house looks wonderful, everything is new. New stove, new refrigerator, and lovely new wallpaper!" put in the cook. "The fire destroyed everything."

"Got out of hand," added Gantry.

"I feel better today," stated Mrs. Hemphill, looking at the lunch tray, then up at Nicole. "No coffee today?"

"Perhaps later," Nicole promised. She put a fresh linen napkin across Mrs. Hemphill's lap, gave a little nod to the visitors, and left the room. Mrs. H was going home Sunday. So little time! She had barely moved her trolley to the service elevator when Mrs. Hemphill's door opened and the two visitors emerged.

"Enjoy your lunch now," called Olla Rhodes.

"And don't forget to take your medicine," reminded Gantry.

The door closed. There was a low, angry murmuring in the hall.

"She looked almost lively. Aren't those damn pills working? We should get some Valium," said Rhodes. "I'm sick of that house, and I'm tired of waiting for my money."

They came around the corner to the elevator just as Nicole wrestled the metal trolley into the service elevator. As the door closed, she saw Gantry staring at her. Olla Rhodes tugged his sleeve.

"Do you think she heard?" she hissed as the door closed.

The elevator started down, and Nicole was unable to hear his reply. She had to get in touch with Beau Jackson. On Sunday Ms. Ann Hemphill would be back at the mansion and subject to any kind of medication that would produce symptoms of Alzheimer's, and subsequent death, given time. What money? Were the servants in Mrs. Hemphill's will? The foxes were already in charge of the hen house, and Mrs. Hemphill would pass on without a defensive squawk if they were successful.

The kitchen was in chaos. Janna and Alice crowded around Big Em, who was wildly clutching her stomach. Big Em's eyes grew large with apprehension, and she bolted up from her chair with great alacrity.

"Get outa mah way! Oh, shit, shit, shit." She waddled from the room as fast as she could, heading for the servant's restroom.

"What's wrong with her?" asked Nicole. She had no idea that laxatives would work that fast when laced with chocolate mousse.

"It's the runs," explained Alice.

The cook threw up his hands. "Why is she sick? Nobody else is sick! Everybody ate the same. She just ate too much. I don't hear any complaints, only from her. Everything I cook is very clean and of very fine quality. Why just this woman gets sick?"

"She ate too much," agreed Janna and Alice.

"Too much," echoed Nicole, stacking her trays. Maybe half a dozen laxatives were too much, she considered, but she's a very heavy woman.

Big Em was not seen for the rest of the day. On her break time, Nicole filled the thermos with hot, sweet coffee, and found a basket of macaroons cooling near the range. She stacked a dozen in a napkin and went up to Mrs. Hemphill's room. Saucy answered her knock because Mrs. Hemphill was playing solitaire on the table near the window and vaguely paying attention to a soap opera.

"I don't know what's wrong with her," confided Saucy, taking the macaroons.

"What do you mean?"

"I mean she's not asleep!"

"You can take your break now if you like. I can stick around," offered Nicole. She picked up the medicine bottle. "Did she have her pills at three?"

"Yes," Saucy answered. She paused and said, "She wants me to go home with her come Sunday morning. She asked me to come with her in front of them, and then, that Olla woman took me aside and said Ms. Ann had enough help at home, and she didn't need me. What shall I do?"

"I think you should go. It's not up to them, it's Mrs. Hemphill's decision. I'll come along and visit a while if she asks me."

"Oh, would you? And it's nearer my home than out here at Meadowlea. Thanks, Nicole."

"Fifteen minutes, okay?" reminded Nicole as Saucy danced over to the door.

"I won again," exclaimed Mrs. Hemphill. "This is the first day I've played in a year. My mind just wouldn't concentrate." She threw down the cards. "Darling! You remembered," she said as soon as she spied the thermos.

They drank the hot, strong coffee and put away several crusty macaroons as they watched the soap opera.

"I believe," explained Mrs. Hemphill, "The woman in black has been married four times, and her daughter married one of the ex-husbands. That child—who it belongs to is anybody's guess."

"What a tangled web we weave, when first we practice to . . . conceive . . ." paraphrased Nicole.

"The word is *deceive*."

"I know. I was speaking of the fatherless child"

Mrs. Hemphill looked at her speculatively. "Just who are you, Nicole, and why are you interested in me?"

"Yesterday you insisted on calling me Sylvia. Today, you are coming out of your confusion, and haven't fallen asleep. Frankly, I believe someone has deliberately created your disoriented condition," Nicole said slowly, "and I want to help you."

"My husband, William, held a high office in the U. S. Government. Are you FBI?"

"No, ma'am. I just want to help you." Nicole repeated. "Saucy thinks that your mind holds a secret that is a threat to someone else. It has something to do with the two fires, but you say about the first one Mr. Gantry was burning trash, and the big fire started from a gas leak, each different from the other, and yet, maybe they were connected."

"Two innocent people are dead."

"Why did those two people go into the kitchen that morning?"

"It was Gantry and Olla's day off. The woman called Alma was to cook, and I guess Mr. Williams would serve breakfast. They had worked for us but three weeks."

"Mrs. Hemphill, I want you to ask Ms. Brown for me to go with you Friday. Tell them I am giving you special physical therapy that you wish to continue at home."

Mrs. Hemphill smiled. "I am convinced you are with FBI or perhaps Secret Service. You're much too clever. I'll see to it."

They heard Saucy out in the hall. "Let's keep this between us for now," suggested Nicole. "We'll talk again."

"Yes, yes!" Mrs. Hemphill agreed, and added, "they traveled with us everywhere for four years," and as Saucy returned, "Thank you for the coffee."

"Are you wanting your nap now, Ms. Ann?" asked Saucy.

"I think I'd like a walk about the grounds. I see little ponds and statues down there."

"Oh, Ms. Ann, it's like a blooming miracle, you wanting to go out!"

Nicole took her thermos and quietly left the room. Three months under constant sedation and now jolted back to reality with aspirin and caffeine! No wonder it seemed like a miracle. The answers lay at Hemphill, the family plantation near Charlottesville, which had borne the family name since prior to the Civil War.

* * *

"Ms. Brown, I am leaving Sunday morning at the end of the week. I'm sorry," stated Nicole.

"It's Emma, isn't it? I heard about the incident with the refrigerator. She has been a lot of trouble for me," sighed Brown.

"Emma?"

"The girls call her Big Em, because of her size, but I remember her as a toddler, you see, her mother worked for my mother for many years, so when Emma asked for a job at Meadowlea, I tried to give her a chance."

"Don't worry about what she did to me. It's the old, helpless guests I'd worry about."

"Oh, Emma wouldn't . . ."

"Yes, she would. She has a cruel streak and a controlling nature, and I've heard rumors about her cruel treatment of at least one of your guests."

"There was an incident of a sprained back, and a foot caught in a wheelchair, but these things happen."

"And a broken arm? Some concerned relative is going to take you to court, Ms. Brown, and sue you right out of that chair of which you're so proud. Let Emma go, Ms. Brown, before you have an unexplained death to contend with."

Ms. Brown turned her chair away from Nicole and stared out of the window. In the tree just outside, a small bird picked at green berries on a parasite vine that had climbed the trunk and spread to low-hanging branches, bearing them down.

There was a knock at the office door, and Mrs. Pritchard, the piano player, pushed her way regally in without waiting for an invitation. She held a small pair of black leather dancing shoes in one hand.

"I thought I saw you come in here, my little friend! Some of the ladies and gentlemen were wondering if you would entertain us again, and I borrowed these from Frieda. She has little feet like you."

Nicole smiled and took the shoes. "It will have to be this afternoon. I will be leaving Meadowlea. I do a little tap number that won a few prizes when I was a child, but I'll need a raincoat."

"'Stormy Weather?'" guessed Mrs. Pritchard.

"No. 'Singing in the Rain.' Do you have the music?"

"For that old favorite? I can play it in my sleep, dear. Later, after lunch?" asked Mrs. Pritchard. "I'll find a rain coat." She hustled out on her new mission.

"You made yourself popular in one short week, Nicole, and you'll be missed," said Ms. Brown. "And you're right about Emma. I must let her go."

"Well, I'll be getting back to the kitchen. I've got to get my trays ready," said Nicole, as she crossed to the door.

"Oh yes, Nicole, Cook said you were the fastest and cleanest dishwasher he has ever worked with."

"I had four years prior experience."

"But you're not a dishwasher, are you?"

"Not by trade, no, ma'am."

She went back to the kitchen and put her lunch trays on her trolley.

After lunch, a crowd assembled in the gathering room. The kitchen staff hovered in the door from the hallway.

Nicole put on Frieda's little shoes, Mr. Henderson's trench coat, and Burberry hat, and as the notes of the joyous song pounded from Mrs. Pritchard's talented fingers, Nicole danced and danced and danced until her audience imagined they could all feel the raindrops.

Chapter Twelve

Waiting for Lily Ann

Sunday

Hemphill, with its ancient brick walls and tall white pillars resembled the O'Hara mansion of literary fame, Tara. It was obvious Saucy Dodd was excited and impressed by its size and beauty, as Carlo, the driver and yardman, drove the old Lincoln up the circular drive.

Nicole, seated in the front passenger seat, had been advised that Carlo was either mute, or he spoke no English, so she had no conversation with him all the way. He was thin and dark, with a furtive way of cutting his eyes around to one side without any movement of his head. Nicole instinctively mistrusted him.

Frank Gantry came out of the front door, greeted Mrs. Hemphill with enthusiasm. Olla Rhodes appeared behind him, all smiles and starched apron. They both looked shocked when, not only Saucy Dodd, but also Nicole, stepped out of the car and helped wrestled Saucy's bag from the trunk. They obviously were here to stay.

"I'm afraid it's a bad time to visit," said Gantry. "The storms of the end of summer have begun, and we had quite a crasher last night. Dreadful lightning circled the house."

"Lost our lights for several hours," put in Mrs. Rhodes. "I wasn't expecting company, Ms. Ann. How many will there be?"

"My niece, Marilyn, and her husband, Paulie and Shelby, myself, Nicole, and Saucy," counted Mrs. Hemphill.

"And will these two be eating in the dining room or the kitchen, Ms. Ann?"

"Why, with me, Gantry!"

"Yes, ma'am."

Mrs. Rhodes pressed close to Nicole's side whispered, "We weren't expecting the two. You won't mind staying in the room with a colored, will you?"

"A colored what?" Nicole whispered back.

"Saucy Dodd. It's back stairs."

Nicole shrugged. "The bed is good, no?"

Mrs. Hemphill was so busy directing Frank Gantry and Carlo about her pictures of her daughter, and when they were to be returned to special places about the house, that she didn't notice Saucy Dodd and Nicole being spirited away to a room beyond the kitchen in the servant's quarters.

The room was bright, decorated blue and cream plaids, two double beds, and a delightful corner fireplace. Old fashion rag rugs lay next to the beds on highly polished floors.

"To think I gave up my room at the motel for this?" Nicole joked, tossing her shoulder bag on the bed nearest the door. "And a telephone!"

"I'll call my mom," said Saucy.

"And I'll call . . . ," Nicole began, and then noticed the pad of numbers under the dial, all connected to a single number. Anyone on the same line could hear any other conversation. It was an old system that had never been changed.

"Your mom?" inquired Saucy.

"No, it would be long distance, and I haven't much money," Nicole answered. She had to get in touch to tell Beau Jackson and Major Whitt that she was no longer at Meadowlea Manor and a collect call could still be overheard and noted on the bill.

"How far is it to town?"

"About three miles," Saucy answered. "Why?"

"I need to get my clothes and my car. Mrs. Hemphill insisted we all come out here together and my car is back there in front of Number Six."

I will run it, Nicole decided, I'll get up as I usually do at 5:00 a.m. and take off as if for my usual run and keep on going. She took out her track shoes and put them on the end of the bed.

Dinner was at seven, with Marilyn and Larry Hewitt and their grown-up children, Paulie and Shelby, who evidently still lived at home, although they appeared to be in their late twenties or early thirties. Nice people, and they seemed genuinely fond of Mrs. Hemphill. They had a home and business in town, Nicole noted. After dessert, they spoke of other relatives, and Saucy and Nicole excused themselves and went to their room to let them catch up on family matters.

As they lay on their beds, Saucy casually said, "I think it was funny, you know, how Ms. Ann started getting better when you arrived. Before, she was just half there, mixing up people, and sleeping all the time."

Nicole sat up. "Can I count on you to keep quiet if I tell you the truth about what was happening to your Ms. Ann?"

"I've been suspicious a long time. Sometimes her head was right, and she'd talk fine, and other times she'd sleep five, six hours a day."

"It was the pills. You gave her sleeping pills twice a day."

"No! It was anti-depressant! It was Prozac, the happy pill. I called and asked Dr. Wardlow myself!"

"But they had been substituted with a strong sleeping pill. When I came, I recognized what they were and replaced them with a generic aspirin."

"And the coffee, hot, dark, and very sweet!" giggled Saucy. "Just like me." Then she added, "Those pills fooled the doctor at Meadowlea. He diagnosed the first stages of Alzheimer's. Nicole, I was so scared she was going to die on me. I went to the police, but they didn't do anything. They made no report. Ms. Ann is so sweet. Why would anyone want to hurt her?" pondered Saucy.

"Money is behind most acts of evil. Find the money, and you've got the perpetrators in most cases."

"There's love, sex, and jealousy."

"We're not dealing with those issues in this case, no?" stated Nicole. "I think I'll hit the showers, and get to bed early."

"Will the TV bother you?"

"No. Watch as long as you like."

* * *

Monday

Before dawn, Nicole was pounding along the edge of the old highway to Charlottesville when she saw a public telephone and stopped to call to Alexandria, even though she knew no one was there at that hour.

"I am at the Hemphill estate, three miles west and south of town. Can you put somebody in the vicinity?" she asked and hung up. She stopped for coffee and a donut, rested, stretched, and ran the next few miles to the motel. By the time, she had settled her bill and retrieved the blue Tempo; it felt wonderful to sit down at last. Muscles were protesting, feet sweating in the track shoes as she drove swiftly back to Hemphill and arrived just as the household was stirring.

Mrs. Hemphill called to her from the sunny terrace at the rear of the house.

"Come have breakfast, and after, I'll show you around the grounds."

Saucy Dodd stood uneasily beside the table. She checked the plates and napkins. She found a hearth broom and swept the terrace, looking around for more make-work.

"For heaven's sake, Saucy, do stop that fussing and join me at the table," demanded Mrs. Hemphill, gazing up at the sky at a gray cloud moving in from the west. "I believe we'll see another storm this evening."

Mrs. Rhodes came in with a fresh fruit platter, little link sausages and scrambled eggs, biscuits and marmalade. Coffee, in an electric pot, sat nearby on a wicker buffet. "The cantaloupe and eggs are local," she announced, as proudly as if she had grown them herself.

"Wonderful! Everything looks tasty. It is good to be home, Olla."

"Yes, we're so happy, me and Frank," gushed the cook. "Is there anything else?"

"Just a moment, Olla," said Mrs. Hemphill. "I seem to have misplaced my prescription bottle. I haven't seen it since I got home from Meadowlea, and I have an appointment tomorrow with Dr. Wardlaw."

Mrs. Rhodes flushed. "I'm sure I haven't seen it. I'm in the kitchen. The upstairs belong to the maids."

"I've asked them," retorted Mrs. Hemphill shortly. "It just seems to have disappeared."

Mrs. Rhodes left the room, and they filled their plates. Saucy poured the coffee and seemingly reluctant to do so, sat down at the table.

"Do you ride horses?" Mrs. Hemphill asked Nicole. "Virginia is horse country, you know, and we keep several Arabians."

"I've never ridden a horse," admitted Nicole. "But I am willing to try."

"Then we'll take the golf cart, just you and I. Saucy Dodd has a thing about cemeteries, and I do want to show you the Mausoleum."

The views from the terrace were breathtaking, stretches of gardens near the house, two guesthouses, a vast barn, and a stable beyond, framed by mountains so dense with pines that one could barely detect the roads that wound their way to the top and steeply down.

"It is so beautiful, no?" murmured Nicole.

"My husband was born in this place. I'm sure he would have never suffered that heart failure if only Lily Ann had come home. I blame myself too. Because of her leaving home, I was in such a deep depression I couldn't see his suffering. And now, when Lily Ann comes home, I'll have to tell her, your daddy is gone."

"You tried detectives?"

"Of course. They traced her to New York, to a series of motels and shelters. They claimed those who knew her said she was addicted to something called crack, and another said heroin, and living with a young man. I know Lily Ann, and it was all lies. At each place, they had moved on—and then nothing!"

"I'll shake your things and hang them in your closets," offered Saucy, "While you are gone."

"And do look for that damn prescription. If you're finished, I'll have the cart brought around," she said to Nicole. She went to the telephone and punched in the number for the garages.

In a few minutes, the golf cart arrived, and Nicole set her coffee cup down hard on the table, trying not to pay attention to the driver. Even at a distance, he looked familiar.

"Now, what is your name?" demanded Mrs. Hemphill. "I declare we have new help every month. I don't know where Gantry finds them."

"My name is Willie Lewis, ma'am."

When Mrs. Hemphill went to the kitchen to see to the lunch menu, Nicole glanced up to see Willie Lewis smiling down at her. Either Beau Jackson or Major Whitt had gotten her message and sent backup. Willie Lewis, in old jeans and plaid shirt was looking healthy, boyish, and fully recovered from his ordeal in Florida. When Saucy Dodd left to go upstairs, Nicole smiled, and said, "Driving golf carts now? I thought you preferred riding in car trunks."

"Great to see you, Nicole!" he said quickly.

Mrs. Hemphill was returning from the kitchen.

"I'll find you later," whispered Nicole, as he turned away and headed for the stables.

Ann Hemphill took the wheel and expertly guided the cart across the lawn, passing by Willie Lewis without a glance, and drove through the garden paths while she pointed out various plantings, then out to the outbuildings, and followed white fencing that enclosed the horse pasture. Several sheep came to the fence as if looking for a handout as she sped bumpily past their enclosure. The lush grass was still damp from the dew as the little cart plowed across the wide expanse to the stone fence that surrounded the cemetery.

"Bad choice, putting the loved ones out here where the drainage is terrible. See how the old graves have sunken. A disgrace! I am so glad William is inside the mausoleum with his brother, his sister, and his parents, of course. Then there are the Grandparents, a widowed aunt, and several babies represented by tiny stone angels. Other family members are buried nearby, and over there on the far side of the fence are many servants and some ne'er do-wells of the Hemphill family from way back."

"Ne'er do-wells?" asked Nicole, curious.

"Non-Christian. Black sheep."

They had arrived at the mausoleum, a tall, white stone structure with double coffin doors of oak that were carved with religious figures. As they got out of the cart, Nicole noticed a small new mound to one side of the broad step.

"That is Boomer, German Shepherd mix. He was William's dog. He came and lay here every day after William died. One day Gantry came and told me that Boomer had also passed away, so I told him to bury him on that very spot."

"Was he very old?" Nicole asked.

Mrs. Hemphill paused. "He was about nine. Always digging up something! One day he brought me a man's cheap quartz watch all covered with mud. But William, and I too, adored that dog. Shall we go in?"

It was freezing cold inside the mausoleum after the warm August sun outside. Hastily, Mrs. Hemphill showed her around and pointed out several empty niches near her husband's space. "For myself, Lily Ann, and other family as we go to join William and meet the Maker. Come, it's too cold to linger in here."

When they came out, they noticed the man, Carlo, engaged in shoveling dirt on the ne'er do-well's side of the stone fence. He saw them, stopped his work, and turned away.

"What is he doing? Go and see, Nicole. It is too wet to drive over there in this soggy mess."

Nicole crossed the grass and stepped over the stile, appalled to see gaping holes where unmarked graves had sunken, some revealing cement, and others rotted wood—coffins? A few had squares of plywood pressed in the earth, covered with artificial turf. Carlo had been piling extra dirt on the two most recent graves, which had already begun to sink. He appeared angry when she stepped over the fence and he motioned her to go back to the other side.

"Whose graves are these, Carlo?"

He leaned on the shovel and glowered at her. He stood in front of the section where he had been shoveling but Nicole discerned two distinct coffin-like shapes in the ground just behind him. Who would bury coffins in such a shallow way? They couldn't be more than two or three feet down below the ground surface, she figured. Did they care too little about the dead to dig down a respectable six feet especially in an area with such deplorable drainage?

"Who lies here, Carlo?" she demanded again.

He jammed the shovel into the mud, turned his back and strode rapidly into the woods. Nicole walked over and gazed down into the shallow coverings. The outlines of two coffins lay side by side and she picked up the shovel. Within a foot of the new dirt, she felt the scratch of metal on top of metal. A small brass plaque on the left coffin read Alma Patty. No birth or death dates. Nicole dug no further. She knew that the other coffin would be that of Ezekial Williams and that these were the two homeless people who had died in the fire that had destroyed the kitchen.

"What in God's name are you doing, Nicole?" called Mrs. Hemphill, impatiently waiting by the cart.

"I'm coming!" Nicole called back, replacing the shovel in the earth. A bit of gold, a twisted circle of glass crunched under her foot, and she reached down and pulled up a pair of eyeglasses, much like the pair of clear-lens glasses she was wearing to alter her own appearance. Quickly, she shoved them into her jacket pocket and jumped over the stile.

"Carlo was filling in the two new graves."

"Already? I told William years ago that was a sorry spot to bury anyone. I vow I will not let another body go into that soggy ground."

* * *

Mrs. Hemphill was invited to a late lunch at her niece's home, so Nicole and Saucy decided to eat in the new kitchen with Kelly and Dorritt, the two maids, and a sullen Carlo, who kept staring at Nicole in as menacing a way as he could muster without speaking.

"Can Carlo speak if he wants to?" asked Nicole, staring back at him.

"Nobody wants to speak to him," giggled Dorritt. Kelly nodded in agreement.

"Maybe he speaks Spanish, Como esta, Carlo? Bueno? Muy loco?" Nicole said, taunting him. "Muy loco?"

Carlo threw down his napkin and stalked away from the table, scowling. The back door banged behind him. It was exactly the reaction Nicole wanted, because now the maids would speak more freely about the Hemphills.

"What did you say to make him leave?" chorused the two maids. "Tell us!"

"I asked him if he was crazy."

"Oh, my Gawd! He'll kill you!"

"Maybe not." Nicole shrugged. "Were you here the night of the big fire?"

"No, the regular staff has weekends off unless there's a party or guests, which there has not been since Mr. William died and Ms. Ann has been wasting away."

"Her daughter was a beautiful girl, from her picture. Too bad she ran away."

"She was wild," murmured Kelly. "She smoked pot in the stable when she was here, and drank booze, when she was just a kid! But I wish she'd come back, for Ms. Ann's sake."

"I think she's dead," whispered Dorritt.

"Why?"

"Because she doesn't write home for money, she maxed out her college charge cards, and that girl never worked for nothing in her life."

As the sandwiches were finished and the Cherry Cobbler devoured, Nicole learned that Olla Rhodes slept with Frank Gantry five nights a week and had a husband in town. And also how they both went into a rage when Mr. William died and left all his money to Ms. Ann, in trust, to disperse in her own will or distribute in her lifetime as she desired. A sum of $180,000 each was suggested to Rhodes and Gantry and smaller sums to other help, but they hadn't seen a penny. If Lily Ann returned, it would all go to her and as Kelly put it, hell would freeze over before that girl would give up a nickel of her inheritance to a bunch of hired help, no matter how many years they worked there.

Saucy Dodd kept on eating without adding to the conversation. She was leaving at the end of the week to return to her job at Meadowlea, and when she completed her year there, Ms. Ann had promised the tuition for nursing school. Saucy had told no one, not even Nicole. Ms. Ann wasn't stingy with her money; she was just careful where she put it.

"How does Gantry know what is in Mr. William's will?" Nicole asked.

"He knows the combo to Ms. Ann's safe better than she does. When Carlo drives her out, he goes into the library. He's not fooling anybody—except Ms. Ann."

After lunch, Saucy went to their room, and Nicole wandered out on the terrace, and then strolled thru the gardens to the stables where she saw Willie Lewis grooming one of the stallions.

"What a beautiful animal!" she breathed, touching the sleek white back carefully.

"Don't stand behind him, he shies."

"They are very tall, no?"

"Major Whitt sent me. No prob getting in here. The Employment Agency in town supplies new help and hire every few months. They can't keep help with Gantry on everybody's back. What can I do?"

"I don't trust Carlo. Could you do something to get him fired?" asked Nicole hopefully.

"He's in Gantry's pocket."

"We'll have to do the best we can. I want you to open a couple of coffins, look inside, and report what, or who you see. I found eyeglasses in the mud. The dog, Boomer, dug up a watch, now he's dead, and he was only nine years old."

"Which coffins?"

"The newest graves, just on the other side of the stile. Oh, oh, here comes Mr. Sweetie Pie. Do you have a weapon?"

He casually patted his loose plaid shirt.

"I'll come down about 2:00 a.m. You dig, and I'll cover you," she muttered as she walked away.

"Aw, I get all the fun."

Nicole grinned at him. "I like the way your nose mended. It has an interesting little hump. You're looking great."

Carlo strode past, motioning to Willie to bring the stallion back into the stable, and Nicole moved along, admiring the tall sunflowers near the gates to the pasture.

* * *

In the late afternoon, it began to rain and continued until midnight. Saucy Dodd watched the late news and as Nicole pretended sleep, Saucy continued her TV marathon with Jay Leno's late night show. Finally, the lamp went out, Saucy used her nose spray, and soon her measured breathing signaled that at last she slept. At 1:30 a.m., Nicole slipped out of bed and pulled on her jeans, leaving her feet bare. She took her revolver from her shoulder bag and stuck it in her waistband.

The rain pounded down as she opened the back door and slipped outside. A single security light was on the roof near the terrace, but she didn't need to go in that direction. However, Lewis would be coming from the stables when he had a break and would come close to it. Don't let him trigger the light, she prayed, as she hovered against the wall and when he appeared out of the dark, she was startled.

"I have a pen light," he whispered.

"Don't turn it on until we are behind the stone fence—just follow me and try not to fall," she directed. She bent close to the ground and began to run across the lawn to the cemetery with Lewis, also shoeless, just behind her.

Neither of them was aware of a third figure that had appeared from the shadows of the big magnolia trees and followed at leisure, aware of the place they were headed.

Nicole and Lewis, sliding on the grass and mud, ran past Boomer's grave, past the Hemphill mausoleum and through the graveyard. Their mucky feet climbed the stile to the far side, and they almost slid into the watery grave of Alma Patty. The coffin of Ezekial Williams sort of rocked up and down, lifting the edges of the excavation that encased the two recent graves. Someone had shoved an 8 × 4 piece of plywood down one side, but it was ineffectual. The torrential storm was winning and William's casket moved freely in the water and mud.

Willie Lewis jumped down beside it in the space between the two coffins, and standing hip deep, pried the cheap lid with a tire iron until they heard the sharp crack of wood and the lid lifted. Lewis peered in as Nicole centered a penlight on the decaying face, the remaining flesh ashy with severe burns.

"Black male, seventy to eighty," he stated. He ran his hand beneath the rigid body and closed the lid. "Nothing under him." He turned to Alma Patty's casket and went through the same routine.

"White female severely burned, sixty to seventy. Don't look, Nicole. Something's been in here."

As he closed the lid and climbed out of the pit, something metal caught on the bottom of the leg of his jeans. He shook it free and picked it up in his hand. It appeared to be part of a headlight for a bicycle or possibly a motorcycle. He jumped back into the pit and felt around.

"There's a bike under the coffins, and I think it was wrapped in plastic—trash bags maybe?" He held up a scrape of green plastic.

"I'll call Major Whitt and tell him we need a heavy back hoe down here. And of course, I'll need to explain to Mrs. Hemphill she has a problem down here," said Nicole, offering Lewis her hand. Bracing her feet apart, she jerked him up on firmer ground.

The figure waiting in the trees trotted quickly to the house and through the back door.

* * *

"Nicole! Come quick!" Saucy called loudly into Nicole's sleeping face. "You wake up! Something bad wrong with Ms. Ann!"

Nicole sat up and blinked at Saucy, her head still fuzzy from deep sleep.

"What?"

"She's real weak, and she threw up!"

Nicole scrambled from the bed and threw on a robe that belonged to Saucy. On bare feet, she sprinted up the back stairs two at a time and ran down the hall to where Mrs. Rhodes and Gantry hovered outside the door, seemingly reluctant to venture inside.

"I can't find it. I looked everywhere." Mrs. Rhodes was saying. She was literally wringing her hands, and her face was flushed.

"Shut up," warned Gantry, gripping her arm. He raised his arm, and she cowered, waiting for the blow, but he stopped in midair.

Nicole brushed past, followed by Saucy, and hurried to Mrs. Hemphill's bedside.

"What happened?" Nicole demanded, placing her hand on Mrs. Hemphill's forehead, which felt cold and damp with perspiration. "What did you have for breakfast?"

"I haven't had breakfast. I think it was a touch of stomach flu. I feel a little better now that I—oh, dear, help me to the bathroom."

Saucy rushed forward and circled Ms. Ann with her arms, hurrying the older woman into the bathroom. Nicole looked into the night table and rummaged through the clutter, eyeglasses, aspirin, Kleenex, notepad, two pens, nothing unusual. She suddenly realized that her bare foot was standing on a damp spot on the rug that trailed under the dust ruffle. She knelt down and looked under the bed. An overturned wine glass was caught in the covers that had slid down on the other side. She rounded the end of the bed, lifted the bedspread and managed to pull it out. A few drops of whitish liquid remained, and Nicole carefully placed the glass on the night table as Saucy and Mrs. Hemphill returned.

"Well, where did you find that?" Mrs. Hemphill asked, looking at the glass in surprise.

"Under the bed."

"Olla has been asking about it."

"White wine?"

"Yes, and there was a plate with cheese and crackers. It seems to be gone now. Olla brought me a little snack about eleven when she saw my light was still on, but it was late, and I didn't really want it. I thanked her and kept on reading my book. It must have been around 3:00 or 4:00 a.m.? I woke up feeling thirsty and sipped the wine, and then I tried to set the glass back on the table in the dark and missed. Where it rolled to, I had no idea, so I went back to sleep."

"And woke later with stomach pains?"

"It must have been the fish, the salmon. I ran into the bathroom and forced myself to throw up, to get rid of it. Oh, such cramps! I thought I was going to die."

A good possibility, Nicole thought, regarding the residue in the bottom of the wine glass.

"I think we should take you to the hospital. It could be food poisoning."

"Oh, they would insist on pumping my stomach! No, no, I don't want that," Mrs. Hemphill said, shaking her head.

"I'll stay right beside you, Ms. Ann," offered Saucy, hovering over the bed, and fluffing the pillows. "Do anything you want."

"I do feel better. Just let me sleep."

"You have an appointment with Dr. Wardlow at two o'clock," Saucy reminded her.

"I had forgotten. No hospital! I'll tell him about my upset. Now, go! Go! Let me rest."

Saucy sat down in the rocker next to the bed. Nicole carefully put the wine glass in the pocket of her borrowed robe, covered it with Kleenex and went out into the hall. Frank Gantry and Olla Rhodes were gone but knowing they were under suspicion, they could be waiting at the bottom of the back stairs. Nicole went to the front, came down the staircase into the huge front hall to find Gantry, a grim smile on his face, standing just out of sight near the library.

"You're out of your league, messing with me, you stupid little bitch," he muttered. "I was a Marine in 'nam before I served my personal hero, William Hemphill, the finest gentleman and best Secretary of Defense this country ever had."

"So, what is your problem with me?"

"You're a woman. You're all garbage. Blood-sucking leeches," he nodded upward. "Look how she's sitting on his money. I did everything for that man—I mean everything! I even buried his dog near his resting place."

"You killed that dog, no?" She challenged him, clutching the wine glass in her pocket. She could feel the moisture of the glass against her leg. "It had more years to live."

"Boomer is with his master," smiled Gantry. "It was a kindness. The same could happen to you. I want you out, you understand me?" Gantry warned, towering over her. He pinched her shoulder hard between his fingers, digging in and holding it until her arm went numb. "And take that nigger with you."

Nicole began to cry. She only had to think of Mimi, the tears always came unbidden, and it worked now. "I'll go," she promised, backing away toward the kitchen. "But I can't speak for Saucy Dodd. Meadowlea sent her for the whole week." She held onto the glass, and forced the tears to flow, because Gantry seemed to get such a pleasure from her pain. "I'll pack my things."

"But first, you tell me why you got that stable boy to open those coffins!"

Mon Dieu! Please God; if you're listening to Nicole please help me now, she prayed silently. She hung her head down, feeling her own tears splashing onto her breast as she waited for the divine intervention that had saved her in so many terrifying situations.

"My grandmother has been missing nearly a year," Nicole found her mouth saying. "She lived on the street. I thought . . . I thought . . . after I read about the fire, the old lady could be my grandmother, calling herself by the name, Alma Patty, because her name is Alma. But it wasn't her."

The story sounded preposterous even to Nicole, but Frank Gantry stood silently as if turning the possibility over in his mind, and she also kept silent making no movement to distract him.

"What does the boy know?" he asked finally.

"Nothing," she shrugged. "I asked him for a favor."

"Did you give him money?"

"He didn't want money. It was personal," she answered away as if embarrassed.

"Slut," Gantry snarled. "Get out! Go back to your whoring, out of William Hemphill's house."

She turned and ran into the back hall so fast she charged into Olla Rhodes, who had been listening in the hallway.

"Slut!" repeated Rhodes, flattened against the wall. "Sex with a stable boy! You don't value yourself very highly, do you, miss?" The voice grew louder as Nicole retreated down the hall. At the door to the back bedroom, Nicole turned.

"Better than that monster you've been sleeping with. You ought to try it."

Olla Rhodes' face grew red, and she screamed, rushing toward the door, but Nicole had slammed and locked it.

Nicole threw her clothes into her tote bag, with the exception of a big loose sweatshirt, clean jeans, and her track shoes. In the bathroom, she put the shoulder holster on over her bra and fastened the knife sheath around the left leg under a tube sock. Fully dressed, she dumped her toothbrush and cosmetics in her shoulder bag and placed the wine glass in a paper cup from the bathroom, covering it with another cup, and securing it with a rubber band. She set it upright in the bottom of her bag, lodging it among the cosmetics.

She looked outside of the one window of the bedroom. Gantry sat a few yards away on a stone bench, smoking a cigarette. She went to the bedroom door and looked through the keyhole. Olla sat on a chair in the hall, facing the door, gingerly holding a large shotgun across her lap. An expression of pure terror marred her soft, round face. Her legs trembled under the white apron she wore over her housedress and her eyes darted from side to side. What if Saucy came down the hall?

Nicole picked up the telephone and pushed the button for the stable. The receiver lifted but no one spoke. Carlo.

"Willie?" she said, listening to silence. She spoke again, this time very loudly. "Willy?"

Nearby a horse whined and stomped.

"Hello, this is Willie Lewis."

Somewhere else on the line there was a furtive click. A third party listened. Nicole went to the door and peeked thru the keyhole. Olla had left her post in the hall to listen in on the conversation.

"Willie, this is Nicole. I can't meet you tonight. I've heard from Dieter. I'll be leaving Hemphill today. Would you come to the back door and get my car keys and bring the Tempo around?"

"Yes, ma'am."

The reference to Bruce Malcom Dieter informed Lewis that temporarily the game was dead and Nicole had to leave quickly. He hung up the saddle he had been polishing and called out to Carlo he was going to the house. Carlo nodded and watched him leave.

Nicole looked out of the window. Olla came out of the kitchen, evidently relaying the telephone conversation, spoke to Gantry, and they stared at Willie Lewis as he approached the house. Gantry strode toward him blocking his way.

"Where do you think you're going?"

"To get Ms. Laurent's car keys, to bring her car around."

"She has a car?" Gantry asked. "She arrived with Mrs. Hemphill in the Lincoln."

"It's parked behind the stable," Lewis told him. He stepped around Gantry and continued to the back door where Nicole was now waiting with her tote bag.

She handed him the keys, and he walked off toward the stable, swinging the keys. In a few minutes, he returned driving the Tempo, passed Gantry and Rhodes, and pulled in beside Nicole. As she got into the driver's seat, she called out to him, "Thank you so much!" They saw her pass something to him, which he shoved in his shirt pocket.

"Just a minute, Lewis, what did she give you?" Demanded Gantry, as he passed.

Lewis reached in his pocket and waved a five-dollar bill. "She tipped me." He kept walking to the stable, feeling Gantry and Rhodes staring at his back. He went into the restroom behind the bunk area, locked the door, and pulled out the note that he had palmed behind the bill.

"Mrs. Hemphill to doctor two o'clock appt. (with Saucy) Replace Carlo. Do not bring them back to the house. I will return. Be very careful."

He read it over several times, tore it into bits, and flushed it down the toilet. At twelve, he and Carlo went to lunch in the kitchen. Lewis ate rapidly, watching the clock. Carlo had a second glass of tea. Finally, they strolled back to the stable and twenty minutes later the telephone rang. Carlo answered, as usual saying nothing, and walked toward the keys near the door.

Lewis came up behind and chopped him in the back of his head, then another chop just below the ear. Carlo dropped where he stood. Lewis touched the pulse in his neck and determined he was alive. He taped his arms behind him and taped his mouth, not knowing what sound, if any Carlo could manage to utter. He picked him up and put him in the last stall, piling up bales of hay as cover.

As he came out of the barn, he saw Gantry on the terrace, and called back over his shoulder as if talking to Carlo, "Take it easy buddy, I can handle it."

He took the Lincoln from the garage and drove up to the terrace.

"Carlo has got the shits. Where am I going?" he called to Gantry. Gantry looked irritated, then angry.

"Where is Carlo?" he growled.

"In the john. Where else?"

At that moment, Mrs. Hemphill waved to him from the front porch, and Lewis drove around, pulling up to the steps. He leapt out, opened the door and handed the two ladies into the backseat. In the rearview mirror, he could see Gantry scrambling down the terrace as if to overtake the Lincoln. Lewis drove swiftly away from the house and sped down the drive to the highway.

* * *

"Dr. Foster at the University of Virginia lab verified the residue in the wine glass as arsenic," reported Nicole.

"Is there a place to land on the estate?" asked Major Whitt. "For a chopper?"

"There are many trees but . . ."

"How clear is the lawn in front?"

"You got to be good, no?"

"I'm very good. I'm leaving for Bolling Air Force Base now."

"I'm going back to the house. They may try to run. Oh, Mon Dieu! Now I remember! Gantry knows the combination to the safe!"

To Whitt's consternation, she hung up. Nicole left the wine glass in a safe at the university where Dr. Foster assured her that it would be protected until a federal agent arrived to pick it up as evidence.

The evening storms were beginning as she left the university. Students rushed past with books and backpacks held over their heads. It was a huge campus, the buildings spread over acres. There was a narrow town street and a shopping center on the left. As she headed out of town, she mused that Thomas Jefferson would have liked his town if he came back today, and would be gratified to know that many brilliant students had gone forth from this university and made the world a better place. She checked to make sure she was heading west back to Hemphill on 250. On the way to town, she had somehow been so preoccupied with keeping the glass upright she had gone further west and found herself in another town, on a mountain, overlooking a spectacular view that stretched out below for forty miles. A kind tourist at the overlook had turned her around and headed her east to Charlottesville, but she had lost valuable time.

The rains were settling in as she drove slowly up to the house and parked the Tempo in front of the door. She got out and glanced down at the garage. The Lincoln, with Lewis driving, and Saucy and Mrs. Hemphill as passengers was, thankfully, still gone. Way in the rear of the garage was Mr. William Hemphill's personal car, a long black Cadillac. Frank Gantry kept it beautifully polished, but no one was allowed to drive it. The farm jeep was there, but the golf cart was missing. No one was in sight. The maids worked half days and were gone by one, but where was Carlo? Where were Frank Gantry and Olla Rhodes?

Nicole tried the front door and found it unlocked. She pushed in and turned on all of the outside lights, on the porch, the drive, and the patio, flooding the grounds with light for Major Whitt. An eerie silence hung over the vast hall, and the only sound was the Grandfather clock ticking. She peered into rooms as she made her way to the back quarters. In the kitchen, a bottle of aged whiskey, half empty and two water glasses sat on the table with an ice bucket of water, where cubes had melted. The tablecloth was hanging down on one side and a dozen paper napkins littered the floor. Down the short hall, she saw a chair propped under the doorknob of the employee's restroom, imprisoning someone inside, but who? There was a noise. What was it? Someone was snoring.

There was a crack of thunder just outside near the terrace, and the rain came down in torrents, but the sleeper snored on.

Nicole found an old plastic slicker with a hood next to the back door and put it on although it was three sizes too large. She looked toward the stable, and although it was getting dark, no light shown through the window. Where was Carlo? Had Lewis convinced him to ride along in the Lincoln? She walked out into the back lawn and discovered the tracks of the golf cart leading down to the family cemetery. Far down near the mausoleum, she saw the golf-cart, overturned and with its back wheels mired in mud. The doors to the mausoleum stood partly ajar and lights flickered inside.

Nicole reached under her sweatshirt and touched the gun. It was difficult to battle the oversized slicker, even unbuttoned. The hood kept falling forward over her face, and she threw it backward, letting the rain drench her hair. The doors pushed easily aside, and she stepped inside the high stonewalls. The angels of the babies' crypts looked down, marble eyes wide, heads bent with the weight of heavy curls, fat marble hands outstretched as if to warn her away from this chill, damp place. Four candles were set, two at the head, two at the foot of William Hemphill's tomb. Nicole stepped deeper into the mausoleum, looking from side to side.

"Gantry, are you here?" she called. "It is you?"

She felt, rather than heard, the doors to the mausoleum close behind her, and turned to see Gantry leaning against them, smiling, smiling. He was dressed for travel in an elegant trench coat, a silk scarf at his neck, a black hat.

"Why did you come back? What a foolish decision to make; I watched you walk down here all alone. No one followed. No other car came."

"I guess I'm curious, no?" she countered. "I want to know why you started the fire, the first fire, that Mrs. Hemphill saw from her window at 3:00 a.m. That fire worries me. No one burns trash at that hour.

And after that you began to slip little things into her food to make her confused. You believed that she recognized something, and that night the voices she thought she dreamed—it wasn't a dream, was it?"

Gantry moved further into the room, pointing up at a niche in the wall. His other hand held a pistol hanging loosely at his side. "No, it wasn't a dream. See that empty niche? It was to be for Lily Ann, but she won't be needing it. I'm sure she won't mind you using it instead. We wrapped them in garbage bags and rolled them into the graves on the other side of the fence. The water bobbed them back up. We rolled the motorbike in on top of them to hold the bodies down, causing the bags to tear. Boomer found his watch."

Nicole stood rigidly, noting the use of "we" and "them." Two did the killing and two died.

"After all those months of waiting for Lily Ann, she finally came home, riding up on the back of his motorbike all the way from New York. I was the only one awake at that hour but Olla woke and came into the kitchen. Shock! We were shocked at the nasty sight of them—her pretty face full of running sores, and her weighing scarce eighty pounds. And him, the same, a face so pocked and then his teeth set out in his mouth."

"Why? What was wrong with them?"

"Full blown AIDS. She had come home to die and wanted to see her mother. We couldn't allow that. The disgrace and at that particular time! Olla fixed food. I put in the arsenic. Burned everything they touched afterward out in the yard."

Nicole listened for the sound of a helicopter, but she heard only the rain. How long would it take Major Whitt to get here from Bolling? Belatedly, she thought of turning on all the lights in the house as she had done for the yard. How else could Major Whitt find the place?

Gantry was not watching her. He had walked over to the tomb and was stroking it. Nicole raised her leg behind her, and extracted the switchblade from its sheath inside her sock, and concealed it in the sleeve of her sweatshirt.

The candlelight picked up the tears that coursed down his face as he spoke to the corpse moldering beneath the cold marble under his fingertips. "Mr. William De Havilland Hemphill, Secretary of Defense, the finest man who ever lived, a former Marine and a true gentleman. We were all aware he was going to get the medal, you understand? Lily Ann and that boy coming when they did just two days before the ceremony in Washington would have ruined everything! A daughter eaten alive with AIDS! Can't you see the headlines? My god!"

"How dreadful," Nicole agreed, moving closer.

"I had to get rid of them. I'm not without compassion. But, I did it for him, to protect his reputation."

"Of course," Nicole agreed.

"I was privileged to drive them to Washington in the Cadillac and attend the ceremony. Such an Honor! I was never so moved as I was when the president of the United States placed that blue ribbon around his neck. There it was! A bronze, five-pointed star hanging from a blue thirteen-star Bowknot with that Navy ship anchor the star hung from. It was a great moment! I swear he looked straight at me and smiled. I knew then I had done the right thing."

"Not long after, he passed away, no?"

"True," murmured Gantry, pressing the cold marble. "About there, he is wearing the medal." He turned slowly and stared at Nicole. "You know you can never leave here alive now."

She stepped back. "But you haven't explained the second fire."

He threw up his hands. "The water washed the corpses to the surface. The damn dog was bringing up pieces. What do you put in a grave?"

"You mean—oh, oh! Mon Dieu!"

"The fire got completely out of hand. Ms. Ana began talking crazy, drawing attention to herself, and I know Mr. William wanted me and Olla to have that money." Gantry took a deep breath and turned toward Nicole. His eyes glittered in the candlelight, and he raised the pistol. "You shouldn't have come back." She listened for some sound outside and realized help would not come in time. Just as he fired, she jumped aside and the bullet ricocheted off William De Havilland Hemphill's tomb, splintering off a large chunk of marble.

Gantry turned and screamed, reaching out to the tomb, horrified at the desecration, then swung the pistol and like an angry child said, "Look what you made me do!"

Nicole thrust upward plunging the switchblade into the palm of his hand. The pistol dropped to the floor. Lily Ann. An unknown boy with AIDS. A homeless woman called Alma Patty, an old black man with a heart condition, all gone at the hands of Frank Gantry and Olla Rhodes. She drew aback and thrust the knife into his heart as he stared in disbelief at the blood that ran between his fingers. He looked up once, startled, grabbed his chest, and fell backward beside the tomb of William

Hemphill. Nicole knelt and touched the pulse in his neck. It faltered and stopped under her fingers. She withdrew the knife, wiped the handle clean, put his hand around it tightly, and sank it back into his chest in the same stab wound. She moved away to the doors and looked back. Suicide at the foot of his master. They'd believe it. Of course, they would.

In the distance, Nicole heard the slow sputter of a helicopter. A searchlight fanned the ground. Major Whitt had arrived.

With the big plastic raincoat dripping blood, she walked back to the house through the rain, across the lighted patio, and around to the front of the house just as the blades of the chopper stopped turning. In the sudden silence, she saw two men jump down and run for the shelter of the broad front porch. There was Major Whitt, and a stranger, hatless and underdressed for the weather, the latter with the harried expression of one hurriedly recruited for a mission of which he had little knowledge.

Nicole stepped into the shelter of the patio wall, took off the plastic raincoat, twisted it into a ball and wrenching an espaliered plant from its foundations, scooped out a mound of damp soil, and buried the coat. She inspected her hands and her shoes and found them cleansed by the rain.

Entering the back door as the major rang the bell at the front, Nicole heard Olla Rhodes crying weakly over and over.

"Frank? Frank, darling, don't leave without me—you need me, Frank—please, somebody—Ms. Ann, is that you? Come on, Frank, don't tease me any more. I love you, Frank—somebody?"

Quietly, Nicole removed the chair that was lodged under the bathroom doorknob and set it against the wall, then ran swiftly through the hall to the front door.

"God, what a downpour!" said the major, shaking off a trench coat and throwing it over a hat rack near the door. "This is Special Agent Rod Cummings, Agent Laurent."

Agent Cummings, middle-aged, slightly balding, and thoroughly wet, shifted uneasily in his navy blazer and tan pants, causing a rivulet on the oriental runner.

"Good to meet you," he muttered, wiping his brow. "Agents in place?"

"One in the house," Whitt told him. "Two on the grounds."

Nicole looked startled. What was he talking about? Two? Who was the other?

"Willie Lewis took the ladies to a safe place in the area," Whitt explained. He turned to Nicole. "I need an immediate report. Where can we talk?"

"In the library. Where is the other agent?" she asked, thinking of Olla Rhodes, locked in the bathroom. Mon Dieu! Not Olla!

"The stable," said Whitt shortly, opening doors in his search for the library.

Carlo! Willie Lewis didn't know that Carlo was in the game either. Why all this secrecy among the agents? They could be helping one another instead of operating separately, and always being unaware of whom to trust.

"We have our reasons," said Whitt, over his shoulder, as if he were reading her mind. "The library—beautiful home, isn't it, Rod?"

"Real old though, maybe couple of hundred years old," answered Cummings. "I like something newer and smaller myself. Must cost a lot to heat this pile of bricks."

Hemphill. A pile of bricks. Nicole felt an intense dislike for Cummings. She chose the window seat far across from the desk, which Whit has appropriated. Cummings chose the chair straight across from him as Whitt placed a tape recorder nearby.

Slowly, Nicole told how Willie Lewis had driven away to take Mrs. Hemphill and Saucy Dodd to a doctor's appointment, and then to the home of Mrs. Hemphill's niece, Marilyn Dewitt—and she spoke of seeing the overturned golf cart near Boomer, the dog's grave—and finding Frank Gantry in the mausoleum.

"He's dead," Nicole informed them flatly. "He died of a knife wound in his chest, and he's lying at the foot of Mr. William Hemphill's tomb. Who knows? He may have liked the idea to die at Mr. William's feet."

"What's that whining sound?" asked Cummings, jumping to his feet. His hand sought the gun nestled in its holster under the navy blue blazer. "It sounds like a woman!"

"Put the gun away," Nicole advised him. "It is just the cook, no? Gantry shut her in the servant's bathroom, and she doesn't know that she can get out now. I removed the chair from under the doorknob."

"Go get her, Cummings. Take her into the kitchen and make sure she stays there—and tape her mouth! She sounds like a dying cat," Whitt directed. He turned to Nicole. "What does the woman know?"

"Everything!" Nicole declared. Then she paused. "Everything except that her lover, Frank Gantry is dead. She'll talk. Just tell her that Gantry planned to leave Hemphill without her. She'll talk."

Cummings scurried out of the library.

"How did Gantry die, Nicole?"

"Suicide," she answered in a flat voice. "Knife to the heart, self-inflicted."

"That's your story?"

"He lost his mind a long time ago. In a fit of misplaced loyalty to the family, he killed the daughter, Lily Ann, when she, and her boyfriend or husband came home seeking help. An autopsy will show they were diseased and incurable."

"What did he do with the bodies?"

"They are under the caskets of the two servants, who died in the fire. In the heavy rain water, the body bags kept rising to the top."

Whitt looked shaken. He put his face in his hands and sat silently for several minutes. "Those poor innocent people died to keep the others in the same grave?"

"And, I believe, a bicycle of some kind." said Nicole.

"My god. My god!" murmured Whitt. He rose and walked around the room. He shut off the tape recorder and placed it in the pocket of his shirt.

"Has Mrs.—what's her name?"

"Olla Rhodes," supplied Nicole. "You want to know whether she had knowledge of this? Yes, she was in on his schemes all the way, and she'll talk her head off when she finds out about Gantry."

"Has she seen you since you came back?"

"No."

"Then I want you to write a note to Mrs. Hemphill and thank her for her hospitality—date it and put the time as early in the afternoon," he directed her, already rustling in the desk for stationery. He came up with a plain note pad and a pen, which he passed over to her.

Nicole began to write, signed her name and asked for a second sheet of paper.

"A note to Saucy Dodd," she explained.

He paced the floor as she wrote. "Now, get your stuff and get the hell out of here. Drive back to my house and stay there until I come."

"My things are in the car," she hesitated. "I'm not sure I can find the house."

"What do you mean?"

"I may go to Alexandria," she decided. "Maybe I can't find this Back Lick Road again," she added, as she headed to the front door.

"Wait a sec! Where is Carlo?"

"He is in the stable."

"Before you leave, show me where the stables are."

He followed her through the front door, around and across the patio. The rain was lessening and the damp air felt warm. The front had passed through, taking the chill with it, and signaling a return to a balmy day to come.

They reached the stables and ventured into the dark. Nicole clicked the switch by the doors but evidently Willie Lewis had unscrewed the bulbs or pulled a master switch somewhere before he left. With only the pale outline from the door to guide them, they made their way slowly into the dark, Whitt's hand on her shoulder, his chest against her back. The horses stomped uneasily, sensing their presence, snuffled loudly, and bumped the sides of their stalls.

Nicole paused. Something dangled from up in the loft above where the grains were stored. A rope?

"Why are you stopping?" whispered Whitt, his breath was hot against her neck.

"There is something brushing my face," she explained. "I think it is a rope." She reached up with one hand, grasped it to push it aside and gave a yank.

Above, there was a loud crack, a hinged compartment opened downward and flooded them both with the next day's supply of loose hay. They fell to the floor. Nicole tried to stand, fell back, and found herself pinned solidly under Major Whitt. The hay continued to fall and their heads were covered with it. The horses whinnied with anticipation. They recognized that sound, and in the dark moved anxiously, knowing the time was wrong for feeding.

Nicole lay pressed into the hay, conscious of Whitt's body covering hers. Something inside sensed what was coming next, and she pushed the hay from her face just as his mouth pressed over hers.

It was like a dream, an awakening. She clasped her arms around his back and felt the tape recorder in his pocket press against her ribs. His tongue pushed her lips aside, and they lay unmoving for a long time, locked in the cocoon of warm hay.

From somewhere, it seemed a voice was calling. Not really a voice, more like an angry growl like a trapped animal. They reluctantly pulled apart and listened to the sound.

"Carlo," she whispered, pushing Whitt away.

"Carlo?" Whitt said, trying to move his legs. He struggled to his feet. "Nicole, I—oh, Nicole—oh, Nicole."

She rolled over and out of the hay, managing to stagger to her feet. Shaking, she held on to the nearest stall. Her heart was beating so loud that she was sure he could hear it, and she clasped her hands over her breast.

"Carlo is back there," she murmured, pointing to the rear of the stable. She coughed and brushed the hay from her hair. "I am going now, Major."

"Yes," he managed to answer. He started to walk toward the sound.

Nicole touched her lips, wanting him, wanting to follow him. He disappeared in the dark, and she heard him call softly to Carlo. "I'll find you. Keep making sounds."

Nicole turned and ran out into the yard, crossing over to the house. She peeped in the kitchen window. Special Agent Cummings had Olla Rhodes bound to a chair, her mouth taped. Her roly-poly body squirmed in protest, her eyes shot fire at the agent, who sat at the table.

On the patio, Nicole uprooted the plant, retrieved the bloody raincoat, and pushed the plant back into place in the soil of the pot. Carrying the coat, she hurried to the Tempo and got in, her hands trembling as she shoved the key into the ignition. As the engine turned over, she looked up at the stately mansion of Hemphill for the last time.

Chapter Thirteen

The Brass Bound Trunk

They stood under the old trees in the church cemetery, like two small black clad witches, their little black boots nestled in the last of the fall leaves. It was cold, but they were reluctant to leave Mimi, Mimi lying beneath the sod in her best dress, and tantalizingly, still wearing the key to her trunk on a fine silver chain around her neck.

Nicole was angry with her mother. In fact, she was furious. First, there was the episode with her hat—Nicole's hat—a black leather beanie, bought to match her new double-breasted leather coat. From the moment she had arrived at Yvette's door to take her to church, Yvette had thrown a fit about the hat, vowing that it was a yarmulke, and it was not right to wear in the Catholic Church. Nicole had snapped back that it was a beanie, not a yarmulke, and Yvette became stonily silent. But she caught Yvette staring at it all the way to the church, and then, as they were going up the walk from the parking area, Yvette had snatched the new beanie from Nicole's head, run to the street and thrown it through the window of a passing bus. Nicole had stood open-mouthed as the bus sped down the street, turned a corner, and disappeared from view, taking her hat with it. Yvette had produced a black handkerchief from her purse and told Nicole to pin it to her hair. Nicole threw the handkerchief to the ground, pulled up the hood to the coat, and marched into the church, leaving Yvette standing on the sidewalk.

And after the service, there was the thing about the silly flowers for Mimi's grave.

"You know Mimi hated anything artificial!" Nicole exploded. "Why didn't you go by the market and get real flowers?"

"These will last longer," declared Yvette. She placed the half dozen silk roses, in a wicker basket, in front of the headstone.

Eerily, as they stood there looking at the grave, a chill breeze blew up. The top branches of the bare trees swayed, and as they watched, a maverick gust of wind descended, lifting up the flowers one by one from the basket. Up and up they went, fragile pink silk blooms drifting about six feet above the ground and finally coming to rest far away, on the oldest grave nearest the church.

"Mon Dieu! Mon Dieu!" Nicole gasped. She reached for the empty basket and turned around to see Yvette, brushing tears from her face, almost running in her haste to reach the Citroen in the parking area. Let her have her cry out, Nicole decided, and carrying the empty basket, strolled aimlessly among the stones. At a distance, she noticed a tall, young man, in some type of uniform, bent in prayer near a recent grave. He reminded her vaguely of Major Whitt, who had called several times. The first call had been very awkward and ended quickly. When she had received the message, almost immediately after returning to Paris, she reluctantly went to the box on the corner near her flat and called the Alexandria office. Whitt answered as if he had been waiting near the telephone.

"Why did you leave on the next flight? We almost had a problem about Frank Gantry's suicide—Carlo found most of Gantry's clothes, and some of William Hemphill's clothes, and Hemphill's personal items—his razor, a nail kit—in the Cadillac, which was all gassed up and ready to go. Gantry was going to split as soon as he said good-bye to Hemphill."

"So, you removed everything, no?"

"Put it all back. Don't sweat it. Carlo took care of it."

"Yes, is there is anything else?"

There had been a short silence and then Whitt, sounding tense, "Why didn't you come back to my house that night? Why did you go to Alexandria and get Derek to arrange the next flight out of the States?"

"Well, I felt I needed to leave."

"It was that kiss, wasn't it?"

"Yes," she had answered truthfully. She fantasized the smell of the hay all around, and his mouth on hers. It mocked her in the day at the oddest times and entered her dreams in the night.

"Are you afraid of me?" he had asked.

"No, Major," she answered. "I am afraid of me."

She had pressed down and cut the connection but continued to hold the telephone close to her breast for a long time. Now, as Nicole stood motionless beside a tombstone, she was forced back to the present at the tremulous sound of her mother's voice, calling from the parking area.

"Darling, I am sorry. I will buy you a new hat. We will go shopping, ma Cherie."

Nicole walked to the car and took her usual place in the driver's seat.

"You are getting more like Mimi every day," Nicole observed. "Throwing my hat into that bus was just like some crazy thing she would do."

"I am her daughter," said Yvette. "And you are mine, and I feel now that you are more than the two of us. You walked at ten months. I remember once Mimi came to visit—mon pere was still living—and you went into the bathroom and managed to turn on the faucet and filled the tub and threw Mimi's red shoes into the water. We were screaming, "Bad girl! You looked up with those big black eyes," pointed at the shoes and said, "Boats!" Oh, how we laughed! We forgot to spank our terrible child. Mimi had to wear my slippers home on the bus. We had no car then. Always from a baby, you had a certain wildness."

You'll never know, Nicole thought to herself, and then said aloud, "Where shall we ago?"

"To our café. Hot coffee and croissants would be good. I want to hear all about your divorce."

"Nothing to hear, Maman. Michael Stern took care of everything." Nicole hesitated. She was almost sure that Stern had made sure the judge, a staunch Catholic, be aware of Rene's secret vasectomy and her own years of waiting for the baby that never came. "It was only a matter of papers—I signed, Rene then signed. I kept all of my jewels and received a nice settlement and gave him all the designer gowns except the two, which were given to me by Ms. Honey Holm."

"A settlement?" Yvette said in surprise.

"Very generous. Rene has sold half the business to Georges and Henri-Paul told me Rene has told Terese's sons to get out and find work. He will no longer support them."

"I always thought the younger boy may have belonged to Rene," ventured Yvette warily.

"Perhaps," agreed Nicole and shrugged. "I have been working in the shop this past month until he can find someone else, but we do not speak except for business."

"How sad!"

"Life never stays the same, Maman. And Maman, don't worry about the hat. Perhaps a little boy will find it and wear it to school and be the envy of his peers."

"Yes! It was a fine piece of leather!" agreed Yvette, always the seamstress.

* * *

The big brass bound trunk has been delivered to Nicole's little flat weeks ago by the Belvoir Bros. And now, it sat against the wall, waiting for a special key, with a short shank and a hole through the center that would fit into the interior turning mechanism. Every day when Nicole came home from work, she reached out and touched the trunk, reminded of Mimi. The only thing in the trunk she had ever seen was the beautiful, old wedding dress, all handmade of a fine cream-colored cotton and lace. A waist length veil of the same material, embroidered with roses, had completed the costume. Mimi had proudly saved it for Nicole for fifty-three years but when Rene heard of the plan to wear it, he absolutely vetoed it, saying it was too old and out of fashion. Nicole had been married in a designer gown that Rene had supervised in every step of the making, consisting of a satin sheath and a tiny satin hat with a half veil in front. Nicole had donated it to a charity affair a week after the honeymoon. It has been the first indication for Nicole that life with Rene would not be as thrilling as Mimi and Yvette had anticipated. For Nicole, a woman from the lower middle class, the obvious answer was a husband. They had so wanted her to be happy and rich and never have to do grueling beadwork for a living. Even after Nicole's extensive education, they had never thought beyond their own living conditions, tedious work, long hours, small pay, small lives, and small expectations, and Nicole, loving them so much, wanted to do whatever made them happy.

This day, she left the shop early and went straight to the counter in the hardware store where the key maker had agreed to create a key to her specific instructions. He presented his masterpiece, showing her how he had to bore the hole to the exact length and then he made a spectacle of polishing it to a shine. They agreed on a price and finally, he handed the key over, reluctant to let it go.

On the drive home, Nicole felt intense anticipation about opening the trunk. The feeling seemed silly since she had seen the trunk for years used as their coffee table—what could be in there? Probably pictures of ancestors, old brown photos with no names on the back to show who they were, faded clothing too good to throw away, newspapers of forgotten events—what else? And yet, the feeling persisted—would it be a pot of gold or Pandora's box—what would she find? She had waited an unusual length of time, arranging for the Belvoir Bros. to bring the trunk from Yvette's place to her own flat, looking for keys in many antique shops, finally having a key made and now, with trunk and key in place, there was no reason left to delay the opening. Yet there was something foreboding, an excitement tinged with trepidation, at what she would discover inside. Deliberately, she stopped by the market and did her small grocery shopping, lingering among the fresh produce, selecting a loaf of bread, and finally stowing her purchases in the backseat of the Volkswagen, she drove slowly along the Seine before turning back to her own flat.

She was washing lettuce for a salad when the telephone rang. When she picked it up, Major Whitt's voice simply said, "Call me." She hung up and went back to the sink, tossing some of the lettuce into a salad bowl. Whitt had called twice in the past week, but she had not called him back. He invaded her thoughts during the day at the oddest times and once when a man with bright blue eyes came in to purchase an expensive gold bracelet, she took a sterling one out of the case by mistake and the customer decided on the less expensive silver, rather the gold, a price difference of seven hundred dollars. Luckily, Henri-Paul was busy with another customer, as he would have certainly run to Rene like the eager little snitch he was. Georges, now half owner of the store, would have been satisfied she made the sale and would have said nothing. And Major Whitt appeared at night in her dreams, his kiss causing her to throw off the covers.

Nicole poured a glass of wine and looked at the trunk. At least I'd better see if the key fits, she decided. Mon Dieu! You would think Mimi had hidden a dragon inside, she thought, the way I'm procrastinating. She put down the wine glass, got the key, pushed aside the sham lock and fitted it into the small interior hole. There was an answering click, and she heaved the heavy lid against the wall, revealing layers of thin white tissue. There was the wedding dress, of course. Nicole pressed it to her face, smelling lavender sachet, and laid it carefully across pillows on the bed.

As she had expected, there was Mimi's Bible, and several old photo albums with solemn people she hardly recognized, and a number of scrapbooks of newspaper clippings, detailing events of English royalty, the marriage of Grace and Rainier, and events of World War II, and many knitted comforters and shawls. A bundle of letters from deceased relatives, and also there was every card and letter Nicole had ever sent over the eight years she studied in America, all bound with ribbon and separated by years. There were many, Nicole realized with satisfaction. Letters for Mimi, cheery letters about washing the dishes with George Archimedes, and standing on the Washington streets selling flowers—and nary a word about the lonely times, the frustration of thinking in French and speaking in English, and putting newspapers in her shoes to keep her feet warm during the chill of the Washington winters.

The floor around the trunk grew cluttered as Nicole browsed through photographs and letters and then she came to the bottom, which was covered with several sheets of faded pink floral wallpaper taped around the edges. She lifted one edge of the heavy paper and carefully peeled it back, revealing what appeared to be large white squares of rough paper with tack marks along the edges, as if they had been pinned to a wall. She drew one sheet out and turned it over. It was a large circus poster with costumed clowns, zebras, girls in sequined tights and overhead men sailing through the air on trapezes. Curious, she drew out the second poster and again there were elephants, jugglers, and a family of midgets. Why did Mimi save these circus posters? And did she go out at night and steal them from telephone poles and fences? Perhaps Mimi thought she would be arrested, and that is why they were hidden in the bottom of the trunk.

There were eight posters of three different circuses, and six playbills for theatre entertainment of the circus indoors type, spanning a period of about four years, twenty-seven to thirty years ago. Nicole gazed at the posters carefully, trying to discern a common bond, reading the names of the performers and staring at the pictures. Two posters had photographs in circles around the edges; the playbills featured the stars in cameo portraits, over a text describing their talents. One name appeared in three posters and three playbills. An aerialist named Nicolas Campion. However, this same man, features altered slightly, appeared also under two aliases.

She went to the kitchen area, found a magnifying glass in a drawer, and returned to the posters spread out on the floor. It was a very young man's face. He appeared to be perhaps eighteen or nineteen years old, extremely handsome, lots of curly dark hair, he was heavily muscled for one so young. She kept staring at his face. Who are you, Nicolas Campion? Sometimes he appeared all in black on a giant web, as Nick the Spider, or in another sort of spider costume. His hair hung to his shoulders, but it was his eyebrows that drew her close scrutiny; they were dark and straight. Nicolas and Nicole. She took one of the posters and crossed to the mirror, placing the poster next to her own image. Her heart was beating so fast she could hear it, and she could feel the heat of tears gathering painfully behind her eyes.

She put down the poster and went back to the trunk, ripping away the heavy wallpaper. An envelope fell out from where it had been stuck to the underside of the wallpaper, and a yellowed sheaf of newspaper clippings spilled onto the floor. There were not many but two were front-page headlines. The circus performer known as Nick the Spider had been arrested. Credited to, or discredited to, Nicolas Campion, was a string of thefts over a period of several years. Famous paintings from museums and private collections, half a million dollars in rare gems and small artifacts, all of which had disappeared under the nose of museum security and from safes inside the fortress-like residences of collectors. Everything chosen was small and easily carried away by hand, even the pictures from the walls. In the museum, he would find a spot high in the air, on a window ledge, or a cornice, climb up and wait. The guards, he discovered, looked around, but never looked up. A window latch or alarm, perhaps in a restroom, had been removed beforehand, allowing a method of escape down a wall. Most of the property was never recovered. Robin Hood had nothing on Nicolas Campion. He gave to church boxes, poor people on the streets, mailed anonymous gifts to anyone he read about in the newspapers, those who were ill, or in sad circumstances. Nuns and monks alike were startled to find packets of cash in their gardens, under their seats, at chapel, and in delivery sacks of groceries. His largesse knew no bounds while Nicolas appeared penniless—he chose to sleep near the big white Percheron horses of the circus, on the hay; he ate circus food, and had only one sign of extravagance, a very nice watch. He was sent to prison Fleury-Merogis, but his sentence was never fully served because he managed to fashion a rope of wire. Each day he would press against the weakest bars until he was able to remove them. The night he bid good-bye, he shoved the bars back into the window sockets with wads of chewing gum holding them in place. When they saw his cell was empty the next morning, the guards on the cellblock panicked and quit their jobs, saying his escape was impossible—alors! Nick had turned into a spider and crawled down the wall! There was a companion clipping pinned to the other one. It was not until the next prisoner in that cell discovered the movable bars, pushed them out, and fell to the courtyard, breaking his legs, that the chewing gum cement was discovered.

Nicole read the old clippings avidly one after the other. Once out into the world, Nicolas had entered another circus, with shorter hair, a little moustache, and a new identity. But he soon became too brazen, too daring, and again he went to prison, the Ile de Re on St. Martin. In time, he escaped again and disappeared.

By 2:00 a.m., there was no more to read. She replaced the clippings and the posters and the handbills, covered them with the wallpaper, and finished filling the trunk as Mimi had originally packed it. She found a small chain in the costume jewelry, put the key on it, and laced it around her neck.

On the counter, the lettuce in the salad bowl was limp and was tossed into the garbage. She found a package of salty crackers and ate them with some cheese. The wine bottle was empty. She opened a new bottle, found her glass on the floor by the trunk and filled it, drank it down and filled it again. The clock read 2:15 a.m.

Feeling angry, depressed, and slightly dizzy, she dialed Yvette's apartment, waiting through eight rings until her mother's voice, heavy with sleep, answered.

"Maman, I want to talk to you!"

"Nicole, are you sick? It is the middle of the night. What is the matter?"

"I am coming over there right now!"

"You cannot come here."

"Why the hell not?"

"Because—Enrico is with me."

"Tell that fat wop to get his fat ass out of our bed and go home to his fat wop wife and his children!"

To her disgust, Nicole heard her own voice break with emotion. She poured another glass of wine, drank it down and continued. "At least his fat wop children know their own father, right, Maman?"

"Nicole, what has happened?"

"You lied to me. No more, Maman. I have opened the trunk."

"Mimi left a letter to you?"

"More than a letter. I have a name, I have pictures."

Yvette screamed and began to sob. Nicole heard Enrico's hoarse, sleep-filled voice call out in alarm, "What is wrong, my darling? Who is that on the telephone at this hour?"

"Shut up, Enrico," yelled Nicole into the telephone. "You are not in this family!"

"Oh, my own mother has betrayed me even as she lies in the grave!" Yvette was screaming. "How could she do this?"

"And you betrayed me! I don't care if my father was a thief! All of my childhood, I wanted a father. I looked into the face of every man I saw, wondering if he could be my father. You should have told me!"

"Calm down, Yvette, my darling," Nicole heard Enrico say. She could hear her mother sobbing in the background as Enrico took over the telephone.

"Who is this? Nicole?"

"This is Nicolas Campion's daughter speaking," yelled Nicole, the wine and fatigue making her incoherent. "Get out of my mother's bed and go home to your children. Act like a husband, you old fat wop—!" Her voice grew hoarse and she slammed the telephone down on its hook.

She fell across the bed and lay there feeling exhaustion in every bone in her body. The telephone began to ring, but she lay flat, listening as it rang on and on. When the recorder cut on, she lifted the receiver and turned it off. She pulled out the plug and lay there in silence, her angry tirade over.

"Mimi," she whispered into the dark.

Sleep wouldn't come; too many things were spinning through her thoughts now that she knew the name and the face of the man she had searched for all of her life. He was alive somewhere and he would be—oh, how old? Maybe only late forties? His face in the pictures looked so young. She got up and put on her black leather trench coat, pulled up the hood and went out into the cold night air to the public telephone on the corner.

The voice of Derek Holland in the Alexandria office came clearly across the line.

"Derek, I have a call for Major Whitt."

"Nicole! It is good to hear you."

"Are you missing Paris, mon petit?"

"Of course, but America is good."

"Yes, America is good."

"Major Whitt is not here at this moment. May I give a message?"

"Tell him I will try to get a reservation to fly out tomorrow and will call from Dulles."

"Perhaps we can share hot chocolate together? It is cold here. Until then, Ma Cherie."

"Adieu, Mon Petite."

Chapter Fourteen

Randolph College

Frost dappled the trees and crunched under foot. Later the sun would come, the early winter pale sun, and melt the frost, making the branches black and the path wet, but at 5:00 a.m., the LeGrand farm lay dark and chilly.

Nicole's head hurt beneath her bright red wooly cap. Her legs in the black spandex suit seemed to be lifting and falling like those of a rusty automaton doll as she covered the seven miles around the farmhouse. The sheepdog, Boncoeur, usually inside the house, watched from the kitchen window, his nose having made a cleared space in the steamed glass pane, and Madam LeGrand waved her dishtowel in greeting as Nicole ran past.

By the time she reached the clearing where the Volkswagen was parked, Nicole felt ill. The wine, more wine, the discovery of the papers in the trunk, the angry accusations she had hurled at her mother, the ugly names she shouted at Enrico! Poor Enrico, who had never been anything but nice to her, who remembered her birthdays and Christmas with stockings and fragrant stationary? In the city, she stopped at the first cafe whose owner was kind enough to let her inside to wait until the bagels and croissants came out of the oven ready for breakfast at six-thirty. Two cups of coffee, two croissants, and a cheese omelet brought the feeling back into her frozen hands and thawed the tip of her nose. She pulled off the red cap and sat near the window, watching people moving quickly past, going to their jobs, to the markets, to school. She would not be going to the shop of Rene Laurent this day. She would call and tell Georges she would not be returning there to work. He would hire the girl called Genevieve, who seemed to be the best of the lot who had answered their ad. Genevieve would sell only. Georges himself would be acting as courier when necessary. Nicole felt she was closing a book. Getting through the last chapter had not been satisfactory, but she realized there were no more pages, no post scrip to study, and no going back for a review.

She paid the café owner, thanked him for letting her come in early and left a generous tip. He handed her a cinnamon crisp in a cone of waxed paper. As she reached for it, he inhaled a whiff of Chanel from her wrist. "You smell very beautiful, madam," he said.

"Thank you. Enjoy this day."

Back at her apartment, she called the airport and managed to get a flight out of de Gaulle at one o'clock due to a cancellation. Her favorite red and yellow cashmere sweater, put aside as much too colorful during the long period of mourning for Mimi, went into her suitcase, with jeans and gray-tapered wool slacks.

She took a couple of the circus handbills and a poster with pictures of Nicolas Campion, and rolled them tightly, fastening them with a rubber band before she tucked them into her suitcase under her underwear. The search for Nicholas Campion had begun. From the news clippings, she had found out that he had come to Europe with a circus from the United States, and he most likely would return to his own country, for what better place to hide than in a country so big it took weeks to go from one coast to the other and always to hear the language of English?

Nicole made her call to Georges, who was not happy at her leaving but was understanding.

And now, Yvette. "Maman, it is Nicole. I apologize for yelling at you last night."

"You distressed me, so I did not sleep."

"Let me speak to Enrico."

"You cannot speak to a person who is not here. In the middle of the night, he left me. He is insulted. He said he will not be called such terrible names."

"I am sorry."

"He is gone, do you understand? Enrico has left me, you ungrateful wench!"

"He will be back, Maman. He cannot live without you."

"He has taken my car!"

"No!"

"Yes. I am alone, and I have no car. You have ruined my life!"

"You can have my car. I am going away, but first I will bring you my car."

"I would not be seen in your ugly little German car. Never, Never, Never!" Yvette shouted angrily, pounding on the telephone for emphasis. "And I am glad you are going away. Go away and don't come back! From the day you are born you have complicated my life!"

The weight of Yvette's words fell on Nicole, and she sat down on the floor, unable to speak. Silence lengthened and then, Yvette began to cry.

"I didn't mean that, Nicole. You are worth more than any man to me. Forgive me, Cherie—listen! Don't go, Cherie!"

Nicole held the telephone close to her chest and finally managed to murmur, "I love you Maman."

"Nicole? Nicole?"

But Nicole had softly hung up the telephone.

* * *

There were the usual flight delays, and it was after nine when she arrived at Dulles. Major Whitt was pacing the waiting area as the passengers disembarked from the flight bus that had brought them in from the plane, and his face broke into a smile as soon as she came through the door.

"I like your hat," he said in greeting. He reached over and pushed the red cap off her forehead so that he could look down into her eyes.

"It's very warm. My hat," she pulled it down.

"Are you hungry?"

"I ate on the plane, someone cancelled, and I am first class. The food is not so bad, no?"

Whitt noticed the fatigue in her walk and the puffiness under her eyes as they went to pick up her luggage from the transfer rack. She appeared not only tired from the trip, but something more, very subdued, and unhappy.

"Are you okay?"

"A little tired, but I am ready for work. You have a job for me, no?"

"Ahhh—sure," Whitt said uncertainly.

She peered at him closely. "I have no other employment. I have given up my job at Rene Laurent, as well as Rene Laurent himself."

"Yes, Beau Jackson relayed that news," Whitt nodded as he retrieved her bag. He had a half smile on his face. He was always intrigued by her choice of explanation and had been especially elated to hear of the passing of Rene from Nicole's life.

"You are staying at my house. I have something to show you," he added.

Nicole felt distinctly uneasy. "I would rather stay at the motel in Alexandria."

"Derek Holland is living there temporarily, and there is another agent being briefed for the next couple of days."

She hesitated. "Very well, but I will take the sofa. I do not wish to share your bed—." She stopped abruptly. "That is, I do not wish to take your bed from you, for myself, that is."

"I didn't infer," he began slowly and then stopped, treading carefully through the sparks of electricity that were ricocheting between them, "that I would be in it—the bed," he floundered.

People brushed past them. Loud speakers crackled announcing flights and arrivals. They seemed glued, unable to move.

"Where are we? The car?" Nicole asked.

"Parking lot. This way."

Whitt suddenly became aware of the bustle of the crowd, of people bumping into them, and he turned to walk swiftly across the terminal to the door to the outside, Nicole hurrying to keep him in sight. When she caught up with him, he was standing by the curb, looking from side to side.

"It's over here . . . back over there."

They gazed out over the sea of cars.

"Let's go find it," she suggested.

"It's in this line near the back."

"Yes? Then what is the problem?"

"I forgot which car I drove here."

"What choices do we have?"

"My jeep. An old Honda, maybe. I can't seem to think straight. Too much on my mind."

She crossed into the lines of cars and walked toward the rear. She knew the jeep. She would recognize that. But it was the blue Ford Tempo that sat waiting on the very last row. Whitt had wandered into different row, and she waved her hand to attract him over.

He looked embarrassed and fished the keys from his pocket. "This is the one you drove on the Hemphill case, right?"

"Yes. It is very speedy, no?"

They drove through the night to the house off Backlick Road and when they reached the entrance road, she noticed that automated gates had now been installed, which Whitt opened with dual switches that operated from a pad on his key chain. Lights sprang on, two on the posts as the gates swung open, and at the front and back doors on the house. Something white moved beyond the growth of bushes by the porch, and two red eyes flashed in the headlights.

"Stop!" said Nicole, opened the door, and got out. A large dog emerged from the bushes, trailing a metal chain, which was attached to one of the pillars on the front porch. It growled deep in its throat, showed its teeth, and then, seemed to wait for instruction from Whitt as his eyes darted from Nicole to the car.

"Good boy," she said softly. "Good boy."

The dog turned its head to one side, listening intently, and ventured closer. She could see its heavy white coat slashed with a few patches of black. In the headlights, to her delight, she could see that this splendid beast had one blue eye and one brown eye.

"Come to me," she whispered. She held out her hand.

The dog approached and offered his head.

Whitt got out of the car. "He is supposed to tear strangers to pieces. Some guard dog."

"What kind of dog is he?"

"A mix of Border Collie and Bearded Collie, the eyes of one, and coat of the other, it seems. He was to have been put to sleep the day I went to the pound. He's about seven months or eight months old."

"Mon Dieu!" gasped Nicole. "Put to sleep!"

"Most people want cute little puppies."

"What is he called?"

"I've had him about three weeks. I don't call him anything actually. I just . . . just say, here, boy, and he comes to me, but he hates Carlo."

"Carlo?" she asked as they walked back to the car.

"He is living over the garage. He's limited at jobs because of his problem, so meanwhile he is acting as a sort of caretaker, chauffeur, whatever."

They drove to the rear, and Nicole saw a lighted window in the space above the garage. A shadow passed and disappeared.

Whitt brought her bag into the house and paused in the kitchen. "Sure you won't take the bedroom? I'm funded to furnish the whole house but never have time to get around to it."

Nicole looked around the empty kitchen. There was still no stove or refrigerator. "The sofa in the library will be fine."

"Well, if you're sure. There's a bath right there, across the hall." He opened a door and turned on a light. "And there's television in the library."

"I'm very tired," she said as she dropped her tote bag beside the sofa that was neatly made up with clean sheets and a comforter, "and very sad. I have quarreled with Maman—my mother—and we said things—is your mother living, Major?"

"Yes, and my dad, too. They live in North Carolina. Would you like to call your mother?"

"In Paris it is not yet dawn."

"Tomorrow then."

"Yes, Good night, Major."

"Goodnight, Laurent."

"You may call me Nicole."

At this, he hesitated in the hall, shifting his feet in his shiny boots, and then stared at her until she looked up and met his eyes.

"I'm thinking of building a stable."

"Then you will need to buy a horse," she countered quickly, pretending not to comprehend his reference to a stable.

"Only kidding, Nicole. Call me if you need me for anything."

She backed into the room and closed the door. In a few minutes, she heard his footsteps going down the hall.

She showered, put on her Mickey Mouse nightshirt, and wandered about the library looking for something to read. Perhaps she should write Maman a letter, apologizing, and asking whether Enrico had returned with her car. It hurt to be estranged from Yvette, especially now Mimi was gone.

Searching for notepaper, Nicole opened drawers in the desk. In the small, right upper drawer, she came across a very curious thing, a photograph of herself, obviously an enlargement from a snapshot, taken several years ago. There was an airport. She was wearing the blonde wig and the de la Renta suit. Where had it come from, why was it here, and who had taken the picture? She placed it carefully back in the drawer, turned off the lamp, and went to the sofa where she snuggled deep in the warmth of the comforter. They stalked me, she surmised. And I was the type they wanted. What type am I, she mused? Finally, sleep overcame her, and she dreamed. Gazar was standing over her, laughing, and he said, "You will become whatever we want you to be, Nicole Laurent."

* * *

At 5:00 a.m., she woke, dressed in the black latex suit, went outside and took the big black-and-white dog off his chain. He readily came out of his doghouse and followed her to the edge of the fence. With a single, excited bark, he ran beside her as they sprinted down to the gates, across the front of the yard, down the other side, behind the garage and back to the house. It was hardly the seven-mile track at LeGrands, but they made the same route around once more in the chill morning air, coming to rest at the back door where a sleepy-eyed major was peering through the pane.

"I'm going to call him Runner!" Nicole exclaimed. "He kept up all the way, sometimes dashing ahead."

"Now he's hungry," she decided, throwing her arms around the big dog.

"I'm hungry," said Whitt.

"You still have no stove."

"The guy showed up when I wasn't here, and he wouldn't deliver again unless I called first and sat here all day waiting for him."

"They're very independent," agreed Nicole. "So what do we do?"

"I'll go get something," he suggested. He struggled into his jacket and went out to the jeep. He came back shortly with a large, white bag with red *good luck* symbols on it in Chinese, and in English, the luck in English represented by horseshoes and shamrocks.

"This is supposed to be breakfast?"

"Well," Whitt hesitated. "There are rolls, egg rolls. You eat eggs and rolls for breakfast, don't you?"

Nicole burst out laughing. "Not in that form. I made instant coffee. At least you still have the office hot plate."

They sat at the table surrounded by paper plates and little white cartons, and dug in with plastic forks.

"My picture is on the desk in the library, an old shot made before I began to work in the game. I was then a courier, delivering jewels for Rene Laurent."

"Gazar put it there. He was absolutely fascinated by you. He had it enlarged from a file photo taken from your dossier. You don't think he picked you off the street, do you?"

"Actually, it was on a plane."

He leaned forward eagerly across the table. "I've got the day planned."

"You will explain my new case, no?" she countered. "I hope it does not take many days. While I am here, I want to do something on my own. I am going to find my father. I have a name, and I have old pictures. Oh! He was a handsome boy!"

"You have old pictures? I think I can send you to someone in our tech office who can help you. There's a photo aging process—the hair becomes gray, or the head bald, and wrinkles appear at the eyes and mouth, a bit of fat around the jowls—."

"Somehow, I believe he is still handsome," Nicole said softly thinking of Nicolas Campion. She looked at the sky through the kitchen window. A butterfly shrimp lay forgotten in her fingers.

Whitt said, "Her name is Charlene."

"That would be wonderful," she smiled, regarded the shrimp in surprise and popped it in her mouth. "It is not fair. You seem to know all about me, but I do not know about you."

"My father is Kelvin Andrew Whitt Sr. I am Junior, and my son is the third, but we call him Andy. My wife is dead, and I have never remarried. I was a Colonel in the Air Force. Did my twenty."

"You were a Colonel?"

"Twice demoted."

"I don't understand."

Whitt looked at the floor, ran his hand through his short sandy hair and then shrugged. "You may as well know. I borrowed a very nice fast plane, an F16, and flew it from Andrews to Asheville, NC without prior clearance."

"You stole it."

"That's how they looked at it. My mother was being operated on for cancer. My dad didn't want to worry me, but my sister called and told me, and I walked out to the flight line, picked out the F16, checked the fuel and flew away, no flight plan, no permission. All hell broke loose.

That night when my mother had come through okay, and when the anesthetic had faded, she looked up at me and said, "Kelly, you're *awol*. Get the hell out of here." I took off in the F16 and two fighters came in, one under each wing and brought me home to Andrews."

"Kelly. She calls you Kelly. And you have a sister!" exclaimed Nicole.

"Yeah, she's a mess, but I love her." So, General Sabine's limo was waiting on the tarmac when I flew in. Two large MPs descended on me, one on each side, marched me to the limo, pushed me inside with the general and stood guard. General Sabine was smoking his pipe, and he stared at me for a full, very chilly five minutes. Finally he growled, "We could have shot you down, Whitt, but the civilians don't like our aircraft dropping on their cities." What could I say? I said "Thank you, sir." He reached over and took my eagles. I was sure I was going to be court martialed, but he motioned one MP to open the door. As I stepped, he said, "Sorry about your mother. Have a good day, Major."

"So, you received a demotion?"

"Two ranks. Docked six months pay for the fuel and curtail of privileges. That was seven years ago and I made it back up the ladder to Colonel before I screwed up again three years later. Conducting a survivor exercise—oh, hell, you're not interested in this, are you?"

"Fascinated." His eyes were the most remarkable blue.

"I had eight tough men. We had to avoid a team of twenty for a period of twelve hours. There was a dock near the far perimeter, beyond the exercise area, beyond it about two hundred yards. I cased it earlier and discovered empty barrels in the loading zone, so I briefed my squad—"Empty your bladders and your butts. Make sure your canteens are full and pick a barrel. Go into a sleep mode. You are a dormouse or you are a koala. I don't want to see you or hear you for twelve hours. I'll take the barrel on the farthest end, so if they come, they'll get me first." So in we went. We slept. We tried to see our watches the best we could. When we finally crawled out, two of my men were still sleeping. The others deployed to the woods to the exercise zone, but I kept banging on barrels until I woke the two Van Winkles—and we were caught. Bounced back to major for leaving the prescribed zone. General Sabine bailed me out again. I guess he likes me. On the day I retired, someone was waiting for me at the gate with a job I had no option to refuse, or they threatened I would be brought up on old charges, and lose my military pension."

"They had been watching you too. What kind of people are we working for?" mused Nicole. Whitt's story amazed and appalled her at the same time. He had been wrong—by military rules—but it was not a bad wrong. There was an understandable honesty in wanting to see his mother and protect his squad, but he had acted on impulse, and a bit of clever deceit. Someone in authority had seen these traits and found them usable. General Sabine? Gazar? The man Hammer? Nicole could see the far-reaching scope of the operation and they, the agents, were caught in the web. And they had done things. She, and the major, and the other agents—Beau Jackson, Maurice Dupin, Willie Lewis, and others she had never met, or possibly never seen—all had done things outside the law.

"If you're not going to finish that fried rice, I'll give it to the dog." Whitt broke into her train of thought. "Eats like a horse."

Nicole shoved the little white carton across the table. "Call him Runner. He has a name. Everything has a right to have a name."

"I don't usually let him in except to feed. He was bought to be a guard dog."

"If it gets too cold, he can sleep with me," offered Nicole.

"The dog gets better offers than I do." Whitt turned, stared at her, and grinned. He put the rice in the bowl, went to the back door, and whistled.

A white whirlwind whipped into the kitchen.

"You didn't mention Desert Storm," said Nicole casually. "Beau Jackson said—."

"I don't talk about Storm. I lost my best buddy on January 25, 1991, in Kuwait."

"I'm sorry." She gathered the bags and cartons, put them in the trash, and busied herself washing the coffee cups and putting them away.

Whitt opened the back door, and Runner, after looking for help from Nicole, reluctantly went back into the yard.

"There's really no hurry about starting this case. The Feds have been on it four or five months without any evidence."

"Why did you call me?" Nicole demanded. "I told you I needed to work."

"What I'm saying is, there's no reason to rush over to the college and get started. We can spend some time together. I've got a nice little Cessna in a private field a couple of miles from here."

"It is your own plane, no?"

He laughed. "Yes, this one is mine. We can fly up to Baltimore and have lunch at Waterside."

As she hesitated, he continued, "Or any place you like."

"I want to get this job done so I can search for my father. Can't we get started, Major?"

"Nicole, what I'm saying here is that I want to get to know you. Hell, I—you—I—."

"Major," Nicole said carefully, avoiding his eyes, "I'm not ready to think about a new relationship."

He paced around the kitchen and stopped at the door, his back to her. "Does this mean you're not interested in me, or maybe somewhere down the line there's a chance that—."

"I'm only just divorced, Major, I need some time."

Also, some time to consider how a very personal alliance would affect our working together, she was thinking, especially with the dangers the game involved.

"But, when you feel ready for a new relationship, would you consider me?" he persisted.

"You'll be the first one to know."

"Hey!" He turned around and smiled. "I can settle for that." He motioned to the library. "Let's go to work."

She followed him down the hall, noticing his rumpled chinos, the denim shirt coming untucked at the back in the middle of his waist, and brown moccasins, without socks. Finding her gone this morning, he had evidently grabbed yesterday's clothes and the first shoes he found near the bed. It was quite a departure from his usual military spit and polish.

"The subject is Jean Ducharme, age nineteen, daughter of former Ambassador Eugenie Ducharme. She is a student at Randolph College, a sophomore, with average grades, shy, few friends. Six or seven months ago, she told her mother she was being stalked. The FBI was called. They had a man at Randolph around the clock, but there was no indication of a stalker except for printed messages, computer messages, typed notes."

Whitt briefed her as he set up a DVD disc and clicked on the TV screen.

"All of the messages she had been getting came from around the campus or area library computers, and they stopped abruptly a few days after the Feds came on the scene."

"You think it was another student, someone who had an obsession with Ms. Ducharme, or was angry at her, or jealous, no?"

"You're looking for a motive, but the Feds suspected maybe Jean was just looking for attention."

"Why do you say that?" objected Nicole, staring at the plain face on the screen. Plain, yes, but the girl's face had a sweet expression, a sort of lovely vulnerability. She was thin with straight shoulder-length dark hair and blue eyes. Her sweater was handmade, obviously expensive, and she wore designer jeans, thick socks, and track shoes.

"Because some of the messages, three actually, came from her own computer."

"I see." Nicole stared closely at the screen; "Who is the skinny youth hanging about—there—and he was there before, trailing along behind the two girls?"

"Simon Wensel. He's just smitten, as they used to say. Isn't that a great word?"

"Stop that frame," Nicole directed. "In the background there is a fat girl, jumping in front of him. Simon Wensel has dropped his books, and she kicks at them—ooh, she kicks him!"

"Dellie Lumbach, self appointed protector of Jean Ducharme. One of several girls who seem bent on hanging out with Jean."

"Like the one who is with her now, holding her arm, and jostling her over to the—what is that? The Science Building? Now Jean goes in—the camera trails the other girl running across the campus—late to her own class? Why did she do that?"

"That is Jean's roommate, Chelsea Clovis. She's very protective. I don't think she wanted Jean to witness the kicking incident."

The film continued to run another thirty minutes. Simon Wensel, waits in the dark, under a dorm window, late at night. Someone, unseen, empties the contents of a shredder on him from the window, and he retreats. Chelsea takes Jean to the local diner. Dellie Lumbach and two other girls arrive and crowd into the booth. Was it her imagination or did Jean Ducharme appear uncomfortable, almost frightened as she was pushed against the wall of the booth? The film also showed class changes. In the dorm, in Jean's room, a DVD comedy played on the computer but no one appeared to be watching it.

"What do you think, Nicole?" Whitt asked as he removed the DVD.

"Peculiar. Something is playing out here," Nicole said slowly, committing to memory the scenes she had seen.

"Do you think drugs could be involved? Jean Ducharme is wealthy, as I recall. Both of her parents have inherited fortunes. She could be the cash source and suddenly got cold feet about the whole thing and wants out."

"The Feds checked bank accounts. The ones she hangs with are solvent. There are no sudden deposits. If they're dealing, they're hiding it."

"Let me read the threats she received. Was there a theme, anger, jealousy, or revenge?"

There were eight messages. Changes in style implicated three different writers. A note indicated that three messages were in the hidden lover category, two were juvenile-type "love" letters with an odd warning "beware" and three were mysteriously ambiguous suggesting that Jean "find her true self and find true happiness." The hidden lover's last letter was sent after the FBI had left the case. And then there were none.

He handed her a printed note in block letters. It read, "Remember who really loves you and cares for you. Do not be deceived and go down the wrong path, for that is where disaster waits. Beware." Nicole read aloud. "Has that kid, Simon, ever been institutionalized?"

During puberty, he couldn't come to terms with his body changes and feelings but that was four years ago. He spent his fourteenth summer at a community retreat. He also went the Ritalin route while in school, but he seems to have his head on straight now except for thinking he's madly in love with Jean Ducharme.

"So the counseling and happy pill worked?"

"Uh, hell no. He just grew up."

Nicole laughed. "That's a big deal, Major."

"Yes, it is," Whitt agreed.

"So what do you want me to do?"

"Stay close to Jean Ducharme."

"I'm too old to be a soph at Randolph College. Shall I drop in and say my mother knew her mother? Which she did, in a professional way."

Whitt blinked. "She did?"

"When Eugenie was Ambassador to France, Yvette made Eugenie a ball gown. It was beautiful of course. Beaded Birds of Paradise. I was a kid, but I remember all of Maman's ball-gown costumes," Nicole said. "However, I must admit that I never met Eugenie Ducharme."

They sat quietly thinking, and then Whitt got up and reran the disc part of the way through until he came to a full-length view of Jean.

"There, look at her feet. Aren't they running shoes?"

"Lots of kids wear those."

"Here, she has on flats, and there, loafers, going to class. Now I'll backup—see the pale light behind her?"

"Before class, early morning." Nicole nodded. "I run in the morning. If she does run, find out where she runs and her regular schedule."

"Will do. I'll put Beau Jackson on it. That gives us a day until he reports in."

"Run the film again. Something is—I don't know—in one place the students are coming toward the camera. Everyone in the same direction," observed Nicole. "Classes are out for the day—but one man, just a sleeve is visible and part of a hat, by that tree, facing the opposite way."

"That's the college security. See the patch?"

"On the sleeve, no?"

"If you are looking at college employees—you might see Carlo working on the grounds."

"He doesn't like me," Nicole said.

"You told him he was crazy. His mind is sharp. He just can't speak," Whitt reminded her.

"I thought he was pretending," she snapped.

Carlo was useless to me when I needed help, she thought silently.

"Would you take me to Charlene in the tech office? I want to find my father!"

"I thought we'd have some time together. Just you and me, but this is important to you, isn't it?"

"Mon Dieu, I have waited all my life!"

* * *

When Whitt and Nicole arrived at the Alexandria office, he parked the Jeep Cherokee in front of the room where Tanya Tzoffke once stayed. Nicole thought of Tanya and hoped she was doing well. They went up the steps and pressed the button. Beau Jackson greeted them heartily from the kitchen and poured two more mugs of coffee. He glanced surreptitiously from one to the other, wondering when these two would discover each other, and if it happened, how would it affect the game.

He was aware that Whitt was sending Nicole into the Ducharme case, a soft job at Randolph College that seemed to have no more basis to pursue.

Derek Holland hurried into the conference area. He was as dapper and handsome as ever in a glen plaid jacket, dark brown moleskin vest and brown trousers. At the sight of Nicole, tears formed in his eyes, and he erupted in a torrent of French that seemed to have been bottled up inside, waiting for another Parisian. Nicole hugged him, and they went into his office where they chattered at each other at top speed.

"I am living here at the motel downstairs in a tiny suite with no room for my wardrobe," he told her. "The apartment didn't work out. The landlady was not told I was a little person."

"Her loss," said Nicole sharply. "Do you have a kitchenette at your place?"

"Yes, small but adequate."

"Perhaps—you have chocolate?"

His small, strong hand reached across the desk and grasped hers in a tight grip. "For you Nicole, I would pick the beans myself, but not necessary! I have chocolate."

"Perhaps I could come tonight?"

"Supper too, then. Come anytime. I will wait for you as long as midnight. Oh, Nicole, your voice makes me homesick for the first time since I came to America."

"You are not happy here, Derek?"

"I am fine." He shrugged and spread his hands.

"What is your room number?" she asked as she heard Jackson and Whitt approach.

"Twenty-one, on the end."

"Nicole," Beau Jackson broke in, "Charlene will see you at three o'clock. Major Whitt will take you. Meanwhile, these are notes on the Ducharme stalking problem, Jean Ducharme's schedule of classes, and mug shots of the six security personnel, and three part-time grounds men."

Jackson handed her a shallow file folder. "Study these faces. Don't want you shooting any of the good guys for following too closely."

"I only shoot the bad guys."

"How can you tell them from the good guys?"

"They have little horns if you look very carefully. Some have tails."

"I see," said Jackson, nodding at the file. "Homework. Get on it. You go to Randolph in the morning." He and Whitt started to walk out of Holland's office and then Jackson turned. "Do I have a tail, Nicole?"

Without looking up from the case notes and Nicole answered without a change of expression, "Big black one."

Jackson and Whitt stopped in the doorway, looked at each other and began to laugh. Derek Holland looked stricken, then joined in the laughter.

"How about me, Nicole?" asked Whitt, sticking his head back around the door. "Do I have the horns of an evil guy?"

"Don't ever forget your hat," she zinged back without a glance in his direction.

Derek looked anxiously from one to the other. "You are not, uh, what is the expression? Political correct?" whispered Derek after the other two disappeared down the hall. Nicole was memorizing the file and didn't answer. On the last page was a small news clipping of the death of a Randolph student two months previously. One Sara Wells had leaped to her death from the roof of the Arts Building. It had been termed suicide, and someone—Beau?—had made a notation, Conclusion: not related. Nicole read it over twice. No local death notice. Sara Wells was from Bay Vista, New York.

Nicole took the file into the conference room, looked around for Whitt, but he was nowhere to be seen, so she folded it opened to the Well's death and placed it in front of Jackson.

"How do you know it was suicide?"

"Sara Wells was a loner. In theory, she was obsessed with pursuing an art career but her drawing talent was minimal. She was thinking of changing her major to music and was trying to learn the flute. Her parents were divorcing and that's always traumatic. One night she took her acrylics, a clean canvas, and an easel, up to the roof, wrote a big *good-bye* on the canvas, and jumped."

"Mon Dieu! It is so sad, no?"

"Sara Well's suicide had no relation to Jean Ducharme," Jackson stated. "That's just a sidenote."

Nicole looked thoughtful. "The messages from the stalker to Jean—did they come before this tragedy, or after?"

"Both. You can check the dates. They are written on those copies." He pointed to the small sheaf of papers. "The notes stopped when Madam Ambassador brought the Feds into it."

"Can you arrange for me to audit some classes at Randolph?"

"It's been arranged." He sat back in his chair. "I'm calling the pizza joint to send lunch over. What's your pleasure?" Jackson reached for the telephone and punched in a number.

"Cheese in the crust. Sausage on top."

"Merci, Madame."

"Speak English!"

"Oui, oui, Cherie!" teased Jackson, then he sat back in the chair and squinted at her through narrowed eyes. "And what do you think of our Major Whitt?"

"He seems professional," she answered.

Jackson kept staring at her. "Everything going okay out at the safe house?"

Nicole picked up the folder and walked out into the hall as the pizza manager's voice came on the line.

* * *

Major Whitt drove to Arlington, and circled a block of old apartment houses before he found a parking space for the Jeep Cherokee. Leaves and dust had settled on the cars along the street as if the owners had parked years ago and settled for the Metro to get them to their destinations in Washington.

They walked to one of the apartment houses, which had been altered with a glassed area enclosing the front porch. Three steps led one to the porch door. Whitt pushed a buzzer by the door. They entered the porch, watched by cameras set on either side of the second door, which led into the hall of the house.

"Come on up, Major," called a female voice from the second floor. A very pretty face smiled down over the railing from above. "So this is Charlene," thought Nicole, I wonder if Major Whitt comes here often. He certainly seemed familiar with the neighborhood. Perhaps he did come here often.

They went up the steps and down a hall to what appeared to be an ordinary, middle-class apartment. There were nice, slip covered couches, a couple of recliners, large television, a small bar, and many bookshelves. Through a doorway was a kitchen area and the smell of fresh perked coffee lingered on the air.

"This is Agent Laurent of the Paris office," Whitt introduced her. "And this is Charlene."

"I thought the Paris office was dead," said Charlene, looking carefully at Nicole and glancing back to Whitt.

"Not dead, just taking a nap. Some players are waiting for a new start."

"I see. Why not . . . ?" Charlene nodded toward Nicole. "She certainly has experience."

"Turned me down flat." Whitt shrugged.

"I have some pictures here," Nicole said, pulling the poster from her shoulder bag. "The major tells me you can do age enhancement, and possibly a trace on this man. The poster is in French and German, but the subject is possibly American."

Whitt noticed that Nicole had not mentioned that the man could be her father, and he understood that she wanted Charlene to handle this as any impersonal assignment.

Charlene looked at the poster with interest. "I can't promise, but tell me what you know about the man. If we know a little about him, it will help us in choosing the probable facial features," she explained to Whitt.

"Let Nicole tell you. It's her project," said Whitt.

"Well, we know he was an acrobat, very agile, doing mostly trapeze work. We know he was with the circus, and they traveled all over the world. We are trying to find out if he is still alive and if so, where is he? This is very important to us."

"For you, Major, anything," promised Charlene, smiling. She touched her sleek dark hair, worn in a bun, and flirted with him over her silver-rimmed glasses. As she headed to the rear of the apartment, she managed to brush against his sleeve.

To Nicole's surprise, Charlene led them into the bedroom and opened a door in the wall that Nicole would have guessed concealed a clothes closet. Beyond the door was the constant hum of machines, and a man and a woman, their backs to the door, appeared to be absorbed in watching computer screens. Charlene went in the room and placed the posters and notes on an empty desk, then came back out and closed the door.

"This is important Charlene. Put Sam on it or handle it personally," Whitt said.

They went back out to the second floor hall and down the stair. The outside door clicked, and they walked through the glassed-in porch into the winter chill outside. The temperature had dropped, and the air felt like the coming of snow. Wind rustled the dead leaves between the cars.

Nicole pulled her fuzzy red cap out of the pocket of her black leather coat and tugged it down over her ears as they hurried back to the car. Whitt put his arm across her shoulders as they moved swiftly along. She hoped Charlene was watching from an upper window and noticed this gesture, a gesture somehow close and tenderly familiar.

As the jeep headed back to Alexandria, Whitt consulted his watch.

"Where would you like to have dinner? It's early still. I can call around for reservations."

"I have a date."

"A date?"

"Yes."

"Who with?"

"I don't have to tell you, Major."

"Where are you going?"

"Nowhere, just take me to the office."

"How are you getting back to the house?"

"Don't worry about it." His questions sounded more like an inquisition, and she was determined to tell him nothing.

"Remember, you leave for Randolph College tomorrow. You need your rest. We need to talk about the case. I want you home by nine."

Nicole burst out laughing. "Yes, Daddy."

Whitt drove the rest of the way through the heavy traffic in silence, obviously upset. At the motel, he pulled into the lot and slammed on his brakes, leaving the motor running. Beau Jackson looked down from above.

"Beau Jackson?" Whitt demanded incredulously.

"No," she answered. "See you later."

The jeep roared out of the parking lot.

* * *

Inside Room 21, flowers were everywhere, on the little table by the window, which was set with motel china and new yellow plastic placemats, on the table by the lamp, and through the door to the bedroom, she saw a few tulips in a water glass on the dresser. Hmmm . . . flowers in the bedroom? Nicole thought, you're not going to get that lucky my little man, as much as I love you dearly.

"I'm going to fix a light omelet, with bits of onion and mushroom, and a green salad," recited Derek breathlessly as Nicole hesitated in the tiny living/dining area. "I would have started sooner, but—" he hesitated. "I wasn't sure you would come, and then I would have to eat all these eggs all week."

"I am here, and I am hungry," stated Nicole. "Can I help?"

"Taste the wine. If it does not suit you, I will throw it out. I have others."

She deftly turned the cork, edged it gently out, sniffed the bouquet, and nodded. "Your best glasses, please. I must toast the host."

Derek placed two motel juice glasses on the table. One had a picture of Bugs Bunny and the other a picture of the Roadrunner. Nicole shrugged. "Ah, monsieur, they're not making these Waterford flutes like they used to!" She poured the wine and lifted the glass. "To my darling friend . . . and to Paris."

"Hear! Hear! To Nicole and to Paris!" echoed Derek, his face flushed with emotion. He downed the wine and turned quickly to the kitchen. "I have television or perhaps music on the CD. I only have Frank Sinatra, and Elvis. Very American, am I not?"

"Édith Piaf, where are you when we need you?" Nicole laughed and put Sinatra into the CD player. In a moment, "Strangers In the Night" wafted on the air.

Dizzying aromas of hot butter popping in the pan, a hint of sharp onion, a cheese sauce in a tiny cup kept warm over a candle—Derek, with a dish towel tied high around his waist, standing on a stool, tossing mushrooms into the eggs—Nicole thought of Yvette and Mimi. How they would enjoy this! They would drink too much wine, laugh, and tell bawdy stories, eat with gusto. Mon Dieu! In a moment, I will cry, thought Nicole, and busily began to gather the plates and silver ware for the table as Sinatra told everyone that he considered seventeen to be a very good year.

The meal was perfect. Afterward, they washed the dishes together and watched two shows on the television. Around ten o'clock Derek made hot chocolate, rich, dark with double marshmallows.

"I should call Major Whitt to come get me."

"You could stay here," suggested Derek. "Not here, of course, but there is now a vacancy in the office suite, and I have the key."

"I'll call Major Whitt. I leave on a case tomorrow and perhaps I need more briefing."

"I hope it is nothing dangerous," said Derek, his brow creased with concern. He threw up his hands. "It is all dangerous, damn it, Nicole! You should get out of this business."

"Not this case. I follow a college girl around who claims she is being stalked, but it is probably nothing."

She dialed the safe house, and the phone was picked up on the first ring. "Come get me," she said.

"It's about time," Whitt said gruffly. "Where are you?"

"At the office in Alexandria."

When the jeep sped into the parking lot, Nicole was huddled on the metal step that led up to the office. Whitt circled the parking lot twice before he spotted her. The black leather hood of her coat was obscuring the red hat. She looked like a gnome, a very small cold gnome, and his heart missed a beat. "God, but she's beautiful," he heard his voice breathe into the empty interior of the jeep.

A lazy snowfall was dusting a thin white surface on the blue asphalt of the lot. She climbed into the jeep and glanced up into the rearview mirror. From the last cabin, twenty-one, an anxious Derek waved a small hand in good-bye.

* * *

Major Whitt had decided to assign Nicole the jeep for her trip to Randolph College, which was located north and west of Fredericksburg. All morning they had poured over the facts of the case, the notes and pictures of those concerned. Nicole had asked for and received more information on the "suicide" of Sara Well. The position of the artist's easel worried her. Up there on the roof, the logical view to sketch would be beyond the parapet, looking outward, but the easel faced a brick wall, near the door leading to the inside stairs. This would mean Wells would have picked up the easel, turned it around, carried it to the door, written the *good-bye* message, then turned back around, crossed the roof and jumped. This roof area was never used for anything. The door was always unlocked. No one ever came here except the security guard on duty. He would open the door, glance out onto the roof, and close the door. He would be seeing nothing out of the ordinary because the easel was near the wall, out of his visual range. Whitt's explanation was that Sara Wells knew that it was going to rain later that night, which in fact it did, and she took the time to place her art supplies near the building so they wouldn't get wet. Why? Why care, if she never intended to use them again?

And now, she was on her way. The wet roads were slick with a coating of ice from last night's snow. Nicole glanced through the windshield and gave a sigh of relief. She had driven about sixty miles in the wrong direction, found herself on Highway 64, heading west to Charlottesville, turned around, and drove back north to Highway 1, where, by pure luck, she found the road near Fredericksburg that led to Randolph College. Major Whitt had secured her a room in the Visiting Teacher's dorm, and she hoped he had not been calling to see whether she arrived. Road maps were such a mystery. There were always little bridges, and the occasional large expanse of water, and numerous small towns, not even mentioned!

At the end of a long paved area, a courtyard, and a circular drive, sat the old red brick administration building. To the right were the classroom buildings and across the wide paved area, facing on the left, were the dormitories. At Randolph, classes were coed, dorms were separate, and the larger old brick building housed the women, which outnumbered the men about twenty to one. Randolph had been an all-girl college until equality laws opened its reluctant doors to male students. Beyond the Ad Building were the cafeteria and the gym.

Nicole was cleared to enter at the gates and was surprised to hear herself announced as Ms. Lawrence. She had temporarily forgotten the slight name change. Whitt had decided she should sound more American. Her ID had been changed, and she had a *visa* and *exxon* card for Nicole Lawrence, a visiting teacher, assigned to the Visitor's dorm on the second floor of the Ad Building. The guard directed her to park at the rear. On the road behind the class buildings, she spotted Carlo, who was piling up ice-coated leaves. He glanced up as she passed and gave an imperceptible nod. She nodded back.

Ms. Kelsey, a secretary in the office, a lady on the shady side of sixty and slightly plump, welcomed her and showed her up to Room 204, a very spacious bed-sitting room, as large as Nicole's apartment in Paris. It had a chintz décor, floral drapes, bedspread, and curtains, couch covers, all faded and worn, but somehow still elegant. A rose carpet was equally fine but threadbare.

"We hope you'll be happy here. Mr. Jackson said you would be auditing the art classes. Perhaps gathering material for a master's?" asked Ms. Kelsey.

"Perhaps," echoed Nicole. "It is a lovely room."

"You're the only visiting teacher here now. A Ms. Holly left just this morning," stated Ms. Kelsey.

Nicole wandered over to the window and looked to her left at the roof from which Sara Wells had fallen, or jumped, and Ms. Kelsey followed.

"We had a tragedy right over there," she whispered, although there was no one else to hear. Her pale blue eyes widened behind her glasses and she brushed back a strand of thin, hennaed hair. "Lovely young woman. Her parents were divorcing, and she could have sought counseling here at Randolph—but she chose—she chose—."

"I read about it. So sad for one so young. Did she have many friends?"

"Sara was shy, stayed mostly to herself, except for her roommate, Vanessa Cole," recalled Ms. Kelsey. "Well, I'll leave you to get settled in. If you want anything, I'm just downstairs. Come by the office in the morning for a class schedule."

The secretary moved to the door, and then seemed to recall something. "Sara had a sort of boy friend, an art student? Yes. Samuel Wensel. No, that's not it, but it is something like that. He's shy, like Sara."

Simon Wensel, Nicole realized with a start, the boy who followed Jean Ducharme.

"Is there a place to run here?" Nicole asked quickly as Ms. Kelsey paused at the door.

"A jogging path. Behind the gym, through the woods all the way to the pond, but why anyone would want to walk there, much less run, is a mystery. In warm weather, there are bugs and snakes. Now, it is simply cold and messy. Stay inside, dear," Ms. Kelsey advised and fluttered her hand in good-bye.

* * *

Students and teachers alike must have heeded Ms. Kelsey's advice because four early morning runs over the first four days had netted Nicole zero in terms of meeting Jean Ducharme or anyone connected to her. It was cold, the path slick, and twice she looked back and saw

Carlo several yards behind her, looking out of place in camouflage jeans, and an ugly open plaid jacket that flapped out behind him. On the fourth day, a beautiful dark-haired woman, nearly six feet tall loped slowly past and waved a brief hello. Nicole recognized Vanessa Cole from a yearbook in the Randolph library, Sara Well's roommate, and cursed her luck that Vanessa had had her run and was heading back to the gym.

The classes were a different story. From the first day, she managed to sit on the back row in Art History, taught by a Mr. Henley, directly behind Simon Wensel, and borrowed a Bic pen, which she purposely kept. Jean Ducharme was on the front row, by the window, and next to her was Chelsea Clovis, her roommate.

During the rest of that week, Nicole watched and listened during the class and made no attempts to talk to anyone, thinking it was better to let the class become familiar with her presence. The first few days, she left the class quickly, returned to her room, and to the library to study and catch up on the class work.

On Friday, when class was over, Nicole stood outside the door until the two women came out.

"Excuse me, did the teacher address you as Ms. Ducharme?"

"Yes."

"Ducharme is not an ordinary name, and I just wondered if the former Ambassador to France could be your mother? I spent my childhood in Paris, and my mother knew Eugenia ages ago."

"Maybe—maybe," acknowledged Jean with some hesitation. "She knows a lot of people."

"She probably couldn't remember a very young seamstress, who made a special ball-gown, all beaded, with a design of exotic flowers, Birds of Paradise?"

"That dress!" Jean exclaimed, suddenly interested. "She only wore it once and gave it away!"

Nicole felt as if she had been stabbed in the heart. Gave it away! She turned and began to walk swiftly down the hall. In seconds, she heard running footsteps behind her. Jean called out breathlessly. "Wait! You don't understand! It was so beautiful, and she donated it to the Smithsonian. She adored that dress!"

The Smithsonian! Maman's design had made it into the Smithsonian Collection and Maman didn't even know. Nicole swallowed the lump in her throat. The Smithsonian! Oh, Maman, what an honor!

"Come on, Jean, we'll be late," insisted Chelsea, pulling hard on her arm.

Jean pulled back. "Your name is Nicole Lawrence, right?" asked Jean, trying to shake off the restraining hand.

"I'm in the Teacher's Dorm in the Ad Building." Nicole managed to convey before Jean was hurriedly dragged off down the hall.

"Damn bitch!" growled a voice behind her. Simon Wensel came out from the stairwell where he had been lurking. "Damn lesbian bitch."

"Oh, Simon!" said Nicole, turning toward him. "Such mean things, no?"

"It's true. They are all gay. That Clovis and Debbie Lumbach and that big dyke, Vanessa Cole. I've tried to warn Jean, but they keep her away from me." He glanced at a large sports watch. "You tell her, Ms. Lawrence. You're older and she might listen to you. I gotta run—I got gym." Wensel loped off down the hall.

"Hey! I've got your pen!" called Nicole. "Meet me in the caff after class."

Wensel stopped and looked around in surprise, then grinned. "Yeah, sure!"

Nicole followed Jean Ducharme and Chelsea Clovis a good distance down the hall, saw them cross to the gym, and watched the door close behind them and at least thirty other classmates.

She waited. No one came back out. They all were changing into red and white gym suits and would play basketball for the next hour. She walked leisurely to the caff, chose a small table, and pulled out her notebook. She popped a Coke from one of the machines and sat down to write a letter to Yvette, which she would give to Beau, or the major, to mail from a post office in Washington, with the return address being a box number. There was not a lot Nicole could convey: "Maman, the translation's is going slowly. It is very cold, and we have snow." After a while, her thoughts ran dry and she started to read a paperback someone had left on the next table. The hour passed. A few students came in and punched packages of munchies and canned drinks from the machines, but Simon Wensel didn't show. Classes were over for the day. Perhaps, he had forgotten he had promised to meet her and had gone to pack some clothes for his weekend at home. Most of the Randolph students left after last bell and spent Saturday and Sunday with families in the areas around Washington, Virginia, or even Maryland and Delaware. Nicole waited another fifteen minutes, walked to the gym, and found it nearly empty. A few stragglers came out of the showers, hair soaking wet, grabbing up their caps and jackets.

"Simon? Has anybody seen Simon Wensel?" she asked as they rushed past.

"No, I didn't see him," one offered. "It's Friday. Sometimes he rides to Washington with Jean Ducharme because their mothers both live at Watergate."

"Thanks!" Nicole answered and ran out, heading for her room over in the Ad Building, where she could look down and see everything going on below in the frontcourt.

The guards at the gate were busy. The gardeners and guards on day shift were leaving. In the line of cars exiting, Nicole recognized the blue Ford Tempo, the car assigned to Major Whitt, and, through the window, the sleeve of the ugly plaid jacket that belonged to the driver, Carlo. As soon as Jean Ducharme was safely in her mother's limousine, Nicole could also head out for the weekend. Seeing the Tempo made her think about Major Whitt, his short hair, and the creases so sharp in his chinos—ah, me, she mused. I think I am caring too much for this man!

There was a steady line of expensive vehicles parading slowly to a stop to pick up students. A long silver Cadillac moved into place, and Jean Ducharme came out of the dorm, carrying a small tote bag. She hesitated, looked around as if seeking someone in the crowd—Simon?—indicated to the driver to wait, and walked toward the boy's dorm. A few minutes later, Jean returned to the Cadillac alone and got in. Nicole scanned the court. A group of three teachers, waiting for a ride, huddled beside the Art Building. A security guard stood near the group, carefully surveying the departing students. Nothing seemed unusual. No other vehicle stationed itself suspiciously close behind the car that contained Jean Ducharme.

The Ducharme limousine drove out of the gate. The security guard watched it leave, turned, and went toward the Ad Building as if his job was done.

Nicole went into the hall, found the communal telephone, and asked the college operator to buzz Simon Wensel's room.

"Sorry, no answer. He probably left," she reported.

Nicole packed a bag, pulled on her red wooly cap and black leather coat, and hurried down to the rear parking lot. The Jeep Cherokee turned over on the first try, and she joined the last of the cars leaving Randolph.

Something was making a sharp patter against the windshield, and she realized it was sleet, little icy pellets bouncing on the dark glass. The car ahead pulled on its high beams, and Nicole followed it out to the main highway where it soon disappeared into the meager traffic.

"Holy Mother, guide my hand," Nicole prayed, hesitating. "I do not wish to be lost. I will say twelve Hail Marys if you take me to Major Whitt."

She headed north, clutching the wheel of the jeep and as the miles flew past, things began to look familiar. Then, there it was: Backlick Road, that crazy name! She hurtled off to the left and slid past the trees—and there were the gates to the safe house, incredibly standing open as if to welcome her inside. The little blue Tempo waited a few yards ahead, and Carlo stepped out of the gloom. Without glancing her way, he closed the gates as she drove through.

Major Whitt waited anxiously on the front porch, holding Runner, the big dog, tightly on the chain. He motioned to her to drive around to the kitchen entrance, and he entered the house through the front door. Carlo followed her to the rear and parked. The sleet had turned to snow and big flakes paused on Nicole's red hat and on the shoulders of Carlo's old laid jacket as they hurried into the warmth of the kitchen.

Major Whitt stood by the table, which was carefully laid for three. Three paper towels and three knives, forks, and spoons. Coffee perked in a pot on the counter, cups nearby.

"Well?" Whitt grinned at them and waited.

"Well, what?" ventured Nicole, struggling out of her damp clothes.

Carlo shrugged.

"We have a stove! It came yesterday," Whitt announced, indicating a gigantic white electric appliance gleaming against the wall. "We're going to have turkey. You guys just go on into the library, and I'll call you when it's ready."

"Turkey?" asked Nicole, gazing at the stove, where only the light of a clock appeared to indicate any signs of activity. Perhaps, White had made everything ahead of time and it was warming in the oven. He looked so happy, so proud, as he reached for a button, and pushed 350°.

Nicole and Carlo went into the library, where they settled in chairs on opposite sides of the room. An awkward silence ensued. Nicole finally rose and turned on the television. An Andy Griffith rerun was on and Carlo made a humorous "Ah oh" noise each time little Opie appeared on screen. Nicole thought she smelled something vaguely like potatoes cooking and found she was hungry, also wishing she had brought nice wine for dinner since the major went to so much trouble.

"Come and get it," came the summons from the kitchen. It had only been thirty minutes.

They went back into the kitchen, and there on the paper towels sat three TV dinners, turkey—yes—mashed potatoes, green peas, and a miniscule cherry cobbler tucked into one division of the aluminum plate. The major handed each a paper napkin. A full bottle of rose wine sat in the middle of the table with three rather dusty glasses.

"Looks good, doesn't it?" said Whitt.

Carlo stared expressionless at the TV dinner and sat down at one place, carefully arranging his napkin on his lap.

Nicole began to laugh. She was so hungry she felt giddy. She laughed and laughed until tears ran down her cheeks. Whitt and Carlo, peeling the hot plastic from the tops of their dinners, stopped to stare.

"Nothing like home cooking!" Nicole finally gasped. She wiped out the wine glasses and poured them each a full glass. "Yum, yum, it must be Thanksgiving!"

Carlo, who had been poised over his meal, damp black curly hair dangling over his plate, rose and went to the calendar on the wall, turned back a page, and grunted.

"Yes," Whitt nodded. "Thanksgiving was two weeks ago. She was making a little joke."

"Ar r gr," growled Carlo and returned to his seat, where he dug ravenously into the dinner.

Nicole finished her glass of wine and poured another. She glanced through the darkened pane of the window at the snow.

"Where is Runner?"

"On the porch in his house."

Abruptly, she got up, went through the long hall, and opened the door. Runner stood expectantly under the porch light, his chain stretched taut, as if he knew she would come. She knelt and unhooked the chain, and he followed her cautiously into the hall. He slumped on a scatter rug just inside as if he knew he was ordinarily not allowed in this house.

Carlo, now finished with his meal, reached inside his shirt and handed Whitt a single sheet of paper, closely written. Whitt took it and shoved it into his pocket.

"Thanks."

Carlo nodded toward his apartment.

Nicole poured Whitt another wine, corked the bottle, and gave it to Carlo. "Buenos Noches. Hasta Manana," she said.

Carlo grabbed his jacket and headed out into the falling snow.

"I don't suppose you have a written report?" asked Whitt.

"No. I will tell you what I know."

"In five minutes, please bring the coffee into the library. Oh, there is cake if you like." Whitt gestured toward the counter, finished his wine, and left the room.

Nicole regarded the cake. It was a flat lemon thing wrapped in plastic. She finished her wine, cleared the table, and dumped the TV cartons into the trash. She rinsed the glasses and cups and unplugged the coffeepot. Runner sidled into the kitchen and flopped against her feet.

"Good boy. Good boy. Want some cake?"

She sliced through the plastic and tossed a large slice on a napkin. She ate the lemon custard topping. Runner ate the slightly dry yellow batter bottom. Afterward, she put her head down on the table for just a minute. She could hear the "tick, tick" of the sleet against the window, and then, she fell fast asleep.

"Are you going to bring the coffee?" Whitt's voice woke her as he entered the kitchen.

Runner, who had been lying against Nicole's feet, lifted his massive black-and-white head and growled a warning.

"Traitor! I thought you were my dog," Whitt muttered. "I see she bought you with a piece of cake."

Runner cast a sheepish look over his shoulder and made his way into the hall.

"Nicole?"

"Hmmmm . . ."

"If you're tired, we will talk in the morning."

"Okay." She put her head back down on the table.

"Come on. Get into bed."

"I bet you say that to all the girls."

"Just you."

She struggled to her feet and wandered off down the hall to the bedroom and sat down on the bed to take off her boots. Suddenly, she was conscious of a very sad song being played on a harmonica. It segues into "You Are My Sunshine," which continued slowly for the next ten minutes. Nicole went into the bathroom, took a shower, brushed her teeth, and put on her Tweety Bird nightshirt. There was silence. She climbed between the cold sheets and pulled the covers over her head. Closer this time, the harmonica whined into song once again, "Somewhere My Love," filled the hall just outside her door. It continued on and on, now softly, now a rising crescendo, until she got up and opened the door.

"What are you doing?" she demanded.

"It's Lara's Theme from Dr. Zhivago."

"I know that!"

Whitt sat with back against the wall. He wore briefs and a huge gray sweatshirt with "Duke University" across the chest. The harmonica was poised, ready to blow.

"I'm awake now! You want to talk?" asked Nicole, marching back into the bedroom and snuggling under the covers.

He followed. "Nicole?"

"Yes, Major?"

"I love you."

She poked her head above the covers and stared at him. "You do? Truly? When did this happen?"

"From the first moment I saw you." He shifted his bare feet from side to side. "Nicole, I'm freezing."

With a sigh, she turned back the sheet and the bed spread, plumped the second pillow, and said, "Get under the covers, Major."

* * *

From habit, Nicole woke a little before 5:00 a.m. Whitt's arm lay across her waist, his face nestled into her neck. She wiggled out from under him very carefully and replaced the covers. He sighed, turned over, and began to snore gently as she crossed to the window. The ground was white, and still a few flurries wafted down from the heavens, turning the world into a frosty, clean, mysterious wonder place. There would be no run this morning, but she decided to wear her tracksuit.

She found the thermostat and turned the temperature to seventy-five degrees, so the house would be warm when the major awoke later. She cleared the pot and set fresh coffee to perking, looked around for breakfast food, and discovered Whitt still had no refrigerator, but there was cereal, oatmeal, and Frosted Flakes. Bread and milk were in Beau Jackson's cooler on one of the counters.

Oh god, what have I done? I've never given myself so lightly, she thought as she poured cereal into bowl and dropped the box on the floor. How can we continue in the business we are in and have a personal relationship? I should leave here and return to Paris, as soon as possible. Mon Dieu, I am a fool!

"Good Morning." Whitt stood in the doorway, sleepy-eyed, a half smile on his lips.

"Coffee is ready."

He went to the window. "If I thought I could get clearance, I'd fly you down to Durham to meet my son, Andy. He's a great guy. Smart. Good looking like his daddy." He laughed and turned to look at Nicole. She had a troubled expression on her face.

"Major. Do you think it is wise . . . ?"

There was a loud knock on the back door, and Carlo came inside, tracking snow from his big rubber boots, a white bag in his hand. He set the bag on the table, and Nicole read the words *krispy kreme*.

"How did you get out of here?" Whitt asked with surprise.

Carlo held up four fingers.

"Four-wheel drive? You took the jeep."

Nicole poured a large mug of coffee and set it in front of the place where Carlo had sat the night before. Carlo's place, she thought and my place. The major sits at the head of the table. Like a family. But it is not a family. She longed to see Yvette's beautiful face.

They ate the doughnuts, finished the coffee, and went into the library where Whitt lit the logs in the fireplace.

"Carlo, you pretty much covered Ducharme on the outside from your report and at no time did she run on the wood path behind the gym that leads to the small pond and doubles back on the same path. You saw Nicole, a couple of male students, one of the guards on his break, and one very tall girl student."

"That would be Vanessa Cole," put in Nicole. "It was cold and messy. That is why nobody came out to run."

Carlo nodded.

Whitt regarded the written report, turned to Nicole, and asked, "And did you see the reflection from the roof?"

"What?" Nicole looked startled.

"On several occasions over the past, Carlo has seen something, a glint from the sun, and when the moon rose, a circle of glass or metal in the area where Sara Wells went off the roof. Carlo, like all the grounds people, is not allowed in the buildings, and has no keys. I thought you might have checked this out."

"I directed my view to Jean Ducharme's dorm room and stayed there until the matron locked the doors at ten minutes past 10:00 p.m. It bothered me that Jean and Chelsea Clovis left the drapes wide open. I could see them in the darkened room watching TV long after lights out."

"So you were concentrating on the dorm rooms to your right and never looked over to the class buildings?"

"I couldn't see that angle from my room. You would have to be in front of the building."

Carlo, his head lowered, appeared to be secretly smiling behind his long damp hair.

Whitt glanced from one to the other. "You two better get your act together. I expect you to be professional on the job, share what you observe, and if there is a stalker out there, you damn well better ferret him out. You are not communicating."

Carlo had stopped smiling and merely looked sulky, avoiding Nicole's angry stare. He whipped out one of his pink post-it notes and printed with his heavy black Sharpie pen, "Stalkers kill." He held it up and glowered at Nicole.

"I can open the door to the roof. If there is anything up there—beer cans probably—candy bar wrappers, condom wrappers—cigarettes, cigars—I'll toss them down to you, Carlo!" she snapped. She took Simon Wensel's Bic pen out of her jeans pocket and placed it on the coffee table. "Here is the pen that probably wrote two of the letters to Jean Ducharme. It belongs to Simon Wensel. He's in love with her. He tries to protect her. Simon is not the stalker we're looking for."

"How do you know?"

"I sit next to him in Art Class. I have observed him on campus. And I have seen him write. I borrowed the pen."

"The Feds pretty much figured that," admitted Whitt. "And the young women—Clovis, Cole, and Lumbach—wrote a few. They want Ducharme to join the RSC, a gay group."

"RSC?"

"Randolph Sappho Club. She must have given them some encouragement, but she has asked to change rooms after Christmas break. The reason she gave was she wanted to move away from Chelsea Clovis. Jean often appears scared to death. I guess she's coming to terms with her own sexuality and realizes that for her, it's a guy thing."

"Well," Whitt paused. "Let's try to wrap this up. Neither of you saw anyone following, watching, making contact, with the subject in any way?"

"No."

Carlo shook his head and got up to leave. He pointed to the window, and they noticed the snow had stopped. He found his jacket and crossed to the door.

"Remember this. There is still one letter writer unidentified. That bothers me," Whitt reminded them. "Clean this up."

"I go tomorrow," printed Carlo on another pink post-it he pulled from his pocket. "Randolph."

"I'll contact you when I get into the door to the roof."

Carlo nodded, picked up the half-empty bag of doughnuts, and left the house.

"Tell me about that man," demanded Nicole. "Is his silence something psychological?"

"Oh, hell, no. He was beaten on a job for Gazar about five years ago. They cut out part of his tongue and cut his throat, leaving him in a dumpster to die."

"I am sorry. But he is so hostile to me."

"He wears turtleneck sweaters to cover the scars on his neck," said Whitt.

"No scars, but look, Major, so do I!"

"Well, there's nothing wrong with your neck. You're beautiful all over, Nicole," he said.

"You know when I realized I loved you more than anything on earth? In France, at your grandmother's funeral. You looked so small, so sad, all in black. I decided I wanted to care for you the rest of your life."

"That—that is the kindest thing anyone ever said to me."

Whitt waited, gazing at Nicole expectantly, but she busied herself picking up the coffee cups and taking them to the sink. After a few minutes, he shrugged and said, "Let's walk out to the gate and see if a brave newspaper carrier has gotten through with the *Washington Post*. And wear that red hat. I even love your red hat. You should wear it all the time, even to bed. Just the hat."

"You are one crazy man, Major." She laughed and went to get her things.

The telephone began to ring and Whitt picked it up, talked for a few minutes, and by the time Nicole returned, he had hung up. As they walked through the ruts made by the jeep, Runner prancing ahead, warm in the snow in his thick black and white fur, Whitt turned to Nicole. "That call was good news. Charlene has the age-enhanced impression of Nicolas Campion."

Nicole pressed her heart. "I have always thought he would be somewhere near in this area. I looked in my college years for him everywhere on the streets."

"I made an appointment for tomorrow."

"Oh, oh! We cannot go today?"

"I've got another case and an agent coming up from Florida. I need to hit the airport and get him settled at the motel in Alexandria. You can come along."

"I will wait here. I want to look at my pictures of the circus, of my father, so that if—no! When I see him, I will know him!" Nicole said excitedly. Impulsively, she leaped up and kissed him several times.

He grabbed her in his arms and turned around and around until they fell in the snow. Runner barked and circled them to see if these crazy people had hurt themselves. He was relieved when they struggled out of the icy drift and continued to the gate.

* * *

Charlene leaned over the railing and beckoned them up to the second floor. Being Sunday, the other two workers were absent for the weekend and the apartment was eerily quiet.

"Come up. I think you'll be pleased. We may have a good likeness, unless, of course, the subject may have altered his appearance surgically or possibly have had a gender change."

Nicole gasped. "Gender change?"

"Criminal types resort to harsh measures to cover their tracks, right, Major?"

Whitt stirred uncomfortably. "We don't know the subject is a criminal."

"Yes, Major, we do! He may even be wanted by Interpol. What a catch!" Charlene gloated. "Come, I'll show you."

Nicole looked stricken. Oh, Holy Mother, what have I done? Whitt moved toward her and gently placed his hand on her back. Nicole pulled off her wooly cap and wiped her brow.

"Here is the age enhancement photo." Charlene handed the picture to Whitt, who studied it briefly. He handed it to Nicole and felt her stiffen in recognition although she remained silent. Her face registered no expression.

"And now, here's what we've dug up via the magic box—he has appeared, and disappeared, in Atlanta, Chicago, Miami, New York, and DC, peddling art and antiques. He has no family we know of and no firm address. He calls himself Charles Wendt, and he is about sixty years old, blue eyes, and gray hair," announced Charlene, triumphantly. She printed and ripped out the copy.

Whitt hesitated. "Where is he now?"

"How did you round up this profile?" interjected Nicole. She stared at the over-aged enhancement.

"We did a picture match. Nothing came up on the name search except four other Nicolas Campions, in various places, who checked out as legit. No, we think it is Charles Wendt. He was last in Los Angeles and San Diego. He has nineteen social security numbers, has never registered as a voter, or owned a car."

"How did you reach the conclusion that this person, Charles Wendt, is the man?" asked Nicole.

"He was jailed briefly—and escaped—so we have the mug shot and the enhancement to compare," Charlene said, with a smile. "And here's the clincher. Twenty years ago, he was using the alias Nicolas Campion. Here's your original file—the poster and circus program. He's your boy, Major Whitt."

"Thanks. As usual, you've been helpful."

"Uh, Major? I have two tickets to the new Broadway show at the Kennedy Center. Are you free Friday night?"

"I'm not sure of my schedule."

"I'll call you," Charlene promised, her hand on his arm as they strolled toward the door. "I'll call you, say Wednesday?"

Nicole dropped her hat on the rug, followed them out and down the stairs. They passed through the door to the glassed-in area. Whitt rolled the printouts and put them in his inside pocket.

"I forgot my hat! I'll just be a sec," Nicole said and hurried back up the steps.

Charlene started after her but stopped abruptly when Whitt quickly asked, "Which Broadway show is at the Kennedy Center? I've already seen 'Cats' and 'Ms. Saigon.'"

Charlene hesitated and turned back to Whitt as Nicole disappeared beyond the landing. The display was still on the monitor. Nicole took out the disk and looked at the title on the sticker, Nicolas Campion/Charles Wendt, and the date the information was entered. She memorized the exact date and shoved the disk back in place.

She snatched up her hat and fled back down the stairs.

"Found it under the chair," she announced, pulling the hat down around her ears.

"Red," remarked Charlene suspiciously. "It should have been easy to see."

"It was."

"Thanks again," Major Whitt said over his shoulder as he headed toward the jeep.

"I'll phone you," called Charlene. She gave a short wave as they drove away.

"I need to check out somebody at the office, the guy I brought in yesterday. It shouldn't take long," said Whitt.

"Good. I can see if Derek is home."

"What's with you and the dwarf?"

"We've been lovers since I was ten."

"Oh, yeah!" Whitt growled.

"He is my friend, and he is lonely. He is in a new country. We speak French. Do you want any more explanation?"

"I'm sorry."

"What's with you and Ms. Computer?"

"She chases me, I run and hide."

"Oh, yeah!" growled Nicole, in imitation.

Major Whitt went up to the motel, his boots clicking on the steel steps to the second floor. Anyone inside could see who was approaching through the slits in the drapes.

Nicole continued down to the last room, number 21, and knocked on the door. A sleepy Derek opened the door and hastily buttoned his shirt, smoothed down his hair, and threw the door wide.

"I'm dreaming or is it Nicole?"

"C'est moi, mon petite."

"I was napping. Sundays, you know. I go to church, have lunch—nothing on TV."

"Major Whitt is in the office," said Nicole. Assured that they were alone, asked him, "Can you do a little hacking, Derek? I want to destroy a file."

"One of our files?" he asked, suddenly awake.

"At the tech office. Can you do it?"

Derek hesitated. "Perhaps, but my obituary would read 'Death by Charlene' if I am discovered. Do you know the name of the file?"

"Of course. Give me a paper." She wrote the names and the date and handed it to him. "I think this man may be my father, but now I need to find him myself. I have put him in danger."

"Wait, wait!" Derek demanded.

"They gave me a picture, but they did not know how young he was when he was in the circus! They added another thirty years! But Derek, I have seen him! He is somewhere near."

Derek stared at her in disbelief, then glanced away.

"The man in the enhanced picture. The eyes are my eyes. His eyebrows are dark and straight. His hair is dark and has some curl, and oh, Derek, I have seen him!"

"Where did you see this man, Nicole?"

"It was dark. I was on Embassy Row on a case, and he was there, in the yard."

"He is one of our agents?"

"No." She sat in silence for a long while. "You see what I've done? I asked for help in locating him, and now, if they find him, they may give him to Interpol. I didn't imagine what they could uncover or that they could use it against him. I just wanted an address! Please help me, Derek."

"Have a glass of wine," he insisted.

"Thanks. The major and I are going to dinner. Come with us, Derek?"

"I have met two Little People, a man and his wife. They're coming at five. We will be going to Chez Avril."

"Another time then?"

"Yes, I'll fix the file before morning."

She put down her glass and kissed him on both cheeks, then wrote on a napkin. "Here's my hall phone at Randolph. Call me after it goes down."

Nicole got up at 5:00 a.m., packed her clothes and without waking Whitt, quietly made her way to the front porch where Runner was snug in his house on a pile of blankets. She undid his chain, brought him into the house, and gave him food and water.

"Take care of the major, sweet boy," she said as she propped her letter to Yvette by the coffeepot. Whitt would see it and get it mailed.

A pale sun was trying to come out, but the roads were still slick; tall black gritty drifts had been piled high on each side by snow plows. The weatherman on the radio promised a high of thirty degrees by noon. The music didn't help. Christmas Carols had begun, with songs of sleigh bells, snowmen, and icicles, celebrating the freezing season.

She turned off the radio and sang "La Vie En Rose" for the next twenty miles, but it made her think of Yvette, so very far away. She would insist that Derek Holland go home to Paris with her for Christmas. It would be a sad Christmas, the first without her beloved Mimi.

The courtyard at Randolph was nearly empty. The workers were arriving and heading for their parking area in the rear. The off-campus teachers would come and last of all, those returning students whose transport could make it on the icy roads.

Nicole took her things up to her room, came down, and was happy to find the door to the cafeteria unlocked. The smell of fresh coffee hung on the air. Something—hot rolls?—was baking. The plump cook put down her newspaper and went to the grill where bacon popped and curled.

"Give me ten minutes, honey," the cook called out, peeking in the oven.

"Yes, I will be back."

Nicole went behind the gym and inspected the jogging path. No fresh prints broke the ice that gathered in the ruts through the woods. All the way to the frozen pond, the snow drifted high and as yet undisturbed. Not even the athletic Vanessa Cole would want to challenge this treacherous trail, Nicole decided, turning back to the gym. She walked around to the cafeteria, and the cook brought out a platter of scrambled egg, hot rolls, jelly, and bacon so hot it still sizzled on the plate. She poured coffee from an urn on the counter and wondered what Whitt was having—a frozen TV breakfast from his new stove? Major, major, major. The thought of him, the sweet smell of his strong lean body, the slight stubble of his morning beard against her neck, and the way his eyes followed her when they were in a room together. He loves me . . . but could I trust him with the rest of my life, she mused, thinking of the men gone before, growing up without a father, her prince marrying his cousin, Rene, and his mistress. Not a happy track record with the men in her life.

After breakfast, she returned to her room and took up a vigil, watching as a meager trickle of cars came in and deposited the students at the dorm. Chelsea Clovis arrived, went up, and threw the drapes wide in the room she shared with Jean Ducharme. Twenty minutes later, Jean appeared in the limo. Others dispersed to the dorm building, but Nicole realized that the weather was keeping half the students off campus.

She went to the courtyard and noticed Carlo clearing the walkways. She nodded and he lifted his eyes to the roof of the Art Building. She glanced up and saw nothing. As she passed near, Carlo pressed a note into her hand. She entered the building and opened the note. "You get the key to roof." He had written in heavy black paint. She tore the note in tiny pieces and tucked them into the pocket of her coat as she went into the Art Class and took her seat at the rear of the room. The teacher, Mr. Henley, waved his arm to indicate the almost-empty classroom.

"Randolph should have closed. Today, we'll have slides and you can write opinions on how you feel about the artist and his work. Tomorrow, I'll tell you how wrong you were."

There was a polite titter as he looked hopefully at the door for more students, but when none were forthcoming, he slipped the disc into the DVD, revealing a self-portrait by Van Gogh. Sad blue eyes gazed out at a cruel world from under a straw hat, and the six scattered students picked up their pens and went to work. Simon Wensel was among the missing. Nicole fingered the new Bic pen she had bought for him and thrust it back into her shoulder bag. After class, she strolled through the halls until she found the door to the roof. It had an older lock, evidently taken from another door, one she could force with a nail file or one of the objects on a key ring that held her room key and the VW key, a three-inch multipurpose knife. A tiny scrap of yellow tape still adhered to a thumbtack, at the left side of the door. It was crime scene tape, which indicated that the police had not immediately bought the suicide theory until convinced by Randolph personnel and parents that it was an accident.

At noon, Nicole walked around the courtyard, noticing that Carlo was doing a thorough job on the walks. She paused at his side.

"Have you seen anything, any reflection?"

He leaned over, tore out a clump of frozen grass, and imperceptibly shook his head. He made a turning notion with his grimy hand indicating a turning key.

"No problem," she told him as two girls approached. "A good job!" she added for their benefit as they passed.

"He can't speak," one of the students said. "He's deaf and dumb."

Scowling, Carlo made an obscene gesture at their departing backs and fell back to work.

"I'll be in my room in the Ad Building dorm on the second floor. If you note anything unusual, drop your hat on the sidewalk. I'll be in touch."

He grunted and gazed after her as she walked away. Untouchable, he thought, major's woman, too skinny, too mean, too smart, for Carlo. He spit on the icy sidewalk and wiped his mouth.

Nicole went to her room and took up her place at the window. Twice Jean Ducharme and Chelsea Clovis returned to the women's dorm, exchanged books, and went back to classes. At four o'clock, two Randolph boys drove up in a jeep. Jean and Chelsea ran out, waving yellow off campus permits, got in the jeep, and drove away, presumably to dinner in Fredericksburg. Classes were over for the day. Carlo looked up, shook his head, and disappeared. He would leave the college grounds at five to go to his room where he was staying at a nearby motel.

Nicole called Simon Wensel's room from the hall telephone. He had not yet returned to Randolph from the weekend break. Many students were still out, some with colds and others using the miserable icy weather and bad roads as an excuse to remain at home with their families. She wandered over to the cafeteria and had the spaghetti special with Italian bread toasted with garlic butter and hot coffee. I am glad Major Whitt is not here—my breath would light a candle, she mused, and I wish I had a nice red wine, but alors! Randolph was very dry. No alcohol, no cigarettes. Of course, the dorm bathrooms hung with blue smoke and beer cans clattered in plastic trash bags.

Darkness came early, and on impulse, she headed for the Art Building, first glancing upward to the parapet. She saw nothing and proceeded inside where she made her way up to the door to the roof. The hall was empty and eerily quiet as she inserted her nail file into the lock, then pulled it gradually back a tiny bit at a time until it found the spot where it clicked. The door swung open to reveal the broad shingled roof with patches of snow banked against the parapet. A huge chimney towered close to the low wall that separated the rear roof area. At the base of the chimney, the heat had melted the snow. Nicole walked over and put her hand on the chimney, which, through the bricks, was pleasantly warm to the touch. She stepped over the low wall to the rear area. Here the snow was level and undisturbed as far as she could see. The sun would reach the front roof during the midday, but the rear remained in shade. She was so absorbed in searching the area for anything that may have caused the reflection that Carlo had reported to Whitt that she barely detected the click that indicated that the door from the hall was opening. A faint wedge of light appeared, and from the doorway, a tall figure in silhouette scanned the darkness with a low-beamed flashlight. Nicole lay down, in the snow, her back pressed against the low wall of the rear roof and waited as the visitor walked to the front.

"Where are you, my pretty one?" a singsong voice murmured softly. Nicole raised her head and listened intensely, but she couldn't tell whether this voice was male or female. Something metallic scraped against the shingles.

She pressed against the wall and held her breath, her hand touching the hard bulk of the gun nestled in the bottom of her shoulder bag.

"Now, Jean, you should have your light on. Where are you? Are you cheating on me? You know I get very angry," continued the whisper.

Jean. Jean Ducharme. Whoever it was, was looking across the courtyard at the dorm directly opposite. The room would be unlit because Jean and Chelsea had left the campus at four, a fact that the watcher was obviously unaware. Still, the visitor waited, occasionally adjusting something and impatiently striding back and forth.

An hour passed. Nicole began to feel as if she were permanently frozen against the low wall. She thought about Major Whitt. She thought about Maman and wondered if she had received her last letter. She would write again—"Maman, I am not doing translations as you think. I am lying on my back in the snow on a rooftop"—no, one did not write one's mother such things; mothers would go crazy.

"Bitch! Bitch!" hissed the voice. There was a hesitation and then, "I have to go, but I'll be back. Don't tease me, Jean!" The last remark took on a threatening tone.

Footsteps thudded across the roof, and the hall door opened and closed. Nicole rolled over, vaulted the low connecting wall, and ran to the door in time to hear the footsteps receding down the empty corridor, then silence. She turned back to the front of the roof where a metal cylinder lay against the parapet. It appeared to be some sort of weapon, the size of a shotgun, but on closer inspection, she recognized a camera tripod, with a Nikon camera screwed onto a base, sturdy enough to hold the heavy long-distance lens.

Not a weapon, but a camera, aimed directly across toward the dorm of Jean Ducharme.

Nicole let herself out into the hall and raced down to the courtyard. From the cover of shrubs at the corner of the Art Building, she scanned the area. At first, she saw no one but moments later, a tall figure rounded the Ad Building and passed under the lamps, and Nicole recognized Vanessa Cole, loping at a slow pace, hunched over, dressed for the chill of the night in a heavy furlike jacket, black pants, and running shoes. Where was she coming from? The jogging path would be frozen at this time of night.

Nicole stepped out and watched as Vanessa Cole disappeared into the dorm building. As the door closed behind Vanessa, a powerful beam flashed against it and just as quickly went off. A security guard, holding a flashlight, stood outside the dorm door as if pondering whether to check inside. Then he turned, noticed Nicole on the other side of the courtyard, and crossed to where she was standing. He flashed the light on her face.

"Good evening," he said pleasantly. "It's—uh, Ms. Lawrence, isn't it? Awful cold to be out tonight. Can I walk you to your door?" He hesitated as a jeep sped through the entrance gate and slid to a stop at the dorm. Jean Ducharme and Chelsea Clovis jumped out, laughed, and waved good-bye to their companions and went inside.

"Ah—the runaways have returned," the guard noted. "Running off on a school night is not good."

"It's quiet around here tonight, but it'll be even quieter next week—all will be gone home for Christmas," said the guard.

He gently placed his hand under Nicole's elbow as if she might slip on the icy sidewalk and steered her toward the Ad Building. She glanced over her shoulder.

At the door, Nicole paused. "Those students—they went in so quickly—wasn't that Chelsea Clovis?"

"Yes, ma'am." He paused. "And Jean Ducharme."

"Oh, of course! They're in my Art Class. Good night, Mr.—" Nicole leaned close to him and looked at the name badge over his uniform pocket. The silver metallic pin read Wilfred Earle. "Mr. Earle. Try to stay warm as you can."

"I duck inside now and then. Good night."

When she reached the hall upstairs, the telephone was ringing and she answered.

"Ad Building. Teacher's Dorm."

"Nicole, is that you?"

"Yes . . . Derek?"

"I'm sorry but I couldn't get into the file of Charles Wendt. It's too tight. I could try a virus, but it would spread and wipe out other information."

"It's okay, Derek. I'll take care of it."

"I'm sorry."

"It's okay. Thanks for trying. Good night, my dear Derek."

She heard him laugh, a lonely little laugh. She could imagine him in the motel room, his only companion a glass of wine.

"Good night, my dear Nicole."

As she undressed for bed, she peered between the floral curtains at the dorm room across the courtyard. For once, the drapes on Jean Ducharme's windows were drawn. She could see the dim, blurred square of blue light beyond the drapes that indicated the television. The watcher would watch in vain this cold night, if he, or she, returned to the roof.

* * *

The Art Class was almost back to normal attendance. Mr. Henley was pleased. He enjoyed teaching. Once a frustrated actor in local plays, he finally realized he would never give Harrison Ford a lost moment of sleep as competition and had turned to education, where every day he had a captive audience and the pay was regular. He could grow to love it. He passed out the corrected papers.

"You guys liked everything he did—the yellow chair, the sunflowers, Dr. Gachet, and hoo boy! You really loved that starry sky! So tell me, why did Van Gogh only sell one painting in his lifetime if he was so hot? Casey?"

"He had a lousy agent?"

The class groaned.

"He was unappreciated in his time," Nicole spoke out. "Theo was the only one who understood his genius. And Vincent was a genius, Mr. Henley."

Henley nodded. "Ahead of his time." He had moved down the aisle to the rear of the class and paused at an empty seat. "Has anyone seen Simon Wensel?"

When nobody answered, Jean Ducharme turned around and stared thoughtfully at the empty chair. "This weekend, his mother was cochairing a charity affair, and when she got home from New York on

Sunday night, he wasn't there. She told my mom he may have gone to his dad's. They're divorced," Jean supplied with a shrug, but she had begun to look worried.

"Tomorrow, we'll review Gauguin. He and Vincent were roomies for a while. It didn't work out," Henley continued. "If anyone sees Wensel, tell him he's got a lot to make up in the next couple of days. Randolph closes for Christmas holidays Friday."

Last Friday was the last time she had seen Simon, Nicole realized. He had not met her at the cafeteria, and she still carried the new Bic in her shoulder bag. The empty seat drew her gaze, and she felt a sudden terrible foreboding. Even if he had visited his father, where was Simon now? Why hadn't he returned to Randolph?

After class, Nicole went to the Business Office and asked whether anyone had heard from Simon Wensel. Ms. Kelsey was not in the office, but one of the secretaries said that his mother had called this morning after discovering that Simon had not been with his father over the weekend.

"Shouldn't you notify the police?" Nicole asked. "He's not in class. He's not at home."

"That is up to the parents. We try to handle student problems without police involvement."

"You mean, like the Sara Wells problem?" Nicole shot back. "Or is that a dead issue?"

"Publicity is damaging to the reputation of the college," stated the young secretary in a singsong cadence, as if the phase had been drummed into her upon employment.

Nicole turned and marched out of the office, wondering whether to report Wensel's disappearance to Major Whitt. Perhaps, Simon had taken off with some friends—she mused. No, not Simon. She hurried to the telephone in the hall near her dorm room and called the Alexandria office collect. Whitt was not there, but Beau Jackson seemed very interested.

"This boy was suspected of being the stalker, wasn't he?" Jackson asked.

"He did follow Jean Ducharme, but only because he was crazy about her. I have a sort of lead on the real one."

"Got a name?"

"Not yet."

There was a silence as Jackson could be heard making hasty notes with a scratchy pen.

"The major will be sorry he missed your call."

"I'm going to follow my lead and get back to you. I need to find Carlo."

"Use that guy!" insisted Jackson. "He's mean and ugly, but you can trust him."

"I hope I can trust him. He doesn't like me, but I do need him. We'll work out something."

"We'll put a trace on Wensel," assured Jackson. "And be damn careful, girl. Got your piece?"

"Yes."

"Don't do anything stupid," he warned her. "I know you, girl! You'd go after the devil himself with a fly swatter."

"Baseball bat," Nicole corrected and hung up. She pulled off the red cap, ran her hand through her hair, and realized it was getting longer and curly, tucking itself into the collar of her black leather coat like a warm wooly scarf. Perhaps, she would just let it grow until summer, she thought, as she looked out of the nearby window down into the courtyard. Students milled about. Mr. Henley seemed to be arguing with a student, the one called Casey, who loved the attention he received from smart remarks he made in class. Ms. Kelsey made her way, wrapped in a quilted down coat, slowly toward the Ad Building. A fall at her age would be disastrous. Further reconnaissance of the area failed to reveal Carlo.

She went downstairs and strolled the perimeter of the courtyard in front of the door to the women's dorm, where she lingered, glancing up at the rooftop across the way. The parapet appeared cold and deserted. The tall chimney gave a thin, hazy spiral of smoke, and she recalled its welcome warmth the night she spent hidden against the rear wall. She would go there again tonight, but first, she had to find Carlo. She walked around to the cafeteria past the Men's Gym, and suddenly, out of the icy, snow-filled jogging path loped Carlo, his long greasy hair flying, his open plaid jacket whipping out behind him—he would have raced past her, but she stepped in front of him. Her hand shot out and hit him in the chest, causing him to stagger back.

"I want to talk to you. Come with me."

He drew his hair back from his eyes and glared at her, his hot breath billowing in the chill air.

"Where have you been?" she demanded, knowing his job was to keep the sidewalks clear.

"On my lunch, I run." He scribbled on one of his pink notes. He showed it to her, and then to her disgust, he put the note in his mouth, chewed it up, and swallowed.

"That's disgusting," she muttered.

He whipped out his notepad and scribbled furiously. He thrust it at her.

"Rule. Written word. Shred it, flush it, burn it, eat it."

"So what? It only said you run at lunchtime. Hardly top secret," Nicole responded. "When you leave at five, wait down the road. I'll follow you to your motel." She walked away as two students approached, and Carlo strode off to the toolshed behind the gym where he kept his shovel.

Up in her dorm room, she reluctantly removed the heavy plaid blanket from the bed, folded it neatly by lengthwise twice, then took it downstairs to the rear parking area where she laid it loosely across the backseat of the jeep as if she had tossed it there.

As Nicole left the parking lot, she noticed Jean Ducharme and Vanessa Cole enter the cafeteria, where there was a lecture on the chronology of artists and art movements. On impulse, she entered and took a seat near the back of the room and watched as students and some faculty filed in to hear the visiting professor. No one paid any special attention to Jean Ducharme or sat nearby or stared. But Nicole now knew the stalker was not a fantasy. Someone did watch from the rooftop, someone who moved stealthily in the dark and who spoke in whispers. Nicole sat forward. Vanessa Cole was leaning over and smiling at Jean—now she reached over and brushed a stray strand of hair from Jean's cheek. Even from her seat at the rear, Nicole could see Jean stiffen at the casual touch and move slightly away from Vanessa. Vanessa smiled and turned back to listen to the speaker.

At four, the speaker concluded his lecture, and Ms. Kelsey invited everyone to stay for holiday refreshments. Cranberry punch and wreath-shaped sugar cookies beckoned from the tables, and the rush was on as Nicole quickly slipped out of the door and returned to the jeep in the parking lot.

At ten past five, she drove past the guard at the gate and out to the main highway. The blue Tempo idled at the side of the road, and as she approached, Carlo pulled out ahead and led her a short distance to Bid-A-Wee Motel. The place was hardly a Holiday Inn, but definitely the sort where Carlo would not cause undue concern with his muteness and odd appearance, as long as he paid on time and did not set his room on fire.

The proprietor looked up as the two cars passed his office and stared at Nicole. He watched as they parked at room nine but quickly glanced away as Nicole paused when she got out of the jeep and returned his stare until he sat back down to continue watching a television program.

Room nine seemed to be designed for children. There were twin beds with faded Superman bedspreads. The drapes across the cold glass window had airplanes and stars on a dark blue background. One hardback chair, one small dresser, an open rack next to the bath for clothing completed the furniture.

On his own territory, Carlo took on a proprietary manner, making his terrible laughing sound. He pointed to Superman, then to himself. He grunted and wiggled his hips in a suggestive grind.

Nicole slung her shoulder bag over her shoulder and walked quickly to the door, but now Carlo was scribbling madly on one of his little pink sheets. He stood between Nicole and the door.

"Joke! Joke!" The message read. "I even breathe on you, the major will kill me!"

Nicole read it and nodded, thinking to herself—the major won't have the opportunity if you make a move on me. I'll do it myself. She turned around and sat in the one straight chair. He continued to stand.

"I'm going up on the roof tonight, and I want you to go with me and cover me from the other side of the big chimney. You will leave your car here at the motel, hide in my jeep under the blanket, and we'll return to Randolph. Someone comes up there—I don't know who—and watches Jean Ducharme across the courtyard."

He nodded and lifted the front of his old plaid jacket, displaying the weapon under his arm and patting it proudly. It appeared to be unusually large, and Nicole peered at it closer.

"9mm Glock? With a silencer?"

"Mmmm," he growled and nodded. He wrote on his pad. "We eat?"

"Oh! Of course! You've had no supper. I'll pick up something. Ready to roll?"

They watched the deserted parking lot. A tenant came out of room five and drove away. Another got ice from a machine near the office and went back inside. The lot was clear. Carlo crept out to the jeep and disappeared under the blanket in the rear seat. Nicole glanced around the room. What a dump! She closed the door, heard it latch, and went out and climbed behind the wheel. Leaving the headlights off, she circled out of the lot slowly in the opposite direction from the lighted window of the motel office.

Two miles down the road, she sighted a Wendy's, drove through the pickup window, and ordered chili, baked potatoes, and hamburgers with two double coffees to go.

The guard at the college gate waved her through. As they passed the courtyard, students were singing Christmas Carols, gathered on the sidewalks. There were fires in metal cans, the flames casting shadows on the snow, and some carolers held white candles, their faces in the light fresh and very young, their breaths like white smoke in the freezing air.

Nicole drove to the rear parking area and gathered up the bags of food.

"Carlo, you will have to find a place to sleep tonight. I'll go up to my room on the second floor. I'm the only one on that floor, the center of the hall. Wait five minutes and come up. The door will be open."

Carlo pressed his shoulder to show he understood and then quickly released it, folding himself under the blanket.

A tall figure in uniform seemed suddenly to rise out of the darkness and appear at Nicole's door just as she opened it, carrying the bags of food.

"Ms. Lawrence?" a deep voice said.

"Yes, is that Mr. Earle?" Nicole asked, peering at the guard silhouetted against the dim light at the corner of the building.

"No. I'm Tom Joyce. Wilfred Earle is off tonight. I'll escort you to the Ad Building. Out to pick up a snack?"

"Tired of cafeteria food. Thought I'd try a burger," she said, hastily closing the door to the Jeep and locking it.

"Don't you need your blanket?" he asked, glancing into the backseat.

"No, I keep it in the back for my dog to sleep on."

Carlo lay motionless. He heard their voices receding as they crossed the parking lot.

"What kind of a dog do you have?" The security guard was asking as their voices faded.

"Just a mix. Black and white," Nicole was saying. "His name is Runner."

Carlo waited and then pushed the lock open, slid through the door, and scuttled to the cover of the nearest bushes, where he lay waiting in the snow. Ten minutes later, he appeared damp and muddy at the door of Nicole's room.

"You're wet."

He shrugged and pushed hurriedly into the room although there was no one in the hall. He was aware that Randolph's rules stated that this was forbidden territory. A yardman found in one of the dorms would be fired. Carlo didn't really care—he planned to be out of Randolph soon in any case. He wanted to complete his assignment for the major.

The food from Wendy's was taken out of the bag and placed on the little table. Carlo suddenly seemed self-conscious, then edged into the chair behind the drapes out of sight, before drawing baked potatoes to his side of the table.

Nicole watched the festivities below from the window. The drapes of Jean Ducharme's window were partially closed, but people passed in the open lighted area, with drinks in one hand, paper plates of food balanced in the other. Several other rooms showed a sort of continuing party in progress, as students prowled the halls in search of holiday spirit and forbidden holiday spirits. The singing and laughter depressed Nicole as she recognized the college life she never really had. Study and work. Study and work. While others partied, she and George washed and stacked dishes at night, sold flowers . . . oh, well, she dismissed the thought. Social life has never impressed me.

"I'm going up to the Art Building roof. Follow me," she directed Carlo. "If there is someone there, we will disable him. Gloves? Pull your cap over your face!" She glanced up. He had covered his eyes. "Mon Dieu! Leave yourself room to see!"

He growled and showed his gloves.

They found the door to the roof locked, and Nicole wrestled the nail file in the keyhole, pushing it forward and back. It didn't open at once, and Carl remained hidden behind a group of metal lockers that lined the west wall. Finally, there was a click, and she beckoned him out of his hiding place.

The roof appeared empty. The tripod, in its wrappings, was missing from the wall near the parapet. Nicole ventured further as Carlo hovered near the door, his back to the wall. A chill wind blew over the drifted snow in the corners of the roof, and Nicole shivered, seeking the warmth of the tall chimney. She motioned to him to find a spot on the east side of the chimney. Perhaps, his wet coat would dry against the bricks while they waited. She leaned against the opposite side, watching the door.

Ten o'clock curfew came and went. The carolers had disbanded and gone inside, but in the dorms, the students partied on. The chapel clock struck eleven. Nicole thought of Mimi, asleep in a Paris churchyard for eternity. She missed Mimi's laugh, her sometimes wildly aggressive behavior when she considered something unfair or shady. She even missed the smell of smoke of the cigarettes that hung from Mimi's stained fingers.

"Huh-uh!" warned Carlo suddenly.

The door to the roof slammed aside. A flashlight shone its beam into the corners and a guard stepped in, pausing silently.

In the light from the hall, Nicole managed to make out the features of the security guard from the parking lot, Tom Joyce. He stood just inside the door without moving, his head cocked as if listening. Then he backed out into the hall, closing the door firmly behind him, and walked away, his boots resounding and then fading. They heard him turning the doorknobs of other rooms all the way to the stairs.

One by one, lights went out in the dorms. Someone was still singing alone down in the courtyard. Nicole recognized the slightly tipsy voice of Casey, the bane of Mr. Henley's Art Class. Tom Joyce approached below, took Casey's arm, and, talking to him in a friendly way, led him to the men's dorm, and saw him safely inside. The moon shone down on the snow. Nicole realized she was standing where Sara Wells must have been standing the last night of her life, gazing up at the full moon, or was Sara suddenly discovering a tripod and a camera directed at the dorm of Jean Ducharme, as the stalker hid nearby, perhaps watching from behind the chimney? Nicole shivered.

"Carlo. No one will come tonight. Too much activity for him, no?"

Carlo came up behind her. He smelled of hot, damp wool and some kind of hair oil or lotion, strange and spicy. He fumbled in his pocket for his notepad, and by the light of the moon, he scribbled, "We will try again. Good night."

"Wait! Where will you sleep?"

Like a wraith, Carlo had slipped to the door, glanced fleetingly about the empty hall and passed through the door. By the time Nicole reached the hall, he was gone.

* * *

It was bitter cold at 5:00 a.m. The announcer on the radio said it was the longest continuous spell of subzero temperature in Virginia since the year of the ice storm. The jogging path crunched under her feet as she sprang carefully from side to side, trying to avoid the icy ruts in the center where water had frozen over. Nicole made it all the way to the pond, a bleak shallow stretch of water so congested with dead trees and clutches of weeds that it was unfit for skating.

"Nasty place, even in summer," said a voice behind her. "Covered in green scum. They should vote to fill it in. Someone could fall in and could drown and be sucked under the mud."

Nicole turned around to find Vanessa Cole standing behind her.

"Yes," she agreed. "Or dredge it out. Put in fish perhaps." She started to step past Vanessa, but the taller woman stood in her way.

"Are you FBI? Are you really here to find out who murdered Sara? She didn't jump you know. She wouldn't have!"

"No, I'm not here because of Sara," Nicole answered truthfully, looking straight into Vanessa's strong, beautiful face.

After a few minutes, Vanessa looked away.

"Do you have any reason to suspect that someone wanted Sara dead?" Nicole asked.

"No," Vanessa admitted. "But someone contemplating suicide does not order a new dress by mail, and it arrives a week after her death, or spend $300 for a flute she does not intend to play. We weren't all that close, but she was nice."

"I'm sorry."

"Well, gotta run. Class at eight. Watch your step," Vanessa advised.

She loped away, hunched against the wind chill, her long legs, legs as long as any man's, covering the icy path at good speed.

Nicole followed at a slower pace. Ahead, at the end of the path, she smelled the aroma of bacon frying and a more subtle fragrance of coffee, coming from the cafeteria. She wandered inside and sat at one of the little tables in the area called the caff while the cafeteria workers prepared for the rush of students for breakfast. She was still sitting there when Jean Ducharme and Chelsea Clovis came in. Jean rushed over to her table, sat down, and began to rummage in her tote bag.

"I'm glad I saw you today. I got a letter from Mom. I told her about meeting you, and she remembered your mom, and the dress, of course!" Jean pulled a manila envelope from the bag and took out a photograph in a folder. "This is for you."

Nicole took it. It was a picture of the dress Yvette had made with the "Birds of Paradise" design, standing there in the Smithsonian collection, more than holding its own against creations worn by famous women and presidents' wives, a thing of unique exotic beauty and delicate craftsmanship. Her throat was full, and Nicole could hardly speak.

"What can I say?" she murmured. "This will mean everything to Maman—my mother. She has started her own business. She will put this where clients can see, no?"

"Come on, Jean, get in line," insisted Chelsea. "It's waffle day and I'm starving!"

"You go ahead. Get in line," answered Jean, remaining in her seat.

Chelsea's mouth flew open. She stepped back and put her hand on one hip, staring at Nicole as if Jean's sudden independent attitude was her fault.

Nicole and Jean sat quietly, waiting for Chelsea to leave, and finally, she turned her back and walked swiftly to where the line was forming.

"Have I provoked her?" asked Nicole.

"She's insufferably bossy, and I can't bear it. Don't tell anyone, but we leave for holiday tomorrow and when I come back, I'll have a room of my own. Ms. Kelsey promised," Jean confided in a whisper.

"I'm happy for you. Thank you for the picture and to your mother too."

"Shall we toddle over and see if Chelsea left any waffles? She was in such a damn big hurry," grinned Jean.

As they waited in line in the front of the cafeteria, Carlo shuffled into the back through the kitchen door, still wearing the clothes from the day before. He had slept in the furnace room. The cook brought a plate to him at the long metal table where the employees ate their meals.

"You need a shave, buddy! You been out with a good-looking woman all night?"

Carlo smiled and nodded his head vigorously.

"Don't butter me, wild man!" said the cook, shaking his head in disbelief. "Who can figure?"

* * *

By afternoon, most of the students and faculty had left the campus. From her window, Nicole watched Carlo scraping away at the icy grass that lined the courtyard sidewalk, pausing in his work to observe the parade as the limos, SUVs, vans, and the occasional sports car picked up the sons and daughters for two weeks of freedom and celebrations.

By five o'clock, the stream of cars had abated, but Carlo lingered on, seeming to invent work in the same area across from the Art Building, shaking snow from shrubbery, brushing the sills of the women's dorm windows . . . Nicole pulled aside the drapes and stood in sight. Almost immediately, Carlo moved back to the courtyard, took off his hat, wiped his brow, and dropped the hat to the sidewalk.

He had seen something on the roof.

She placed her hand against the window to show she understood and partially pulled the drapes, feeling that tingle of anticipation that came when the game was going down. Standing in the darkened room, she watched as lights came on in the dorms that were occupied. She saw Jean Ducharme pulling clothes from her closet, emptying dresser drawers, and scooping cosmetics into a bag on the bed. Chelsea Clovis had departed moments before in a minivan. Jean Ducharme was alone.

Carlo, having retrieved his hat, took his broom and shovel and made his way slowly toward the Ad Building, then disappeared from sight. The dim courtyard lights flickered on, casting their pinkish glow on the snow. After the carols and parties of the night before, the silence seemed ominous, the sidewalks deserted, empty.

Nicole took her gun from her shoulder bag, preparing to fit it into the leather holster, when the telephone in the hall began to ring. She impatiently went out and answered.

"Ms. Lawrence here."

"It's Beau, Ms. Whoever. Where the hell you been, girl? I called every hour up till 1:00 a.m. Nobody answered."

"I'm the only one on this floor, probably the only one in the building."

"Hey! That's not good. When you coming in?"

"Randolph closes tomorrow."

"Well, see Ducharme outa there and head on in. You got anything to report?"

"Something's cooking," she relayed cautiously as she gazed around the hall.

There was a moment of silence, then Beau growled, "Well, get it outa the pot. We'll be looking for you."

"See you soon, no?" she answered and started to hang up.

"Wait! There's something you gotta know. Major's talking Christmas in Asheville."

"His family is there."

"And he thinks you're gonna be there too. I already told him he's being hasty making plans for Nicole."

"Holy Mother! I cannot go!"

"He's crazy for you. He wants to show off his little French souvenir from Paris to Mama and Papa—and Uncle Zeke and Aunt Petunia—and—"

"No! No! No!" she protested. "I must be with my mother, or she will be alone. It is the first Christmas without Mimi. You—please, Beau, talk to the major."

"His head is as hard as yours, baby."

"You get me two tickets to Paris and tell Derek to pack his things. Good-bye."

She hung up the telephone, leaned against the wall, and pressed against the cold tile. Oh, Major, I asked you to give me time, she whispered into the wall. For several moments, she stayed that way, thinking of the night he sat outside her door playing love songs on his harmonica until she let him in, the touch of him, the smell of him . . . the sweet pain . . . of desire.

Abruptly, the reverie ended. A shadow figure holding some type of pole had slipped silently down the hall and was standing in the light of the door to her room.

"My gun is on the bed" was her first thought as she sprang away from the wall.

"Uh-huh" came the familiar sound.

"Carlo!" she gasped. She ran down the hall and shoved him inside the room.

He had taken out one of his pink notes and was scribbling furiously as she went to the bed, quickly grabbed the weapon, thumbed the bullet chamber, and set the safety. She strapped the holster across her chest and fit the gun just beneath her armpit.

"I'm getting careless!" she said angrily. "Mon Dieu, you could have shot me with my own gun! I am a fool! A fool!"

He nodded solemnly in agreement and handed her the lengthy note.

"Someone is on the roof. Something reflects. Come and go since four o'clock. I watch the roof door. Comes out. I follow to kitchen. Eats now."

She read hastily.

She grabbed her jogging jacket and zippered it part of the way to the top, took up the note, flushed the scraps down the toilet, and waited as the water arose clean.

"Let's go."

He picked up his broom, clutched her arm roughly, and pulled her behind him, motioning that he would go first. The broom, of course. If Carlo were found inside, they would assume he'd been called to clean up something. He raced to the stairs, glanced down to see if the way was clear, then plunged downward, his ugly plaid jacket flapping behind him, Nicole close on his heels.

Moments later, they circled the Art Building; one at a time, they entered the foyer without being seen and made their way to the door to the roof.

Nicole pressed her ear against it, listening for sounds within. She inserted the file and located the trip points before she beckoned to Carlo. The knob turned easily, and they slipped inside, each reconnoitering a side of the roof divided by the chimney. The tripod, with camera mounted, stood by the parapet facing the women's dorm. Through the lens, Nicole could see partway into Jean's room; visible was Jean's feet and part of her legs, propped on a recliner. One hand held a bowl of something. The television was on. The drapes, partially closed, obscured the rest. Nicole indicated to Carlo to take the right side behind the chimney. She decided to climb over the low wall and hide where she had hidden during her first vigil. Her foot touched something and sent it rolling away from the tripod. She followed, picked up a black plastic thirty-five-millimeter film can, which she jammed down into her jacket pocket, then stepped over the dividing wall where she lay with her back against the bricks. We came to find Jean Ducharme's stalker, and tonight we will get him, she anticipated with satisfaction. She listened carefully to see if she could hear Carlo at his post some fifteen feet to her left. Not a sound.

Time dragged by. Her legs cramped. She endeavored to see the watch, but the moon was hazy tonight, covered by drifting clouds, and she wondered if this dark sky with clouds in motion was the last thing Sara Wells saw that night. Nicole finally stood up and stretched just as the key turned in the lock. She dropped to the rooftop as someone slipped inside, briefly shone a flashlight around, and moved over to the camera.

"Hello again, my beautiful Jean," the voice whispered. "Move over. I can see only your legs. Maybe, later tonight I can touch them, lick them, with my tongue, until you scream with pleasure. I can barely wait."

The camera clicked, advanced, clicked, advanced, clicked.

"Tonight, little Jean, you will fulfill my dreams. That bitch, Clovis, has gone. And when the last light goes out, you'll be alone. I've waited a long time for you, princess." The voice droned on. He groaned aloud.

Click, advance, click, advance.

"What dear little toes! I could eat them. Perhaps I will, Jean."

There was a pause. "Where did she go? Bathroom?" For a while, there was only the sound of heavy breathing. The camera was still.

Nicole rose and drew her gun. She could see the figure in the uniform of a security guard hunched over the camera.

The light in Jean Ducharme's window went out. The drapes twitched together. Only two other lights still beamed from the dorm, one above and the other was the room immediately adjacent to Jean's, indicating that its occupant was still awake.

The guard watched the lighted window and paced back and forth, stomping his feet, growing more agitated as the light remained on, a beacon in the dark building. He dismantled the camera, folded the tripod, and wrapped the equipment. He looked around the floor and then patted his pockets, searching for the other roll of film. The flashlight came on; he scanned the roof, just as a giant sneeze broke the air in the vicinity of the rear of the chimney. Twice it came again, shattering the silence.

Carlo!

Nicole leapt over the small dividing wall, the sound of her boots thudding on the roof, causing the confused guard to swing back in her direction. He wrestled the pistol from his belt. She plunged into him and crushed his wrist with the butt of her own gun. The guard dropped his flashlight and screamed out in pain, but he had managed to hang on to his weapon. Carlo stepped from behind the chimney, and sensing a new enemy, the guard swung around ready to fire. Nicole brought the butt of her gun down hard just behind his ear, knocking off his cap. He fell forward onto the roof where he lay still. Nicole turned him over.

"It's Wilfred Earle."

Carlo stood by, his hair hanging over his face and the big Glock with the silencer hanging down by his side. He shook his head back and forth. He seemed ashamed that he had reacted too slowly.

Nicole felt for the guard's faint pulse in his neck. It beat erratically, fluttered, stopped, and then started again. She stared down at him for a full three minutes and then stood up.

"He'll be out cold for a while. You get lost for now. I'll call 911 in about thirty minutes and report a light on the roof." She made sure the flashlight's beam would be visible from the courtyard below. "The cops can find him and the camera. If we let the locals handle it, I can be out of here first thing in the morning. Meet me at the jeep at 5:00 a.m., and I'll take you back to your motel."

Carlo pointed across the courtyard at the dark square of Jean Ducharme's window. The light on the other side had gone out.

"I think we may have saved her life, Carlo."

He nodded, looked down at Wilfred Earle, and nudged him with his foot. He touched the chest beneath the uniform, searching for a heartbeat; then he began to take out one of his pink notes, but Nicole waved it away.

"No time for that. Wait three minutes and follow. We've finished our part of the job. Now we get out."

She opened the door to the hall, peeked out, and, seeing no one, raced for the stairs. Five minutes later, she was letting herself into her dorm room and flinging herself down across the bed, cold and exhausted from the hours on the roof. She wanted to sleep. Her back ached from lying behind the dividing wall, but there was no time. There were things to be done. In the bathroom, she inspected her gun and found one round blob of blood on the butt where it had dug into the area behind Earle's ear. There was a circle of blood in the palm of her hand, still bright red and wet. She stood by the sink and washed the gun and her hands over and over, rinsing them in Listerine, which some previous visitor had left behind in the medicine cabinet. Clorox was better, but there was none. She stood over the sink until the water ran clear.

Had Carlo had time to leave the roof and return to his sleeping place? She carefully dried the gun and returned it to the bottom of her shoulder bag, took off the jogging jacket, and rolled the holster inside, then shoved it into her open suitcase. How much time had passed? She looked across at the roof of the Art Building, but she was unable to discern even a glimmer from the flashlight. Even from this angle, some dim glow should be visible. Had Carlo forgotten and taken the flashlight with him or simply forgotten her instructions and turned it off as he exited the roof? Had they left anything, overlooked anything?

A feeling of unease crept over her as she tried to retrace the events of the night, but nothing stood out as a blatant error. They had not had to fire their weapons, and Wilfred Earle had not had time to use his. The scuffle was brief and almost noiseless. Still Nicole had a feeling that something had gone terribly wrong. She looked again where the flashlight ought to be seen. The rooftop was dark. She went downstairs, walked along beside the women's dorm, and gazed up at the Art Building across the street. There was no light, but a dark trickle of water ran down the side of the building. Possibly, the snow was finally melting off the roof, she surmised. The temperature felt the same, and yet perhaps, it was a bit warmer.

She moved quickly around the Ad Building to an area near the cafeteria, where there was an outside telephone booth. The door stood ajar, and she didn't close it as she punched in the numbers.

"911? Randolph College. There may be a burglary at the Art Building."

"Who is this calling?"

"Ms. Kelsey," she mumbled.

Nicole abruptly hung up and cleared her throat. It had been a poor imitation of the elderly secretary, and she hoped nobody ever reviewed the tape.

Back in her room, she sat in the dark watching from behind the drapes. The pinkish lights in the courtyard showed no movement below for almost forty minutes until an official-looking dark sedan came through the gates at the entrance. The guard on the gate appeared to be trying to reach someone—Wilfred Earle?—and, being unsuccessful, climbed into the car on the passenger side. The car moved leisurely down to the Art Building and a searchlight on top of the car scanned the face of the building and finally settled on the water now pouring from the roof. No longer a trickle, it was more a stream, and a spreading puddle reached out over the grassed area, inching its way onto the courtyard.

A sheriff's deputy and the gate guard got out and inspected the creeping deluge.

Nicole raised her window to listen.

"You got a key?" asked the deputy.

"Outside door stays open. For the cleaners. I got a pass key for the rooms."

They went inside. Hall lights blinked on, progressed upward from floor to floor, and finally, the beam of a flashlight appeared on the roof where Nicole heard loud shouts of surprise. The lights flashed on the chimney, up and down the parapet. There was more shouting.

They've found him, Nicole thought. They've found Wilfred Earle. She undressed in the dark, listening to the sound of voices, and, incredibly, the sound of laughter, as the men returned to the deputy's car in the courtyard.

"Man, you don't need a cop, you need a hellava good plumber! What happened is that the outlet valve to the fire sprinkler system somehow got turned loose and she's flooded the roof. You better hope that mess doesn't freeze before morning."

"Sorry to have brought you all the way out here. Some of the girls musta heard the water and didn't know what it was."

"Well, you better get it fixed."

"First thing. Thanks for coming out."

"It's my job, buddy. Get in. I'll take you back to the gate."

The car drove away. Nicole closed the window and sank down on the edge of the bed. There was no way they could have overlooked Wilfred Earle. And the camera! Holy Mary, Mother of God! She got under the covers and curled into a ball. We had him, we had the stalker, and he got away. What will I tell the major? she groaned and covered her head. She slept briefly, dreamt of drowning, fought her way up to the surface, gasping for breath, only to be pulled down again. Shaking, she woke up fighting her way out of the covers and sat in the dark, watching the little red numbers of the bedside clock tick away the minutes until four o'clock. She showered and finished packing, looked around the room at the faded floral drapes where she had spent so many hours watching the activities of Jean Ducharme and the students of Randolph, and left, locking the door behind her for the last time.

As she finished putting her suitcase in the back of the jeep, Carlo materialized from the bushes, climbed into the second seat without looking at her, and covered himself with the plaid blanket. She drove to the gate, gave a big wave at the guard, and sped out to the highway. Five miles down the road, the familiar golden arches beckoned. She pulled around to the drive-in window and ordered two McMuffins and two coffees. The parking lot was almost deserted at this early hour, and she parked as far from the building as possible, the jeep half hidden behind a green dumpster.

"Sit up and talk to me, Carlo!" Nicole demanded. "What did you do after I left?"

Carlo grabbed the coffee eagerly, wincing at the heat as he gulped half of it down in one swallow. He unwrapped the sandwich and put it on his knees as he reached for his pad of pink notes.

"Wait here three minutes. Leave roof. Sleep behind furnace. Wait for jeep open."

Nicole read the note and sipped her coffee. Either Carlo was lying or Wilfred Earle had recovered and managed to get his self and his camera off the roof before the guard and deputy arrived. If that was the case, Earle was still on the grounds of Randolph and so was Jean Ducharme!

Abruptly, Nicole put her coffee on the dashboard and hurried to the telephone booth at the side of the building. She breathed a sigh of relief as she heard Jean's sleepy voice answer.

"This is Nicole Lawrence. I just called to say good-bye and wish you a wonderful holiday!"

"Oh, it's so early!"

"When are you leaving for home?"

"Around nine or ten."

"Thanks again for the lovely picture."

"Merry Christmas. I'll miss you!"

"Me too. Take care."

Nicole stood by the booth, considering calling area hospitals to see if anyone had been admitted with head injuries, then decided against it and returned to the jeep to find Carlo peering over the seat, hungrily regarding the McMuffin.

"Don't even think about it!" she warned him, tearing off the oily paper. She ate without caring what it was and downed the coffee.

"You will go back to Randolph, no?"

"Shave. Clothes first," Carlo wrote and threw it over the seat.

Nicole nodded. Even from here, he is getting pretty ripe, she noted. She drove to the end of the lot, tossed thrash into a can, and left the window open.

At the Bid-A-Wee Motel, she dropped him by the blue Tempo and drove away. At the exit, she looked back. Carlo had unlocked the door to his room but had turned around facing the parking area to watch her leave. He stood there, looking like a particularly evil scarecrow, watching. And smiling. Carlo knew something, the smile said.

Nicole hesitated and then drove off.

She continued back down the highway, passed the entrance to Randolph, and proceeded to the parking lot of a shopping mall. It was too early for the mall to be open but as time passed, employees, sleep-eyed and walking slowly toward their stores, filled the outer spaces. Nicole pulled forward, facing the highway. In the increasing morning traffic, she did not see the Ducharme limo as it passed on the far side going to Randolph, but she caught sight of it coming back. It stopped at the stoplight. Jean was leaning forward, talking to the driver. Beside her was a beautiful older woman, very thin, dark haired—former Ambassador Eugenie Ducharme. The light turned green. The limo drove on.

Nicole continued to the office in Alexandria, only getting lost once in a maze of confusing construction at Springfield. She stopped for lunch at Hunter Motel and got directions. Beau Jackson, in the office, glanced up in surprise when she finally entered.

"How you doing, girl? Thought you'd be heading out to the major's."

"I must make my report, no?"

"Oh, yeah. Wrapped it up, did you?"

Nicole paused uncertainly. "Jean Ducharme is safe for now. She's on her way home."

"What's the matter then?"

"We had him—I mean—Carlo—Mon Dieu, I don't know where he is!"

"Carlo?"

"No, the stalker."

"Nicole," said Beau. "You lost the perp?" He pushed his chair back and stared in disbelief. "It seems to me you lost one before, and he hasn't turned up to this day. You got to stop misplacing people, Nicole."

"Where is Derek? Did you get our plane reservations for Paris?"

"Derek is at lunch," Beau said and reached into a desk drawer. "I didn't have anything to do with these reservations. The charge is on Nicole Lawrence's temporary Visa, you understand?"

"Perfectly. Give me some paper. I'll file my report," she muttered halfheartedly.

"Is that Remington in the broom closet?" She dragged out the dusty typewriter and was picking away, desperately reluctant to make this report, and apprehensive as to how her experiences on the case would compare to Carlo's. What would he write about Wilfred Earle?

Beau Jackson sealed her report in a manila envelope and locked it in a file cabinet adjacent to Derek's desk, just as Derek burst through the door.

"Nicole! I saw the jeep, and my heart bounced with joy!" Derek exclaimed. "I am ready!"

He kissed her cheek and threw off his custom-made cashmere overcoat and the matching cap and hoisted himself into the seat of the nearest chair.

Nicole took out the reservations and looked at them for the first time. "Sunday," she read.

"Ah-h-h, Paris—I miss her more than I ever thought," Derek began, then his eyes slid to Jackson and he added quickly, "But I like America."

Nicole looked over at the conference table, where the major usually sat. His notebooks, pens, and telephone were aligned exactly. A small American flag decorated a jar of pencils, and a picture of his son, Andy, stood next to his computer. She felt a wave of desire, wishing him there.

"He's in Germany watching a potential recruit," Jackson volunteered, picking up her thoughts.

"Then there is no one at the safe house?"

"Gregor, a watchman. And tonight Carlo is due to return for the weekend."

"This Gregor, he is trusted to feed my dog, no?"

"Gregor has been with us twenty years. He doesn't do cases anymore. He got caught in a crossfire. But he'll feed that dog."

"What time do we leave?" asked Derek. "I have to pick up a suit from my tailor. I must impress that I am wealthy when I visit my mother."

Nicole checked the reservations. "11:00 a.m. Too bad. I will miss church." She took the gun and holster from her bags and handed them over to Beau Jackson, who looked the gun over carefully before locking it in the safe.

"Not fired," he commented.

"No, not fired."

"The one who got away."

Nicole said nothing as she gathered up her things and prepared to leave.

"We have a room here for you," said Beau seriously. "Take either one."

There was something in his voice that made her hesitate. She wanted to confront Carlo about Wilfred Earle and determine whether he was lying. She had never trusted Carlo, and this Gregor, she didn't know him . . .

"I'll take the one on the front." She decided and started down the hall.

"Dinner tonight?" Derek called eagerly. "I'll cook! Filet Mignon! Fresh fruits!"

"Put my name in the pot," she answered.

Chapter Fifteen

I'll Be Home for Christmas

It was still cold but sunny as the plane lifted off from Dulles, and Nicole thought to herself, I never thought I'd be anxious to see the Eiffel Tower, that venerable monument visible from everywhere in the city, but Mon Dieu, I have missed it!

Derek sat beside her, his short legs covered by the tray he had lowered. On the tray was an envelope with no address, and Nicole glanced at it curiously. The plane climbed into the clouds, the seat-belt sign went off, and the movie went on. They had opted not to see the movie, and Derek turned to her, his handsome face lit with anticipation as he handed her the envelope.

"A little early Christmas gift. I've been working on my own all week."

She peeled away the plastic seal and took out a sheaf of papers. Some appeared to be pictures from newspapers.

"Most fugitives take the identity of a friend or retain their own names with subtle changes. In this case, Nicolas Campion had two middle names—Dana and Lee—sometimes he was one and sometimes another, as you'll see," explained Derek. "This is your father."

Nicole stared at the painstaking paper trail going back almost twenty years, including minor arrests, teaching in a private school, real estate sales, product demonstrations at merchandise shows, and a bad-check conviction, which was dismissed when he made restitution, and here he was, saving two little babies from a fire! Nicole pushed ahead to the last few years, and there he was at antique shows as an appraiser among other appraisers—sort of a poor man's Antiques road show attraction, at small towns all over the east coast.

She felt faint. That face! *I look at the feminine version of that face in the mirror every morning*, she realized. *And I have met him. He gave me a bracelet on the embassy lawn because he assumed I was a thief—like him—on the night I rescued little Charlie Brown.*

Derek was watching her intently.

"It is him," she admitted. "I never looked like Maman or Mimi. I was the dark one, the wild child."

"I'll help you if you want to find him," Derek offered. "That is, if you want to."

Nicole looked out at the clouds and, as if memorizing his face, pushed the curls back from her own forehead and traced the straight dark brows beneath her sharp, short bangs.

"I think so. What shall I call him? Papa, Father, perhaps, just Nicolas?" she mused. "What will he call me?"

"Daughter," said Derek, touching her hand. "These are from the *Miami Herald, the Post, Constitution, Time-Dispatch*!" Nicole noted names and dates. "Look, some are very recent."

"I spent about three hours every night scanning. In those product demos, he even appeared in TV ads as Nick Dana. As an appraiser, at shows, he is Nicolas Lee. As Lee, he has a little mustache and is gray at the ears."

"Yes, that's him."

"I felt I owed you this—to find him" was Derek's odd remark. He thought of the secret he had kept from Nicole about Nicolas and the circus, and Nicolas in prison. Even after all these years, he prayed he was doing the right thing.

"You don't owe me anything!" Nicole protested.

"I mean, of course." Derek hesitated. "Bringing me to America." He settled back in his seat and pretended to nap.

When they landed at Orly, Nicole immediately went to check on their baggage as Derek dawdled behind, looking for some small but expensive trinket to take to his mother. He purchased a set of spray cologne and bath products and was passing the newsstands when his eye caught a familiar name in a small square at the bottom of the front page of an American paper. He quickly purchased the paper and hurried after Nicole. He found her surrounded by their luggage, in a telephone booth, talking to her mother. Then they located the car rental where they signed up for a new Volkswagen.

Once they were seated in the rental car, he handed the paper to her.

"Major put a trace on this young man, and he found nothing. He is still missing from Randolph College, where you were posted."

Simon Wensel.

The short piece reported that his divorced parents, each believing Simon to be with the other, finally realized the frightening truth that their son was missing and contacted the school. College security and local police searched his room and found an outfit of school clothing. Coat, boots, and wallet were missing. His roommate confirmed Wensel had been assumed to leave the campus on early-holiday leave, two weeks previously.

Simon Wensel.

Nicole rapidly went through the rest of the paper, searching for news of the security guard, Wilfred Earle, but found nothing.

She sat behind the wheel, feeling angry with herself. Never before had there been so many loose ends and such a disappointing feeling of a lack of closure on a case as this one. She kept coming back to Carlo. She had left him on the roof with the unconscious guard. Carlo was supposed to leave immediately after she did. The local police were supposed to find the guard, the camera, and the film. Case concluded. However, it hadn't gone as planned. Something had happened after she left Carlo on the roof. There was nothing concrete to prove to the major they had even been on the roof.

Mon Dieu! Nicole remembered suddenly that the other roll of film was in the jacket pocket of her jogging suit!

"Nicole, your mother is waiting," Derek reminded her gently, hesitant to interrupt the fierce look of concentration on her face.

"You don't suppose my car is still where I left it, in the alley behind Rene Laurent? I expect it is long towed away, no? You may have this splendid Volkswagen. It is called New Beetle."

"The pedals are too short."

"Yes, the pedals," she agreed. Neither mentioned that perhaps, it was Derek who was too short, but they were both smiling.

At the apartment building, the first change Nicole noticed was a discreet professional sign in her mother's window, *Yvette Longet, couturier*. And, in the Longet parking space was the beautiful blue Citroen, gift of Enrico Garibaldi. Nicole had known that Enrico would not remain away from Yvette for long. He would as soon give up eating, and Enrico loved to eat.

Yvette flew through the patio door and snatched the car door wide open. "Ah, my darling, you have brought your petite friend! You did not tell me he was handsome, and these lovely clothes—such good wool! And the cap!"

For a moment, poor Derek, caught in her fragile embrace, thought she was about to undress him and examine the seams, but she only took his trousers between her fingers and peered at the top of his head.

"Maman, you are embarrassing Derek! Now, perhaps a kiss for your daughter?"

Yvette held her back, looked her over, and noted the yellow sweater, with the red hat. "Not together, darling, red with yellow. The leather coat is nice. Maybe I'll find one second from my business. I can run you up something."

They clung together.

"I missed you, Maman. You got my letter?"

"Yes. Don't worry about Enrico. He came back in two days, and you see, brought my car, and it is now registered to Yvette Longet!" she announced triumphantly. "And several bottles of very good wine. As-h-h, men!"

She had prepared a lovely meal of tiny filets, three vegetables with three different sauces, and a strawberry ice. She instructed Derek how to uncork the Rothschild without spilling one precious drop.

After dinner, Derek called his parents, and an old black touring car arrived a little after eight and whisked him away. One small leather-gloved hand waved good-bye. Yvette gave an audible gasp and put her hand to her heart as the car passed. On the door, plain to see in the gleaming black finish, was definitely a faint gold crest.

"He is royalty, is he not?"

"I do not know Derek's family, but what does it matter?" Nicole shrugged.

"Did you touch his trousers?"

"Oh, Maman!"

"Did I tell you Rene has been calling? I told him I am very independent now and he must no longer pay my rent—he seemed very confused, but he agreed since I am not his mother-in-law."

"Maman, I have always paid your rent," confessed Nicole reluctantly. "Not Rene."

"Oh, you silly girl, you have no money! Why do you lie to me?" Yvette threw up her hands. "Yes, Rene still loves you! And a policeman from America called twice."

"What!" exclaimed Nicole.

"My English is better than his French. He sounds like an ignorant schoolboy!"

"A policeman. What did he want?"

Yvette put her hands on her hips, pursed her lips, and mimicked, comically, "'Ma-dam Lo-rent, sil vous plait,' and I say in perfect English, 'She is not here.'"

"Then what did he say?"

"His French is depleted."

"Did he give a number, a name?"

"No number. Name? Mr. Right."

"Are you sure he didn't say Major Whitt?"

"Mr. Right, Major Whitt, all the same. Those in authority sound alike."

Nicole began to laugh. "Maman, you sound more like Mimi every day."

"Thank you, darling, my mother was a saint. We will go to church on Sunday. Tomorrow, I have two holiday dresses to finish."

"And I have shopping to do," Nicole said, thinking of a photo shop where she could quickly get the roll of film processed and expedited quickly back to Alexandria.

Together, they washed the good dishes and put them away, and after many kisses, Nicole drove the New Beetle back to her own apartment and parked it next to her own VW. Suddenly, her own little Bug appeared faded and decrepit next to the shining new-model rental.

"Don't worry," she assured her car, giving its dusty hood a pat. "I'm not trading you in."

The telephone was ringing as she came through the door, but she let it ring until she threw open a window to let the closed, musty smell out into the chill air.

"Your mother gave this number under threat of death."

"Major!"

"God, I miss you! I'm leaving for Asheville Tuesday and I wanted you to go with me, but I understand. Really, I understand."

"Yvette said you had been calling."

"There have been developments you and Carlo need to know. A jogger found one black shoe at the pond end of the path. It belongs to one of the guards."

Nicole sank down into the nearest chair and gripped the telephone.

"Tom Joyce," Whitt continued, "identified the shoe as belonging to another guard, Wilfred Earle. We're expecting a little thaw, and on

Monday, crews are going to try to break through the ice and start to drain the pond."

"They think Earle is in the pond?"

"He's missing."

"And Simon Wensel too," she said faintly. "I saw a newspaper."

"Carlo will be in tomorrow. I hope he'll have some news."

"Has he made his written report?"

"Yes, and its identical to yours. Earle was unconscious on the roof when Carlo left, and he went to the boiler room, where he slept, hidden behind the furnace, until morning."

"Just curious, Major, who found the shoe?"

"An early jogger, Vanessa Cole."

* * *

At 5:00 a.m., Nicole was dressed in her black jogging suit and headed out of the city in her old VW—that after three tries, the engine miraculously started. The air was crisp, with a hint of snow, and the path at LeGrand's farm was soggy with the remains of a recent thaw, but she plodded the tough half circuit around the farm before stopping in front of the house. The truck was gone. Boncoeur came to a window and gave a welcome woof as Nicole placed packages on the porch swing, a bottle of good wine, and a box of dog cookies. Then she sprinted back to the VW in the clearing and drove into the nearest commercial area. The Quick-Photo shop wasn't open, so she drove around until she found a cafe where a few early birds were gathered for breakfast.

At nine, she waited in the Quick-Photo for an hour while the roll of film from the roof was developed and two sets were speedily printed and bagged. The Indian technicians manned the machines without curiosity at the contents, Nicole noticed. One rang up the sale, and said, "Merci." She left the shop without a backward glance. She hurried to the Volkswagen and drove out to a park that had spaces overlooking the river. Few people were there on this cold day enjoying the view. She removed one set of twenty-four prints.

The first few were daylight shots, and from the light, it was afternoon—there was the heavy girl, Dellie Lumbach, shoving Simon Wensel, Simon following Jean Ducharme and Chelsea Clovis, and what appears to be an evening long shot of the darkened, women's dorm building. Next frame, lights come on. Here, the lens had been changed to 70-210, and zeroed in on Jean and Chelsea. The camera abruptly pans back to a tall figure near the entrance to the dorm for the next shot. Whoever it was then entered the dorm. Jean and Chelsea have changed to nightwear. Jean wears short pajamas and is bare foot, Chelsea wears some kind of short gown, and they sit on the bed playing a board game. A long shot reveals Simon Wensel is at a corner of the Art Building, holding binoculars. The next frame is out of sync, as if the tripod was jostled, and the lens picked up part of the parapet of the roof, and a pale circle in the background, which could be the full moon. At different time periods, successive frames, ten through twenty-four, were taken after the heavy snow, window shots at night, which were not too successful, due to haze on the lens.

There had been another roll of film in the camera that night she and Carlo were hiding on the roof. She had heard it when the shutter clicked, advanced and clicked, but that film was missing, and the camera and the guard's gun, which he had aimed directly at Carlo and Wilfred Earle himself, vanished as if that night had never happened, as if he never existed.

Nicole shivered and pulled her red cap around her ears. The old car had no heat, but it was the deep sense of foreboding that gave her a chill when she carefully selected the picture of Simon, standing in the courtyard, with binoculars, directed upward toward the lighted square of Jean Ducharme's room. This, then, was probably the last sighting of Simon before he disappeared. Immediately afterward, the camera was tipped over, and no more pictures were taken that night.

Nicole divided the two sets. One went into the pocket of her jacket. She went to the post office, purchased an 8 × 10 manila envelope with bubble padding inside, sealed the other set of pictures with the negatives, and addressed it to Major Whitt at the Alexandria office. He would deduce much the same conclusion. The main stalker, Wilfred Earle, had removed the one person he believed to be his competition. The package of prints would not arrive in the States until after Christmas. Let the major have his holiday.

On the way home, she bought a few gifts at the shopping mart. From the florist, she purchased a pink poinsettia, and four red and silver balloons to decorate Yvette's apartment. In the confines of the little car, she began to sing, "I'll Be Home for Christmas."

* * *

The snow held its promise. Christmas Day, it wandered down in big, wet flakes, just enough to give a lovely, clean look as it clung to tree branches and melted when it reached the ground. Here, in Paris, there were none of the freezing temperatures and drifting that had plagued the States for the past month, and Nicole was grateful to be away from the deadly ice that downed old trees and froze the ponds and rivers.

As she drove to Yvette's, dressed in her red jacket with the brass buttons and black shirt, she couldn't help thinking of the pond at Randolph. Had they been able to drain it? She brushed all thoughts of America aside. Today, she would be there for Maman. She prayed to herself, "Holy Mother, let us on this day be happy, and I will say twelve Hail Marys."

To Nicole's surprise, Rene's BMW was parked in the lot beside Yvette's Citroen. *Why had Yvette invited Rene?* Nicole wondered. *Certainly, not with any idea she and Rene would get together again.*

Gerta Mueller, who had been Mimi's lifetime friend, and her two daughters, had also arrived early. They had brought great tin pans of bread, roasted apples, German Potato salad, and two kinds of strudel.

"Mama, am I late?"

"No," Yvette said, sounding flustered. She basted the goose and closed the oven door.

"Everyone else is early, Cherie," she glanced at the red-and-black suit Nicole was wearing. "Go to the bedroom and take off your clothes. I stayed up until one, putting in a hem for you. That suit is lovely, but it is old, maybe five years old!"

"Oh, Maman!" Nicole exclaimed "But first, the balloons and the poinsettia and a present for you, Maman."

"Later, I will look," said Yvette, peering curiously at the square package wrapped in silver paper.

"Rene, you are looking well. Joyeaux Noel," Nicole said as he rose from the sofa.

They embraced somewhat awkwardly, and she passed her attention to Gerta and the two beautiful buxom Mueller sisters, Helga and Marta, who exclaimed over how thin she was.

In the bedroom, Nicole found a white silk blouse, with tags still on it, and an emerald green velvet skirt, long and plain, with slits on either side to the knee. Nicole smiled to herself as she touched the skirt. The material looked familiar. It was the same as one of the holiday dresses

Maman made for a client. She took off her suit and tried on the new silk blouse. The skirt looked elegant and fit perfectly as she turned around in front of the cheval mirror. *I wish major could see me, I wish he was here, I wish . . . I could touch his face . . .* Nicole stared at herself in the mirror . . . *Mon Dieu, I think I am in love!*

The doorbell rang, and she quickly cut the price tags off the blouse and went into the living room.

Derek stood uncertainly in the doorway as the sisters leaped about him, laughing, and clasping their hands together in delight.

"It is a Christmas dwarf in a tiny red vest. Come look!"

"Ahh, he is adorable!" Gerta stretched out her arms as if to pick him up.

"Don't touch me," warned Derek, backing off. He held two small gaily-wrapped packages in front of his chest like a pathetic shield.

Nicole came to the rescue, pulling Derek into the room. "This is my friend, Derek Holland. We work together in America."

"Sit with us!" begged the Muellers. "Such beautiful brown eyes and a strong chin. Such dear little shoes!"

"Are you married?" inquired Gerta, examining Derek closely. "Engaged?"

"No, madam," mumbled Derek. He handed the packages to Yvette. "For you and Nicole."

"I did not know there would be others."

"This is Rene Laurent," introduced Yvette, giving Nicole a sly glance. "He is Nicole's husband. He has his own business."

"Yes, I have been in his store. Georges has helped me," Derek nodded.

"My ex-husband," Nicole clarified. She laid her arm casually across Derek's shoulders. "And this is my very good friend. He is an accountant, very smart, wealthy too."

"But he is a—a—a dwarf!" the words burst out of Rene's mouth. "Nicole!"

"And so charming," Nicole continued, "that after ten minutes with Derek, one tends to forget."

Rene, who had risen from the sofa, abruptly sat back down. One of the Mueller sisters took the seat beside him.

"I have been in your lovely store, but the jewelry in there—ah, so expensive! Perhaps you could suggest something a poor girl could afford?"

"Perhaps, a watch for children," Rene said, dismissing her abruptly as he rose and followed Nicole across the room.

"I have missed you," he said in a low voice. "I never knew I'd miss you so much. On Fridays, you made Quiche, the best Quiche I've ever eaten."

"And a green salad," Nicole recalled.

"And in the store, you were invaluable! The stones have not been inventoried since you left. Nicole, I made the biggest mistake—."

"The goose is done," proclaimed Yvette loudly, dragging the big roast from the oven.

"Nicole, my big platter. Rene, open the wine. And you, my little man, put the napkins in the rings, if you please!"

The dinner went amazingly well, mainly because the goose was done to perfection, the wine was seriously aged, Gerta's potato salad—hot and covered with crispy bacon—was a surprise to the palate, and the strudels, gorged with fruit and covered in thick cream, caused them to groan and feebly push their plates away. Later, Derek had given Nicole and Yvette slim silver-colored name bracelets, which Rene recognized from his own stock as platinum. Georges had been helpful indeed.

The early darkness of winter descended and the sated guests filed out into the dwindling snowfall. They stepped carefully across the wet parking area, waved good-bye, and drove away.

The mountain of dishes had been washed and put away. Even the goose-roaster had been scrubbed and again hung in its place near the kitchen stove.

Nicole took off the new blouse and skirt and put on a robe of her mother's. Yvette laid, in feigned exhaustion on the sofa, with her feet propped on the arm, pillows under her head and back.

"Never," said Yvette, "will I go to all this trouble again. Without Gerta, I could not have managed!"

"She is better than gold in the bank."

Yvette laughed. "Gold is good too, Nicole. Oh, I forgot—so much to do, so many people—I forgot to tell you that policeman called in the night. Does he not know the time?"

"Police? Oh, you mean Major Whitt. His time is six hours different, Maman."

"What does he want with you?"

Nicole hesitated.

"Are you in trouble with the police?"

"No, Maman. I explained to you before that Major Whitt is not a policeman. He was in the military, the United States Air Force. I like him very much, and he likes me. He likes me very much."

Yvette sat up and stared at Nicole.

"Would you like the radio," Nicole suggested, "or the television on?" She rose and walked over to the set.

"No, no TV." Yvette said. "I invited dear lonely Rene to my place today in the hope he would see you and fall in love again. He has asked of you so many times. Oh yes, he has called here hoping to see you. What could I do but ask him to come today."

"It is over with Rene."

"Such a nice man. His suit was Armani," Yvette pointed out. "Did you notice?"

"No."

"And you, acting silly with the little man, as if he were your lover."

"Maman, I think I will go now," said Nicole, sharper than she had intended.

She went into the bedroom and dressed in the red jacket and black skirt, put her new outfit into a plastic cleaner's bag, and returned to the living room to find Yvette looking small and unhappy on the sofa, hunched over a pillow held close to her chest.

"I'm going. Thank you for the beautiful velvet skirt and the blouse. I don't know how you had the time to sew it."

"It was nothing."

"Maman, I love you."

"Yes. Thank you for the flower and the balloons."

Suddenly, Nicole remembered the silver-wrapped present, still sitting next to the pink poinsettia, forgotten in the busy preparation for the dinner.

"Oh, Mon Dieu!" Nicole rushed over and swept up the shining square tied in scarlet satin ribbon.

"This is for you, Maman!"

Carefully, Yvette accepted the gift, admiring the wrappings, as she took out an ornate silver frame in a repousse pattern. At first, she didn't seem to understand.

"Who is this?"

"The dress, Maman. Look at the dress!"

Yvette stared at the photograph for a long time. "Birds of Paradise! Very heavy, that dress. Real beading is heavy, you know, and none of that nasty, glued—I sewed every bead by hand. Where did you find this picture, my darling?"

"Jean Ducharme, the ambassador's daughter, gave it to me. I visited the college where she goes to school."

"And you remembered Madam Eugenie Ducharme from so many years?"

"I remember the dress, Maman! You will be so thrilled! It is in the Smithsonian, the most important museum in America. Look, I have written on the back of the frame where it is, who it belonged to, and of course, created by hand by Yvette Longet."

Yvette smiled. "An honor, no?"

"Yes, yes, an honor."

"One day I would like to go and visit this important museum and see my work and the people stopping to admire."

"I will take you, Maman!" Nicole promised.

"But I am so afraid to fly in a plane!"

"I would be with you. Nothing to fear."

"Yes, perhaps I would be safe with you, Nicole."

Nicole drove home to her own apartment, the pale headlights catching the lazy flakes in the beams. Because she unlocked the door, she heard the telephone cease ringing. She felt like talking to no one. She kicked off her shoes, and stood, looking for a moment at Mimi's trunk. It smelled of sweet lavender, age, and cigarettes. She touched the top of the trunk.

"It is Christmas again, Mimi, and we miss you so much. Goodnight. Sleep in peace, my angel."

Chapter Sixteen

The Muddy Depths of Randolph Pond

In the weeks following, Major Whitt called every other night. The telephone would ring at midnight and they would talk ten, maybe, fifteen minutes. Nicole would yawn, and he would ask her if he was boring her, and she would remind him of the hour. He would protest.

"I tried calling in the day, but you are never there. Where do you go every day, Nicole?"

"Sometimes I shop, I jog, the library, and of course, I visit Yvette."

"I called your mother's apartment."

"Please don't call, Maman!" Nicole objected. "She is working very hard in her business and she has no time to talk to you."

"She oughta get to know me. She is going to be my mother-in-law." He paused and there was silence. "I love you, Nicole. Good night."

"Goodnight, Major."

"Say it, Nicole, say it." He sounded very lonely.

"Goodnight, Major."

She would hang up and lay across the bed, looking out at the stars, feeling guilty for everything—for being unable to commit, to even admit to herself that she loved him too. He stayed in the background of her mind, no matter what else she was doing. He was the last thing she thought about before she went to sleep, his sweet mouth, the stubble of his short GI-haircut, his neat starchy clothes, even his big feet, and the man-sweat of him when they made love. Then, she would dream.

There was a reason that Nicole couldn't be found during the day, and she had decided not to mention it to Whitt, or Yvette, who would react in different ways to the news that she had temporarily gone back to work for Rene to do inventory work that had not been done by anyone since she left. It was important for the insurance coverage. Rene wouldn't allow anyone else in his personal work area, and he simply did not involve himself to do anything he considered as menial, even trivial, as counting and keeping records. Nicole had spoken confidentially to Georges, who was now a partner in the firm, and he had begged her to come in—a week, maybe two, until he convinced Rene to do it himself. So Nicole came in at ten and left at four, had dinner, and spent evenings going over the folder on Nicolas Campion. Derek had gone beyond names. He scanned faces, and on at least three occasions placed Nicolas on a spot where his name was not in the cutline under the photograph. Nicolas had saved two babies and left the scene; he lifted the roll bar of an overturned jeep from a soldier's neck after a traffic accident; he beat a purse-snatcher and held him for the police, disappearing in the crowd while the officer cuffed the snatcher and put him in the police car. Nicole never got tired of looking at his face. "Someday I'll find you," she promised.

On the last week of January, Major Whitt called at midnight with some unsettling news.

"Nicole, they have found a body in the mud in Randolph pond. The ice has finally melted, and they managed to drag the fallen trees from the water. Wensel was caught about three feet under in a mass of debris."

"Oh no!" Nicole cried out. "Oh, he was only a boy, a nice boy! Who could hurt a boy like that?"

"You saw the film."

"Yes."

"There's your motive. He was competition for the attention of Jean Ducharme. He was her peer, with wealthy parents, and the right background. He was killed by Wilfred Earle, the security guard."

"How can you be positive about that? We don't even know where Earle is. I told you exactly what happened on the roof. He was there when Carlo and I left, but he must have recovered—."

"When they pulled Simon Wensel's body from the pond, his fist was closed around the name plate from Wilfred Earle's uniform jacket. A piece of heavy twill was still attached," reported Whitt. "He put up a fight."

"And the black shoe that was found on the path?"

"Wensel was wearing size twelve, white Reeboks. The black shoe is Earle's." Whitt paused. "Nicole, I suspect Carlo is involved. We gave him a polygraph last Sunday. He gave no verbal answers, but we were able to record his reactions to the questions—that's the crux of polys anyway, you know. But, I know the essence of Carlo. If he were knocked down by a truck, the truck would rollover and Carlo would get up and smile."

"I've seen that smile," Nicole admitted.

"You know he's in love with you."

"No, he is not!"

"He stole the picture of you, the one of you in the blond wig that was in the desk drawer in the library. I don't know how he got it but when he went back to Randolph I went to his room and there it was in a beautiful frame, with his rosary arranged over it and a candle on each side."

"Mon Dieu!" Nicole felt sick. "Did you take it away?"

"No, I left it there. We need to get inside of Carlo's head."

"How?"

"You could turn him, Nicole. You had him writing more notes than I've gotten out of him in a year. He would tell you his part in this mystery of the missing men."

"Where is Carlo now?"

"Still working at Randolph. Here at the house on weekends. He has a Green Card but I'd like to send him back to Ecuador."

"You are using me, Major. I know it is my job, but—."

"Don't say that, Nicole!" shouted Whitt. She held the telephone at arm's length. "If you talk to Carlo, I'll be at your side every minute! I'd never put you in harm's way—oh god—please!" She could hear him groan in the silence that ensued. She said nothing. Finally, he said plaintively, "Nicole?"

When she spoke, the chill in her voice was evident. "I will come speak with Carlo on my own time, one on one. You will not be there."

"Oh yes, I will!"

"Then he will tell me nothing."

"I don't want you to ever be alone with Carlo again. He's not predictable, and whereas he can be smart, even clever, no one knows how much his injuries affected his—his thinking—I will be there, Nicole, if you confront him about Wensel and Earle."

"Give me time to think about it."

"Is there anything I can do for you? Forget about Carlo. The hell with it."

"Do you have your harmonica with you?"

"In my pocket." He sounded surprised.

"Would you play, "Somewhere, My Love?""

She heard a rustling noise as he pulled the harmonica from his pocket, and over the telephone, the haunting notes filled her small apartment. She felt empty and very alone. When the song ended, he said, "I miss you so much. Will you come, Nicole? Forget Carlo. I need you."

"Thank you for the song. Good night, Major."

"Say it, Nicole, say it," he pleaded.

"Good night, Major."

She went to the window and sat looking out at the dark sky. There was no moon. No stars. It would rain tomorrow if one believed the clouds. She glanced at her watch and saw that, indeed, it already was tomorrow, after one o'clock, and yet she wasn't sleepy. She crossed to Mimi's trunk and got out the circus posters. There he was, Nicolas Campion, a boy really, flying through the air with the greatest of ease. She pressed the brittle papers flat with her hands on the bed and gazed at them for a long time.

*　*　*

On Friday, Nicole handed Rene Laurent the completed inventory. He wanted her to teach the newest saleslady how to do this tedious paperwork, but Nicole urged him to take on the job himself.

"There is always the risk of theft. Rene, a few stones here, a few there—"

Rene paled at the thought. "I guess I must do it all! You can trust no one in this business! Except you, Nicole. I always trusted you."

"Thank you, Rene."

"I must pay you for this work. You are no longer my wife, no longer Madam Laurent. Oh yes, many times since I have wished you were with me. No one wears a designer gown better than you. Never have diamonds looked more exquisite than on your beautiful neck."

Nicole looked at him. "If you had spoken to me like that, and if you had told me about the vasectomy, perhaps things would have been different."

"I thought it made me less of a man," he ventured, avoiding her gaze. "But, we had our good times, you must admit."

"Yes, we did," she agreed.

"And now, I'd like to pay you for the work you've done on the inventory. Tell me how much. Make a price."

"I don't want money, Rene, but there is a watch I admire."

"Take it, my darling, but be sure to write a ticket. Let me find it for you." Rene put his arm around her and led her to the glass cases near the front. "Now which one pleases you?"

As they stood close together, looking into the glass cases full of watches, she was aware of him, the familiar scent of exotic aftershave. He was wearing a gray suit, the color of his hair. She felt a wave of nostalgia for what used to be. Rene was looking down at her as if he were sharing the same thoughts.

"Which one pleases you, Nicole?" he repeated.

She pointed to a watch with two dials, set about an inch apart, on a gold stretch band. "That one."

"But, that is a man's watch. You don't need a heavy piece like that."

"It is for a friend. May I have it?"

"But," again Rene hesitated. "It is not expensive. It is what is known in the trade, as a novelty. See? You set one dial for personal use, and the other one, any place in the world you wish to know the time."

"Yes. I know that. We sold many to tourists," she reminded him.

"It is for that dwarf, isn't it? I saw how fond you were of him at Christmas."

"May I have the watch?"

"Much too big for such a little man. He will fall over. Oh, well, shall I wrap it?" Rene threw up his hands.

"I'll write the ticket."

* * *

On Sunday, after church, Nicole told Yvette she would be returning to the States to do some translation work, and as usual, Yvette protested, telling her she could find plenty of work in Paris, perhaps she was not too old to model. Yvette would inquire.

"No, Maman," protested Nicole. "The girls today are fifteen, and only allowed to weight as much as a goat."

"Alors!" and the makeup! So much black on the eyes, like pandas!"

Nicole drove Yvette home in the Citroen and retrieved her own Volkswagen. They kissed many times and said good-bye. Enrico

Garibaldi waved from the window, and seeing him there, Nicole was glad, because Yvette would not be alone.

When she reached her own apartment, the telephone was ringing. She hurriedly unlocked the door, ran in, and picked up the telephone in time to hear the long distance operator ask the caller if he wished to continue.

"Yes! Yes! I am here!" Nicole answered breathlessly. "Who is it?"

"It is Derek. I have big news about your father so I am calling—."

"Will you accept the charges, madam?" the operator cut in.

"Yes, I will. Go ahead, Derek."

"I'm sorry. I didn't want to call from the office. This is for your ears only. I have a schedule for Nicolas Lee for the next three weeks. Can you come to the States very soon?"

"A schedule?"

"He is traveling, doing appraisals. There was a notice in the window of an antique shop. I went back to the classified ads in the *Post* and there it was in last Sunday's edition. I know where Nicolas Lee will be for the next three weekends. That is the name he uses for this occupation."

"Oh, Derek!" she managed, as she dropped down on the bed. Then she laughed. "What are you doing in an antique shop?"

"I have rented half a house. You know, two stuck together?"

"A duplex?" she guessed.

"Yes. I move from the motel in thirty days. My friends helped me find it." His friends, the Little People, he meant, and she could hear in his voice the excitement of finally having a house of his own.

"That's great. I'm anxious to see it, and Derek, say nothing to the major about Nicolas. Please let this be our secret. I will contact you soon," Nicole said. "I love you a bunch, Derek."

"Don't wait too long. He'll be gone."

"I understand. Good-bye, dear one."

"Good-bye, Cherie."

She fixed a sandwich, a glass of wine, and a cup of tea, and spread the contents of Derek's folder on the tiny table by the window. Because she ate her lunch, she carefully went over the news clippings and looked at the grainy pictures of Nicolas. *Soon, I will find you.*

She changed from the black suit she had worn to church, hung up the white silk blouse that had been Maman's gift, and put on jeans and a pale yellow turtleneck sweater and a suede jacket.

The afternoon was spent wandering about the city streets, window-shopping. At a bookstore, she purchased a fat Sunday newspaper and headed home. A Sunday afternoon with nothing urgent expected of her was a luxury, precious empty hours all her own. It felt strange, but delicious. She put on a robe, piled up the pillows, and sitting cross-legged on the bed, pulled out the Style section. Working her way leisurely toward the crossword puzzle, she felt a sense of irritation when the telephone began to ring insistently. On the tenth ring, she picked it up.

"Nicole?"

"Yes, Major. You're calling early. It's barely seven."

"I think you'd better come in as soon as possible. They just dug the body of Wilfred Earle out of the mud in Randolph Pond, about twenty feet from where they discovered Wensel. No bullet wounds, no knife wounds, on either body."

"How did they die?" The newspapers slid to the floor, but she didn't notice.

"It's a tough one. The cold temperatures, the covering of ice, the immersion in the mud as the ice melted, make it hard to pinpoint the exact time of the deaths. It's a miracle they were found at all. That pond is deep in the middle."

"Like dinosaurs," Nicole said quietly. "They could have—I'm glad they were found."

"Yes, but now comes the mystery. How did they get in the pond?" Whitt posed the obvious question. "I think Carlo knows more than he has told us."

"Perhaps he wasn't involved at all, Major. I was with Carlo, and I saw nothing."

"But you left the roof first. You don't know what happened when you left Carlo alone with Wilfred Earle."

"Why would he do anything? He knew I was calling the police. He had to leave."

"What was the time element—ten minutes? Twenty? After you left?"

Nicole thought about it and couldn't remember exactly. "Maybe twenty? I didn't use the phone at the dorm. I went out to a pay phone."

"Would you wear a wire and get Carlo to talk about that night?"

"Talk?" Nicole laughed. "You want a miracle, no?"

"You could ask questions and indicate his nods and reactions by repeating what he does into the wire," insisted Whitt. "I have to be in Germany a couple of days this week on this new recruit I'm following, but I'll be back Thursday the latest. Can I arrange a reservation for you?"

"No," she answered. "I'll take care of it."

"God, I've been missing you! I'm practicing some new songs on the harmonica. Do you have any requests?"

"How about "Love Me Tender?""

"Anytime, baby, anytime. I love you."

"Good night, Major."

"Say it, Nicole, say it," he begged.

"Good night, Major."

After Nicole hung up, she pushed the crossword puzzle aside and concentrated on the conversation. Whitt wanted her to bait Carlo into some kind of confession, without any evidence that Carlo was involved. It didn't seem quite fair. And yet, there was that smile, that smile was hiding something.

I'll go, she decided, on my own terms. No wires and no major.

* * *

When the plane came in at International on Tuesday afternoon, Nicole had only one goal in mind, to locate Carlo and talk to him as one agent to another. Technically, they had done their specific job. The two men who appeared to be stalking Jean Ducharme were dead. How and why they died left a gaping hole in the case and until there was closure, it could not be packaged and filed as report completed. There had been others, open-end cases, but this one Nicole wanted to wrap-up herself.

She went to the nearest telephone booth and called Personnel at Randolph College.

"I'm sorry, Carlo Arana has been terminated as of last Friday. We are letting some grounds staff go due to the continuing bad weather, and we'll possible rehire in the spring."

"Mon Dieu, have I come all this way and missed him," she thought desperately. Major had mentioned something about sending Carlo back to Ecuador. She tried the safe house and a guttural voice with a heavy accent told her, "Major gone. Carlo gone. Only Gregor is here."

"And how is Runner?" Nicole asked wistfully, wanting to see the dog again.

"You know this dog?" Gregor chuckled. "He is the best dog in the world. Who is this, know my dog?" Gregor demanded.

"No! My dog!" Nicole bristled. "In my heart, Runner is my dog! I'm a friend of the major's. Good-bye." She replaced the telephone and stood thinking where to turn next. Carlo was no longer at Randolph, and he was not at the safe house. He never went to the Alexandria office except on direct orders, but there was one place he could still be if he had not left the country.

She picked up her tote bag. It felt light, with only an extra pair of jeans, a couple of sweaters, underwear, and running shoes. Her shoulder bag felt light too, and she felt a sense of foreboding. What was missing was the gun and knife now locked away under the watchful eye of Beau Jackson.

The car rental agent offered a deal on the more expensive models because they said they had rented the cheaper ones. People seemed to be tightening their financial belts as the dreams of the new tech generation faded and stocks went up and down like kites in a windstorm.

"So, you can drive your pick of our Cadillacs, Buicks—how about a Lexus?" the clerk suggested as she looked at him with her dark, no-nonsense gaze, his smile became uncertain. "Just what did you have in mind?"

"Something with four tires and a steering wheel." she told him. She still had her Nicole Lawrence credit card but this trip she was on her own. She pulled a roll of bills from her pocket. "How much?"

"We do have a Jeep Cherokee. Not new."

"I'll take it," Nicole said. She rather enjoyed driving the one assigned to the major, so it would be familiar, and you never knew when you'd need four-wheel drive she reasoned.

With only two short excursions in the wrong direction, Nicole managed to find the main highway that led past the entrance road to Randolph College, and then continued down to the Bide-A-Wee Motel.

The blue Tempo sat in its usual spot in front of Carlo's room. She pulled into the empty space beside it, locked the jeep, and casually peered into the Tempo's back seat. The ugly plaid jacket was there, a full green plastic trash bag and a pair of muddy boots. A plastic statuette of Jesus, badly painted, with a brown cross and red lips and liberal red blood on the hands and feet, lay across the clothing as if to protect it from theft. Nicole was appalled and made the sign of the cross across her chest.

"Precious Mary, Mother of God, I apologize for all humanity for this monstrosity. Forgive them," she intoned in a whisper. "For they know not what they do."

She knocked on the door. No one answered, but she knew he was inside, so she rapped sharply on the window glass.

Carlo pulled the drape slightly aside and motioned for her to go away.

"I need to talk with you!" she called out loudly. "Open the door, Carlo!"

The door to the next room opened just a crack and a voice from inside announced, "My name is Billy Dee Williams, like the actor, but I'm not him. I'm Billy DeWayne Williams, for your further confusion. Whatcha want with that old ugly man next door, pretty girl like you?"

A seedy character, thin and bearded, red suspenders hanging down over filthy trousers ventured out of the next room. The apparition opened a toothless mouth and commented, "That one is deef. Deef and dumb. Somebody beat that sucker. Scars all over his face. You don't want to go in there, lady."

Carlo threw the door open, raised his closed fist to the other roomer, and made his horrible animal sound. The man jumped backward into his own room, and they heard the chain as he double-locked the door. Nicole pushed past Carlo and entered his room.

Clothes littered the bed, some clean shirts in a neat pile to one side, and some baggy, but clean dark socks. A new, open vinyl bag held a few toilet articles. Carlo was ready to travel, and he was traveling light. A new navy peacoat hung from the closet door; new black shoes stood beneath it. From all appearances, he would have been gone within the hour but now that Nicole was here, he was obviously upset and angry that she had arrived before he could complete his packing and leave.

"We need to talk," Nicole stated bluntly, and placing the clean shirts into the suitcase, made room to sit on the bed. "I want to know what happened to the guard after I left the roof. He was lying there alive, I felt his pulse."

Carlo held up his hand and scribbled something on a pink note.

"He was dead. You killed him."

"No! I saw him breathing," Nicole insisted. "Now they've found him dead in Randolph Pond. I did not put him there, no?"

He sat down on the other side of the bed and stared at her silently. She realized she could see his eyes. His long oily hair had been cut to his shoulders and trimmed a bit around his face. He appeared somewhat younger, and she wondered at his age, thirty, thirty-five?

"Why don't you write it down for me, just for my own knowledge?"

Carlo made his laughing noise and scribbled. "Major sent you."

"No, he didn't," she answered and foolishly added. "He doesn't know that I'm in the States."

His eyes shifted and Nicole realized she had made a mistake. He got up, moved, and sat down on the radiator, which was under the window near the door. Nicole pretended not to notice and busied herself looking through her should bag. She drew out a plain white notepad.

"Please, for me, Carlo. Write it out. Did you know Earle killed the boy, Simon Wensel?"

Carlo nodded and made scratching motions with his nails at his face, held up his hands.

"DNA under Simon's nails?"

Carlo nodded.

Nicole noticed a candy bar in the open suitcase and realized she had forgotten lunch. Through the gaps in the drapes the light was fading to late afternoon and she though longingly of dinnertime. As if he picked up on her thoughts, Carol reached over, picked up the candy bar, broke it in two, and he handed her half.

They sat munching silently, and he wrote on one of his pink notes.

"Picnic. You and me, like friends."

She finished the candy and stood up to go. Her white note pad lay on the bed and as she reached for it to put it back in her shoulder bag, Carlo placed his hand over hers. He indicated that she sit back down. He picked up her pad, went to the vanity chest and turned on the lamp. Hunched over the pad, he seemed to stop and think a moment about the wisdom of this confession, then gave a faint sigh and began to write.

Nicole sat on the bed, looking at Carlo's back as he wrote steadily. It grew dark in the room except for the glow of the lamp. Night descends early in the winter. A dim orange flow from outside indicated the parking lot light had come on. The Bide-A-Wee sign read vacancy.

After twenty minutes, she said, "Restroom?"

Carlo nodded and bent to read what he had written so far.

Nicole went into the bathroom, turned on the faucet, and let the water run as she used the toilet. She washed her hands and drank from the cold-water spigot, all the while looking around for anything that could be used as a weapon in case Carlo decided he didn't want her to leave. She thought about what major had said about Carlo stealing her picture from the drawer of the library desk, and the votive candles, homage to a saint. Saint Nicole, she considered with amusement, not likely. There was nothing at all in the bathroom. Even his toothbrush was missing.

Carlo had finished writing and sat waiting for her to return, the papers dangling from his hand. His hair fell forward over his face, and she was unable to gauge his thoughts.

"I may read this now, no?"

He laid the papers on the desk and indicated that she should take the seat by the lamp. While she read each sentence, and committed it to mind in case he took it back, he completed his packing and sat patiently on the bed.

"This is true?" Nicole finally asked. She was amazed and appalled. "How could you—?"

Carlo made his laugh and waved his hand as if to say it was nothing. He wrote scratchily on one of his pink notes.

"I am hungry now. You?"

Nicole hesitated. "Yes, I'm starved."

He picked up his suitcase put it near the door, and put on the new pea coat and new shoes. He opened the door for Nicole as she stepped out onto the sidewalk; she almost fell over the old man, Billy Williams, who had been listening near the door to Carlo's room. A lit cigarette fell from William's hand as he threw himself into the room next door and slammed the door.

Carlo snarled and kicked the door. He snatched up the burning cigarette and smashed it against the glass in the window, making a series of angry sounds. The drapes on the other side trembled as if the old man were holding them together to keep Carlo from crashing inside. Although there were lights on in a few rooms, no one ventured outside.

"Come on. You are hungry, no?" Nicole said, pulling on Carlo's sleeve.

He stood for a second, looking into the blue Tempo, then marched around to the passenger side of her jeep rental, and waited for her to unlock the door.

"If I'm to drive us, you must give me directions to a restaurant," Nicole insisted.

"H-aagh," he growled, pointing south down the highway.

About three miles on the right was a sort of rustic roadhouse with a DIN—the "e" was missing; a light 'N' dance sign in orange neon flashing at the far end. There were only three other cars in front of the place, and three others parked near the rear. It appeared very dark inside, but there was the sound of voices and a jukebox playing Patsy Cline, dishes rattling on a cart.

On entering, Nicole looked around the one vast room, with a bar at one side, a cluster of metal tables and chairs next to it, and a scruffy dance floor. An older woman, and a boy of about eighteen, both in jeans and plaid shirts, pushed slowly around the floor, their boots dragging out of step with the music. The only lights were those behind the bar, on the walls in blinking violet signs advertising beer, and the candles on the tables.

"You have eaten here before?" Nicole asked, seeing no food being served.

Carlo shook his head and sat down at one of the tables. The bartender looked at them suspiciously, opened a door behind him and called for Maria, a summons that brought a sulky looking Latino woman from the kitchen. She fished two greasy menus from under the bar and waddled over to their table.

"I'll choose for both of us," Nicole decided as Carlo pulled out his pink notes. There were two choices of entrees. The hamburgers and fries seemed the best choice, winning out over chili and cheese dogs, the other selection. She ordered coffee and apple pie. Maria wrote laboriously on her yellow pad, her small black eyes flicking interested glances at the silent, hunching Carlo.

Nicole went to the bar and ordered two glasses of red wine.

"Not from around here, are you?" asked the bartender. "What's the problem with your boyfriend, hair hanging down like that?"

"He's shy." Nicole leaned close across the counter as she picked up the drinks. "But don't make him angry. If he comes out of his shell, he breaks things—it's terrible!"

"I ain't planning to ride him," the bartender assured her. "Those drinks are on the house if he don't make no trouble."

"How kind. Merci, Monsieur!"

"See, I knew you wasn't from around here."

The hamburgers were large and juicy, the fries hot, the coffee black and strong, and the apple pie very cold, as if hastily yanked from the refrigerator. Nicole felt they didn't have a big dinner hour.

Carlo ate steadily, motioned for more wine, and stared at Nicole through the flickering candle. At times, he seemed depressed, his head bowed, and once he reached across and held her hand, then squeezed it gently and let it go. She sensed he was almost apologizing for something, perhaps the shocking details of Wilfred Earle's last night on earth.

Nicole controlled a shudder, drank the last of her wine, and reached for her billfold.

"Uh-h-h-h-!" Carlo objected and pulled a roll of bills from his pocket.

"Thank you. It was—uh, hot and tasty."

"I drive," he wrote and held it up to see.

Nicole shrugged. Why not? He drove the jeep assigned to the major occasionally and this rental was the same model except for color, this one being black, instead of navy blue. At the cash register, she picked up a handful of mints and dropped them in her coat pocket then handed him the keys without argument. When they went out to where the jeep was parked, she realized she didn't know whether the way back to the Bide-A-Wee was north or south. Being stuck on an unfamiliar highway half the night with Carlo as she headed in the wrong direction was not a desirable option. She climbed into the passenger seat.

Carlo backed out, expertly flicked on the headlight without looking at the dashboard, drove to the highway exit, and turned south. Trees on either side. A white house far back from the road. Cattle standing by a wire fence on the left. Something was wrong!

Nicole tensed and looked around. There had been billboards on the way to the roadhouse, large billboards advertising a sort of flea market and general shops in a complex, which would have been twenty miles beyond the roadhouse, and now they passed a billboard that said fifteen.

"We are going in the wrong direction. Turn around, Carlo!" Nicole said sharply.

He lessened his speed and peered through his dangling hair, a curious smile hovering on his lips. She had surprised him. He shrugged and pulled to the next turn off, pointing the nose of the jeep back North. The engine idled, letting a few cars pass. Nicole looked back to the left.

"It's clear on this side. We can go."

She felt the sudden movement from the driver's seat but couldn't turn back in time. A needle-like object plunged in just below her jaw line, one short piercing stab. Her vision clouded, and she found herself unable to speak. In a second, she knew what had happened because she had been forced to use this method on a felon in a prior case, to keep from being followed. It was not a needle at all but a shard of bamboo the size of a large toothpick, the sharpened end encrusted with a paralytic. Easy to carry, efficient to use. It could be worn under a lapel or a shirt collar. It was a powerful but temporary drug that paralyzed speech, caused peripheral blindness, and induced a sense of falling. The muscle of her arms and legs felt like marshmallows, great soft things attached, and yet useless. Her mind struggled to call up the length of the effect, but she had lolled back against the seat, her pulse slowed, and she stared ahead through the windshield at the stars.

Carlo pulled onto the highway and headed back north, looking into the darkness (from side to side). About a hundred yards before the entrance to Bide-A-Wee Motel was an over grown road leading back to an abandoned stable.

Once, a small farmhouse had stood beside, an outhouse, and a sty, but now they were heavily charred from a night fire and fallen into various stages of collapse. A mile south, in a grove of trees, another house, about 80 percent complete, was taking form, but was yet unfinished.

Carlos drove slowly back to the stable, stopped the jeep, and removed the keys. He walked inside, past six stalls, all empty, and by the light on his key chain, he saw what he had observed previously the two times before that he had, out of curiosity, wandered down the road behind the motel. On the far wall, were two metal rings. Each ring held a chain about ten feet long. Rusted water bowls and half gnawed bones indicated that two guard dogs had once been quartered here. Two locks, without keys, lay on a ledge above the rings. Carlo put them in his pocket, shone the tiny beam around the stable and into the stalls. Each stall remembered the old days when the horses snorted, stomped, whinnied—sucking up the grain with their great soft lips—the faded cross posts read star of wonder, star brite, becky's shining star, belle's star, jett star, and star of the night.

He tried to find a bucket for water but all the bottoms had rusted out. By the pump outside, he found a soiled brass one hanging on the wall, got the creaking pump going, rinsed the bucket clean, filled it, and took it back to the area of the chains. In the open rafters overhead, something moved. Carlo flashed the light overhead but saw nothing. He stood in the middle of the stable and groaned aloud, tearing at his hair, angry with himself for what he was doing. I'm sorry—I'm sorry—I'm sorry!

Nicole lay against the seat in the jeep, now in the fully unconscious state where she would sleep for several hours. Carlo lifted her gently, lay his cheek against her curly dark hair, hair so dense and round like a little fur cap. He longed to kiss those perfect pink lips, the eyelashes that lay flat on her cheeks, to touch her. He growled at himself, ashamed, and hurried into the stable, laying her down on several bales of musty hay. He locked one chain around her left arm and one chain around the boot top of her left ankle. The water bucket was nearby. He went back to the jeep, got her tote bag and shoulder bag, and hung them on a nail just inside the stable door. As an after thought, he walked back to where Nicole lay and placed the tiny flashlight in her hand.

* * *

The pale sun, first pink, then gold, pushed its way through the heavy fog and entered the partially open door of the stable. Pearls of dew hung from the high grass just outside.

Nicole woke and watched the sun inch across the ceiling. She had fallen between four dusty bales and vaguely recalled pulling handfuls of hay over and around her to make a nest to keep warm during the night. Her body ached, there was a spot of dried blood under her chin, and she couldn't seem to move. With tremendous effort, she pushed herself up from the hay and that is when she became aware of the shackles. She looked about for a place to use as a bathroom and struggled as far to the right corner as the chains would reach. Still unsteady, she staggered back to her nest, fell asleep, and when she woke again, the fog had lifted. The interior of the stable was lit with brilliant sunshine. She was able to read the horses' names on the cross posts and wondered when their owner would bring them in—had they been here while she slept last night? She rubbed her eyes.

The water buckets, rusted through and lying on their sides, the lack of tackle hanging on the walls, made her pause. The chains—where were the stable dogs? No one was coming. No one knew she was here, only Carlo, who may be out of the States by now.

"Hello? Is there anybody out there?" she called out. "Hello? Can anybody hear me?"

The length of the chains took her halfway to the door, and she called louder. Her voice disturbed something in the rafters, and she stopped to listen. A faint movement continued, winding its way forward. It passed overhead. A few grains of oats filtered through the narrow cracks above marking the creatures pace, and Nicole remained motionless. The sound stopped at the window over the barn door where the sun made a circle of warmth and light. I'm not alone, Nicole thought, but whatever creature it is, is mysterious, noiseless. She laughed. Sounds like a description of Carlo, she thought, and then—he will tell major I'm here, and he'll come for me—perhaps today. But I can't be sure of that, she realized.

She called out again, but her voice resounded hoarsely in the dusty stable. The water in the brass bucket near the sleeping bales looked fairly clear except for a black skate bug ricocheting on the surface. She slapped it out of the bucket and drew up a handful of sweet well water, letting it trickle down her throat, and then another. She walked to the length of the chain and called once more.

A rusty pitchfork hung from one wall, and she struggled to dislodge it, until it fell from the nail. Picking it up, she went back behind the bales and began to force the tines under the ring that held one chain. Nothing gave in. The rings appeared to be affixed by screws. On a second try, the tines of the pitchfork broke off, but she continued to pry until the remaining fork broke from the handle, and she threw it down in disgust. Far in the front, high in the dark corner, to the left of the door, she could see her shoulder bag and tote bag where Carlo had hung them from a hook. In the shoulder bag were her nail kit, two plastic charge cards, and some other items that could be converted into usable tools if only she could reach them, but the pitchfork handle was at most four feet and wouldn't reach that far.

She went back and sat on the bales, searching the pockets of her coat that yielded two bobby pins, a handful of tissues, and six foiled-wrapped peppermint candies. Food was not as big a priority as escape so the candy went back into her pocket with the tissues. The bobby pins were stretched flat, the gummy ends bitten off and the flat end forced at the hole in the lock, where it met an obstacle almost immediately and stuck. She gently wiggled it out, reversed the pin to the rippled side, and tried again with the same frustrating result.

The closest stall was "Star of the Night" on the right side. Nicole pulled the half-open door to a wider opening and searched the inside thoroughly but found nothing. The next one was "Jett Star," and it had only a large, moldy green horse blanket, soiled and moth-eaten. The stalls on the left, "Belle's Star," and "Becky's Shining Star" were equally empty, and Nicole couldn't reach the two the farthest toward the front near the door.

Toward two o'clock, she ate one of the mints, drank some water and lay down on the bales, wondering where she was. She rubbed her left arm and leg. Her foot felt as if it had swollen inside the boot, and the chain was too tight to remove it.

"Holy Mary, Mother of God, I beseech you to give me the strength and knowledge to find my way out of this barn—," Nicole prayed, speaking loudly into the darkness of the rafters overhead. "Forgive my sins and ask of me any—"

The unseen creature moved from the circle of light by the window. Dust drifted down, the motes in the sunlight appearing as flecks of gold. Movement ceased about halfway.

"Hail Mary, full of grace, blessed art thou—oh, blessed—Mary. Oh god, what is it moving around up there?"

Afternoon came and went. The sun completed another day and disappeared, giving way to a cold and starry night.

Nicole was in a half sleep when the sound came, the sound of hooves on damp ground crackling with frost. Someone on horseback was coming to the barn!

"Hello. Who is it? Help me!" she called out.

There was an excited whinny at the stable entrance and the largest black stallion she had ever seen paused in the door, huge puffs of white steam issuing from his nostrils, hooves pawing at the ground, head going up and down in agitation as he sought the sound of the strange voice in his stable.

Nicole crawled into her sleeping hole between the bales of hay and lay quietly. There was no rider, only a very large stallion, unhappy about her presence.

"Mother Mary, you are not hearing Nicole," she whispered. "Have I sinned?'

The horse stomped up and down, and finally, quietly entered the last stall. He stood perfectly still, his head went down, and he slept. So this then, was Star of the Night.

Nicole peeked up above the hay, saw the sleeping stallion, settled into the bales, and fell asleep.

Toward morning, Nicole heard the horse moving in the nearby stall and fervently wished his owner to come looking for him, but no one appeared. Star of the Night backed out, shook himself, slapped his long black tail across his back, and ambled sleepily toward the barn door.

Something on the far wall had caught his eye, and he paused, one hoof extended. He stood, staring at Nicole's bags, which Carlo had hung there.

Nicole watched as the big horse maneuvered closer, kicking at troughs, some wood crates, and a piece of rusted farm machinery, a cultivator that barred his way. His head reached out and tried to dislodge her shoulder bag. It swung to one side. He snapped his teeth. His long nose pushed it aside. He turned around; his back hooves went up and out, kicking the cultivator. The shoulder bag swayed just out of reach. Star of the Night pounded his front feet into the ground, shook his mane, and raced out into the light. What was he trying to do with her things, Nicole wondered? Did he resent foreign objects being in his stable and was attempting to get rid of them? His actions had left her curious. None of the other horses had come back to this place.

This day passed slowly, with hunger pains, and a frightening lack of feeling in her left foot. Willing herself to keep moving, she walked the ten feet up and ten feet down until she could wiggle her toes in the entrapping boot. She went back to her bales and sat there, nibbling on two of her four remaining peppermints and drinking water. Two peppermints left. Half a brass bucket of well water.

A fat field mouse skittered into the stable and began to eat greedily at the little piles of grain dislodged from above, puffy little jaws working, beady eyes so interested in finding the dusty loot that it didn't notice Nicole, sitting motionless on her bales. Then it happened. Like a flash of lightning, a heavy patterned body dropped to the floor. The mouse shrieked, but it was too late to run. The big snake's head shot forward; the mouse disappeared inside. Its frantic tail hung momentarily from the snake's mouth, wiggled once, and was still. The snake laid in casual, lazy lumps, neither coiled, nor straight, the interior juices already beginning to digest its prey. So, this was the creature that inhabited the rafters above. It had an interesting pattern, with red spots lined with black, and a sort of tan background on a well-fed body, perhaps five feet long. As Nicole observed, it progressed leisurely to an upright post and hunching and winding its body, slithered upward to the welcoming darkness of the rafters.

With such a tenant as that living upstairs, I will never have to worry about mice, no? Nicole laughed, thinking she had inherited Mimi's dry humor that spouted forth in the direst circumstances. She remembered when their water was cut off for non-payment, and the rain came through the roof of that dreadful third-floor flat, Mimi thought it was God's Providence that the leak was directly over the bathtub, and cheered. Yvette had cried, "What can we do?" Mimi suggested that they eat the last three cheese croissants and go to the circus. So they did.

For the first time since she had been in the stable, Nicole felt helplessly alone. Tears are a sign of weakness; she seemed to hear Mimi say. The water in the brass bucket was very low. She took just enough to wet her lips and throat and fell back on the bales. Her right hand flung out behind her, hit something metal. That's how she found the big iron hook embedded in the next bale. It had a handle and a shank that curved into a sort of J. It was a little rusty, but strong, capable of lifting a heavy bale into a pick up truck, or maybe onto a tractor. Wrenching it back and forth, Nicole pulled it from the hay and looked up at the rings that held the chains. The hook was stronger than the wood behind the rings, she felt certain.

Someone was singing, far down the road, something country, or maybe gospel, off-key, reedy, and as it came closer to the stable, Nicole realized the owner of the voice was male and drunk. She still held the hook in her hand. Sitting down on the bales, she secreted the hook in her sleeping hollow, and waited until a slight figure appeared in the doorway. The silhouette in the afternoon light was vaguely familiar. It staggered into the stable and gazed at the wall.

"I knowed there was a pitchfork on that goddamn wall. Now where it is? I done sold the hammer. I done sold the posthole digger. Somebody done been here and beat me to it. Damn thieves everywhere."

"Billy D. Williams, is that you?" Nicole called.

"Jesus, good god-a-mighty! Who is it want to know? Scare the bejesus out of a body hiding back there!"

"My name is Nicole," she told him and added reluctantly. "Carlo's friend at the motel."

"The pretty woman," he recalled, peering myopically past the stalls. He ventured to the back, stopped, and stared when he saw the chains.

"Please, can you help me? Do you have anything to eat or drink?" she pleaded.

"Want a cigarette?"

"No! No! No cigarette." Nicole shuddered, looking around at the dust bales of hay.

As Williams stared at the chains, he sized up just how vulnerable was her situation. His booze-muddled brain was battling to figure out how to take full advantage. "You got any money maybe I could help you?"

She stood up and turned out the pockets of her coat. The last peppermint fell out. "Carlo took everything. Do you know where Carlo is?"

"At the Bide-A-Wee. I ain't seen him but his blue car is in front of his room." Williams looked doubtful. "I ain't messing with him. He's crazy."

"Could you call somebody for me?"

"What'll you gimme?"

"I don't have anything!"

"Ohhh—you got something, lady," Williams leered as he pulled down the zipper of his filthy trousers. He loosened his red suspenders. "Pretty lady don't have no AIDS, do you?"

Nicole reached down, and her hand closed around the hay hook holding it out of his sight. If he tried to touch her, she could take his head off. The Evil Imp wished he would. As he hesitated, Nicole heard a sound coming from the right, across the fields, hooves striking cut over ground. Star of the Night was coming home to sleep.

"You better leave, Billy D. Williams. My horse doesn't like strangers," Nicole warned. "He bites, He kicks. And Mon Dieu, you're standing near his bed! He won't like that. Run, Billy D.!"

"You ain't got no horse." The old drunk grinned and shook his head.

Star of the Night appeared, filling the door with his huge black body. He lifted his head and the shrill, piercing whinny burst forth and filled the rafters with sound.

Billy D. Williams whipped around, pulled up his suspenders, screamed, and dove into the stall marked on the cross posts as "Bell's Star." He reached over the door and pushed the latch down, threw himself in the farthest corner, and laid shaking, tears of fright coursing the deep creases in his cheeks.

Star of the Night clattered into the stable, head up, sniffing the sweat smell of fear that hung in the air near his stall. He went into his sleeping space, assured himself no one lingered there, backed out, and nervously raced up and down. Hooves like thunder. Voice of doom. Once he appeared to go to the outside door as if to leave but then he turned back, came along to "Belle's Star" stall and lifted his tail, and dropped a huge steaming pile in front of the latched door, and cantered daintily into his own space. His huge head dropped forward, and he slept.

Nicole watched the whole scene in amazement. Williams could hide, but he couldn't run. The black horse knew where the intruder was hidden and left his calling card. She tried to go back over what had happened. Before Williams arrived, there had been no sound of a vehicle of any kind, so he must have walked here. He also knew about the pitchfork, so he'd been in the stables before. The motel had to be somewhere nearby. That's how Carlo knew about the stable. And Williams had told her that Carlo's car, the blue Tempo, was still in front of his room. It's a decoy, she surmised, Carlo is not there. He has made his getaway in my rental jeep. If only I could get to the motel, I could hotwire the Tempo and find my way to Alexandria, but first I've got to break out of these chains.

Her ankle was on fire from the pressure of her boot, and she took the sharp tine of the hay hook, stuck it into the edge where the sole met the vamp, and sawed back and forth until a deep split appeared, releasing her swollen toes. Her foot appeared blue, but it still had mobility. Although she could now feel the sudden cold air on her toes, she worked the split wider, freeing her instep, which gave her some relief. Tomorrow she would attack the rings on the wall. It had to be soon. She felt weaker every day.

About 2:00 a.m., Nicole heard a slight squeaking sound as the door to the Bell's Star stall pushed furtively aside. She rose up and watched as Billy D. Williams crawled out and into the pile of manure that Star of Night left behind.

"Aaaah," the old man groaned. "Shit! Shit! Shit!" He struggled to his feet and waving his hands as if to throw them from his body, ran as fast as he could from the barn into the cold, moonlit night.

Star of the Night stomped his feet and whistled through his nose. Nicole lay laughing in her hay bed between the bales. The snake in the rafters moved to the circle of light under the window. And they slept.

At dawn, the big black horse backed out of his stall and made his way toward the door. Again, his eye sought Nicole's bags hanging on the wall, and this time he gauzed the distance behind the cultivator. He kicked it with his front hooves and the aging metal yielded, dropping rusty parts into the dust, and opening about a twelve-inch space closer to the wall. This was all he needed. He lifted his long nose and caught the straps of Nicole's shoulder bag in his teeth. He reared up, and it lifted easily from the hook.

"Come on, boy, bring me the bag!" Nicole called frantically. "Please..."

Dragging the bag by its long straps, Star of the Night, delirious with his triumph, reared several times, and raced from the stable with his treasure.

She could hear the sound of his big hooves fade away. Of course, he wouldn't come to her. He wasn't a dog! Now there was a new dilemma. Without her nail kit, she couldn't remove the locks even if she pulled the chains from the wall. That crazy horse had taken everything with him.

She dipped her fingers in the brass bucket and wet her lips and throat, then drank a handful of water, realizing that her fingers were touching bottom.

"Mother Mary," she prayed. "Send rain."

It was getting hard for her to stand, but the effort had to be made, to pry those rings loose while she still had the strength. With the hay hook in her hand, Nicole forced the heavy tool under the screw that held the ring to the wall. The wood splintered behind the ring. The muscles in her upper arms shook, but she continued the pressure until the wall, screeching in protest, reluctantly spit out the ring. The chain attached to her wrist fell to the ground.

"Excuse me, miss," said a man's voice from the doorway. "I'm Ben. Ben McEnery. If you're looking for your pocket book my horse brought it home."

"Ben?" Nicole repeated faintly and sank down on the hay bales, still holding the hook. Mother Mary, she prayed silently, please don't let Ben be drunk, lecherous, or crazy. I can't bear it.

The man came closer, bent forward, and exclaimed when he saw the chains, "Who did this to you?"

"I don't know. A stranger."

He turned immediately and ran back outside. In seconds, he came back with a flat rock and a hammer.

"Put your arm here on this rock. I promise I won't hurt you," he directed. He put her hand on the rock, and to protect her, placed his own hand over hers.

The hammer came down twice on the lock, and it jerked open. Her arm was free. The relief was so great that she felt hot tears surge to her eyes. He awkwardly took her torn boot and tenderly lay her swollen foot on the rock. The hammer fell, and the lock broke into two pieces. This time Nicole screamed out and clung onto the burly farmer who hovered over her, tossing the chains aside. He put his arms around her and rocked her side to side.

"You'll be alright. You're free now," Ben assured her, rubbing her shoulders.

He smelled like a warm kitchen. Coffee and bacon odors carried in his wool jacket. He must have just come from breakfast at a farmhouse nearby.

I could eat his coat, mused Nicole, burrowing her face in his chest; I am so hungry. How long had it been since supper with Carlo at the dine and dance?

"Let me carry you to the truck," he insisted, and lifting her as easily as a hay bale, he hurried through the stable.

"My things—" Nicole said. "If I leave them, the man from the motel will come back and may steal them."

"He was in here again?" Ben said gruffly, nimbly sidestepping the pile of manure lay there by Star of the Night. "Hmmmm, gotta get one of the boys down here to muck that out! I'll put you in and come back for your other bag. They house some homeless men down there, and they prowl around to find stuff they can sell for cigarette money." He set her into the passenger side of the pickup and went back inside the stable.

Nicole glanced around breathing in the fresh air and seeing for the first time in the distance, by the highway, the back of the long white building—the Bide-A-Wee Motel. About hundred yards from the stable was the foundation of a burned farmhouse. All that remained were charred uprights and two freestanding brick chimneys.

The sun was shining. It seemed too bright after the dark end of the stable, and she covered her eyes.

Ben McEnery climbed into the driver's side of the truck and held up something small, a cylinder of black plastic.

"Is this yours? Sorry I stepped on it."

"What is it?"

"A little flashlight." He flipped the on/off button. It flickered erratically.

"No, I had no light."

As they sped along the dirt road, Ben said, "I better call the sheriff, and you can tell him how you got into such a mess. Maybe the guy who brought you dropped this flashlight."

Carlo, Nicole thought. She could not involve Carlo. Agents took care of their own.

"I do not wish the sheriff," Nicole said. "I will call my husband and he—"

Ben was glancing at her suspiciously and he broke in, "Your husband did this to you, is that it?"

"No! No!" she protested. "My husband would never do such a thing! But he will know what to do about this."

"Then he knows the guy who did this to you?"

Nicole thought quickly. Maman had always been convinced that Major Whitt was a policeman from his authoritative tone of voice.

"He is a policeman, my husband. I must tell him everything, no?"

McEnery seemed to mull this over, and they drove along in silence until they turned into the graveled drive leading to a sprawling gray frame house. The house appeared new, as did two out buildings and a dog run.

"Here's home. I'm going to get my wife, Belle, to rustle you up something to eat, get you cleaned up, and then you're going to tell me the whole truth about how you ended up in my stable."

"Of course," Nicole agreed, her fertile imagination already fast at work. "Why did your horse take my shoulder bag?"

Ben laughed. "It's black leather and has a strap. He thought it was his nose bag, and he wanted it back."

Nicole laughed. "He is a beautiful animal."

"He likes women. Don't care for men. He just tolerates me because I feed him. He was born in that stable, and he still goes back there to bed down."

"He saved me. My ankle was in very much pain. Not so my arm because the chain was over my coat sleeve. Mon Dieu! I am so tired!"

"Hello, I'm Belle," came a voice from outside the truck. A tall, thin woman, wearing a wool cap over a long light brown ponytail, was smiling through the truck window. "Come on in the house. We looked in your wallet and saw your name on the credit cards, Nicole Lawrence, and then Ben said, Night brought this home, I bet somebody is in his stable, maybe somebody hurt."

Ben came around, and although Nicole protested that she could walk, he picked her up and carried her into a bright, yellow kitchen. Belle followed, carrying Nicole's tote bag.

All Nicole could think of was the notepad containing Carlo's account of the night on the roof of Randolph College. It was in the concealed compartment in the bottom of her shoulder bag, the place that usually held her gun. Had they rummaged through everything?

"I'll bet you're hungry. Let me fix you up some eggs and sausages," insisted Belle. She snatched off her cap and turned to the stove.

"Please, nothing fried," begged Nicole, her empty stomach suddenly churning at the thought of food. A plate of biscuits sat on the table. "Do you have tea?"

"Why, yes, honey! A nice cup of tea! Those biscuits were just baked two hours ago. They'll go down real easy," agreed Belle, busying herself with good china and yellow cloth napkins.

Ben settled himself on the other side of the table, observing Nicole. "This policeman husband of yours. How do I reach him?"

Nicole tentatively nibbled a biscuit and recited the number of the office in Alexandria. "Ask for Major Whitt."

Ben wrote the number on a paper napkin but made no motion toward the telephone. "His name different from yours?"

"I kept my own name," Nicole informed him. She reached eagerly for the steaming cup and added two sugars. She inhaled the vapor fragrant with orange and cinnamon, and smiled her thanks at Belle, who pushed the plate of biscuits closer.

"He must be on pins and needles, your being gone like that," sighed Belle. "Ben would be calling the doggone FBI."

Nicole nodded. "Except he didn't know. I went to Washington to do some shopping, and major drove me up, but he had to go back to work, so I rented a car. He knew that I was going to visit an old friend at Randolph College for a couple of days."

"That's just a whoop and a holler down the highway," put in Belle. "Rich kids."

"I never got there." Nicole rubbed her forehead wearily, pacing her story carefully, aware that Ben was watching every move.

"I missed the entrance to the college. I have a problem with directions, and I kept on going until I got to a sort of restaurant. It was very dark when I pulled into the parking lot."

"What's the name of the restaurant?" asked Ben. "I know most places around here."

Nicole paused. "I never saw a name, just a sign that said dine and dance but on one letter—the light was out—a man came out and saw me looking at a map in the light from the dash and asked if I needed help. He pushed his way into the jeep—my rental car—and his arm went around my throat. I felt something cut into my neck, like maybe a big ring on his finger, and I lost consciousness—"

"Ben! Ben! That's enough," objected Belle, who placed her hand over Nicole's. "If it's painful, you don't need to go on."

"I believe you," said Ben. "I know that dump. Never been in it, but I've driven past it plenty. Rough characters hang out around there. And you're right, the E is missing—the light is missing on the sign. I'll just make that call now."

He got up and walked out to the hall. They could hear him dialing the telephone.

"Did he rope you?" whispered Belle.

"No. He just chained me in the stable and ran when the big horse came."

"Star of the Night. He's my horse. I'm the only one can ride him."

"I think he was afraid of the horse."

"Yes! Night doesn't like men."

Ben returned to the kitchen. "Major Whitt is not there, but I spoke to a Beauregard Jackson and gave him directions. He's on his way. Hope I did the right thing."

"Don't think she heard you, Ben. She's plumb wore out, poor thing," said Belle softly. "Can you carry her to the couch?"

Nicole had fallen asleep, a half-eaten biscuit in her hand. Ben carried her into the living room and laid her gently on the couch. Belle removed Nicole's boots and gasped at the swollen foot and ankle.

"I'll fix an ice bag for that."

"I'll do that," offered Ben. "You stay here in case she wakes up." He went into the bathroom closet and found the ice bag and an old soft towel. In the kitchen, he emptied the ice tray. As he leaned against the sink, he was aware of something in his pocket, and pulled out the little flashlight he had found in the stable. He shrugged and threw it into—the everything drawer by the sink.

Belle and Ben kept watch from the window as Nicole slept, and two hours later, a large black unmarked Buick swept up the driveway. A powerfully built black man stepped from the car, unbuttoned his suit coat, and scanned the area around the house and out buildings before approaching the porch.

Ben came outside. "I'm Ben McEnery."

"Beau Jackson." He extended his hand and Ben glimpsed the holster strap across his chest. "I understand you have something for me?"

Chapter Seventeen

Carlo speaks

For the first thirty miles, the ride back to Alexandria was one of stony silence inside the black Buick. Beau Jackson seemed both angry and relieved at seeing Nicole alive, and Nicole kept tending to drop off into five-minute naps to make up for the nights deep in the hay bales. It was only when she pulled a crumbling biscuit from her pocket and began to chew hungrily that Jackson pulled into the parking lot of an exclusive little café, Chez Revier.

"You want lunch, girl?"

"I'm not going in there," protested Nicole. "I am five days dirty. My hair itches, and I am wearing Belle's boudoir slippers, two sizes too big."

"You've got hay in your head," he observed.

"McDonalds," she suggested.

"You keep those folks in business."

"Drive through. Cheeseburger and soda."

"I've seen a few expense records. You eat as cheap as Willie Lewis. I thought I'd please you with that Frenchy place. You better take advantage of me being nice because major is going to boil your hide for this trick, and he's due in from Germany today with that new recruit. You got another job in mind? Major just might cut you loose altogether."

"What trick are you speaking of?"

"Switching cars with Carlo."

"He stole the jeep!"

"We had a tracer on his ride, the Tempo. We had one in a button of his plaid jacket and one in a penlight on his key chain. He took the jeep and returned it to the rental agency at the airport. We had to play repro-man and pick up the Tempo. The jacket was in the dumpster behind the motel, and only God knows where that penlight went . . ." Jackson informed her angrily, pounding the steering wheel for emphasis, as he drove back out onto the highway.

God and me, thought Nicole, and Ben McEnery, but I will not involve those kind people and that wonderful black horse that thought my shoulder bag was his feedbag. She regarded the bag. It was dusty and had large teeth marks both back and front, where Star of the Night had carried it in his mouth, making a deep, distinctive embossed pattern. She ran her hand down into the bottom of the bag and confirmed that the sheaf of papers that Carlo had written was safely inside.

"Where is Carlo now?" Nicole asked.

"Major had an envelope, with Carlo's name one it, with a one-way ticket to Ecuador, and some cash. Carlo picked it up from Derek the day Randolph College let him go. We haven't seen him since, but he cashed the plane ticket!" Jackson peered out of the car window. "I can't find McDee's around here. How about KFC?"

When they reached the motel office in Alexandria, Nicole went through to the farthest room of the suite.

"Don't bother me," she said. "I am going to take a long bath. Maybe two hours, no?"

"Wash your head or learn to sing, "We're Off to See the Wizard." You look like the scarecrow," Jackson suggested gruffly, disengaging a piece of hay from her collar and dropping her tote bag in the bedroom.

* * *

Major Whitt and the new recruit arrived at the motel, about ten o'clock. The recruit looked about nervously and ran his hand over the blond fuzz that barely covered his head. He was in his late twenties, tall and deceptively slim. Behind his wary blue gaze, he appeared furtive, and terrified, and perhaps he was, thought Beau, wondering how Gazar, now retired, Hammer, and Whitt found these people, strong-willed, passionate, and flawed. They all had a story.

Whitt did not introduce the recruit. No need. The German was on probation. He could disappear as quickly as he arrived or stay and save your life in the months to come.

"Where is she?" Whitt asked.

"Front," Beau nodded toward the hall.

The recruit jumped to attention and started to follow Whitt down the hall.

"You stay!" barked Whitt, pointing to the chair. "Can you find him a beer? He likes beer. Just one. I need to wean him."

"I have wine, and I have Sprite."

"Wine is for Frenchies and Italianos," snorted the recruit in perfect English.

"Sprite then," decided Beau as Whitt strode down the hall, "and better watch your mouth. We got one of those Frenchies under cover," he paused and laughed at his little joke, "and she's dangerous when she gets angry."

"I fear no one. My grandfather was SS."

"Let's keep that our secret," growled Beau. "You're in America now." He went into the kitchen, popped the tops on two cans of Sprite, and sat one in front of the recruit.

Whitt opened the door to the front bedroom, saw Nicole asleep on top of the bedspread, went in and closed the door behind him. Even from here, he could smell the sweetness of bath salts, and her dark curls were still damp from a shampoo. She wore a red Mickey Mouse sleep shirt, there was a tantalizing glimpse of white lace panties, and on her feet . . . Whitt moved closer. He felt a hot surge of desire that made his hands sweat, and he gazed down at her until he couldn't stand it anymore. He had never thought he would feel like this again. The bruises on her ankle made him wince and the deep circle, like a bracelet on her arm, brought a groan to his throat. He backed out of the room and closed the door.

"She sleeping?" asked Beau, crushing the empty Sprite can in one massive fist.

"Yes. You will be here all night?"

"Uh huh."

Whitt beckoned to the German recruit, and they headed for the outside door. At the last moment, Whitt turned and asked, "What are those big things on her feet?"

Beau chuckled. "Those are bood-wah slippers, Major, bood-wah!"

Whitt said, "See you first thing in the morning, eight o'clock. Holland will be here?"

"Derek, yes. He had off today to supervise some painting at his new place, but he'll be here tomorrow."

"Goodnight."

* * *

At eight sharp, the major arrived alone at the office, and with a barely civil "Good Morning" to Derek, and Nicole, motioned Beau into the first bedroom for a private briefing on what had expired while he was out of the country. He listened carefully while Beau told him of Nicole coming to the States to confront Carlo and being chained in the stable until discovered by Ben McEnery.

"She operated on her own after I had suggested a similar plan, with her wearing a wire, and being covered at all times—instead, she did it her way and got caught big time! I can't have it," stated Whitt. He rose from his chair and strode around the room.

"We've had agents go off before for physical," Jackson hesitated, "or psychological, reasons. They had to be terminated, one way or another. I'm positive Nicole took out another agent down in Florida, but he's still listed, unofficially, as missing."

Whitt sank down at the desk and put his head on his hands. "What do I do, Beau?"

"Well, if it were anyone but Nicole, I'd say cut her loose, return her to Paris. An agent who doesn't follow orders, doesn't play the game as a team, is a wild card. But we're talking Nicole Laurent here."

"It's killing me, Beau."

"Let's sit on it for the present. She has had Derek run off copies of Carlo's statement on the Ducharme case. We should see what he has to say."

"He chained her up and left her! Why? So he could leave the country? No! At least, he didn't go to Ecuador. And he was smart enough to use her rental car. He bypassed all tracers."

Jackson laughed. "Sounds exactly like someone we could use in our business."

"Yes," said Whitt, cracking a wry smile.

They looked at each other and got up to leave the room. Whitt paused at the door and turned around. "You know I'm dead in love with her, don't you?"

"Heard it on the grapevine, man, seen it on your face. Let's go."

There were three copies at the conference table. Nicole sat at the counter bar that divided the kitchen area. A glass of milk sat before her as she reread the original script on the notepad, as written by Carlo. randolph college, agent carlo arana Subject: jean ducharme, daughter of former ambassador eugenie ducharme I was sent by major kelvin whitt to the college and was hired as a yard worker, where i could observe ducharme. prior to my employment, a student, sara wells, had jumped or was pushed from the roof of the art bldg. i observed a reflection from the roof on several occasions and told agent laurent someone was on the roof. agent laurent expedited an entry. on the first occasion we waited for several hours and no one came at that time. it was very cold. on the second occasion we found a camera on a tripod pointing directly to the room of the subject and we had located the stalker. i made a noise and drew attention. security guard wilfred earle pulled his weapon. i pulled my weapon but before earle could fire agent laurent broke his wrist with a blow from her weapon. he raised his weapon. agent laurent opened a large wound on sgt. wilfred earle's head. he fell hard. laurent took a pulse. he lived about three minutes after that. i tried to write and tell but laurent said to run and she did run. sgt. wilfred earle was dead. when police came they would look for his killer. i was afraid to be caught carrying him out of the building. i threw him off the roof. i threw the camera and tripod. footsteps of the struggle was in the snow. i opened the sprinkler valve to flood the roof and ran. no one was in the courtyard. i ran. i carried sgt. wilfred earle and things down the jogging path and beat a hole in the pond ice and pushed him in the water. if he didn't die we could walk when my job was up but the blow killed him. I hope agent laurent is not in trouble. I, agent carlo arana, swear this to be a true account. i had nothing to do with any other deaths at randolph college. now, i go away.

They all sat silently, staring at the notes before them.

"We could have handled it," said Jackson. "He acted on impulse instead of asking for help. And this business with Nicole—was totally—what was he thinking?"

"Can't be trusted again," echoed Whitt, angrily. "Completely irrational."

Oddly enough, Nicole came to Carlo's defense. "He couldn't run to the telephone and get a crew out there before the body was discovered—Carlo doesn't talk. He tried to write a note. I brushed it off. I am as much at fault as he is!"

"How can you take up for him after what he did to you? You could have died out there in that stable!" Shouted Whitt.

"I was nearly loose when Ben came," she answered, not mentioning that she had been that last day so weak from hunger and lack of sleep that she was harboring the same thoughts. She reached down and pulled up her white socks and Whitt noticed that she wore only one track shoe, none on the left foot.

"Did you see a doctor about that ankle?" he asked.

"I don't need a doctor. It is only a few bruises, no?' she shrugged. "Tomorrow I put on my other shoe. What do we do about Carlo? He ran because he was afraid if he stayed he would get the blame."

"Earle killed the Wells girl. We know that now. Her blood and artist's paint were found in the crevices between the laces and tongues of his shoes. The weather changed, and the guards began to wear their winter uniforms, which meant a heavier uniform shoe with a thick, patterned rubber sole. He threw the other shoes in the back of his closet," stated Jackson.

"And Simon? What of Simon?" asked Nicole.

"That case is still working."

Nicole thought of Simon, his boyish uplifted face in the light of the courtyard, gazing at Jean Ducharme's window, unaware he was being watched from the roof. Her mind wandered to thoughts of Mimi, and she felt a terrible sadness for those who had gone before; one old and one so young. Death had no respect for age.

Whitt went over to his desk, which was a rigidly neat area at one end of the conference table. He shuffled through a few pieces of mail that had arrived while he was in Germany. He picked up one square envelope, stared at it, then went back to look at the copy of Carlo's "confession."

"When did this come in?" he demanded, noting the printed stamp, passed.

"Early in the week," ventured Derek. "It was hand-printed and had no return address. It went to the tech center for scanning and came back yesterday."

Whitt tore it open. A single, white sheet of paper, and a pink note fell out onto the table. He unfolded the white sheet to reveal a map.

"Carlo sent the exact location of the McEnery stable, the road to it, the distance from the motel—it's all here. If I had been here, when this letter arrived, we could have had Nicole out and safe three or four days ago! Damn it to hell!" Whitt turned on Derek, whose face was ashen. "Didn't you recognize Carlo's printing? Why did you send it to tech?"

"I was following procedure. It had no identification. We look for plastiques! This is a dangerous business!"

"He was doing his job, Major," Nicole broke in quickly. "What does the note say?"

Whitt looked down at the pink paper. "It says the keys to the Tempo are taped to the underside of the third drawer on the left—if this is so, why didn't the sensor pick up the signal from the penlight on the key chain when we went to the motel?"

They remained silent, mulling this mystery over for several minutes.

"Perhaps, it was somehow broken, or the battery went dead," suggested Jackson.

"Maybe a big, black horse stepped on it," Nicole muttered and broke into unexplained laughter.

"Or it was swallowed by a mouse who ran away!" added Derek, hoping to liven the tension and take the attention away from himself.

"I saw a squirrel on the highway the other night with this tiny—" began Jackson getting into the act. He was mumbling, "Who stole my cashews?"

"Enough! Beau, you want to take a run out to the Bide-A-Wee and check that room?"

Jackson rose. "If we'd had that letter, we wouldn't have had to repro that Tempo. I'm on my way." As he passed Nicole he said, "Take it easy, girl, and stay off that foot."

As Beau Jackson plodded heavily down the metal steps to the parking lot, Whitt turned gruffly to Derek. "The party is over. Shred these documents except for the original and put that in the safe." He turned to Nicole. "You want to file a report on your little adventure?"

"I was on my own time," she answered.

"You won't get paid."

"I know that."

"As long as you know that—"

"That is not fair," Derek argued. "Carlo told her what happened, so we could close the Ducharme case."

"You stay out of this," said Whitt.

"Leave him alone!" snapped Nicole.

Hastily, Derek gathered the copies and ran them through the shredder.

"I'm putting the German into the front room. See that the maid cleans. He'll be here this afternoon about three."

"This is my room," objected Nicole.

Whitt put on his jacket, gathered his briefcase and prepared to leave. "You'll stay out at the safe house."

"I will stay here!"

"You want to see Runner, don't you?"

"Yes," she admitted. "He is really my dog. He loves me better, no?"

"I have to admit that, but he's getting very fond of Gregor, who feeds him. Dogs like the ones who feed them," Whitt informed her casually as he went out the door. He clattered down the steps.

They went to the window and watched his tall figure cross the parking lot and settle behind the wheel of the jeep.

"He is a puppet master," observed Derek soberly. "He pulls your strings. Is it such a wonderful dog?"

"I'm afraid he has my heart," Nicole admitted, turning away from the window.

"You love him then, the dog?"

"Yes."

"The dog," Derek repeated. "Quel Veinard?"

Nicole laughed, and said nothing. She went to the front bedroom and began to pack her things.

When she returned to the conference room, Derek was busy at the end of the conference table, but he stopped his work and drew out a slip of paper from the pocket of his jacket.

"This is the last schedule that I have for Nicolas Lee. He will be in Atlantic City—well, he's there now actually—tomorrow is the last day."

"I can fly!" she interrupted.

"I have called, but they can only offer standby. You could be there for hours."

"Major has a plane. Perhaps?"

"I wouldn't involve major. There is one more show north of Myrtle Beach, SC, and Nicolas will be there, a place called Cherry Grove for two days, Friday and Saturday. How's your foot?"

"Don't worry."

"I do worry, Nicole. If you want to go to this place, I will take you. My car is very comfortable, and I will do all the driving," Derek offered.

"You are my dearest, dearest friend in the world." Nicole kissed his cheek.

"And that will have to be enough," sighed Derek. He pocketed Nicolas Lee's schedule and turned back to his work, his large handsome head bowed over the desk, avoiding her eyes.

* * *

At ten of three, Whitt returned to the Alexandria office and left the sulky, young German, who brushed past Derek, almost knocking him over, in his haste to take his heavy, canvas sack to the front bedroom.

"Don't go out," ordered Whitt. "Eat here, or order in." He turned to Derek. "See he stays in. He has a smart mouth and could get in trouble."

"If he tries to leave," grumbled Derek, brushing off his jacket. "Can I shoot him?"

Whitt seemed to think this over although Derek was obviously joking. "Just once. The neighbors may complain. Nicole, if you're ready to leave?"

The drive to the safe house harbored a tense silence. Whitt stopped at a grocery store and came out with a cart loaded with bulging plastic bags. Nicole, who had opted to stay in the jeep, noticed one bag loaded with Skippy dog food. At least, Runner was being well fed.

"You don't have to scream at me in front of the others," Nicole said, once they were on the way. "I came on my own. You don't need to pay me."

"I'm not going to pay you for acting like an idiot and getting yourself chained up."

"An idiot!"

"Yes. You could have died out there. Nobody knew where you were but Carlo."

"Billy D. Williams knew. He would have gotten drunk and told somebody."

"Who?" Whitt gave her an incongruous look.

"A homeless man at the Bide-A-Wee Motel," stated Nicole. "Or perhaps Carlo would have come back."

"Carlo lied to you in the confession."

"He did not!"

"Yes, he did. There was water in Wilfred Earle's lungs, from the pond. Your blow with the gun didn't kill him. The toss off the roof didn't kill him. The autopsy proved he drowned."

Nicole sank back against the seat and tried to comprehend what Whitt had just told her. It would explain why Carlo had confined her until he could get away. If only he had left Earle on the roof for college security, or the local police to find! Jean Ducharme was safe. Their assignment was done. As if he were reading her thoughts, Whitt said, "Carlo was at Randolph before you came. Maybe he knew something about Sara Well's death and saw the opportunity to even the score." He gave a deep sigh. "Too bad. If he turns up, we'll never use him again, but it's my belief, even with his unusual appearance, he's managed to leave the country, possibly through Mexico, who knows?"

"Did you remember the wine?" Nicole asked, glancing over her shoulder at the grocery bags.

"Had he altered his appearance?" Whitt continued. "He's very distinctive."

"New clothes. What are we having for dinner?"

"Chicken. It's a roasted chicken, fully cooked. What kind of clothes?"

"White wine then. Like sailor's wear. A pea jacket, dark blue."

"And potato salad. French bread. Did he have a hat or cap?"

"A new cap. Did you buy a dessert?"

"Ice cream."

"Then hurry! It will melt. The cap was also dark blue, like some sailor's in winter. In shape, perhaps like a Greek cap, no?'

"I hope you like peach."

When they reached the gates, Gregor and Runner were waiting just inside, the dog jumping and racing around with excitement, his beautiful white coat in motion. Gregor tipped his cap, and stared hard at Nicole, but his features, blunt, square, and with the rough texture of a person who has lived most of his life outdoors, showed no emotion.

The watchman and dog followed the jeep around to the back door. Nicole got out and extended her hand. He simply nodded.

"I am Nicole." She withdrew her hand.

"Me, I am Gregor. I stay back here." He nodded behind him at the out buildings.

"Come for dinner. I am told it is chicken, and peach ice cream," she offered, "and perhaps, wine."

"I have my own supper."

"Another time, then."

Gregor walked away. Runner darted from one to the other and then stood trembling with indecision. Which person should he follow? The grocery bags won out, and he followed Whitt into the kitchen, thrusting his nose into the enticing smell of bread and doughnuts.

"I asked Gregor to join us for dinner," she relayed to Whitt as she dragged two loaded plastic bags into the kitchen. "But he declined. He is another odd one, no?"

"Can you put some of this stuff in the refrigerator?" he suggested, then added, "I'd rather we have this time alone."

"Me too, if you won't be angry."

"I'm not angry. I was scared," he said.

Nicole picked up a massive package of hamburger and stuck it in the freezer compartment. Then she added the packages of sausage and two pounds of bacon.

"You never buy in quantity, do you?" Whitt asked as he hauled it all back out. "Sausages and bacon in the meat keeper—this plastic thing—and split that ground beef in four—," he handed her a roll of Saran Wrap, "packs."

She laughed. "Maman shops every day. Fresh everything in her little string bag."

He ran his hand through the tangle of dark curls at the nape of her neck, bared a spot, and covered it with kisses. His arms went around her waist, and he held her close as she deftly tore off squares of plastic and plopped the red meat neatly in four exact piles.

"Does this suit your majesty?" she asked, whipping the plastic tightly together.

"You could throw it on the roof for all I care," he murmured in her ear. "Lets go to bed. God, I've missed you much!"

"The ice cream, for the freezer, no?"

"For the freezer, yes. Come on, Nicole."

"We eat first," she insisted. "Let's make a picnic. Make a fire in the library. Put a blanket on the floor and pour the wine."

"God, you're bossy!"

"Jump to it, Major. It'll be fun."

"We can eat fast. Paper plates. We can throw them in the fire and hit the hay."

"Don't say hay to me."

"I forgot. I guess you've had enough hay to last a lifetime. I'll replace that.

"Never mind. Take the chicken, the bread, the potato salad, the chips . . ." She looked through the drawers in the kitchen counter for a tablecloth, but there was nothing. On an upper shelf were two dusty red candles in old bronze candlesticks. She added them to the food on a large silver tray.

Whitt poured the wine. Their glasses touched. He hesitated, unsure what to say.

"To us," Nicole said.

"I'll drink to that. Let's get married."

"Let's eat first."

"It's always something!" he sighed. He finished his wine, picked up the tray, and made his way down the hall to the library.

Nicole made coffee and by the time she followed with the china and silver, the fire had caught the logs and was crackling briskly. One lamp was lit on the library table under the window, and she placed the red candles on each end of the mantelpiece.

Whitt was arranging the food on the blanket. He poured more wine. "This was a great idea. Want some music?" He reached over to an old console and turned on the classic music station. "Claire de Lune" murmured softly in the background, its high notes wafting to the tall ceiling of the old house.

They ate leisurely, tossing the chicken bones into the blazing fire, and listening to the hiss as the flames consumed bits of fat. From the radio came the theme from "Phantom of the Opera."

"Heard Michael Crawford sing that," Whitt said. "He was the perfect phantom."

"I saw Claude Rains."

"You did not!"

"Maman, Mimi, and I went to all the old movies, and Claude Rains was the phantom. He scared me so much that I could hardly tap dance."

Whitt burst into laughter and poured the last of the wine. "You tap danced in the movies?"

"After the movies. I won money for Maman in the talent contest. I am so sleepy."

"No ice cream?"

"Save for tomorrow. Is good, no?"

"Is good, yes." He piled the dishes on the tray and pushed it aside. He shook the crumbs into the fire and spread the blanket on the rug.

Nicole pulled the small throw pillows from the sofa and tossed them on the blanket. She curled up facing the fireplace and in a moment, Whitt dropped to his knees beside her. He studied the play of light on her face until she turned to look up at him.

"Nicole, I can't live without you in my life. Just tell me what you want. I'll move to Paris. I can head the Paris office, or give up this crazy business all together. Please—give me something—some hope—something!"

She turned over and held up her arms. He lay down beside her and rocked her body close to his. Their mouths touched, at first softly and then in a frenzy of wanting, the urgency of desire. He tugged at her clothes, but she pushed him aside.

"Let me do it," she murmured. She stood up and slowly, as if performing a ballet just for one, she removed her jeans and underpants, kicked off her heavy socks—one landed on his shoulder and he put it to his mouth—he caught the other sock and put the two of them into his shirt pocket. At last, she removed her fuzzy yellow sweater and bra and stood nude in the firelight, turning slowly in a pirouette.

"Monsieur, shall we dance?"

Whitt reached up and grasped her waist, pulling her down on the blanket, covering her face with wet kisses. She unbuttoned his shirt and bit him lightly on his neck.

* * *

Outside the window, beyond the dim glow of the lamp on the console, Gregor stood silently watching. His rugged face betrayed nothing, but he was sweating profusely under his wool jacket, and beads of sweat formed on his forehead under his heavy cap. He had seen no woman in a very long time, and this one was, at once, like a she-devil and an angel, a temptress unlike anything in his experience.

He could see their bare legs and feet beyond the sofa, but the movement of the shadows cast on the library wall silhouetted an orgy in pantomime. The woman lifted herself over the man and, as if stretching, raised her arms above her head—he rose up, enveloped her, and drew her down—the music played—there were eerie flutes and pulsing drums—the rise and fall of the shadow figures continued, a kaleidoscope of reds and golds twirling on the wall behind them. The waning fire crackled into hot, dying embers. Finally, the blanket lifted, the two forms melted into one. All motion ceased. The players had fallen asleep, and the room grew dark.

It had begun to rain. Gregor held out his hand and caught the cold drops in his palm. He took off his cap and wiped his face with the water, turned away from the window, and made his way across to his own lodgings. He stopped and gazed up at the place he called home. There was no light in the window. No woman waited for him. He pulled his cap low against the rain and fumbled for his key.

* * *

A red sun pushed another day onto the horizon. Far away in the front hall of the house, a clock tolled 5:00 a.m. Nicole woke and gently moved one arm and leg from under Whitt. The fire was out, and the library had a damp chilliness that caused her bare skin to shiver. She adjusted the blanket over Whitt, kissed his shoulder, and gathered yesterday's clothes, crept into the hall, and down to the bath just off the master bedroom. By the time she showered and got into her jogging clothes, the winter sun was making an effort to bring about the new morning. Its feeble glow spread palely across the sky.

She hurried around to the front porch to find Runner awake and stretching his fine white feathery legs. She took off his chain, and he followed her to the fence. The grass was wet from a night shower and she hesitated. Could she trust the weak left ankle, or would she slip and fall?

Runner led the way, racing ahead, and coming back to her. Gingerly, she started out at a slow measured pace and made it down one side of the fence, then across the gate, and mailbox area, which reminded her she must write to Yvette. Her trot became a walk on the other side. The pain was very slight now, but still, she was conscious of it and this was her first run. Coming in toward the house, she saw Gregor watching her and the dog. As they approached, he stepped in front of them, obstructing the path to the kitchen door, and held up his hand.

"I wish to speak with you."

"Certainly," Nicole agreed, curious at the stern look on the old man's face.

"The major is a fine man. He gave me this job. You should go away."

"What? Why do you say this to me?" Nicole demanded. "You are angry, no?"

"Carlo said you were his lady friend."

"Carlo?" Nicole frowned. "He is nothing to me!"

"He had your picture. The hair was blond but it was you! And he has written your name over his bed, maybe one hundred times, upside down, like he lay in the bed and wrote on the wall. The German stayed there. He said to me, what name is this, old man? I pretended not to know."

Nicole stood silent, her mouth slightly parted. Finally, she shook her head. "I don't know where he got my picture. It's an old one and I am wearing a wig. I used to change my appearance because I didn't want to be recognized. I was a courier of valuable jewelry and coins."

Gregor seemed to think this over.

"Carlo—he's still out there somewhere. He did not go to Ecuador. You must be very careful. A man wants something from a beautiful woman like you; he will do crazy things."

"I know," Nicole said bitterly. She rubbed her arm where the chain had been. "If he should come here, or you see him, tell me at once."

"I will tell the major," Gregor grunted. With that pronouncement, he turned and walked away, leaving her standing near the kitchen door.

Nicole looked about the place. Beyond the fence were cleared areas of about fifty yards, and then the forest began. Anyone approaching on three sides would be seen. The main road ran parallel to the front-gated area.

"Good morning, beautiful! Come on in. I've got the coffee going," Whitt called from the kitchen door. His hair was wet and stuck up on his head. He wore an air force sweatshirt and baggy gray sweatpants.

"Your eyes are very blue and shining this morning," she teased. "Sleep well?"

"Get in here so I can kiss you."

"Okie dokie." She hopped into the kitchen.

He had some cereals arranged on the counter, the sugar bowl, and a gallon of milk nearby. The smell of coffee filled the air.

They had nearly finished breakfast when Whitt suddenly snapped his fingers. "I almost forgot. I've got a present for you—two, in fact. One was for Christmas actually. Be right back!"

He placed a pair of red furry bedroom slippers by her cup. Stuck in one slipper was a small festive package. "Now you can send those yellow jobs back to the nice lady with the horse—way too big, baby!"

The package contained Channel #5.

"You remembered my perfume!" she exclaimed, sniffing the square glass bottle. She pinched off the little black string that released the top and touched her ears.

"Lovely!" she breathed. "I feel beautiful!"

"Easy for you to say." He looked at her seriously. "About last night—"

"I have something for you too," she told him. "It's in my shoulder bag. I'll be back in just a second."

She returned with the package from Rene Laurent and watched him open it. "It's not expensive, just fourteen carats, but it will tell you what time it is. Remember how late you called me in Paris? I'd lie on my bed hoping the phone would ring before I fell asleep."

Whitt held the watch in his hand, examining the band and the two dial faces. "Two different times?"

"Yes. One is the time of the United States. Six hours later, it is France. You will always know the time where I am."

He put the watch on the table and walked to the window. She picked it up and thrust it back in the box.

"I'm ashamed!" she said sadly. "Rene told me it was a tourist thing. I will buy you a much better, I promise. A Rolex or—."

"It's not the watch, Nicole. I love you. I don't want you to be in another time zone. I want you in my time zone. People who love each other ought to be together!" He turned from the window, and she saw the anguish on his face. "Don't you feel something for me?"

"Yes."

"Then say it, Nicole, or I'll die."

"I love you, Major," she murmured softly.

"Say it again."

"I love you, Major!" she shouted, and burst out laughing.

"Then we don't need two dials, do we?"

"I'll take it back and get another."

"It's okay. I travel a lot and it might come in handy." Whitt took off the watch he was wearing and put on the new one. "Now, about last night—I think we should at least get engaged. What's your ring size?" He paced about the kitchen, stopped at the coffeepot, and refilled their cups. He stood there with a steaming cup in each hand and grinned. "Say it again? That love thing?"

"You're so silly."

"Kisses then. God, I feel, I feel happy!"

The telephone rang and since it was nearest to Nicole, she reached over and answered it. "Bon jour—I mean, good morning. Who is calling, please?"

"Who is this?" answered a woman's voice. "I must have the wrong number. I'm calling my son, Kelly Whitt."

"He is here. One moment!" Nicole handed the telephone over to Whitt.

He started to laugh. "Yes—I know it's early in the morning. Sorry, Mom, you shouldn't be asking that. She's a very special lady. I want you two to meet." There was a long silence. Was it question and answer time? He ran his hand through his hair. "Her name is Nicole Laurent. Is she pretty? Hell, no! She's got green hair, and a big wart on her nose, weighs two hundred easy, and you should see the tattoos—who's kidding?"

Nicole was laughing. She threw a handful of napkins at him. They flurried over the table like snow in the wind.

Runner, who had been sleeping in a corner, suddenly came awake and leaped to see if there was food in the napkins. Nicole gave him a handful of Frosted Cheerios under the table.

"Maybe we can buzz down in the Cessna this weekend. Andy will be there? Great! Love ya, Mom."

Nicole waved at him frantically, but he had already hung up the phone.

"You're going to love them," Whitt said. "And you can meet my son, the doctor-to-be."

"I can't go," stated Nicole flatly.

"Why not? The weather is going to be perfect for flying, and Dad was saying something about killing the fatted calf—a reference to the fact I haven't been home since Christmas. What do you mean you can't go?"

"I told Derek I would go somewhere with him. And I must do it."

"Derek," muttered Whitt. "Derek is a dwarf." He stated the fact as if she were unaware.

"Derek is a man. You say dwarf like there's something wrong with him."

"Well, the guy is four feet tall on his best days. Where are you going?"

"I don't have to tell you."

"Why not?"

"Because it is a personal thing, and I'm not sure how it will turn out. If it is a good thing, then I will share it."

Whitt swept the fallen napkins off the table. "I don't like it. He traveled with you at Christmas—"

"His parents live just outside Paris."

"Where are you going with him that I can't take you?" Whitt demanded.

Nicole stood up and began to clear the table. She carefully retrieved the scattered napkins and aligned them in a neat pile. She unplugged the coffeepot and began to wash the dishes. Whitt sat at the table and studied her movements at the sink—small, strong hands deftly rinsing the bowls and cups in water so hot it steamed the kitchen window. She flipped the damp dishcloth over the sink and turned so suddenly it caught him by surprise.

"Do you have a new job for me, Major? If not, I'll be leaving the States on Monday. I don't think this—what we have between us—is going to work. I am used to making decisions for myself and being independent. That is how I am."

"You said you loved me."

"And I do. I truly do," Nicole said. She crossed the room and sat in his lap, laying her head against his shoulder.

Whitt held her close enough to feel her heartbeat, and after a few minutes, he stroked her hair. "Agent Laurent," he murmured in her ear. "We have a problem."

"Yes," she answered. "Isn't that our job, solving problems?"

"This one is personal. I can't send you out anymore. I can't see you strap on that shoulder holster, walk out of the office, and into uncharted situations where you could be killed. You don't do that to someone you love."

"I saved Charlie Brown, that precious little boy, and brought him back to his parents. I took Madame Tanya home. Life was better for them because of me." She stood up and stretched.

He pulled her back and kissed her several times. "We'll find a way, because I can't think of the years ahead alone, with you always on my mind. I'd be the lonely old, crazy American wandering about the streets of Paris, looking for a lady with the most amazing dark eyes and the most perfect mouth in the world."

"I would sit at a little outside café, with a special bottle of wine, until the old crazy American found me."

"I love you, Nicole."

"Kiss me, Major."

"Say it, Nicole, say it!"

Nicole felt the big white furry head of the dog press itself under her hand. She fed him another handful of frosted Cheerios and scratched behind his ears.

"I love you—Runner."

"Tell me where you're going, Nicole," Whitt insisted. Half jokingly, he added "I guess I'll have to beat it out of Derek."

"Leave Derek alone!" she warned.

"I'm only kidding, but let me remind you what happened the last time you went off on your own—if it hadn't been for that horse—."

"Just leave it, Major. I'm not one of your military personnel. Give me room!"

She left the kitchen and went into the library where she ran her hand over the shelves, and she was surprised to discover one of her favorite books, *When I Grow Rich*, by Joan Fleming. When Whitt glanced in a little later Nicole was deep in the world of Nuri Bey, a Turkish scholar, his ancient friend, Madame Miasma, a retired member of a harem, and her eunuch servant, Hadje and she didn't glance up in his direction.

For the next hour, Nicole immersed herself in the exotic environs of Istanbul, one place she had never been, and for the moment, put aside her own problems. Finally, she marked her place with a leaf from a wilting plant on the console table by the window. As she tucked the leaf into the book, she happened to glance at the ground outside the window, and there in the still damp grass was the deep imprint of a man's heavy boots. Someone had stood there for a long time in that spot. Gregor? Why, Gregor? She felt a sudden chill, knowing that Carlo was still out there somewhere and he had once lived here. He may still have a key to the gate or found a way to get over the fences without setting off the alarm. She pondered sharing her suspicions with Whitt, but perhaps the night visitor was simply the curious old caretaker, Gregor, who had stood there watching, perhaps even watching them make love by the fire—a lonely old man.

I'll ask Beau Jackson for my weapons, Nicole decided. Better to be prepared. She went into the kitchen and shook the coffeepot. It was empty. She glanced through the window and saw that Whitt's jeep was gone from the back parking area, but the tempo stood in the shadow of the garage and the key hung on a peg near the kitchen door. She would find a shopping center and buy something really nice to wear on her trip with Derek, a pretty outfit with a skirt, something feminine—something daughterly . . . for Nicolas Lee . . . Nicholas Dana Lee Campion. Would she like him? More importantly, would he like her?

Chapter Eighteen

Nicholas Campion

Nicole stood in the hall of the safe house, waiting for Derek. He had called and told her Whitt had sent him on an errand, and he would be late picking her up. She glanced at her watch and realized that at eleven o'clock, they had already lost half a day's travel to South Carolina. Was the delaying errand deliberate? Whitt was against the trip from the beginning, not knowing where they were going, not wanting her to leave. He had reminded her that Carlo was still out there somewhere and when Whitt left the office, Nicole asked Beau Jackson for her gun. He gave it to her, with extra ammo, and without asking any questions.

And now, waiting for Derek, she looked in the hall mirror and checked the fit of her new jacket, a longer length brown wool—the salesperson had said, "Honey, you don't need a twelve," and Nicole had insisted, "Yes, I do," and noted how the jacket fell loosely over the shoulder holster. Everything was new, tapered pants, shiny loafers with tassels, and a shoulder bag in the same style as the one that bore the print of the big horse's teeth, but this one was natural leather instead of black. In the suit bag was another new outfit for tomorrow. When Nicole returned to Paris, Yvette would be thrilled to see her daughter in something other than jeans and boots, but tomorrow this sudden chic was for Nicolas. Nicole glanced in the mirror and pressed her dark spiky bangs into place. Was something missing? Hat! What kind of hat? She had no hat.

The light on the wall near the front door went on, indicating a vehicle at the gate, and Gregor came from behind the house, followed by Runner, and made his way slowly, moving in no particular line, toward the small blue car waiting just beyond the gate. Nicole could recognize Derek's cap as the car window lowered, gathered her things for the trip and hurried outside.

"It's for me, Gregor," she called and the gates swung open. At the sound of her voice, the large white dog raced to her side and followed her across the yard. "Tell major, I plan to return Sunday or Monday." She bent and kissed Runner's head. He tried to leap into the car, anxious to go along.

Gregor acknowledged her message with a curt nod and grabbed the dog's collar, wrestling him back inside the gates as Derek drove away.

"You are looking very fine," he said. "Did you toss the purse with the teeth marks?"

"No, I have it. You look fine yourself. That jacket and cap are cashmere, no?"

He nodded. "Sorry I am late. The major remembered the jeep needed to be inspected. I had to stay to answer a call from Germany."

"You know the way? It is many miles to South Carolina. America is such a big country. We may need to stop by night, no?"

"Highway 95 is very fast." Derek answered, glancing sideways. "I think we might make it in ten hours if there is not much traffic." He seemed flustered at the thought of staying the night at a motel. He glanced her way again. "What is that on your finger?"

"A ring. A sort of college ring," Nicole answered without further explanation.

Derek turned his attention back to the road. He had seen that ring on the major's finger ever since he came to work in the Alexandria office. He drove on in silence as Nicole turned toward the window and gazed out at the scenery.

So many trees in America, so much green, Derek thought in wonder. It was his first trip and he felt at once anxious that he drive well, and trepidation that he misunderstand the rules and do something embarrassing. The car itself, a small Ford Escort, was several years old, and as yet unfamiliar. It had been adjusted for his legs and seemed to be comfortable so far, but it would be a long drive. When he became more knowledgeable about the streets and highways in the United States, he would transfer funds from his Paris bank and buy something a little more upscale, Derek decided. Meanwhile, he wished he had been able to leave the office earlier in the morning.

Nicole placed one hand over the other, thereby cradling the oversized ring out of sight. The United States Air Force Academy, Colorado Springs. She gazed at the pine trees along the highway and thought about the major. They had watched the news, and gone sleepily to bed, but once they lay together they turned to each other—one kiss led to another—he tugged her Mickey Mouse nightshirt over her head and they made love slowly, sweetly, until they fell asleep wrapped in each other. About 3:00 a.m., Nicole woke feeling cold air on her back and shoulders, and struggled into her nightshirt. Major woke and raced naked down the hall to reset the temperature control for the furnace. When he came back, he took hold of her hand and put his ring on her finger. "First time in twenty years, it's been off my finger. Now, it's yours," he told her.

It rolled off and rattled across the floor.

"Damn, that was a short engagement!" he exclaimed and went to retrieve the heavy ring from under the dresser. He went into the bath and when he returned, he put the ring back on her finger, the underside wrapped with a giant wad of adhesive tape.

She had reached behind the bed and turned on the reading lamp. "Are you sure you want to give this up? It is important to you."

He kissed her. "Now, get some sleep."

—Derek broke into her thoughts. "Nicole, did you have lunch? It is after two o'clock."

"I'm starved," she admitted. "The sign up there says Petersburg, next right. Take the right lane."

"There has been a motorcycle one car behind for the last thirty miles," Derek stated. "I'll be glad to get away from that noise."

Nicole glanced into the rearview mirror. "I see it. I think it's a Harley. Big one."

Derek edged over and took the off ramp. The car directly behind continued down 95, but the motorcycle slightly dropped back, and then followed the Escort down to the road that led into the city, keeping several yards behind.

"Can't get rid of him that easy," said Derek. "See any place you like?"

"Over on the left—look, little picnic tables set up outside! You can go up and order at the window, and it's warm in the sun. Notice how much the temperature rises as you go south?"

"Not exactly the Champs Elysee, Nicole," Derek suggested. "They also serve inside. If it is windy, on the outside the cups and napkins blow away."

"It is an adventure, no?"

"With you, always," he sighed. "For you, I will eat outside!" He drove to the window and was surprised at the variety of different foods offered. "But there is not wine, Nicole. I know you enjoy your wine."

"I'll have coffee, the chicken salad plate, french fries, and the cherry pie," she ordered.

"The same for me but no fries," Derek added, speaking to the waitress in the window.

"You can share mine, no?" she offered, and then looked to the back of the line. Several cars waited, and she saw the motorcycle, idling, last in line. She could see the white helmet and shiny black jacket of the rider, his face hidden beneath a shield. "He is here. The Harley person."

Derek nodded and drove to a sunny spot at the edge of the parking lot. Other drivers dotted the area at nearby tables. A young boy at the nearest table had a small radio playing rock music as he downed a milkshake and large fries.

Nicole noticed that the rider on the motorcycle had picked up a bag of food from the window and rolled his machine to a table at the edge of a small wooded section. As he dismounted and walked the few steps to the table, Nicole paused, her plastic fork halfway to her mouth. The piece of cherry pie dropped to her plate unnoticed as she stared at the man's back. Something about his walk, something about his boots, appeared familiar, and she froze.

"Excuse me," Derek was saying. "I will go look for the restroom. You'll wait here?" He gathered their cups and plates and threw them in a nearby trashcan. As he strolled away across the parking lot, some people stared and a small boy ran to Derek and touched his coat, laughing to see a grown-up so small. Derek said something to the boy, patted his head, and disappeared into the restaurant.

Nicole crossed to the table where the boy was playing his radio. He looked up and smiled.

"Would you like to make five dollars?"

"Doin' what?"

"I want you to go over to the man with the Harley and ask him the time."

"That's it? Ask him what time it is?"

"Yes."

"No sweat! And you'll gimme five bucks?"

She took the money from her shoulder bag and held it in her hand as he considered the offer. Temptation won out, the boy picked up his radio, and started walking toward the table under the trees. The man, who was sitting with his back to the other diners, turned slightly as the boy approached from behind.

A car and trailer pulled out and passed in front of Nicole, moving slowly. It stopped at a trashcan and discarded paper cups, then dumped the contents of an ashtray, all the while obstructing her view of her messenger.

The boy strolled back, his head leaning into the radio, feet stomping to the music.

"The time is five minutes to four," he reported, and held out his hand for the five.

"Run through it for me. He told you the time?"

"What do you mean?" The boy looked baffled.

"He spoke to you?" Nicole asked.

"No, he just showed me his watch."

"Here's the five. And thanks."

"Why did you want me to do that? You got a watch," the boy indicated Nicole's watch.

"I thought he may be someone I knew," she explained, speaking quickly as she saw Derek coming out of the restaurant.

"Well, he sure wasn't friendly," the boy said. "I asked him about his bike, and he just growled at me so I beat it." He noticed Derek walking toward Nicole's table. "Your boyfriend is a dwarf?"

"Yes."

"You sure know some weird people, lady."

"Thanks for your help."

"Ready to move on?" Derek asked anxiously. "We're not going to make it to Myrtle Beach tonight. I should have started sooner!"

"Don't worry about it. We can find a nice motel and arrive tomorrow in plenty of time. Go sit in the car and study the map while I visit the restroom," she instructed him. She looked across at the hunched shoulders of the motorcycle rider. He was reading a road map, head lowered, his fingers seemed to be tracing a highway. His shoulders had the stiff appearance of someone who was concentrating on the sounds and movements of those behind him.

"Get in the car," Nicole said sharply. Even with other people seated close by, she hesitated to leave Derek sitting at the table alone. "You look a little chilly. Get inside where it's warmer. I'll be right back."

She hurried to the restaurant. Looking back when she reached the door, she was relieved to see Derek climbing into the driver's seat of the Escort. The motorcycle rider still sat, studying his map, across the lot. In the booth of the restroom, she reached under her jacket and placed her hand inside, reassuring herself the gun was in place. Nothing must happen to Derek. She was the reason he was here in this country, miles from Paris, away from old friends and his family.

Maybe the rider wasn't Carlo. She had not actually seen the rider's face. It could be anyone—and yet—he had not spoken aloud to the boy. "He growled at me," the boy had said. He had done what Carlo would do.

When she came out of the restaurant, Derek sat calmly in the car reading the map. Over by the trees, the table was empty. The motorcycle was gone. Nicole breathed a deep sigh of relief, ran, and jumped into the Escort.

"Let's hit the road and see how far we can make it before dark. I don't like these big highways at night."

"If you see a nice motel in North Carolina, we'll stop," Derek agreed.

As they continued on, she glanced back from time to time.

* * *

The sun was setting beyond the trees, its dazzling orange glow signaling the end of day. They had progressed another sixty or seventy miles south, and she noticed that Derek appeared to be getting very tired. Nicole started looking for a sign on 95 indicating food and lodging.

"Just ahead is a place called Roanoke Rapids. Take the next ramp, there, 173 Exit, off to the right. Are we in the next state?" Nicole said in surprise. Her attention had been diverted from time to time to watching the traffic behind them in the rearview mirror on the right side. Other motorcycles had passed but none with drivers in a white helmet and black leather jacket.

They came down into a busy intersection, and within a mile Nicole spotted the Hampton Inn and nearby was Cracker Barrel, a restaurant chain known for its southern fare. She recalled having lunch with Beau Jackson several months ago in a small town in Virginia in a similar one.

"I'll see if they have two vacancies," Derek said, wearily unlatching his seat belt. "Look, there's a pool. Too cold for that!"

Nicole grabbed his arm. "Derek, could we get just one big room and share it? They all have two very large beds and I don't think I snore." Maybe I do, she thought belatedly, but the major has never complained.

Derek looked stricken. He was a very private person. His face turned ashen, then red. "Why would we do that?" He suddenly threw up his hands as he thought he understood the only possible explanation. "If you have forgotten your money, my darling Nicole, I have plenty with me!"

"It's not that. After seeing that man on the motorcycle—well, I believed he was following us—I am very nervous, no?"

Derek shook his head. "Two rooms! You have not one nerve in your body, Nicole."

"I do. Please?"

A half smile of embarrassment played across Derek's face. "You are not afraid of me? I am a lecherous little man."

"One room. Two beds. I trust you."

Derek shrugged. "You are right to trust me, my darling Nicole. You see, I am thirty-nine years old, and I have never spent an entire night with a woman."

"That's very sad. Now you will have a new story to tell," she teased. "Just don't mention my name. It would be all over Paris and Maman could not show her face."

He went into the motel and the desk clerk peered down over the counter, then she tried to see through the window who was waiting in the car outside. Nicole waved. The clerk withdrew her gaze and handed Derek the key as he returned the register. Derek twirled the key around his finger, came back, and plumped himself into the driver's seat.

"Congratulations," he laughed. "You have just become my wife." He waved the receipt and flipped it into her lap. "Monsieur and Madame Derek Holland, Room 104."

"Mon Dieu! I must have had too much wine. I don't even recall the wedding!" exclaimed Nicole. "Is 104 the Bridal Suite? I simply won't settle for less. And did she give you one of those little cards that says do not disturb?"

"She was very discreet. She wished me a pleasant evening."

"And what did you say to her?"

"Nothing. I just winked."

Nicole laughed. "I know that wink. Remember when I used to see you in the Paris office and I would—."

"Cross your eyes and stick out your little pink tongue," Derek nodded. "That little routine of yours made me smile all day."

"I miss those days," Nicole admitted.

He pulled into the slot in front of the door and looked around at the partially empty lot. Behind them, the water in the swimming pool lay cold and dark, reflecting the overhead lights. He got out and unlocked the door as Nicole pulled their small luggage from the backseat and placed it on the sidewalk.

She walked to the end of the block of rooms and scanned the parking areas adjacent to the buildings. It was off-season and several rooms were dark; in others, lamps gleamed from the windows denoting occupancy. She walked back to a locked door. Laundry. There were ice and drink machines. Everything looked normal. When she returned to 104, Derek stood uncertainly in the middle of the room.

"Which bed do you prefer? You can see the TV from either side."

"Next to the window and door," Nicole answered, tossing her shoulder bag on the queen-sized bed and kicking off her shoes. She unpacked her Snoopy nightshirt and put it on the pillow.

They watched several news programs, went to Cracker Barrel, and had a delicious chicken dinner, with hot butter cornbread, and a sliced apple covered ice cream dessert. Nicole bought a small, fuzzy bear dressed in camouflage fatigues for major in the gift shop, and scented notepaper for Maman. She loved giving gifts and wondered what would be suitable for Nicolas, but she did not yet know Nicolas. She bought Derek a tie with tiny little sailboats. Tomorrow she would meet Nicolas! She felt excited but apprehensive. What would they have to say to each other after thirty years, she wondered!

They strolled around the parking lot in the brisk evening air, noting the license plates from so many states, as far away as Vermont and California. On the other side of their building there was a motorcycle parked, but it was red, small, and light, almost as light as a bicycle, Nicole reasoned. As they made their way back to Room 104, she tried to shake off her feeling that Carlo was out there.

They took turns in the bathroom, undressing, and getting ready for bed. Derek found on TV an old movie that even in black and white was more interesting than the inane sitcoms.

As they became drowsy, Derek said casually, "Nicole did you ever—hmmm—were you ever curious about how it would be to make love to—hmmm—a dwarf?"

Nicole became wide-awake. Actually, she had never given it a thought. Derek? Handsome, charming, and kind, he was—but as a lover? The desire was not there!

Finally, after an uncomfortable silence, she answered, "It would break up a beautiful friendship, no?"

Derek sighed. "It is the major, isn't it?"

Nicole twisted the huge ring with its soggy wad of adhesive tape. "Yes, it is the major."

Later, when the Tonight Show signed off, Nicole heard a soft, little snore from the other side of the room and knew that Derek had fallen asleep. Leaving the television murmuring in the background, Nicole rose and took the Smith and Wesson from the shoulder holster and placed it under the second pillow on her bed. She turned off the TV, and lay down facing the window, reached across, and touched the cold blue steel. *Carlo is out there somewhere*, was her last thought before she fell asleep.

* * *

A little past seven, Nicole slipped out of bed, gathered her clothes, and tiptoed to the bathroom to shower. She dressed in a new rose-colored sweater and matching skirt. The boots were also new, natural leather, zipped up on the inside, and had a narrow strap and buckle at the ankle. Would Nicolas be impressed? She crept quietly out of the bathroom, shrugged into the shoulder holster, and covered it with the new, long brown jacket. Buttoned it up, and then hesitated. What if Nicolas gave her a hug? He would surely be curious about the bulk near her left shoulder. Nicole pulled off the holster and put the gun in the bottom of her shoulder bag.

Derek was still sleeping. Even with stubble of dark beard, his handsome face, in repose, looked like a boy of nineteen. He had partially rolled out of the covers, and Nicole glanced down at him. He wore Burberry plaid pajamas and one small foot lay bare in the bedspread. She gently pushed the cover over it. Derek woke at her touch, sat up in the bed, and consulted his watch.

"It's almost eight. Why didn't you wake me? I like to drive in the early morning when it is less crowded."

"The bathroom is all yours. I will take a little walk while you dress."

"You look very pretty," he sighed.

"It's for Nicolas. Last night when I thought of meeting him, I could hardly breathe!" she confessed. "Oh, Derek, what will I do if he doesn't want to know me?"

"Then we shall call the police and have him certified as hopelessly insane," stated Derek. "And I shall take you back to Virginia, where we shall get drunk on the finest of wines, sup on filet mignon, and go to the opera."

"Perhaps, I won't see him."

"We have not come all this way to abort this mission, my dear girl."

"I kind of like the idea of getting drunk and going to the opera," she laughed.

"We will do that too," promised Derek, heaving himself out onto the floor. "And now I shave."

"I'll get coffee; to eat here will be quicker," decided Nicole. She hesitated. "Lock the door. I will knock when I return."

He looked at her. "Why lock the door, Nicole, for maybe twenty minutes?"

She sat on the edge of the bed, wondering how much she should tell him. "That motorcycle rider yesterday—I think it may have been Carlo."

"He was given a ticket to Ecuador," Derek said. "He is miles away."

"He cashed the ticket, Derek."

"If you think he is after you, we should call the major at once."

"I don't know where Carlo is. There is no other big motorcycle visible in this area, only a small red one, because I have looked—at least—early last night, before we went to dinner."

"We need to be careful," agreed Derek.

"Lock the door, please? For me."

Nicole slipped outside and waited until she heard the chain jangle against the doorjamb. She strolled around the area. Sleepy people were loading their cars and checking out of the motel, heading north or south to homes or vacations. Dads were throwing boys into vans or station wagons; moms were herding reluctant children. She crossed to the Cracker Barrel and joined the hungry line.

Back at room 104, Derek was peering through the window. He quickly unlatched the door, took the carton of breakfast food, and placed it on the small table under the window.

"It's just pastries and coffee."

"Smells magnifique!"

"We can eat and be on the road."

Twenty minutes later, they were heading down 95 south toward Rocky Mount and had covered about thirty miles when Nicole glanced down at her hand.

"Mon Dieu! Derek, stop the car! We have to go back. The major's ring—I mean, my ring is gone!"

"Oh! Oh!" exclaimed Derek, looking wildly around for a place to turn off, but of course, this meant exiting the highway. "I must go into town, circle back to the North—oh, Nicole, the ring was so heavy—why did you not miss it? Why did I not miss it?"

"I'm so stupid. It must have fallen into the tub when I took my shower. I am so stupid, no?"

Derek, tight-lipped, didn't answer but glanced at his watch as he veered off onto the exit ramp. He clutched the steering wheel. "We will be late. Now we must go thirty extra—no! Thirty-four miles—there is the sign. How could you not miss something so big?"

"I washed my hair. Perhaps the shampoo?"

Derek raced up the ramp to the northern exit and darted back into the traffic headed north for Roanoke Rapids.

"I'm sorry, Derek, but I cannot lose that ring!" Nicole said. It was the first time she had ever seen Derek so upset. From the corner of her eye, she happened to glimpse a large motorcycle on the other side of the highway. It was partially hidden behind two long semis, but she could see the rider well enough to see his white helmet and black jacket before a passing van obscured her view. When she turned to look back again the motorcycle had disappeared.

Had it exited the Rocky Mount ramp? White helmets were common, she tried to reason. Many riders favored the big Harleys and wore white helmets. In any case, it could be going in the opposite direction so there was no need to alarm Derek, who was pushing the Escort to the speed limit.

The miles flew by in silence, and they soon were back in Roanoke Rapids. As they drove back into the motel parking lot, Derek turned to her.

"You must understand. I am not upset with you, but we have miles to go and perhaps all our trouble will be for nothing. I do not know where Nicolas will go after this. First, we start late, and now this delay because the ring is lost. Sixty-something extra miles we could have been heading south!"

Without answering, Nicole got out of the car and went into the motel office. The desk clerk came forward.

"We stayed in Room 104 last night. The name is Hall, and I lost a ring. It may be in the tub somewhere. My hands were slick from shampoo."

"Would you describe the ring?"

"It was from the Air Force Academy and wrapped with lots of adhesive tape."

The clerk laughed, reached under the counter, and took out a plastic bag. "I thought you'd be back. The maid found it sitting on the top of the drain. Air Force, huh? I guessed it didn't belong to the little fella, little short for the military."

"No," said Nicole, looking down at the ring sadly. "My brother. You understand?"

The clerk's smile faded. "Vietnam?"

"Desert Storm. Thank you, and here is something for the maid." She pressed a twenty-dollar bill into his hand.

"Maria, she found it. I'll see she gets this. She can use it. Y'all come back anytime, you hear?"

"Thanks again."

"Have a good trip now."

Derek was looking forlornly out into the parking lot, and when Nicole returned, wearing the ring, he turned to her and smiled. "Sorry, I yelled at you."

"You had good reason. Now we must start again because I was careless," Nicole admitted, looking down at the ring.

"Put it on a chain around your neck," Derek suggested as he put the car into gear and drove quickly from the motel, anxious to make up for lost time.

"Do you want me to drive?" offered Nicole. "I know we have lost time."

"No, your knees would hit the steering wheel," said Derek. "Besides, I have heard stories about your great sense of direction."

"Touché. I shall read my book about Nuri Bey and the great city of Istanbul."

The miles droned by. Again, they approached the Rocky Mount exit and sped on down the highway toward Wilson, then on to Smithfield, where signs indicated the turn off into Raleigh.

"I have a headache, Nicole. I think we should stop for lunch and I will have a couple of aspirin. Raleigh is a big city, I think?"

"The map says so—this big orange spot, but it appears twenty-two miles west. Perhaps something is closer? Our destination, Cherry Grove, should be to the east."

Derek continued past the Raleigh exit, slowed down somewhat and got into the right lane, watching the signs as they passed.

"Lumberton is east," announced Nicole.

"Are you sure?" Derek demanded.

"We must go there," stated Nicole. "And from there, we go onto a different highway that leads to the ocean because that is where Cherry Grove is—the Atlantic Ocean."

"Nicole, you better be right or we are going to be too late. A different highway? I will look at the map myself as soon as I find the way off from this 95," Derek insisted, scanning the exit signs. "Every state in this country is as big as a single country in Europe, is it not?"

Nicole nodded as Derek sped off the ramp to the right and found himself facing several roads leading in different directions, but he was immediately attracted to a small country restaurant he could see just a few yards away. He turned the car to the left and bumped along a minor bypass into the parking lot.

"Our pancakes are world known. Our beef barbecue is like no other. Come in and try Grannie's Cookin'." The sign was large and beckoned invitingly from the road, but only two pick-ups and a van were parked outside as they drove in.

"Way past lunch time," mentioned Derek, consulting his watch. "Bring the maps."

The restaurant, rustic from the outside, was a pleasant surprise. Partly pine paneled and partly wall papered in a small floral pattern, it had maple tables and chairs with clean white tablecloths, shelves of copper pots, and twinkling brass chandeliers. A brick fireplace at one end gave a warm atmosphere to the dining area.

"Good afternoon," said the waiter, a young man in a denim shirt and Dockers. "We are out of barbecue. Sorry. Big lunch crowd."

"You serve breakfast all day?" Nicole asked.

"Yes, ma'am."

"What I'd really like are crepes, but I guess pancakes are close enough. And little sausages and coffee. Derek?"

"We make crepes," the waiter interjected.

They looked at him in disbelief.

"With strawberries or cherries?" he added.

"Strawberries," said Derek. "Not too many, and please, no whipped cream!"

"Coffee and sausages for me also."

"Grannie must be in the kitchen knocking herself out—crepes? Mon Dieu!"

"I'm Grannie," the waiter confessed. "The original passed on twenty years ago." He closed his pad and whipped away to the kitchen at top speed.

"Crepes!" said Nicole. "God has brought us poor French aliens to this place."

Derek consulted the map. "You think we are in North Carolina still, this Lumberton? Oh yes, here is number 41, to the South Carolina line. We find this place, Mullins, and go east to the ocean, perhaps forty to fifty miles?"

"So big this country!"

The crepes were perfect, the coffee and sausages steaming and sizzling. They ate in silence, hurrying, as outside the day dwindled down, the sun low into the sky.

As they came out of the restaurant, Derek looked toward the west. "I hope we make it before the show closes. We should have started sooner."

Nicole also felt anxious about the time factor. To be so close to finding Nicolas and miss him was too painful to contemplate. "Do you wish me to drive, Derek?"

"You watch for signs, Nicole. Leave the car to me. Look for number 41."

"I can drive very fast," she insisted.

"I have heard of your driving," he argued and hastily got behind the wheel.

Avoiding the ramp back on the super highway, they found the secondary road, which led to the South Carolina line and triumphantly grinned at each other as they entered the next state. In another hour, maybe less, they would reach the coast and find the place called Cherry Grove, just north of Myrtle Beach. Nicole felt exhilarated and still apprehensive. She looked down at her new sweater, skirt, and the new boots. She pulled down the little overhead mirror, stared at her face, and decided a little more lipstick would help. She put on lipstick and combed her spiky dark bangs into place.

There were few cars on this road as they traveled south. Derek turned on the headlights and looked to the right for signs, so occupied with reassuring himself they were headed in the right direction that at first he wasn't aware of the sound of the siren and the flash of pale blue lights coming up fast about a mile behind them on the dark and empty road.

"Pull over! Pull over on the side, Derek!" Nicole warned him. "It is the police."

Derek wrenched the Escort to the right, his small hands fighting the steering wheel as the car crunched onto the shoulder of the road, his face ashen with guilt.

"What have I done?" he cried. "Was I speeding? Oh, Nicole, I will go to jail!"

"No! No! They are not chasing us Derek, it is something else," Nicole assured him.

A light motorcycle, red in color, whizzed past at a high rate of speed. Close behind came the state police car gaining on the fleeing cyclist, as it shot past.

Derek laid his head on the steering wheel and attempted to regain his composure. His hands still gripped the wheel. "I thought the police were after us," he groaned. "But, I did not know why—a burned out headlight; perhaps the wrong license?"

The siren faded and in the distance ahead, they heard the sound of a crash, the scream of brakes, and the shattering of glass. Nicole sat frozen in place, her mind repeating the sight of the motorcycle as it passed in the headlights of Derek's car. The fleeting vision lasted but a second, but it was enough to see that the rider wore a white helmet. She clutched her hands together tightly to stop the trembling.

"Perhaps we can be of help," suggested Derek, relieved that his personal crisis was over, and he was no longer in danger. He turned to look at Nicole.

Finally, she said yes. She cleared her throat. "Go slowly. We do not know what is ahead."

Derek carefully looked both ways and the Escort crept into the dark road, but there were no other vehicles in sight. He gained a little speed and about three quarters of a mile ahead he saw the flashing light of the police car, which seemed to have sideswiped a massive oak tree at the side of the road. The officer had climbed out of the vehicle and was peering over the edge at something unseen, below in a culvert. As the Escort approached, he halfheartedly waved them on, but Nicole pressed Derek's arm.

"Stop, I want to see what has happened. The officer may need us to go for help. This police car appears to be damaged."

"He waved us to proceed."

"Stop, Derek!" she demanded.

"No, I will not stop. We are so late. I am sure this trip has been for nothing. You let me oversleep when I prefer to drive in the morning. You drop your ring. I am sick of your delaying tactics, Nicole!" Derek exploded, his face flushed with unaccustomed anger. "You know what I think? You are afraid of meeting your father. You are afraid of finally seeing Nicolas."

Nicole looked shocked. "Listen, little man, who made you a psychiatrist? If I did not want to meet Nicolas, why did I come with you? Now, stop this car!"

Derek looked straight ahead, and smarting over the "little man" remark, he drove fast. "No stops!"

"I need to go back!" she screamed at him as she made a grab for the steering wheel. Defiantly Derek sped up and she glanced in the rearview mirror. The blue light on the police car was a tiny dim spot in the darkness now half a mile or more behind. She reached over and grabbed the keys from the ignition. Momentum propelled the car for a few yards and it stopped. Derek lurched forward on the steering wheel, pushed himself back, and attempted to grasp the keys from her hand but Nicole had opened the door and leaped to the side of the road. She threw the keys into the backseat.

"Go on then, go to Cherry Grove! Go back to Virginia! I can take care of myself," Nicole shouted, as she turned away from the car and ran as fast as she could toward the pale blue beacon at the side of the road. She could feel the weight of the gun in the shoulder holster beating against her chest but she fell into her best speed, the muscles in her legs responding even though her jogging routine had become sporadic the last few weeks. Her breath was coming in short spurts by the time she reached the accident scene.

The officer looked up in surprise. He cradled a cell phone in his hand. "Where in hell did you come from, lady?"

"I was jogging and I heard a crash."

"You just stand there a minute 'til I get off this phone," he ordered.

"Bob? I went down and got his ID. Let me read you this so you can get a trace with the Virginia DMV Yeah, it's a Virginia license. Fellow's name is Billy Dewayne Williams, resident of the Bide-A-Wee Motel—Yeah, I'll spell that for ya."

Nicole ran to the side of the road and stared through the darkness. About fifteen feet below, resting in a culvert, was a lightweight red motorcycle, and beside it lay a still figure in a black leather jacket and a white helmet, the visor still pulled down, shading the face. She climbed down from the shoulder of the road and clinging to some fragile growths projecting from the torn earth that denoted the path of the bike, she scrambled to the prone figure of the rider. She pulled back the visor. He lay with eyes shut, arms flung out to the sides. One leg lay in an awkward position, broken at the hip joint, cast aside as if it not longer belonged with the body. Was he dead?

"Carlo." Nicole said. "Carlo."

At her voice, his eyes opened and he gave a crooked smile. He made one of his unintelligible growls as his hand reached out as fast and strong as a striking rattlesnake and locked itself around her ankle, trying to drag her down. The grip tightened and he made an effort to raise himself toward her. "Let me go, Carlo," she warned, trying to pull away. Instead, his fingers dug into her boot. His eyes glittered as his fingers wrapped around her ankle like a steel cable. "Stop it! I'm warning you!"

He clung on, squeezing with all his strength.

Nicole raised her other boot and kicked him in the head twice. Carlo grunted and dropped back, his eyes closed, the grip on her ankle relaxed, and his hand fell aside.

She heard the officer calling from above. "Lady—lady, you come back up here! There is a crime scene. You goin' to be in big trouble with the law you mess with my crime scene! Bob? Bob? I got a nut loose here. Wake up Danny and get him over here with the tow truck. My cruiser has no headlight on the left side." The officer tucked his cell into his shoulder strap and huffing with the unusual exertion, half slid, half fell down the embankment, cursing the dirt and mud that clung to his uniform.

"Lady, what are you doing down here?"

"I thought it might be somebody I knew."

"Well, he ain't from around here. That cycle was stolen from North Carolina, and Mr. Williams here, from Virginia, is the deceased."

"He's breathing," Nicole pointed out.

The officer leaned forward, produced a small mirror and held it under Carlo's nose. Gingerly, he felt the rise and fall of Carlo's chest. "I'll be damn. Better call an ambulance. He looked like a goner to me." "The leg appears broken," Nicole said.

"Did you witness the chase?" he probed, looking unhappily at the embankment that he had to climb to get to the road. "Did you see him go over?"

"No."

"Well, get out of here and don't mess up my crime scene if you got nothing to report."

"Yes, sir," she agreed quickly and scrambled up the rough furrows made by the motorcycle on its way down. She could hear him cursing and grunting as he tried to follow and kept sliding back.

Once on the road, Nicole began to run toward the Escort and breathed in relief when she saw it still parked at the same place, Derek pacing up and down beside it. When he saw her approaching, he opened the door and got in.

"You didn't leave," she panted as she flung herself into the passenger side. "Let's go!"

"I knew you'd be back," he said casually, making no move to turn on the ignition. "What's your hurry? You timed your little escape long enough. Nicolas won't be there. He will be gone, perhaps forever."

A police car, followed by an ambulance, careened past, lights blinking, sirens screaming into the night.

"What did you do down the road, Nicole? Beat up that policeman?" Derek said with heavy sarcasm. "Burn down a house?"

"Start the car, Derek," she commanded. "Or I'll shove you into the road."

"You wouldn't," he dared her.

She just looked at him.

"Yes, you would," he decided and slipped the key into ignition. He drove off at a high rate of speed, hoping whatever chaos Nicole had left behind would not catch up with him. He had no chance now of reaching Cherry Grove in time and he was filled with a genuine sorrow. It would have been good to see Nicolas again after all these years. Had the glamorous man of the flying trapeze ever thought about the old circus days and a nine-year-old dwarf who clowned with the dearest, funniest, mentor in the world, Beez-bol? Probably not, he sighed, pushing the Escort to the limit.

"If you see a telephone booth," Nicole said, "Please stop. I have an important message for the major. It concerns another agent." She would report the whereabouts of Carlo Arana—he would not be going anywhere with a broken leg—and the major would come to the hospital and take "Mr. Williams" away. She could still feel Carlo's painful grip on her ankle, the same ankle injured by the chain in the stable.

"There—on the other side of the street," Derek said. "Where's the maps? I think this town is Conway."

"I can't ask anyone. They're asleep," Nicole noted, glancing at the quiet streets. She crossed to the telephone booth and called the safe house number collect. A sleepy sounding Whitt answered, and he became instantly alert at the sound of Nicole's voice. He groaned as she related the news about finding Carlo.

"He has a driver's license in the name of Billy Dewayne Williams, Bide-A-Wee Motel, probably double-laminated with his own photo. He has a broken leg and possible concussions—check hospitals near Mullens and Conway, and pick him up before he can escape."

"Nicole, why didn't you tell me you were going after Carlo?" Whitt asked anxiously.

After Carlo? He thought she had gone after Carlo! For a moment, Nicole didn't know what to say.

"Why not take me?" Whitt insisted. "Why Derek, for god's sake? He won't even carry a weapon."

"We can talk this out when I get back. Go after Carlo."

"I'll find him," Whitt promised. His voice softened. "Hurry home, Nicole, and be careful."

She imagined his face. Beautiful blue eyes that could be warm enough to melt her soul, cold enough when angry to bore holes in a flak jacket.

"I love you, Major. I'll be back soon. Goodnight." Reluctantly, she hung up the telephone and leaned against the booth, for one sweet moment wrapped in his voice, and then she hurried back to the car.

"I hope we still have our reservations at the Beach Cove," said Derek. "Sometimes motels don't hold them after six. I doubt we will find Nicolas, but on the chance it may be open, we'll head for the Flea Market first."

"We're close, no?"

"A few miles."

She looked down at her skirt and picked a few burrs from the wool, a few more from her sweater. Her boots looked muddy from climbing up and down the embankment. This was hardly the impression she wanted to make when she saw Nicolas—if they did find Nicholas.

At first glance, the Flea Market appeared deserted. In the long wooden building a few dim lights burned but the big double doors were locked. Through the windows they could make out long rows of tables, some empty, and others piled with merchandise shrouded in heavy plastic. On the outside were about a dozen or more picnic-type tables. Newspapers, shredded for packing, blew across the empty field. Little pale green popcorn insulation balls crunched underfoot, discarded as the china and glass they had protected had been sold and taken away. At the far end of the field, faint gleams of light shone from the windows of a trailer parked under two giant pine trees, and as Nicole and Derek made their way toward it, someone had been watching from inside and the door swung open. Briefly, a man was silhouetted in the glow. He peered into the parking lot.

"Show's over, folks," the man shouted. "Y'all come back next week."

"Excuse me," Nicole called. "I'm trying to locate Nicolas Lee, the appraiser. Could you tell me where he is staying?"

"Just a minute." The door closed, reopened again to reveal a middle-aged red-haired woman in a chenille bathrobe, followed by a tall, teenager in cut-off jeans, and a white tank top. As they approached, their bare feet kicking up dust, it was obvious they had come out to get a better look at Derek, who stood firmly waiting, his cap pushed back, his handsome face wearing his most charming smile.

"Daddy said there was a midget out here," giggled the girl, gazing at Derek. "We thought he was a-lyin'—and he won't."

"Just the cutest little thing I ever saw," said the red-haired woman, walking around Derek, her robe flapping to reveal chubby white legs. "I bet you got a cute little pecker too, ain't you, sweetheart?"

"About Nicholas Lee," Nicole quickly interjected. She put her hand lightly on Derek's shoulder. "My husband and I have come a long way to see Uncle Nicolas—we were in a terrible wreck—that's why we're late."

"Husband? He your husband?" both women said at once. The older woman folded her arms over her heavy breasts in a sudden show of modesty. "I seen Mr. Lee at his table, a good-looking man, but he's gone. They all gone hours ago. Sorry." She turned and headed back to the trailer.

The girl lingered, smiling at Derek. "I never seen no midget up this close before, only in "The Wizard of Oz" and like that." She glanced briefly over her shoulder. As the older woman went into the trailer, she came closer to Nicole. "I know where Mr. Lee is. He come in a trailer like one of them silver bullets, with a man and a woman that do a rodeo act, Tessie and Buck, and Daddy told them they could park it down near Murrell's Inlet, cross from those big gardens, 'cause our lot was full."

"Where is that?" asked Derek "Murrell's Inlet?"

"You talk just as regular!" exclaimed the girl. The big gardens—I went once and all those stone people make me crazy. I thought they were going to come alive and walk up on the back of me! I walked around a corner, and there was this little stone statue boy just sittin' there on the ground. He looked so real I almost said, "Where's your Mama?"

"North? West?" Nicole urged.

"You go South, down the road a piece, maybe fifteen or twenty miles, on seventeen, past the Grand Strand."

"Thank you, thank you," said Nicole. She put her arm around Derek's shoulder. "Come on, honey. Uncle Nicolas will be worried sick."

The girl rolled her eyes and giggled. "You tell Mr. Nicolas Lee, Brenda say hey." With this, she turned and ran toward the trailer, her long white feet leaving prints in the dust.

They hurried back to the car, Nicole doing her best to keep from laughing aloud. Derek marched along briskly, muttering under his breath with every step. He unlocked the car and climbed up into the driver's seat.

"What are you laughing about, Nicole? My humiliation?" he demanded.

"She thought you were cute."

"Well, my little wifie, if you can contain your snickering long enough to read the map and tell me how to find this trailer park, I'll just turn on the ignition and take my cute little pecker down the road!" he puffed. With his cap pulled down to his eyebrows, he sat staring stonily through the windshield.

"I'm—I'm sorry. Oh, Derek, you should have seen your face! Mon Dieu, I thought she was going to ask for a peek!" Nicole laid her cheek against the cold window glass and unsuccessfully tried to stifle her laughter.

In a few seconds, Derek joined in.

"You are used to stupid people asking questions by this time, no?" Nicole looked at the maps. "Which is the south—this way?"

"No, Nicole, don't direct me," he decided. "That is west. I'll look for signs."

"Perhaps that is best. I once drove the major all the way to Atlanta, Georgia."

"I hear it is an interesting city."

"But we were going back to Alexandria," Nicole admitted. "He was very nice about it."

Already he was falling in love with you, Derek thought, as he sped down the highway. To his left hung a full moon. A full moon, and a beautiful woman at his side—life was never perfect, he mused, but it could be very, very good at times.

The Grand Strand was a lively stretch of highway, lined with brightly lit motels, restaurants, and shopping centers. Derek stopped at a fast gas and shop to fill up the Escort with gas, and ask directions. Nicole rushed into the convenience store and came back with coffee and sandwiches.

"The place where Nicolas may be staying is on the left side. It's called Huntington Beach State Park, and the gardens are across the road on the right," Derek explained, one small finger pointing to the maps. "Watch for a sign that says brookgreen."

Nicole paused, the sandwich halfway to her mouth. "Derek, what if he's already left?"

Derek considered this, drank his coffee, and replied, "Then we have had a trip together, had a change of scene, and we made the effort."

Nicole seemed to relax. "You are wise, Derek. When I was a little girl and things got tough, Mimi used to tell me to live for the day—don't worry about what is past, and the future is still unknown, no?"

Derek started the car, and Nicole gazed intently through the window as they left the lighted area of the Strand and entered the comparative darkness of the highway heading south.

"Here! Here!" Nicole exclaimed, as the sign suddenly loomed large and white to her right. "Ooh, we are passing the gates so soon! You must turn around."

"Damn trees—so many damn trees," Derek complained as he made a wild U-turn and slowed down until he found a road leading back toward the ocean.

Tucked in among the pines and heavy undergrowth were cars, vans, and trailers. Some had awnings, and outside picnic tables, the smell of barbeque and grease from small metal grills still lingered on the air although it was after eleven o'clock. Little squares of light from trailer windows indicated television. A few hearty men braved the cold night breeze form the Atlantic to sit on the hood of a car passing a bottle back and forth between them. The Escort approached, and the bottle disappeared as Nicole stepped out of the car. "Pardon me. We are looking for Nicolas Lee. Would you direct us to his trailer?"

There was a muted conjecture among the men about how wise it may be to expose the whereabouts of a neighbor. One was overheard to say "I bet they come for all that Civil War stuff Nick bought off that woman" "And that gold joory"—"How 'bout them watches"—"That Nick is slick"—and lastly, they agreed, "Don't tell 'em nothing!" Within a few minutes, the muttering ceased, the bottle reappeared, and Nicole gave up and got back into the car.

"We know what it looks like—a silver bullet and it must be large because there is a man and woman with him," the girl at the Flea Market, Brenda, said.

Derek drove deeper down the rutted paths between the trees, made a half circle, and on a secondary road they spied it, looming like a ghost, in a clearing lit by the moon. A small outside light shone by the door of the trailer and three metal steps that led up to it, and another dim light filtered through lace curtains. Lace curtains, Nicole though, a woman's touch.

"Go with me, Derek. I have this strange feeling like I want to cry—he's in there—I know it," Nicole whispered. "In there!" She pointed to the darkened end of the trailer, to the one window without lights but made no effort to move.

Derek got out, marched around the car, and flung open the door to the passenger side. "Come on," he ordered. "Get out, Nicole." He reached out his hand and she took it.

As they started toward the metal steps, the door opened and a very tall woman in a satin robe called out, "Is that you, Buck?" she peered out into the door. "Oh, who is it?"

"We're looking for Nicolas Lee," Derek said, stepping into the light by the door so that she could see him clearly.

The woman hesitated. "I'm afraid, Mr. Lee has gone."

"Oh no, madam!" Nicole cried out. "Everything has gone wrong this day! Please tell me where he is!" She also stepped into the light and the woman appeared startled—gazing at Nicole several moments.

"Why do you want to see him?" she finally asked.

"Because—" Nicole hesitated.

"You're kin, aren't you? I should have known. Only family would have those brows and that hair." She opened the door and invited them into the trailer. "People sometimes find him and want to buy their old heirloom stuff back. Nick is not supposed to make his little deals, just do appraisals, but—"

"Is he here, then?" Derek broke in, looking about the neat but crowded interior.

"I'm Tessie Houston. Yes, Nick is back there in his room asleep. Who did you say you were?" Carefully holding the satin robe together, she shook hands with Derek, but she directed her glaze at Nicole.

"My name is Nicole Laurent and this is my friend, Derek Holland. Shall we knock on his door?"

"Heavens no! He's got so much junk in there you couldn't sit down." Tessie hurried to the door at the rear and rapped on it sharply several times. "Get up, Nick!"

"Sleeping. Go away," came a groan.

"It's kin, Nick. You just come and see!"

"I have no family," the voice answered.

Nicole stepped up to the door and put her hand against it, her heart leaping with the knowledge that the hunt was over. He was just on the other side of this door, the man she had been searching for all her life.

"Do you remember a beautiful French girl with blue eyes and blond hair? She met you at the circus thirty-one years ago in Paris—her name was—"

"Yvette," came the voice, from behind the door, suddenly clear. "Give me a minute."

Nicole was trembling. Derek put his arm about her waist as if to protect her and led her back to the front of the trailer.

"Have a seat, dear," Tessie said, indicating the foldout bed, made up as a sofa. She turned off the television. "Can I get you something to eat? A drink, maybe?"

They shook their heads and sat stiffly on the sofa, their eyes riveted on the rear door.

The quarry appeared. Nicolas Dana Lee Campion was of average height. Dark hair hung just below his ears. He had pulled on gray sweatpants but his feet were bare and he held a gray sweatshirt in one hand. His chest and arms were heavily muscled, his hands not particularly large, but wide, and appeared tough. He stood in the doorway for a moment, then pulled the shirt over his head, and came over to the sofa. He looked down curiously at Nicole.

"She looks like you, Nick," Tessie stated.

There was a long, tense silence, and then Nick asked, "Who are you?"

"I am Yvette's daughter. I am thirty years old. I believe you are my father."

"If this is so," Nick said guardedly, "I had no knowledge of you, of your existence."

Derek suddenly leapt up and pushed Nick in the chest. "For god's sake, man, just look at her!" He seemed ready to jump on the sofa and punch Nick in the face. "Can you possibly deny the likeness?"

"And who the hell are you?" demanded Nick.

"I am her friend!" Derek shouted. Even to his own ears, the word, *friend*, seemed much too weak to express how he felt about Nicole, and Nick immediately sensed it.

"My name is Derek, and I know you, Nick Campion—older, but just the same tricky Nick! I was just a clown's foil in those days—nine years old, you may not remember me, but I know you!"

Nicole's mouth flew open in surprise, and she looked from Derek to Nick. What was Derek saying?

"What the hell is going on?" Nick groaned. "How do you know me? From the circus? I worked with a hundred dwarfs. How can I recall one?"

"My clown was Beez-bol," Derek murmured. "You must remember him! My clown was Beez-bal, the best clown in the world. We worked all the little shows in Europe."

Nicole was speechless. Everything was going so fast. She looked from one man to the other. Derek seemed to be pleading with Nick to remember this clown, and Nick was wiping his forehead in confusion as if attempting to draw up the past. Temporarily, they appeared to have forgotten why they were here. Why she was here!

"I'll make some coffee," offered Tessie. She looked out the door. "Buck is missing all of this. Won't he be surprised?" She crossed over to the window and stood anxiously, looking into the dark. "Wonder why Buck is taking so long? That man in Space Five came by this afternoon, talking about some wild cat running loose up there in the bushes—a wild cat! How about that coffee?"

"No coffee, thanks, Tess," said Nick. "I've got to be on the road early in the morning."

"Find us a spot in Savannah near the stores," suggested Tessie. "Buck has been gone near an hour."

Nick sat down at the table close to a basket of fruit, idly picked up an orange and two apples, and began to juggle them without paying attention to the rapidly revolving arc going higher and higher. He seemed lost in trying to bring to his memory events of thirty years ago.

Nicole was mystified. Why was Derek referring to baseball, and clowns, and acting as if he had already known about Nick? Absentmindedly, she picked up an orange, placed it on her shoulder, and rolled it down the length of her arm, flipped it into her hand, and tossed it to Nick.

He caught it and the orange joined the other fruit in motion. "Where'd you learn that?"

"I could always juggle. No one taught me."

Nick put the apple and oranges back in the basket and leaned forward toward Nicole. "We need to talk. Will you take a walk on the beach with me?"

Derek stood up.

"I need to talk to Nicole alone," Nick insisted. "If she is my daughter, we have a lot of catching up—thirty years of it."

"It's okay, Derek."

"If you're sure," Derek agreed reluctantly. "I will be in the car if you need me." He turned to Nick. "No one who ever saw Beez-bol's routine would forget him. I'm not convinced you are Nick Campion."

"He's Nick." Tessie said. "We've been doing the circus together five months of the year for the past three years; closer than most families in the trailer."

"Thank you for your hospitality," said Derek formally, put on his cap, and went briskly out of the door. "Good night."

They heard the car door open and slam.

When Nicole and Nicolas left a few minutes late, she noticed Derek had bedded down under a blanket in the backseat and appeared asleep or on the way to being asleep.

"He drove all the way, poor fellow. I have exhausted him," commented Nicole, as she followed Nicolas down to the wide, damp crusty beach that seemed to stretch endlessly in both directions.

"There are some stones down near the big house where we can sit," Nicolas offered. "Is the breeze off the water too cool for you?"

"No," she answered, and paused to peer through the dark. "What house?"

"Atalaya—it was the summer home of Anna and Archer Huntington years ago. She was a very talented sculptor and some of her work is across the road in the gardens. If I weren't leaving for Savannah, I would take you there tomorrow."

"Can't you stay one more day?" Nicole pleaded.

"I just wish you had come sooner," he said. As if he couldn't get enough, he kept staring at her. He touched her cheek, her chin.

"You do accept me as your daughter? I realize it must be a shock, and I wouldn't blame you if you didn't believe me—suddenly bursting into your life."

He smiled and threw his arms around her. They stood like this, a long while, feeling the sand under their feet, hearing the waves slapping against the shore. The bright moon lent a surreal sense to the scene. He finally kissed her on one cheek, then the other, then leaned back, and cocked his head to one side.

"You gotta belong to me, kid," he laughed. "It's written all over your face." He kept glancing her way as if puzzled about something. He paused, squinting in the moonlight. "Have we met before? The circus? You said you went to the circus—you look—familiar, and yet—"

"I was very small when you were in the circus, and we never saw you perform."

"Yes. I haven't done high wire in twenty years."

Nicole turned away and hurried ahead. Of course, it had been in the yard on Embassy Row. Nicolas, the thief. Nicolas, the thief.

They walked along the beach for several hundred yards and to the right the place he called Atalaya house came into sight. The low walls of the house seemed endless, and there were towers and trees within the walls, the whole house forming a huge courtyard.

"It's almost sinister," Nicole observed, stopping suddenly. "Ghosts live there now."

"Perhaps the Huntington's, Anna and Archer. It has quite a history. You would like it better by daylight."

"Perhaps. We will sit here on these rocks where we can talk, no?" Nicole climbed up and sat facing the ocean.

Nick sat close by. "You're wearing a man's ring but no wedding band. I can't believe some guy hasn't grabbed you up by now."

"I was married. I am divorced. And you—you have someone?"

"I married one lady in Belgium. It lasted three months. The next one lasted a while longer, a year and something—in London," Nick told her. "I get restless and always want to move on."

"And are there children?"

"No," he said, turning toward her. "Just you, kiddo. And damn, you're a pretty one!" At that moment, she realized there was more similarity than just dark eyes, straight nose, and curly hair between herself and her father. At twenty possible years older, Nicolas had no ties. He traveled part of the year in a tiny room in a trailer; he had no home, no significant other, no children, no address, or telephone. It was like holding up a mirror to her future life, and what Nicole saw made her very frightened. Where will I be in twenty years, she wondered. She reached across and squeezed his hand. I will be his anchor, she promised.

He was staring again, as if sizing her up. "What kind of work do you do?"

Nicole hesitated. She had never even confided in Maman the truth of what she actually did in America. The accepted story for years was always that she did translations, incredibly, now she decided she could confide in Nicolas.

"I am an undercover agent."

There was silence, then broken by sudden laughter. "You don't have to make up a glamorous profession to impress me, Nicole. No, come on, why don't you tell me what you really do?"

She turned and looked at him.

"You're pretty enough to be a flight attendant," he added "or a model."

For a few minutes, she sat speechless, wondering what to say. He had rejected the truth. What else could she say?

"I—I'm a dishwasher. I wash dishes in a restaurant," she finally told him.

He gave her a hug. "Any honest job is not to be embarrassed about, Nicole. I hope you wear rubber gloves. You've got nice little hands for such a hard job." He took one of her hands in his as if to comfort her. "Tell me about Yvette. Is she still beautiful? Is she happy?"

"She is beautiful and very smart. She has started her own business, designing, and making custom clothing, and is doing quite well," Nicole told him. "She never married." Her eyes were drawn to the strange movements of something down the beach from the way they had come. A small dark animal of some kind was running toward the waves and was being thrown back onto shore, where it ran crazily in circles.

"I can't believe it, Yvette is not married!" exclaimed Nicolas. "I want you to know I really loved your mother. There was a little garret room where we used to meet—those were the sweetest times of my life. We would have gotten married, especially if I had known about you, but I never knew!"

Suddenly angry, Nicole burst out. "Why didn't you come for her? We looked and looked everywhere for years. Maman and Mimi took me to every circus that came near Paris, but she couldn't find you!"

Reluctantly, Nick murmured, "I went to prison. I didn't want her to know."

"She loved you. You should have written and told her where you were. She would have understood! The decent thing, no?" Nicole, distracted, pointed down the beach into the darkness. "Do you see that animal? It is staggering like it is sick, no? Is it a cat?"

Nick stood up on the stones and looked in the direction she was pointing. He watched the animal intently as it moved closer up the shoreline, darting into the water, reeling back.

"It is drinking salt water!" he exclaimed. "Bigger than a cat. We'd better go up and return to the trailer by way of the road. That thing acts as if it is rabid!"

Nicole got to her feet and shook the sand from her skirt. The movement seemed to be a signal to the animal, which had become aware of the presence of creatures other than itself, and had begun to run toward them staggering, falling, flipping itself madly in the air but still progressing rapidly in their direction.

"Hurry, Nicole!" Nick called out. "We've got to find cover!" Without hesitation, turned and ran for the road. "For god's sake, come on! Can't you see that thing is sick out of its mind?"

Nicole stood still. She could hear the stones scatter as her father scrambled up the bank behind her. Up close, she could see the animal clearly. It was long and black, its coat wet from the surf. The tail was circled in white. Its eyes flashed red; the needle sharp teeth were bared in a foamy rictus. Rabies. "Poor creature," she whispered. Her hand unzipped her shoulder bag and sought the gun buried in the bottom. Without looking, she flipped off the safety and drew it free. "Poor creature."

The animal hissed at her and leapt forward.

The shot rang loud and clear on the deserted beach. In the cold, damp air, a tiny puff of blue smoke rose from the barrel, and she held the gun ready for a second shot, but it was not needed. She walked the few yards to the body. It lay on its back, legs stiffening. There was a small, almost bloodless hole between its eyes. It had died at impact.

"Baby, baby, are you all right?" Nick panted, coming up behind her.

"See the tail? It is a raccoon, no?"

"Dead? Are you sure?" He approached the wet, still carcass with caution, nudging it gently with his foot. "God! That was a brave thing to do. Why are you carrying a gun, Nicole?"

"Never know when you'll need one."

He stood back, looking at her uncertainly. "Let's get the hell outta here. Somebody may have heard that shot."

Nicole stood looking down at the raccoon. "We can't just leave it here. A child could touch it." As Nick stood by without moving, she added, "I will bury it. You can go back to the trailer."

"No, no, I'll help," he decided. He looked warily around to see if they were still alone. No one was in sight. No light appeared beyond the trees. He salvaged a piece of driftwood caught in the rocks.

"Where shall we bury it, Nicole?"

She took the driftwood and marked a square close to the body. "Here. The tide will not come up that far. The sand will be firm under the top layer, then easier. Too deep and we may hit water." She began to dig, piling the sand neatly to one side.

Nicolas found a rusted can and scooped the sand to the other side. At about two feet in depth, using the driftwood as a shovel, they wrestled the raccoon into the hole and piled the sand back into place until they could no longer discern the square.

Nicole stepped back and made the sign of the cross over the general area, turned abruptly, scrambled over the stones, and up to the road where she began to walk rapidly back toward the trailer park. She could hear Nicolas running to catch up behind her.

"You did that so efficiently! I mean, about the layers—like you bury dead things on the beach all the time. Have you done this before?"

She walked faster, her thoughts going back to a night in Florida on a much larger body than a raccoon. Was he still there, the agent known as Bruce Malcolm Dieter, sleeping that last sleep, under the beach house of Gazar? She began to run, the weight of the gun in her shoulder bag beating against her side. Memories were not a good thing to keep in her line of business. Move on, Nicole, move on!

By the time they reached the big silver trailer, Nicolas had caught up with her, and they both stopped to look into the backseat of the Escort where Derek slumbered on, wrapped in his blanket, his cap pulled down over his face.

Nicolas grinned. "He's the only guy I know who can sleep full length on the backseat of a car."

"I must wake him. We must go back up north and you must go to Savannah. Look, out there over the ocean, the sun is coming. See the pink spreading on the horizon? Already it is a new day."

"Nicole, I have some money," Nicolas began awkwardly. "I can help you. I want to know you, to be in touch. Please, always tell me where I can find you. A phone number, an address, anything."

"I don't need money, and I move around as my job takes me," Nicole said. "But here is my Paris address." She found a piece of paper, wrote her own name, but added the address and telephone of Maman's apartment. "Do not give it to anyone else, promise?"

"Absolutely." Nicolas laughed. "If captured by the enemy, I will eat it!" He tore off an end of the paper and scribbled on it. "This is Tessie and Buck's home in Texas. They usually know where to find me."

"Nicole?" came a scratchy voice from inside the Escort. Derek peered thought the car window and rubbed his eyes. "Is that sun?"

"Yes, Derek, it is a new day."

Nicolas put his arms around Nicole and held her tight for a long time, then released her, and traced her face with one finger. He cleared his throat and started to try to speak.

"Don't say good-bye," she whispered.

He turned quickly, ran up the steps to the trailer door, and let himself in.

Derek struggled into the front seat and turned on the ignition. He straightened his cap and smoothed his leather gloves. He fiddled with the radio, and still Nicole did not come to the car. Finally, in the rearview mirror, he saw her turn, walk away from the trailer, and open the door to the passenger side. She slid heavily into the seat and looked straight ahead.

"Are you all right?" Derek asked. He slipped the car into drive. "Buckle your seatbelt." He drove swiftly through the trees, passed the spaces of other trailers, and headed up to the highway.

Nicole turned around once and looked back. "Yes, I am all right. I have met my father, and I am complete."

"The major will be wondering where we are. He'll be angry, and then he will be so happy to see you, he will forget!"

The major. Nicole placed her fingers over the big air force ring. She ached to see him, to tell him about Nicolas. She wanted to build a fire in the library, lose herself in making love, run with the big white dog. Life had closed a circle. She was free.

The End

Edwards Brothers Malloy
Thorofare, NJ USA
September 27, 2013